# Praise for *The Artist Colony*

"*The Artist Colony* is a sumptuous ride through Carmel-by-the-Sea as Sarah Cunningham attempts to uncover the truth about her sister's mysterious death. Atmospheric and delicious, FitzPatrick delivers a thrilling page-turner woven with artistic flourish. This exquisite novel does not disappoint! Highly recommended!"

—Michelle Cox, author of the Henrietta and Inspector Howard series

"It's 1924 and a young woman journeys to Carmel, California, to learn more about her sister's sudden death. She soon learns that the bohemian arts colony is anything but idyllic, as she's confronted by flagrant racism and intimations of murder. FitzPatrick has written a vivid historical novel with an absorbing mystery at the center of it, and I was riveted."

—Elizabeth McKenzie, author of *The Portable Veblen*

"The dramatic landscapes of Carmel, beautifully depicted by FitzPatrick, are central to the plot, whose blow-by-blow story keeps us gripped to the final revelation of Ada's murderer . . . a must-read novel for anyone who loves historical fiction, art, detective stories, and the West Coast."

—Maggie Humm, author of *Talland House*

". . . FitzPatrick keeps the pot stirred nicely, with revelations popping up like whack-a-mole. There is also a nice sense of scene, capturing this idyllic place on the Monterey peninsula. . . . [This] tale delivers an escape to gorgeous Carmel and an engaging mystery."

—*Kirkus Reviews*

# Praise for Joanna FitzPatrick's
## *Katherine Mansfield*

Bronze Winner of the 2021 Independent Publisher Book Award (IPPY) in Historical Fiction

"A historical novel reconstructs the life of Katherine Mansfield as she becomes a noted short story writer and critic while battling tuberculosis. FitzPatrick's heavily researched novel . . . truly gets into the head of the innovative writer as she balances career, a shaky marriage, and a fatal illness while struggling financially . . . the author deftly captures Mansfield's fervent dedication to her craft and her unwavering hope that she will overcome her illness. A well-informed, intuitive account of a singular modernist writer whose life is cut short."

—*Kirkus Reviews*

# THE ARTIST COLONY

# ALSO BY JOANNA FITZPATRICK

*Katherine Mansfield*

*The Drummer's Widow*

# THE ARTIST COLONY

## A NOVEL

### JOANNA FITZPATRICK

SHE WRITES PRESS

Published 2021
Printed in the United States of America
Print ISBN: 978-1-64742-169-4
E-ISBN: 978-1-64742-170-0
Library of Congress Control Number: 2021904267

For information, address:
She Writes Press
1569 Solano Ave #546
Berkeley, CA 94707

She Writes Press is a division of SparkPoint Studio, LLC.

*For Ada Belle Champlin (1875–1950)*

Ada Belle is the ghostly inspiration that set me off on this particular fictional path and the shade and shadow behind the characters and events in this book.

*We owe respect to the living; to the dead we owe only truth.*

—Voltaire

*The tide, moving the night's*
*Vastness with lonely voices,*
*Turns, the deep dark-shining*
*Pacific leans on the land,*
*Feeling his cold strength*
*To the outmost margins: you Night will resume*
*The stars in your time.*

—Robinson Jeffers: *Night*, 1925

# INTRODUCTION

I f I hadn't inherited a landscape painting by my great-aunt, Ada Belle Champlin, and if I hadn't moved to Carmel Valley, California, because of that wondrous landscape, I would still be in Manhattan and I would have written a different story.

After my husband, Jim, and I moved into our new home, I hung Ada Belle's landscape over the stone fireplace. I wondered where in Carmel she had stood to paint the country road bordered by a row of eucalyptus trees in a golden pasture lit by a blue sky brushed lightly with white clouds. In the background, a range of mountains graced with purple splendor.

I am not a painter but I think *The Artist Colony* started on a blank canvas, not a blank piece of paper. I had a palette of vivid ideas. As I brush-stroked layer upon layer of pigments onto that imaginary canvas, it evolved into an historical novel set in 1924 when Carmel-by-the-Sea was a thriving women's art colony.

I became very curious about an art colony populated by women who, like my great-aunt, had become painters at a time when it was declassé for a woman to do anything artistic beyond needlepoint. Women were expected to marry and make babies, not art. I wondered how Ada Belle succeeded as a painter under these restraints.

Soon I was deep into a mystery plot, interweaving the history of Carmel's artist colony with the actions of my characters. As my research expanded, I added real people—the poet Robinson Jeffers and his wife, Una; the painters Armin Hansen, William Ritschel, and August "Gus" Gay—and had them meet my fictional characters in

1

the locations where they had lived. Then I stepped back and let them tell their story.

I became a location scout and went in search of the many historical locations in Monterey where I could set my characters, like the Hotel del Monte, Point Lobos, Monterey Wharf, La Playa Hotel, and Carmel Beach.

One autumn evening, my scouting led to Block CC, Lot 13, on Camino Real, where, based on a very old town map, I thought my great-aunt had lived. I must admit that I had low expectations. There are few original houses left in Carmel. (Those that have survived have been enlarged until the original homes are hardly recognizable, if not torn down.)

After Jim and I had cocktails at Carmel's La Playa Hotel bar, we walked down Camino Real in search of Lot 13. The surf was breaking against the rocky coastline a few blocks away and I inhaled the same brisk, salty air that I imagined Aunt Ada Belle had breathed in when Carmel was an undeveloped coastal village.

Night was falling as we approached a parked car with the headlights left on. Jim knocked on the front door to inform the owner. A man in his early sixties came out,  switched his car's lights off, and thanked us.

We told him we were looking for a cottage where my great-aunt Ada Belle, a painter, might have lived in the 1920s. He pointed at an unlit cottage directly across the street and said he'd lived on Camino Real his entire life. One artist had lived there when he was growing up, and then another artist had moved in around 1973. He gave us her name and phone number. I couldn't believe my good fortune.

The next day I called Belinda Vidor-Holliday, the current owner of Block CC, Lot 13. I introduced myself, said her neighbor had given me her phone number, and told her that my great-aunt might have been the original owner of the studio-cottage where she now lived.

"We must meet," she said immediately. "Where are you?"

"I'm in Carmel."

"Then come over now."

My heart beating fast, I drove down Ocean Avenue to Camino Real and parked in front of Lot 13. Even in daylight the cottage was barely visible behind a wooden picket fence and under the cover of leafy oak canopies. I had just unfastened the seatbelt when there was a tap on my window. I rolled it down and said hello to the elderly but still lovely Mrs. Holliday. After quick introductions, she invited me to come inside.

Stepping over the threshold was like entering another world, another time. I looked up at the lofty multipaned windows and skylights on the north-facing wall. A shaft of sunlight illuminated a paint-stained easel propping up an abstract painting layered in vibrant colors. Used paintbrushes stuck out of glass jars on a tray of metallic oil tubes. All my senses took in this painter's paradise and I felt the spirit of my great-aunt applauding my arrival. I could've shouted for joy, but I didn't want to scare my hostess.

Mrs. Vidor-Holliday was well-informed about the history of the cottage, as she too had been curious about its lineage, but she doubted that my great-aunt had built it. I hid my disappointment and asked her if I could see the files documenting the cottage's history she'd mentioned.

She brought me into a small side room furnished with a trundle bed and desk. While she looked for the files, I hoped I was standing in the room where Ada Belle had slept.

Mrs. Holliday couldn't find the documents she was looking for, but she asked me to join her for a cup of tea in the studio. We found we had much in common and were soon calling each other by our first names.

When I told Belinda that my great-aunt had been a founding member of the Carmel Art Association, she said there was a photographic portrait exhibition of past artist members currently on display at the gallery. I had only seen a blurry, pixelated photo of my great-aunt, and the prospect of seeing what she actually looked like gave me goose bumps.

"Let's go," Belinda said with a twinkle in her bright blue eyes, as if she'd read my thoughts.

In the gallery, we slowly walked along the rows of photographs honoring deceased CAA members since its inception in 1927. Belinda, a longtime member, pointed out several artists she'd known. We were disappointed not to find Ada Belle's photograph.

On my second visit, Belinda told me she'd found the Architectural and Historic Survey from 1922. My heart stopped when I saw "Owner Block CC, Lot 13: Ada Belle Champlin."

"Look, Belinda!" I said pointing to Ada Belle's signature on the deed.

She was as thrilled as I was.

Standing at her printer and copying the documents that proved my great-aunt's ownership of Lot 13, I felt certain Ada Belle was peering over my shoulder. Every time I return to visit Belinda, who is now my good friend, I feel the same rush of excitement I had that first time.

After I told Belinda the name my great-aunt had given the cottage, she had a wooden sign carved and *THE SKETCH BOX* now hangs from her front gate. She said it was "the right thing to do."

—Joanna FitzPatrick

# SATURDAY, JULY 19, 1924

## —1—

The screaming iron wheels of the Overland Express awakened Sarah to her alarming circumstances. She blinked several times until her eyes accepted the morning light. Normally, she would've admired the radiant emerald green and amber patterns cut into the stained-glass window of her Pullman compartment and considered how to capture their radiance on canvas. But today wasn't normal and she doubted her life would ever be normal again.

Not after receiving a telegram at her garret in Paris informing her that her sister, Ada Belle, had drowned in the Pacific. And now here she was in a tiny room on wheels coming to a halt at San Francisco's Union Station.

Two weeks ago this death-by-decree telegram from the marshal in Carmel-by-the-Sea showed up under her door just as she was raising her paintbrush to her canvas to start the final painting for her one-woman show at the prominent Nouy Gallery in Paris, and her first measurable success as an artist came to a screaming halt just like the wheels of the Overland Express.

She shut her eyes, returning to the imagined palette she'd been blending pigmented oils on.

*Shame on you, Little Sis,* she heard Ada say as if she was in the berth above her, rather than lying cold in a casket. *Always thinking of yourself first. Try to remember that I am the one who will never paint again.*

*Your death is not my fault,* complained Sarah, gulping down an emotional cocktail of resentment mixed with grief and guilt.

She stretched out her cramped legs and stepped down onto the cold floor.

"San Francisco. End of the line. All passengers disembark!" shouted the Pullman porter as he rapped loudly on her door.

Observing her pale, pathetic face framed in the washstand mirror, she said critically, "You will never do!" Her painter's hand penciled in the brows and painted the lips ruby red like it was her own self-portrait in need of a touch-up.

A crimson jersey skirt and matching jacket hung in the closet. The chic outfit had given her the appearance of a House of Chanel model stepping out from behind the curtain into the limelight. Only three weeks ago she'd bought it in expectation of wearing it at her first exhibition. But now it seemed unpleasantly cheerful when she felt so miserable. If only she had a black veil to hide behind, but it was too late to think of that now.

The porter rapped again and called out in his Southern drawl, "Ma'am, are you awake?" She asked him what time it was, then wound back the hours on her deceased father's pocket watch from 6:00 p.m. to 9:00 a.m. and stood up straight and tall, feigning confidence. She pulled down her cloche hat over her bob of unruly auburn hair stopping at her penciled brows.

Her hand froze on the doorknob, suddenly afraid to face the world without Ada. The Pullman compartment had been a safe, dark theater where she had projected their shared memories like a silent movie while the Overland Express whisked her across the country: Ada cuddling her when she fell and scraped her knee. Ada teaching her how to hold a paintbrush and blend oils on a palette even before she taught her how to read.

Sarah stepped down onto the railway station platform. From living in Manhattan and now Paris, she knew her way around hectic train stations. In normal circumstances, she would've saved a dime and proudly made her way through the terminal on her own, but not today.

A red-capped Negro porter, easily identifiable in a sea of white faces, piled her valise onto a handcart. "Where to, ma'am?"

"Del Monte Express," she said, remembering the directions Ada's friend Miss Rosie McCann had cabled when inviting Sarah to her lodge in Carmel.

"Follow me!" The porter pushed his way into the dense crowd of suit-and-tie men and white-gloved women, indistinguishable faces shaded under fedoras and sunhats. Seconds later, she was drowning in the rush of marching feet. She stood up on her toes, painfully squeezed into Parisian pumps, and saw the red-cap disappear down a long corridor.

At the Del Monte Express ticket booth, he was waiting with his hand outstretched and a wide grin. She tipped him gratefully and purchased a one-way ticket to the Monterey depot where Miss McCann said she could catch an autobus to Carmel.

Above the din of blasting train whistles, a newsboy held up the morning paper in his hand and yelled, "Read all about it! 'Inquest Verdict: Famous Artist Commits Suicide.'"

Sarah gaped at her sister's enlarged photograph filling the front page. The ground beneath her tilted and she leaned against a post to stop the train station from spinning. Her hand shook as she fumbled for her coin purse, paid the newsboy, and pressed Ada's photograph to her thumping heart.

The conductor of the Del Monte Express saw her stumble on the boarding platform and picked up her baggage and then helped her onto the four-car train just as it was whistling its imminent departure.

He found her an empty compartment and she collapsed onto a wooden bench. She stared at Ada's golden smile under the ominous headline. The familiar photograph of her sister had been taken by a

journalist at the Metropolitan Museum of Art in New York. There
were very few paintings by women hanging in any museum, and
there'd been a huge to-do about Ada's seascape *Carmel Point* being
displayed. Sarah remembered standing next to Ada and feeling very
proud of her big sister's success and wishing someday her own painting would hang at the Met.

As the train lurched forward, a dapper middle-aged man wearing
a gray pinstripe suit and a gaudy pink ascot slid open the door to the
compartment. He tipped his fedora, stepped in, and plunked himself down on the opposite bench. He stretched his long legs across
the narrow aisle and buried his face behind his own copy of the
*Examiner.*

Sarah pressed down her skirt, squeezed her knees together to stay
away from his outstretched legs, and began reading the lead story:

*When the renowned art critic Mr. Arthur E. Bye was asked why he
thought the famous painter, Miss Ada Belle Davenport, 36, took
her own life, he said, "Women artists cannot sustain the force, the
strength, the power of concentration, the prophetic insight that
genius demands. To create a child is the greatest aspiration of a
woman's life."*

*Mr. Alvin Judd, marshal of Carmel-by-the-Sea, added, "Yes. If
Miss Davenport had aspired to motherhood and left art-making to
the men, she might have avoided such a tragic end to what would
have been a fulfilled life."*

*You idiots!* she cried out to herself. *My sister did live a fulfilling life.*
Sarah knew from experience the prejudice that the fraternity of
art critics held against professional women painters, but for a man of
the law to use her sister's career as the motive behind her suicide was
outrageous.

The article ended with the inquest. An inquest that was supposed to be held after Sarah got there, not before, or so promised Marshal Judd when she wrote back to say she was coming immediately.

Within a few days she had exchanged all the francs she had in the bank for US dollars, bought her tickets, packed a few garments, and boarded the HMS *Majestic* to New York and then the Overland Express to San Francisco.

And now she was gripping her bench and looking down at the rugged Pacific coastline as the miniature-like train sped around a bend in the cliff. Through the salty foam dripping down the window-pane, she imagined Ada reaching out her bare arms toward her, calling out her name. An ocean wave crashed over her head and dragged her under.

*How horrible those last seconds must have been. If only I'd been there, I would've stopped you. Why, Ada, why?*

She pulled down the green window shade to shut out the vision, but it only conjured up another image: Ada lying facedown on a beach. Seagulls pecking at her flowing red hair spread out like angel wings. The carmine embroidered roses of her black flamenco shawl buried in the wet sand.

Ada had visited her in Paris the previous summer and bought the flamenco shawl when they went shopping on the Champs-Élysée. Sarah had admired her purchase and Ada, always generous, at least with her gift-giving, bought her an identical shawl. Sarah often wore it and even now it was folded in her valise.

The Del Monte leaned into a sharp curve and the *Examiner* slipped off her lap onto the floor. A patch of sunlight fell on the black-and-white copy of Ada's painting of *Carmel Point*, bereft of its silvery pink sky and glimmering jade sea.

"Tragic waste of talent," said the gravelly voice of the stranger seated across from her.

"Yes," she mumbled, picking up the newspaper and folding it into her satchel.

She turned back to the window, snapped up the shade, and looked at the passing view, only to be confronted by his reflection in the glass, his dark eyes pinned on her from behind. His pearly white teeth below a pencil-thin moustache.

He was like one of those older Parisian men in the Jardin du Luxembourg who would block her path and try to start a conversation. As if she'd be interested in high-fashioned dandies. Her French girlfriends called them *les dragueurs* and warned her to ignore them. Easily done on a path in a garden, but it was difficult with one sitting across from you in a cramped train compartment, his legs grazing yours.

"I see you're traveling with an artist's sketch box," he said, ignoring her obvious, though silent, request to be left alone. "Have you come here to study art?"

She had no wish to tell him she was here to bury her sister, and she kept her eyes on the pastoral scene of grazing cows now that the train had left the coastline.

"I have a gallery in Carmel-by-the-Sea and I'm *always* interested in helping young women painters like yourself. Why don't you come visit me and bring some samples of your work?"

Was it only a year ago that her heart leapt at such offers? She would spend days choosing which paintings to show the prospective art dealer, hoping he (it was always *he*) would admire her work and advance her the money she needed to pay the rent, restock art supplies, and buy something fashionable to wear at her first exhibit in his gallery. After a few off-handed comments about her work, he'd invite her to dinner. When she was full of wine, caviar, and false promises, the seduction came. She was certain this pin-striped dealer's offer was no different.

But she was different. She now had a reputable dealer in Paris who had offered her a one-woman exhibition and with her advance she'd bought the Chanel suit she was now wearing.

The yearning for a cigarette and a need to be away from this *dra-gueur* brought her to her feet. She excused herself with a side glance, stepped over his extended legs, and closed the door behind her.

Two cars down, she entered the parlor and found one empty seat facing the window. She searched in her satchel for a packet of Gauloises and ordered a black coffee.

*Suicide, Ada? For god's sake, why?*

Sarah's thoughts turned to when she'd last seen Ada six months ago in Manhattan. She and several other selected art students from Académie Julian had come to New York for a collaborative exhibition of their paintings at the Whitney Studio Club, a significant modern art gallery.

Ada had been waiting at the gangplank when her ship docked at Chelsea Piers and had immediately swept her away to Keens Chophouse for dinner. "Please, Sarah, promise me," Ada had pleaded until Sarah said yes, not knowing it would become her sister's dying wish.

*Keens on East 36th Street was famous for its members' long, thin, clay pipes that hung from rafters over the regal, walnut-paneled dining room. These exclusive members were financiers, mobsters, and celebrities, and their pipes were identified by numbers. The celebrated painter Ada Belle Davenport owned number 806.*

*Keens' maître d' had ushered us into the crimson Lillie Langtry Room, so named for the actress who sued the restaurant for not allowing women to dine there—and won.*

*A Negro waiter appeared at our reserved table carrying two champagne flutes on a silver tray next to clay pipe #806, and a small packet of tobacco. With great finesse, he popped the champagne, wrapped it in starched linen, and filled our flutes. Several of the other diners, mostly men puffing on their own pipes, stared openly. I was uncomfortable, but you, never one to avoid making a spectacle of yourself, were equally amused by my discomfort and the admiring stares.*

*The attentive waiter returned with a tray of raw oysters on the half shell, placed them in the center of the table, shook out napkins in our laps, and slipped back out of view.*

*In between dipping the juicy morsels in a spicy red sauce and slurping them down, I told you about my recent work in Paris, my teachers at the Académie Julian and my experimentation in complementary colors that had changed my palette and encouraged new ideas onto my canvas. It had to have been the bubbly because I was usually not so forthcoming, particularly with you, who so often found fault in my work.*

*When only a few oysters were left on the melting ice, you leaned toward me and said, "I have a small favor to ask you."*

*I was immediately suspicious. When you asked me for a favor it was never a small one.*

*You then raised your glass and said, "Ars longa, vita brevis—Art is long, life is short."*

*I asked you what this Latin phrase had to do with what you wanted me to do for you.*

*"Don't you see. An artist's life is short," you said, "and I need to trust someone to carry on my legacy after I'm dead." You waited until the waiter refilled our champagne glasses and then added, "Didn't John Middleton Murry publish his wife Katherine's lifelong work after she died?"*

*You knew I was an admirer of Katherine Mansfield and would know the answer. "Yes, but Katherine's dying wish was that he publish only her best work and destroy everything else. He's a cad. Instead, he published every scrap of paper she ever wrote. He did it for the money."*

*You relit your pipe. "Okay. Maybe he's not the best example. What about Vincent van Gogh's brother, Theo? When life became too difficult, Vincent shot a bullet through his heart. It had to make it easier to kill himself knowing his brother would keep his legacy alive."*

*"We still don't know if he did kill himself," I said. "Maybe someone*

shot him. Suiciders seldom aim for the heart; their preference is shooting themselves in the head."

"But what does Murry or Theo have to do with your small favor?"

"I'm about to write my will and I want you to be the executor of my artist's estate. So if something were to happen to me, I'd know my legacy was in reliable hands."

I felt trapped. I'd moved to Paris to get away from your consuming demands for my attention, which often interrupted my own work, and now I was being dragged right back into your orbit.

"What about your dealer, Paul deVrais? Isn't he reliable?"

Your reaction was unexpected. "No!" Then with a swish of your hand as if swatting a fly, you said, "Believe me when I say he's a worse cad than Murry. I would never entrust him with my life's work. In fact, I'm about to break our contract."

You then covered your hands over mine and said, "You're the only one I can trust to carry on my legacy. Please, Sarah, promise you will do this for me."

I wanted desperately to say no, but the deep scars on your hands stopped me. After our parents died in a Manhattan hotel fire and you barely escaped the same fate by sliding down a rope, you cared for me like I was your own child though you were only six years older than me.

"All right," I said, "I promise to be your Theo."

"Thank you, Sarah. I couldn't ask for a better Theo than my own little sister."

The word Peace engraved on the pendant hanging from your neck glimmered in the candlelight and my heart sank.

Many years ago, when teaching at the San Francisco Art Institute, you had been upset about the exclusive Bohemian Club of poets, authors, and artists not letting you join their club. They wouldn't allow any women in their club. They still don't. So it was just like you to start La Bohémienne Club for women only. The creed was similar to the Bohemian Club. If any member failed in achieving artistic satisfaction

*they could choose death by suicide, a morally acceptable escape from*
*melancholy or disgrace or plain boredom.*

*The pendant hanging from your neck carried a lethal dose of cya-*
*nide. All the Bohemienne Club members wore one. I asked, "I don't*
*expect there'll be anything I have to do anytime soon. Right? You're not*
*planning to do anything foolish, are you?"*

*You let go of my hands and rubbed the pendant between your fin-*
*gers. "You needn't worry about this, Little Sis. I only wear it because*
*of my loyalty to the Club. You really should become a member. It's a*
*fabulous group of talented women artists."*

*"No thanks. I don't believe in suicide pacts."*

*"It's not a suicide pact. It's just a reminder of life's transience. I'd*
*never really swallow it."*

*You took out a small key from your bag. "This opens my safe deposit*
*box at the Wells Bank in Monterey. I've been spending so much time on*
*the West Coast that I set up an account there. I'll put in a copy of the*
*will, an inventory of all my paintings, and any other legal documents*
*that might be relevant. Only you will have a key."*

*You opened my fist and placed the key in my palm. It felt like burn-*
*ing coal and I dropped it into my bag.*


The Del Monte Express took another sharp curve and the tasteless
cup of American coffee that had gone cold splashed across Ada's photograph on the *Examiner*'s front page. Sarah patted it dry and looked
closer. Yes, there it was. The pendant engraved with *Peace*.

Her eyes came to rest on what was left of her cigarette. She pinched
the end of it and dropped it in the almost-empty packet. There might
not be any Gauloises in the remote village of Carmel-by-the Sea.

The pinstriped *dragueur* was asleep when she returned to the
compartment. She stealthily stepped over his legs again, hoping not
to wake him.

Outside the window, blurred rows of purplish green artichoke plants passed by in straight lines across vast, flat fields. They were tended by groups of men, women, and even children moving slowly between the rows. It was the first time she'd actually seen the plants growing on black-stained fields or the immigrant laborers who were harvesting them hunched over in the hot sun. Ada had romanticized their labor in her many paintings of Central Coast California agricultural scenes, scenes that had made her famous. Wealthy collectors who had never toiled in the hot fields bought them.

Asian children in tattered clothes looked up at the train passing by and waved.

To fill the remaining time on the train to Monterey and to divert her thoughts, Sarah brought out her drawing pad and began sketching Daumier-like caricatures of Mr. Pinstripe. She put a top hat on his head and gave him a rotund belly like Daumier's satirical drawings of the fat bourgeoisie.

The drawing helped her forget her misery. Sketching had that effect. Particularly now.

A sudden jerk by the train knocked Mr. Pinstripe's knees against hers and the drawing pad fell on the floor. Her caricature grinned up at them with a toothy smile under a thin moustache. The likeness was obvious. Unamused, the dealer stood up and took down his attaché case from the luggage rack.

Sarah closed the pad, placed it on the wooden bench, and brought down her valise. When she reached for the leather strap of her sketch box and started to hook it over her shoulder, he stepped toward her. "Here. Let me carry that. I know how heavy they can be."

"Thank you, but that won't be necessary," she replied firmly.

He let out a laugh. "Oh dear. You just arrived and you're already sounding like all the other independent ladies who flock to our artist colony to make paintings, though I really think it's to escape the clutches of chivalrous gentlemen. Won't you give me a chance to help a damsel in distress?" He grinned and reached again for her sketch box.

"I'm not in distress, sir," she said as she squeezed by him through the narrow doorway.

He caught up to her at the exit door and held up the drawing pad with *Sarah Cunningham* written on the cover. "Did you forget this?"

Grateful that she hadn't lost the pad, she thanked him, and put it under her arm.

"I should've recognized you right away," he said, "but your face was half hidden under your cloche and I could never get you to look at me until now."

"And why should you have recognized me?" she asked, irritated at being at a disadvantage.

"Why your sister's portrait of you, of course. Such a strong likeness."

She reddened. Who was this man who had seen Ada's portrait of her? A portrait that she herself hadn't seen.

He seemed not to notice her distress—or he was enjoying it—and continued. "Ada told me that you went by your mother's maiden name, Cunningham, to distinguish your artwork from hers, and I've been expecting your arrival, but I hardly thought I'd be lucky enough to share a compartment with you on the Del Monte."

He took off his fedora and, leaning into her, lowered his voice. "My deepest sympathies, Miss Cunningham. I was very distressed by the facts leading up to the inquest verdict. I knew Ada at times was, shall we say, 'down in the dumps,' but I never thought her melancholy would drive her to suicide."

His hot breath and presumed intimacy were stifling, but there was no space in the small corridor to move away from him.

"How do you know my sister?" she asked, feeling woozy from the drageur's cologne.

"Know her," he said, seemingly offended. He pulled a business card out of his lapel pocket and handed it to her. "Ada was my most valued client. I've been her art dealer for many years. But certainly you know that?"

Sarah held his card between her hands and reread it several times to avoid looking into the eyes of Paul deVrais—the art dealer who Ada had accused of stealing her artwork and her entire legacy if he could get away with it.

She forced a smile and, shaking his offered hand, said with feigned politeness, "Why yes, Mr. deVrais, my sister told me all about you."

"After you get settled, please come see me at my gallery. Shall we say Saturday morning? Come early and I'll make sure we're not disturbed. We have much to discuss."

To Sarah's relief, the train came to a stop and the door opened onto the Monterey depot.

"Where are you staying?" the dealer asked, while helping her off the train.

"Miss McCann has offered me a room at her lodge."

"What a pity. I'd take you there myself, but I have a previous engagement." He pointed to a muddy, elongated yellow sedan with viewing windows on the sides and a gaping open roof. "There's your ride. You'd better hurry. José doesn't like to wait."

She declined his offer to carry her baggage to the autobus, he smiled, tipped his fedora, and walked away.

When she handed her valise to José, out of the corner of her eye she saw Paul deVrais get into a smart two-seater Ford driven by a gorgeous, young blonde. Sarah adjusted her lopsided cloche, shouldered her sketch box, and climbed aboard the bus.

With her thoughts on deVrais, it wasn't until the rickety bus started climbing up a steep incline that Sarah paid any attention to the well-heeled tourists. They had boarded at the Hotel Del Monte depot and sat in their reserved front-row seats as if it were their moral right to do so. The Asians and Hispanics were crowded into the back of the bus. Sarah was embarrassed. Negros were also forced to sit in the back of New York City buses while she and the other whites sat in the front. She lacked the courage then and the courage now to say anything.

The racial discrimination in Monterey was not unknown to her. One of her fellow students at Académie Julian, a Chinese American girl, Moon-Li, was only six years old when her Chinese fishing village was burned to the ground by their white neighbors. Moon-Li's homeless family then moved to San Francisco where her father helped rebuild that city's Chinatown after the 1906 earthquake. Later, Moon-Li had worked as a maid on cruise ships to pay her way to Paris, where she could study art in a city where people didn't discriminate against her because she was Asian. That was not to say the French were racially tolerant—only that they had chosen others to discriminate against.

The bus strained to reach the top of the hill and then turned sharply and started a breathtaking crawl for ten minutes down a bumpy dirt road. The panoramic view of Carmel Bay beneath a cobalt blue sky was just as Ada had painted it.

They dropped down into a small village with scattered shops on either side of the road, rustic cottages and barren lots shaded only by a row of pine trees whose foliage was hardly mature enough to offer more than dappled relief from the bright sunlight.

Ada had told her that Carmel was only one square mile in area, but it was densely populated with painters, mostly women, who came there to create art in peaceful surroundings. Ada had complained about the railroad tracks that the immigrants had laid down between San Francisco and Monterey, paid for by the robber barons of the Southern Pacific Railroad so the upper classes could conveniently spend their holidays at the neo-gothic Hotel Del Monte resort in Monterey. The current tourist pamphlets advertised Carmel as a must-see artist colony, as if Ada and her contemporaries were exotic, caged animals to gawk at in a zoo. But she also admitted that the paintings made by the local artists were sold at the Hotel Del Monte Art Gallery and that put much-needed money in their pockets.

How ironic, thought Sarah, staring at the bobbing heads in front of her, that she and Ada had also been tourists at the Del Monte, but with their parents. Their father, an avid golfer, had played the golf circuit from San Diego to San Francisco to the Del Monte in Monterey with his two daughters tagging along. She had only been four years old, but she still held a sweet memory of their family holiday.

Ada had often told Sarah that because she was such a wee thing, as light as a doll, she could carry her across the hotel grounds to play in the Arizona Gardens and the Mazes. That's when Ada had started calling her "Little Sis."

Ada would always start the story by saying, "I'm sure you don't remember—" which irritated Sarah, even now, because she did remember. She also remembered what happened the following year after their idyllic summer in California.

Sarah lay her head back on the bus seat and let Ada tell her again as if she was sitting next to her, still alive:

*You were only five, but because I was eleven I got to go to New York City with our parents to watch the St. Patrick's Day Parade.*

*We were watching the Fifth Avenue parade from the fourth-floor balcony of the Windsor Hotel when we first smelled smoke and then there were flames climbing up the building.*

*It was before the law that required fire escapes on all tall buildings, and the only way out of the Windsor Hotel was to slide down ropes, which hung outside the windows for such emergencies.* Ada would always explain these facts first as if that would make the story less horrible. It never did.

*Father helped me over the ledge and told me to grab the rope and slide down. My hands got burnt by the chafing rope and were bleeding when I dropped to the pavement below. Mother started down next, but the rope snapped under her weight and she fell several floors. There were no ropes left so Father leapt into the waiting arms of the firemen.*

*Horse-driven ambulances rushed them to Bellevue Hospital but they were dead on arrival. The last time I saw our parents was through the front display window at Bellevue where corpses had been laid out for identification by their families.*

*I would trace the scarred burns on your hands,* Sarah interjected, taking over their story. *I'd predict a happy future for both of us, but you would press your hands together and shake your head solemnly. You began spending days at your easel. I gave up trying to get you to play card games like we used to, or having make-believe tea parties. Desperate for your company, I'd prop up my own easel and paint alongside you.*

*Our grandparents became our guardians, but it was you who mothered me. And it was you who made sure I continued my art studies, our mother's cherished desire for both of us. When you were accepted at the Art Institute of Chicago, I went with you, carrying our lunch bags. I'd sit cross-legged on the cold studio floor and sketch along with you and the other older students.*

*How different you were after the fire,* Sarah added, lifting her teary eyes to the white clouds hovering over the bus. *It wasn't just the wounded hands. There was a yearning in your eyes when you looked off in the distance, as if expecting someone who was just out of reach. I hope you are no longer yearning for our parents and are with them now.*

The Monterey autobus came to a sudden stop, bringing Sarah back into the present. The view before her was identical to Ada's seascape hanging on her wall in Paris; it brought continuous sunshine into her dimly lit fourth-floor garret. Ada had discovered a painterly paradise in Carmel and she shared it with Sarah and everyone else who viewed her landscapes.

What could have happened, wondered Sarah, to change this paradise into an early grave?

"Last stop!" shouted José. "Carmel-by-the-Sea!" The passengers climbed down and started off in different directions.

Sarah stepped onto a wooden boardwalk and scanned the deep blue waters that spread out beyond the end of the road. *Is that where they found you? Under the cobalt blue sky? The cypresses? The waves crashing against jagged rocks? That white pristine beach?*

The brilliant colors faded to black when she lowered her head and whispered, *I'm so sorry, Ada. I've come too late. Will you ever forgive me?*

Ada's silence was deafening.

José had put her valise on the boardwalk and was climbing back onto the bus when she cried out, "Stop. Please don't go!"

He turned around and pushed back his wide-brimmed sombrero. "Is something wrong, Señorita?"

"I have lodgings, but I don't have an address."

"People living here don't want to be found. There aren't any street addresses in Carmel, Señorita. Does it have a name?"

"McCann's Lodge."

"Oh." He smiled. "That's easy." He pointed toward the sea. "Head straight down. Turn left on Camino Real. Three blocks up from the ocean. Big white house with green shutters. If you step onto the beach, you've gone too far."

She looked down the deserted street. On a Saturday afternoon in Paris there would be a dozen taxicabs competing for fares. She felt ridiculous but asked, hopefully, "Taxi service?"

"Nope. Just Critter," José replied, motioning toward a two-story wooden building. A lanky young cowboy leaned against one of the porch posts underneath a wooden sign: CARMEL HOTEL - STAGE AND TRANSFER AUTOS FOR HIRE TO ALL POINTS.

"Hey, Critter," yelled José. "Can't you see this fine lady needs your help? Show her the way to that boarding house. You know, where all those pretty paintin' gals live." Critter pinched the lit end of his cigarette and dropped it in his shirt pocket. The spurs on his muddy boots jingled as he strolled over to Sarah.

"Howdy, ma'am," he said, tipping his broad-brimmed hat. "This way."

Without another word, he picked up her valise with ease and strode down the hill. Sarah slung her sketch box over her shoulder, gripped her satchel, and did her best to keep up with him. Her Parisian pumps—often silenced by the crowded, noisy boulevards in Paris—banged loudly against the hollow, wood-planked boardwalk. The few passersby glanced suspiciously at the new arrival in a red Chanel suit.

# —2—

In the entryway of McCann's Lodge, a short, buxom woman welcomed Sarah with a most agreeable round face framed by silver-white hair pulled up loosely into a bun on top of her head. A gingham apron hung around her ample waist. Her eyes were like dabs of ultramarine pigment and she had full, pink cheeks that dimpled when she smiled—just like Ada had described her.

Rosie McCann asked Critter to put Sarah's valise down next to the staircase and after handing him a few coins, he sauntered off and she gave Sarah her full attention.

"Oh my," she said with a gentle Irish brogue, "you are a blessing for my sore eyes. And the spittin' image of your lovely sister. May she rest in peace."

"You're very kind, Miss McCann," said Sarah, relaxing in the presence of a sympathetic soul after her long journey.

"It'd please me if you'd call me Rosie. Now come into the parlor and take the weight off your feet while I put the kettle on."

Sarah followed Rosie into an old-fashioned pale yellow room. A bouquet of burnt-orange marigolds posed in a ceramic vase on a green tablecloth. The fresh oranges and apples stacked in a bowl next to it reminded her of a Paul Cézanne still life that she'd copied in the Musée de l'Orangerie. She'd made studies of its every stroke, shadow, and hue.

Rosie disappeared behind a swinging door into the kitchen.

Sarah's curiosity was drawn to the crowded bookshelves. What an impressive collection, she thought, recognizing the works of Agatha

Christie, Arthur Conan Doyle, and Dorothy Sayers. There were also many lesser-known mystery writers.

The next shelf down was a *Who's Who* of modern literature: Edith Wharton's *The Age of Innocence*, which Sarah hadn't been able to put down until she found out what happened to Countess Olenska. And there were other memorable authors who had inspired her to seek her own independent path: Rebecca West, Virginia Woolf, Willa Cather, Kate Chopin.

Ada had preferred the romantic poets so they never had to argue over sharing books. They argued over more serious things, like "I didn't say you could use my sable paintbrush" or "You stole my tube of cerulean blue."

There was an *A–Z Encyclopedia Britannica*, a *World Atlas*, and many history books, including *Becoming American; The Asian Experience*. If Rosie had read all these books, she was a well-educated woman and her opinions should not be taken lightly.

Sarah picked out *California Impressionism* from a stack of art books and brought it over to a comfy couch upholstered in yellow roses. She'd just sat down when a small dog ran in and made an incredible leap into her lap.

"Behave yourself, Albert!" said Rosie returning from the kitchen to find the dog jumping up and down on her guest's lap and sniffing her neck and face. Sarah cupped his head in her hands and looked into his black agate eyes, "So you're Ada's Albert," she exclaimed.

He was just like the watercolor her sister had sent. A barrel-chested, short-legged, tri-colored Jack Russell terrier. He had a frisky white face with a brown patch that spread down over his furrowed brows. Wrapped around his white torso like a saddle was a black patch, and on his rump a black inkblot. She scratched behind his floppy chocolate-brown ears. He looked so pleased she could've sworn he was grinning when he exposed a row of teeth that she knew were designed to be sharp enough to pull a fox out of a deep hole.

"Usually he's suspicious of strangers," said Rosie, "but your voice is so like Ada's."

Albert tilted his head at Rosie and then curled up in Sarah's lap.

The kettle whistled and Rosie bustled into the kitchen again, the door swinging behind her.

As Sarah stroked her furry friend, she admired the stained-glass lampshades of amber, rose, and jade that gave a burnished elegance to the frayed furniture and spread warm hues over lace doilies on the backs of chairs and tops of tables.

Two needlepoint footstools by the fireplace drew her back into her grandparents' parlor in Chicago where she'd sat on a stool with a drawing pad in her lap and a charcoal pencil in her hand. Ada was on the other stool, bent over her own pad. They were earnestly copying an Albrecht Dürer drawing in an art book propped up in front of them.

Now, in Rosie's comfy parlor, white chintz curtains danced with a sea breeze wafting through the open bay window. Sarah sighed. Ada hadn't exaggerated when she said it was so quiet in Carmel that at Rosie's lodge, a ten-minute walk from the ocean, you could still hear the surf breaking on the shore. She breathed in the brisk blue air that her sister had found so inspiring.

Albert rolled over in her lap and asked for a belly rub, his paws fanning the air.

"Look out, he'll never let you stop," said Rosie, bringing out a porcelain tea service on a tray and placing it on the low table in front of them. "I expected you'd be hungry so I baked blueberry scones for your arrival."

Albert sat up and wiggled his black-patent nose. "Your treat is in your bowl, young man," said Rosie. As if understanding her, he jumped off Sarah's lap and pushed himself through the swinging kitchen door.

"It warms my heart to see him perky again," said Rosie. "He's been mourning his mistress and having you here is a godsend. He spends his waking hours at the front door waiting for Ada to return or paces the entryway with his tail down as if it's his fault she went away."

Sarah felt a similar guilt.

Rosie poured black tea into delicate cups decorated with shamrock leaves, then looked up. "After Ada found Albert wandering on the beach, and when no one claimed him, she adopted him. They were as thick as thieves from that moment on."

"How could anyone abandon a cuddly, adorable dog like Albert?"

"Don't let him fool you, he might look like a stuffed animal, but he can be as tough as nails. Jack Russells are known for their strength."

"That's what Ada told me," said Sarah as she took a bite of the warm flaky pastry. Blueberry juice dripped down her chin. She wiped it off with a napkin. "This is so delicious!" Between bites, she thought to bring up the inquest verdict, but they'd get to it soon enough, and she was suddenly ravenous.

"How long have you lived in Carmel?" she asked. Rosie let go of the white pearl necklace she was rubbing between her fingers and sat up. Her bright eyes met Sarah's.

"Coming on twenty years. I moved here in 1906, after my home in San Francisco was destroyed in the fire that burned parts of the city after the earthquake. The land developers of Carmel offered homeless artists and university professors, like myself, generous loans to build houses here on inexpensive lots."

"You were a professor?" said Sarah, impressed.

"Yes." She smiled. "It runs in the family. My father was a history professor back in Dublin and my mother taught young children. There weren't many opportunities for educated women in Ireland, so my parents encouraged me to come to America for my graduate studies."

Sarah glanced over at the bookshelves. "Your library is first-rate. Have you read all those books?"

"Most of them," she said, looking over at the books as if they were her best friends.

"Where did you teach?"

"At Berkeley College. My main subject was California immigration, starting with the Chinese immigrants who arrived at Angel Island in San Francisco and went in search of gold, but ended up building our railroads. Many settled in San Francisco, but others came to Monterey for employment, and so did the Japanese, the Italians, and the Portuguese. I taught my students to respect their contributions to our country and to have empathy for the suffering they endured to settle here, as they were not always wanted. I still give lectures on immigration at the local libraries, but since the war they are poorly attended. Monterey has a lot of immigrant stories to tell and they're not all good ones."

Rosie stopped talking to bite into a scone, and agreed with Sarah that they were delicious.

"Several of the other Berkeley professors came here with me to look at the vacant lots by the sea. When our horse-drawn carriage came over Carmel Hill and dropped us into a fogbank, it moistened my parched skin like a healing balm. I felt safe, far away from the threat of another destructive fire." She drained her teacup. "Your sister's first impression of Carmel was similar. She too found safety in the fog."

"She never told me that," said Sarah, with a bit of jealousy that Ada would share this intimate feeling with Rosie and not her. She'd often wondered why Ada had wanted to move to this remote village, forsaking New York City where she'd thrived as a renowned artist. But "safety in the fog" made sense. After their parents died in the hotel fire, Ada was afraid to even light a match and it took several years before she would light a wood-burning stove.

Sarah felt Ada's spirit in the room urging her to get down to why she was here.

Sarah opened her satchel and brought out the San Francisco *Examiner*. "I suppose you've seen this," she said, holding up the news-paper. Ada's photograph stared out at them from under the suicide headline making both women upset but for very different reasons.

With a turned-down mouth, Rosie took the paper and dropped it in a nearby wastebasket. She folded her short, thick arms. "I'm sorry you saw that, Sarah. I wanted to be the first one to tell you, not to have you read it in the papers."

"It was quite a shock. The marshal's telegram had been brief. I had assumed my sister's death was an accident."

"An accident? Saints alive, my child! You of all people should know better than that. Ada would never have gone out swimming at night fully dressed. I don't want to upset you, but your sister didn't commit suicide.

"She was murdered."

Sarah put down her scone, having lost her appetite. It took her awhile to respond. "But the article I read said that the handwrit-ing expert confirmed the suicide note was 'in Miss Davenport's handwriting.'"

"Poppycock! Anyone who knows anything about crime investiga-tions knows that suiciders seldom write notes. It's a forgery."

"A forgery? But why would anyone want to kill my sister?"

"I don't know, but I do know the inquest was a bloody sham from the start. Marshal Judd handpicked witnesses who had the same biased opinion of Ada's state of mind as he did. The marshal just wanted to get it over real quick. That's just the way he is. If it was a murder he'd have a lot more work to do. If it was a suicide it'd be a lot easier for him." She rubbed her pearls with such irritation that Sarah thought they might break. "My testimony had absolutely no effect."

"You did what you could," said Sarah, still stunned by this older woman's astonishing revelations. She didn't look insane, but her accusations were bizarre.

"Evidently not enough," said Rosie, hotly. "When I asked him if he had found any evidence of foul play, he glared at me as if I were an old Irish harpy. I hope you don't think so."

Sarah looked down at the wastebasket and the crumbled newspaper.

"Now that *you're* here, Sarah, maybe you can pound some sense into him."

Sarah couldn't think of an appropriate response and turned away to look at a magazine on the side table. The cover illustration was a masked man holding a knife over a kneeling woman's bare chest as she gaped up at him, pleading for her life.

"Bloody awful cover, isn't it?" said Rosie, flipping the magazine over. "Though I have to confess it was a nail-biting story. I didn't figure out who did it until the end. Do you like a good mystery?"

Sarah pulled her eyes away from the pleading victim and onto Rosie, who suddenly reminded her of Agatha Christie's Miss Marple, an amateur detective with an active imagination living in a small village.

"Sometimes. They don't usually carry them in Paris kiosks."

"Well you can catch up while you're staying here. I have lots of them."

Rosie's fascination with detective stories troubled Sarah and her talk of "foul play" upset her even more. She had only just found out that her sister committed suicide and was hardly prepared to take on the possibility of a murder.

Rosie poured her another cup of tea. When Sarah picked it up, it took both her hands to hold it steady. She put it back down.

She suddenly sensed her sister watching them from the entryway and turned to look, but of course she wasn't actually there.

"It was very brave of you to come all this way, dearie, not knowing what you'd have to face when you got here."

"I don't think I had a choice," Sarah said with unexpected irritation.

Rosie's brows furrowed at her tone and was about to say something when Sarah said, "I'm sorry. I didn't mean that. I'm very glad to be here and I'm grateful for your invitation. It's just my sister's death was a terrible shock and then to find out it was a suicide. And now for you to suggest it was a murder is a bit too much for me to take in right now." She shifted to the edge of the couch and was about to cross her legs when Albert came bounding back into the room and jumped into her lap as if she'd called him.

"It's me that should be apologizing," said Rosie. "I shouldn't have brought this up when you just got here."

She brought out her blue packet of Gauloises and looked around for an ashtray. "Do you mind if I smoke?"

"Not you too! Why do all you girls have to smoke those stinky coffin nails? I can't stop you, but I do have my rules and one of them is: No smoking in my home."

Sarah slipped the packet back into her pocket and tried not to show her irritation.

Rosie stood up and straightened her apron. "Why don't you and Albert take a walk on the beach? Get to know the place a little." She smiled down at the small dog who jumped off Sarah's lap and stood in front of Rosie wagging his tail. "He'll be pleased to show you around." Albert cocked his head at Sarah when she stood up.

"That's what Ada would do when she needed a cigarette," said Rosie. As if on cue, Albert ran into the kitchen, came back with a leash hanging from his mouth, and balanced on his hind legs. Ada had told Sarah how smart Albert was and how quickly he learned, but seeing him actually do such an entertaining trick made her laugh, which was a relief to both women and probably Albert, too.

"Go on now, dear girl," said Rosie. "An afternoon constitutional is just what you need. I'll show you your room upstairs when you get back. Tomorrow we can talk about Ada. I'm here to help you in any way I can."

— 3 —

In Rosie's front garden, a budding scarlet rose caught Sarah's attention. It was a pigment found in the cinnabar mineral used in Renaissance paintings, an expensive pigment she coveted in her sketch box. She breathed in the various fragrances. Monet's impressionistic pigments of yellow, orange, vermilion, crimson, violet, blue, and green were all visible in the blooming garden. This was her world and she hesitated to step out of it, but Albert was leaning against her leg, the leash still in his mouth. She bent down and clipped it on his collar.

Outside the fenced garden, Camino Real was an undulating dirt road that stretched in either direction. In the afternoon light the Bay's cresting waves could be heard and seen between a few cottages widely separated by scrub-covered empty lots. She felt uneasy, even frightened by these isolated cottages, where behind their walls cruelty could easily go unnoticed.

She recognized the Monterey cypresses from Ada's paintings. The sinewy silver trunks made strong by coastal gales, their masculine limbs twisted into mythical forms by the forces of nature.

Nose to the ground, Albert pulled Sarah across the road, stopping to sniff the wide trunk of an ancient oak.

Sarah lit a cigarette and exhaled the blue-gray smoke skyward through the oak's gnarly limbs.

Albert stopped in front of the closed gate of a brown-shingled cottage. Weeds were beginning to sprout on the pebble path leading up to its covered porch. The geraniums planted in pale blue window boxes had lost their blooms, their leaves burnt to a crisp under the relentless hot sun. The locked and shuttered windows indifferent to their thirst. No one was at home to care.

The little dog scratched on the gate and whimpered. Sarah knelt down and anxiously said, "What's wrong, Albert?"

And then she saw it. A rough wooden plank was nailed to the gate. Its carved letters spelled out THE SKETCH BOX. Her heart clenched. It was the name Ada had given her cottage. Albert was begging Sarah to open the gate so he could go home.

Across the road, on the second floor of Rosie's lodge, a curtain fluttered in an open window. The bedroom window where Ada had written letters to Sarah describing the Sketch Box as it was being built. Sarah's grief erupted into anger and resentment. This is the cottage that had been built with the money Ada made by selling their apartment in Manhattan, and Ada had never asked Sarah's permission to sell it. As always, she'd never considered what Sarah wanted, and then assumed her sister would enjoy hearing about the construction. Sarah never wrote back.

She saw a shadow behind the curtain. She waved, but it was just a trick of light. No one waved back.

Albert kept scratching on the gate and moaning. Sarah's unwilling hand opened the latch and he ran up to the front door. He barked and jumped up trying to turn the doorknob.

Sarah ran up to him. "She's not here, Albert. Ada's not here. She doesn't live here anymore. Nor do you." He wasn't listening.

She finally had to pick him up and didn't set him down until they were back on the other side of the closed gate. Fortunately, Albert perked up when he saw a squirrel and took off with Sarah holding on to the leash. She stumbled over the knobby roots of oak trees as he chased after his prey. If only she could be so easily distracted by a squirrel when her feelings for her sister turned into unwanted resentment and bitterness.

When they reached the dune overlooking the beach, Sarah dropped down on a bench in front of the Carmel Bath House to catch her breath and fan her flushed face. The wood-framed structure was spacious and had a gorgeous view of the Bay through its wide, glass windows. Ada had told her the Bath House was a gathering place for Carmel's artist colony. Through the open door, she watched carefree men and women laughing. Near a radio console, two young women were singing along to Al Jolson's hit song, "California, Here I Come."

A seagull cawed and soared over the turquoise surf breaking on a beautiful stretch of white sand. Swimmers and sunbathers were scattered along the beach to the south. Sounds of delight were carried in the breeze from children as they flirted with the waves and threw sticks to their dogs to fetch.

"Carmel Bay is a rich palette of blues and violets and titanium white hues worthy of a thousand or more brushstrokes," her sister had written. "You have to come see it for yourself. You'll be so happy here."

It was her attempt to reach through Sarah's resentment with their shared love of pigments, another attempt to share her artist paradise with her sister.

Sarah looked up at the cloudless sky. *I'm sorry, Ada. I should have answered your letters, but I couldn't forgive you for selling our apartment, not even now.*

The sun's rays were hot and Sarah took off her jacket and let her blouse hang outside her skirt. *What was the point of raking over the past*, she thought. *I can't change what happened.*

Directly below and to her right, a dozen or so young women stood in front of sketch boxes unfolded into easels propped up on tripods stuck in the sand. They dipped their paintbrushes into large hand-held palette boards and brushed dabs of paint across their canvases.

She and Ada had often spent summers on the New England coast painting together like this. *And now you're gone and I've come to bury you. Why did you do it, Ada? When you had so much to live for? And why, when I so desperately need you to talk to me, are you silent?*

Sarah frowned at her shiny black patent pumps, unbuckled the straps, stuffed the stockings in the jacket pocket, and dug her cramped toes into the warm sand while watching a slightly stooped gentleman in a Panama hat stop behind each painter, point at the canvas on her easel with a teacher's pointing stick, speak briefly, and move on to the next student. All the women nodded deferentially when he spoke.

She recognized Henry Champlin, the renowned pleinairist and art teacher. Sixteen years ago, Ada was a student at his summer art school in Rhode Island.

When her sister came home, brown from the sun and feeling sassy, she hung the portrait she'd painted of him over her bed and pointed out to Sarah his handlebar moustache and rusty orange beard that ended in a sharp point on his chest. "His upper whiskers tickled when he kissed me. He'd get so angry when I giggled."

Fourteen-year-old Sarah, still too young to have been kissed, was put off by the thought of Ada kissing a man twice her age. She wouldn't have wanted his scratchy whiskers anywhere near her face, or Ada's face for that matter. But his portrait had been painted by her talented sister and she made a study of it as she did with all of Ada's paintings.

It was Champlin who had introduced Ada to Carmel. He had closed his Rhode Island school and taught here in the summers. When he offered Ada a teaching position, she jumped at the opportunity.

By then, Sarah and Ada were both living in New York with Aunt Helen, their mother's sister. She'd offered to share her Manhattan apartment with them after Ada had graduated from the Art Institute of Chicago and gotten her first teaching job at the Art Students League on 57th Street.

Sarah had been jealous of Ada's first summer spent in Carmel while she stayed behind in the stifling hot apartment to take care of Aunt Helen, who had become an invalid. After their aunt died, Ada continued to teach summer classes in Carmel and Sarah, never invited to join her, found work in Manhattan on her school vacations.

Albert tilted his head and gazed curiously up at her as if to say, "Why are we stopping here? I want to run on the beach."

Sarah freed him from his leash and he scampered down the sand dune. She contemplated the steep drop and decided to take the rope handrail that led down through the sunbathers to the water's edge.

As she dipped her feet in the water, a hefty wave took her by surprise and splashed water on her skirt. She laughed, pulled the skirt above her knees, and pedaled backward like the children dancing and laughing around her.

As children, she and Ada had often played like this on Lake Michigan. Ada had taught her to swim, if throwing her into the water and letting her fend for herself was teaching. If not a swimming lesson, it was certainly a lesson on survival.

But now Sarah shrank back from the waves, afraid of the strong current that had dragged Ada underwater.

She walked southward along the shore, throwing a stick to Albert who happily retrieved it over and over again. Eventually a granite promontory, half buried under the incoming tide, blocked their progress. Another Ada painting, she thought. Being in Carmel was like walking through an exhibition of Ada's work.

They turned back.

When Sarah saw the student painters again, the mid-afternoon sun had cast their shadows across the sand. Several were sitting and others were standing, posed like Georges Seurat's painting *Un Dimanche après-midi à l'Île de la Grande Jatte*—Parisians wearing sunhats and straw boaters or berets, staring out at the sailboats on the Seine river.

Women's fashion had noticeably changed since Seurat's pastel painting of corseted silhouettes. These women on Carmel Beach had lived through the Great War, had earned their right to vote, and thrown away their corsets, bustles, layered underclothes, padding, and somber fabrics. Their blazing red, yellow, and orange blouses were like freedom banners waving in the sea breeze.

Several men in shirtsleeves and rolled-up trousers were squatting nearby next to a rocky outcrop. Their hands were underwater and when they brought up large black shells shaped like human ears, they raised them above their heads and shouted, "I got one!"

Sarah was fascinated by the colorful beach scene and would've sketched it if she'd brought her drawing pad.

Albert seemed to recognize some of the students lounging on a beach blanket next to their folded-away sketch boxes. He hurried over to say hello.

A robust young man came over to Sarah wearing a wide grin. "Hi! My name is Tony Mac Ginnis. My friends call me Mac." He stuck out his hand, ready to shake hers, seemingly not intimidated that she towered over him.

"Sarah Cunningham," she said, brushing the sand off her hand before shaking his.

"Well, you arrived just in time, Miss Cunningham. We're just about to fry up some abalone."

"I'm not sure I know what that is?"

"What is abalone? Holy cow! Where have you been?" His eyes roamed curiously over her couture suit and her polished pumps hanging by their straps in her hand. "Hmm. A stranger to our exotic shores I see. C'mon over and meet my friends."

"Are you sure it's all right? I don't want to intrude on your party."

"Don't worry. There's more than enough abalone to go around."

"Hey everyone, we have a visitor," announced Tony. "This is Sarah Cunningham. Pour her a glass of wine and make her welcome while we men fire up the barbecue."

"Wine?" As an expatriate living in Paris, she was often teased about the absurdity of Amendment Eighteen. If there had been laws in France outlawing alcohol consumption there would've been another revolution. "I thought it was illegal to drink alcohol in the States?"

"Why, Miss Cunningham," said Tony, "you really are new here. Carmel is wine country. It's not illegal to harvest your own grapes and drink your own wine."

The women lounging on the beach were very friendly—not like in Paris or New York where people were generally suspicious of one another. She returned their smiles and took the generously poured glass. They made room for her on the blanket and she tried to make herself less conspicuous by folding her pale legs under the tight skirt that was far more appropriate on the Champs-Élysée than on the beach in Carmel, California.

The students were discussing the paintings of the abstractionist Arthur Dove, whom Sarah had met in Manhattan. At seventeen, she'd been lucky enough, with her sister's help, to get a job as a receptionist at Alfred Stieglitz's gallery, 291, on Fifth Avenue. Dove frequently visited 291, a magnet for modern artists whose work wasn't accepted at the more traditional galleries. When Stieglitz exhibited Dove's abstract paintings based on natural forms, it was a revelation for Sarah—the first time she'd seen any work similar to what she was trying to express. Dove and the other artists she met at the gallery were a major influence in her decision to study modern art in Paris. But then the war came, and she didn't have a chance to fulfill her dream until several years later.

It seemed odd that Henry Champlin's students were talking about Dove with such enthusiasm, when the traditionalist believed you should paint only what you see and not express what you feel inside. She listened to the women while driftwood logs crackled in a nearby fire pit and sparks flew through the azure air. Her body finally relaxed.

Tony and the other men brought their abalone catch to the fire pit, scooped out the shells, hammered the flesh, and laid them on the red-hot grill where they hissed and sizzled.

As promised, her host brought her slices of grilled abalone, their luminescent shells for plates. She made the mistake of asking for a fork.

"A fork?" He laughed. "What do you think this is, the Ritz? We eat it with our hands. It tastes better that way."

The abalone puckered its slimy gray lips and Sarah's stomach turned over in revolt. When she finally managed to fight off her revulsion and bite down on the crunchy gray shellfish, her bravery was rewarded with a satisfying buttery taste.

"This is really good," she said between mouthfuls.

"Spoken like a local," said Tony. "That's why the Japanese and the other immigrants came here in the first place. And us poor artists, too. We all feed off the Pacific. You can't tell by looking out there, but all of Monterey Bay is a giant fishbowl. You can eat a different kind of fish every day if you're clever enough to catch them. Then all you need is a vegetable garden in your backyard and you'll never go hungry. A working artist's paradise, I'd say."

She held up the empty abalone shell to the sunlight. It reminded her of the inlaid mother-of-pearl cigarette lighter that Ada had lit their cigarettes with at Keens; she said it had been a gift from deVrais. After Sarah had admired it, Ada wanted her to have it. But after Ada had told her what a despicable person he was, Sarah gave it back.

Her thoughts were interrupted when Henry Champlin squatted next to her on the blanket. He was as overdressed as she was, maybe even more so. A finely weaved Panama hat, a buttoned-up dark brown waistcoat, and rolled-up linen pants similar to what he wore in his portrait. Way too archaic for an art class on the beach, but he was known for his eccentricities. She hid her smile at the incongruity of his bare feet.

Up close, the manicured moustache that had tickled Ada's young lips sixteen years ago had thinned and the orange beard had faded to gray, but his light brown eyes hadn't lost their teasing, mischievous glint that Ada had duplicated so well in the portrait that Sarah had copied.

He leaned toward her. "Hello, I'm Henry Champlin."

"Sarah Cunningham," she said, reaching out her hand but then quickly pulling it back when she realized it was covered in abalone juice. She refused his offer of a pressed linen handkerchief and wiped her hand on the corner of the blanket she was sitting on.

When she settled back down, he put on his monocle and leaned uncomfortably close. "Haven't we met?"

"No," she replied nervously, "but you knew my sister, Ada Davenport."

An awkward silence fell between them.

"Why of course," he finally said. "The likeness is obvious. You must think I'm an old fool not to recognize you even with this silly contraption." He put away his monocle. "I am so sorry, my dear girl. Every day I ask myself if there wasn't something I could've done to prevent Ada from—"

*Kree-aaahh, kree-aaahh.* Sarah looked up to see an orange-billed tern sweep over their heads and plunge into the sea. Before she could ask him when he last saw Ada, he pulled a gold watch and chain from his waistcoat pocket and said, "We must speak more about Ada, but I can't miss tonight's train to San Francisco."

He pushed himself up and adjusted his waistcoat. "Ada told me you were a modernist." She nodded. "Well then, you might learn a thing or two in my class about the rules of technique. Ada did. Of course, soon after we worked together, she received that first prize at San Francisco's Palace of Fine Arts Exposition and she did whatever she wanted. Are you as talented?"

"I don't know," Sarah murmured.

He brushed the sand off his trousers, picked up his spats and shoes, and swung a suit jacket over his shoulder. "Let's find out. I'll see you here at nine sharp, Monday morning. We'll have time to talk after my class."

Before she could accept or decline, he was halfway up the dune.

She had just stretched out on the blanket to take a much-needed nap when she felt a spray of icy seawater on her face. The perpetrator was a petite boyish-looking girl of eighteen to twenty who was standing over Sarah shaking her wet bob of shaggy black hair.

"Sorry," the girl said, looking down at Sarah. "I didn't mean to get you wet." Sarah wasn't sure that was true.

A smile graced the girl's heart-shaped face when she plopped down on her towel. Sarah thought of violet petals pressed into powder when she looked at her eyes. The face was bronze from spending time outdoors. The girl stretched her short, muscular legs out on the sand, still wet from her swim.

The students got up to leave and took the beach blanket with them. The girl offered Sarah a dry corner of her towel.

"I'm Sirena. A student in Mr. Champlin's plein air class, like them." She pointed to the departing students. "My back ached so much from standing and painting I took a swim."

Sarah introduced herself and said, "Mr. Champlin just invited me to come to one of his classes. What's it like?"

She kicked up sand. "Boring! First he put us through a week of lectures on theory in his miserable dark studio, and then we had to make studies of *his* marine paintings. Today was the first day he let us out. Why should I have to sit and listen to a lecture on painting? I already *know* how to paint."

She jumped up and crouched down next to Sarah. Her black, bushy brows disappeared under her bangs. "Between you and me, I don't think he wants to be on the beach after what happened. It reminds him too much of Ada. You see, they were close, *close* friends, or they used to be, if you get my drift, and her suicide—"

Sarah raised her hand to hush the girl. "Before you say anything else, you should know Ada was my sister."

"But that's why I'm telling you. Miss McCann told me you were arriving today and who else would be sitting out on the beach in a very chic suit other than Ada's sister from Paris?"

Sarah laughed in spite of the girl's sassiness. "How do you know Miss McCann?"

"I live at the Lodge," she said as if Sarah should know that. She dug her hands into the sand and started building the foundation of a sandcastle. Sarah liked the girl's creative playfulness and began to dig a moat around the rising castle to protect it from the incoming tide.

With agile hands the young girl sculptured wet sand into a turret and lay it on the castle roof. "How long are you planning to stay?" she asked, interrupting their silent work.

"I don't know."

When the rising tide had almost filled the moat and started to capsize the castle, Sarah asked, "How did you know Ada and Mr. Champlin were close friends?"

"Buggers! Don't you know who I am?"

"I guess not."

"I was Ada's studio assistant. I knew her pretty well. I'm surprised she never mentioned me."

"She didn't tell me much about the people she knew here."

"I don't know why not. We're a pretty interesting group. Anyway, that's why I know about her relationship with Mr. Champlin and that's why Marshal Judd asked me to be a witness at the inquest."

"You were a witness?" asked Sarah, becoming more and more interested in this odd girl. "Was it difficult? Being a witness, I mean."

"Not really." Even though Sarah had dug out a deep moat the sandcastle was sinking under the incoming tide. Sirena knocked down the crumbling remains with a push of her hand. "Except that

Miss McCann was cross with me. She has this silly notion that Ada was murdered, but we all know it was a suicide."

Sarah looked over at the circle of five or six young men who were still talking loudly around the fire pit. If everyone knew it was a suicide, why did Rosie concoct her own story of foul play? Was it an overactive imagination or could Rosie just not find it in her heart to blame Ada for her self-inflicted death? Hadn't Sarah felt the same sense of denial when she saw that headline in the newspaper?

"What did you say at the inquest?" asked Sarah.

"Oh, just things. Don't worry. I didn't tell the marshal about you."

Sarah snapped around. "What about me?"

"That Ada was furious when you told her you wouldn't come to Carmel."

*How like Ada to complain about me*, thought Sarah, *when I'm not around to defend myself.* "What else did she tell you?"

"Just that you're stubborn and unforgiving."

To hear this spoken out loud, even though it was true, was like a slap in the face.

"I'm sorry," said Sirena, seeing Sarah redden. "I shouldn't have said that. Don't take it too seriously. Ada was probably just kidding. She was like that."

Sarah raised her stinging eyes to the orange sky as the sun's disc slipped below the horizon.

"I better be getting back." She jumped to her feet and brushed the sand off her skirt. "Miss McCann will be wondering what happened to me."

"I'll come with you," said the girl, oblivious to the pain she had just caused Sarah. Either she was incredibly insensitive or just very young, thought Sarah, watching the girl jump up and shake out the towel.

On Sarah's second call, Albert ran over from the fire pit where a few stragglers were scooping sand onto the last embers. When she picked him up, he licked her salty cheeks. Sarah was grateful for his sympathy and hugged him to her chest.

When they reached the top of the sand dune, she realized she'd left her shoes on the beach.

"I'll get them," Sirena said, running back down. She returned seconds later with the patent pumps in her hands. "I wish I could afford shoes like these. They're the bee's knees. Did you buy them in Paris?"

"Yes, but they weren't expensive," said Sarah, putting Albert down. She brushed the sand off her feet, leaned against a fence post and put on her shoes.

"You know it was Miss McCann who found her," said Sirena.

"No, I didn't know that. On this beach?"

"No. Over there." Sirena pointed south where Sarah had walked earlier with Albert. "See that rocky outcrop? It's called Carmel Point. On the other side is a clamshell-shaped bay. Your sister's body was found on the beach near where the Carmel River flows into the sea. She often went to paint there. She said that's where she wanted you to paint by her side like you used to. Before you got pig-headed and went off to Paris to paint on your own."

*Enough*, Sarah wanted to scream, but instead put on her jacket and buttoned it up against an approaching wall of fog that had followed them up the sand dune and crept under her clothes.

"You seem to know a lot about my sister and me, but I don't know anything about you."

Sirena shrugged. "There's not much to tell. Your life and Ada's are far more exciting than mine could ever be."

"Did you two come to the beach often?"

"In the mornings we'd go for a swim and then if there was an approaching fogbank, like this one, Ada would run into it and act like a *banshee*." She laughed and raised the towel over her head like a cape. "Watch. I'll show you." She flew into the dense gray cloud and started wailing.

A clammy fear gripped Sarah. When she was a child, Ada would read her stories of Irish folklore; the banshee, a female fairy, was a predictor of death in a family. Ada enjoyed wailing like one because it frightened Sarah, who had slept with a light on in her bedroom ever since.

Sirena reappeared and dropped her cloak when she saw Sarah's face. "Sorry. I didn't mean to scare you."

The temperature had dropped and the girl started hugging her chest and shivering. Her lips purple. Her bathing suit still wet from her swim in the ocean. "Here. Take this," said Sarah. She pulled her rosebud shawl out of her satchel and held it out.

Sirena turned away and started running up the road. She shouted back, "Thanks, but I like the cold."

Albert had run between Sarah's feet when Sirena had wailed and was still trembling. Through the dusky light she could barely see the girl and ran to catch up to her, Albert running close behind as if attached to her feet.

# SUNDAY, JULY 20

## —4—

Upstairs in Rosie's Lodge, Sarah had been up since dawn reading through the packet of letters she'd brought with her. Letters that Ada had sent her that might give her some indication as to why Ada would kill herself.

She reread the last telegram Ada sent her on June 20: *I'm in deep trouble, Little Sis. It's about my portraits and only you can get me out of this mess. Come now. Please.*

At the time, Sarah had thought it was just another ploy, though the most compelling one to get her to California. She knew Ada meant well, but she wasn't about to leave Paris, where she was finally getting her first real break.

Proud of herself for standing her ground and not being swayed by Ada's theatrics, she'd put away the telegram and forgotten about it. But rereading it now, she heard the desperation in Ada's voice for the first time and wondered why she hadn't noticed it before.

She had written back, assuring Ada that it was only jangled nerves and that her collection of portraits would be a tremendous success. She promised to come to her October exhibition in Manhattan, adding that she was to have her own exhibition in Paris the month before. Sarah hadn't told her sooner because she didn't want her showing up and stealing the limelight as she'd done back in January at the Whitney Studio Club.

On the night of the school exhibit, Sarah had waited and waited for her sister to arrive. When she finally did show up her fans hovered over her, demanding autographs. Ada was only too happy to oblige. She only glanced at Sarah's submission, which had won the first prize for originality, and mumbled, "Interesting."

*I could've killed you*, thought Sarah, blowing smoke from her cigarette out the bedroom window. Surprised by her own animosity, she quickly said, *I didn't mean that, Ada. I promise I'll never think that again. Yes, I resented your indifference to my work and yes, I was jealous of your successes, but I never stopped loving you. I never wished you dead. There were just those moments when I didn't like you very much. The competition, the broken promises, the put-downs . . .*

None of that mattered now, she told herself. What did matter was that she keep the promise made at Keens. She was Ada's executor, and it was up to her to ship Ada's portraits to Eric Crocker's gallery. He'd already been in touch with Sarah and said he'd have to cancel if they weren't delivered soon.

She hurried downstairs and burst in on Rosie in the kitchen making her lodgers breakfast. "Do you have a key to the cottage?"

Rosie smiled. "I was wondering how long it would take you to ask me for the key. As my Da used to say, 'Your feet will bring you to where your heart is.'"

"Sorry, Rosie, but I don't know what you mean."

Rosie opened the kitchen sideboard and handed Sarah three keys dangling from a yellow ribbon.

"Your heart belongs in that cottage. You just have to get your feet to take you there. If you'll wait a moment, I'll finish rolling this loaf of soda bread and come with you."

"Thanks, Rosie, but I'd prefer to go on my own." If Rosie was disappointed she didn't show it. It was the little dog who looked up at Sarah plaintively. "Come join me when you're done here and please bring Albert with you."

A gust of wind rustled through the sprawling oak in the front yard of the Sketch Box as Sarah passed under it. Whispering leaves fell down around her. She knocked at the pale blue front door foolishly hoping Ada would swing it open and say, "Thank goodness, Little Sis, you're finally here."

Her nervous hand shook as she took the keys out of her pocket, slid the latchkey into the lock, turned it counterclockwise until it clicked, and stepped inside. Ada's well-worn tweed jacket hung on a hook in the entryway; the vanilla fragrance of *Shalimar* still lingered on its collar, as if Ada had just taken it off. The reality of Ada's death hit her hard in the stomach—her sister was never going to wear that jacket again.

She pushed away her grief and, not taking any time to stop in the living room, rushed through an archway that Rosie said led into the kitchen and that the studio door was set in the wall to the right of the sink. Despite her impatience and the obstinate padlock, she finally got the door opened.

The odor of linseed oil, turpentine, and cobalt chloride escaped from the studio and tickled her nose when she stepped inside. Slanted rays of the morning sun drifted through a skylight and illuminated the landscapes that were hanging from the white plastered walls. Sarah's eyes crossed the paint-splattered cement floor to a grand window framed in the northern wall, a window as important to a painter as pen and paper is to a writer. Its mellow light cast a soft glow over the canvases propped against the other walls.

The studio was an immense space with a large storage loft at one end, and even though Ada had described it in detail, Sarah was still impressed. No wonder Ada couldn't wait to show it to her.

Few artists ever had a studio of these proportions. In Paris, she was cramped in a communal Académie studio where the students had to share splinters of light coming through one window.

"This is simply glorious," she whispered, arching her back to look up through the blue, blue sky framed in the skylight. Her eyes followed the stream of dust motes down onto a large canvas propped up on an easel. She wondered if it was something Ada was working on before she died and walked over to it. She recoiled. It was not Ada's work.

Thick brush strokes of oily ebony paint had created monstrous waves that seemed to be flailing down on a narrow strip of beach. The blood-red sky above the waves was like the underworld in Dante's *Inferno*. She touched the crest of a foamy black wave. The wet oil stained her finger and sent chills down her back. The canvas had been recently painted.

On the sink was a wide brush soaking in a Mason jar of muddy turpentine. A smaller paintbrush was lying on a palette of red and black oils. A shuffling noise came from the loft above her head and she froze in fear.

She heard Rosie calling her name and ran out of the studio into the kitchen, slamming and locking the door behind her.

"What's wrong?" asked Rosie, seeing Sarah's pale face.

"Does anyone have permission to use Ada's studio?"

"Not anyone I know of, though it's certainly possible. Why?"

"Because someone is in there right now. Where's Albert?"

Rosie called him and he came running in from the living room. Sarah unlocked the bolt. Albert ran in ahead of them, barking.

"Why, it's gone," said Sarah, staring at the empty easel.

"What's gone?" asked Rosie.

"There was a painting here on the easel."

"Are you sure?"

"I know what I saw, Rosie," she snapped, "and I heard someone up in the loft."

"It could've been mice."

"No, Rosie! Someone was just in here. Look at the sink." She held up her blackened finger. "The canvas was still wet. The paintbrushes. The palette."

On the far side of the studio, Albert was sniffing and scratching at the alley door. She ran over and flung it open onto an empty lot. Albert took off barking down a flagstone path that led to the front of the cottage and the road. Rosie called after him, but he was already out of sight.

"What is this side door used for?" asked Sarah.

"Ada used it to bring in art supplies or to carry out her finished paintings. Otherwise she kept it locked."

A ladder was leaning up against the loft. "Well, someone else has a key. Look at the splotches of black fingerprints going up the rungs."

"There must be some explanation," said Rosie. "Ada could've loaned her studio to one of the students to use while she was away and gave them a key."

"But she isn't *away*, Rosie. She's dead and everyone must know that. And why hide in the loft and then grab that horrible painting and run off?"

Rosie put her hands on her waist. "I don't know. Maybe they were too embarrassed to be caught."

She made a quick decision. "If you don't mind, Rosie, I'd rather we keep this to ourselves. I'm going to Henry Champlin's art class tomorrow. I'll look at the other students' work to see if anyone paints canvases like the one I saw and, if so, I can deal with that person directly without filing a complaint with Marshal Judd. Meanwhile, would you help me look for the portraits? They have to be in here somewhere." She walked over to the stacks of canvases leaning against one wall and started flipping through them. Rosie started looking through another stack.

Disappointed with her search, Sarah climbed up the ladder and started to look through the canvases in the loft.

Twenty minutes later when she came back down, she shrugged and Rosie raised empty hands.

"Where else could Ada have stored them?" asked Sarah. By now she was frantically looking in every corner of the studio.

"There's the upstairs bedroom."

They hurried back through the kitchen and turned to the right at the end of a hall. Rosie waited below while Sarah climbed up the spiral steps. The pretty room contained a bed covered in a quilt, a round rug across the wide-planked polished floor. The bay window had an unobstructed view of the Pacific. A door stood open revealing an empty closet.

She came back downstairs. "It's lovely up there, but no portraits. Is that where Ada slept?"

"No. She meant that room for you. She had the window built especially. The architect, Mr. Murphy, said, 'Windows aren't made that way here on the coast.' He swore it would crack in a harsh winter storm, but Ada insisted."

"Too bad she never lived here long enough to find out," said Sarah with such sadness that Rosie put her arm around her shoulders.

"You've had quite a morning, dearie. I think we both could do with a cup of tea in Ada's kitchen. I brought some in my thermos."

"Thank you, Rosie, but I can't settle down with a cup of tea, not with the portraits still missing. I've got to find them. Where could they be?"

"Maybe you should ask Sirena? She was responsible for cataloging Ada's artwork. Maybe she knows."

"Good idea," said Sarah, heading for the front door.

"Hold on," said Rosie. "Sirena went out. She won't be back until this afternoon." She held up the thermos and smiled. "Let's have that cup of tea, shall we?" Sarah followed Rosie back into the kitchen.

She had been in such a hurry to find the portraits that she hadn't noticed the hand-painted royal blue and emerald green peacocks painted on the walls. She was sure it was Ada's handiwork. Ada was convinced the peacock symbolized resurrection, renewal, and immortality. She often used their pigments in her paintings.

Feeling her grief overcoming her, Sarah opened the window above the sink and looked out at the sea view, breathing in the salty air Ada might have painted. She filled Albert's water bowl and not knowing what else to do, sat down on the blue banquette to watch him drink.

"Everything is so modern," she said, glancing at the gas stove. A far cry from the hot plate in her garret in Paris where she boiled water to pour into a claw-foot tub that doubled as a breakfast table when she put a panel of wood on top.

"It wasn't always so modern in Carmel," said Rosie. "When I first moved here, the homes didn't even have plumbing."

Rosie took down two canary yellow mugs from a wooden shelf, washed them in the sink, filled them with tea from her thermos, and placed them on the table next to a vase of dead daisies that she dropped into the waste bin.

Sarah sipped the warm, comforting tea, thanked Rosie for bringing it, and turned to gaze out the nook's window. The sky and the ocean met in a precise horizontal line. Ada looked at this same view, she thought, and then painted it.

"Rosie, you're right. My heart is here. I'd like to stay here while I'm in Carmel and, if it's all right with you, I'd like Albert to stay here with me."

Albert stood up on his hind legs and put his paws on Sarah's lap.

"Of course, dearie. This is where you both belong. Ada would want you here."

Sarah picked up Albert. "You are such a comfort to me, Albert. And so are you, Rosie." Her eyes were welling with tears she couldn't hold back, and she turned back to the window to brush them away.

Rosie squeezed Sarah's hand, handed her a hankie, and got up to leave, "I need to go back to the lodge and finish my baking. And what about yourself? You didn't have any breakfast. Can I make you a sandwich?"

"Thanks, Rosie, but I think I'll stay here awhile and open up the house. It needs a good airing."

"Suit yourself. There will be sandwiches on my kitchen table when you do get hungry." She looked down at Albert. "You look after your mistress and don't let her get too down in the mouth."

Sarah pulled back the damask curtains in the living room, opened the windows, and folded back the blue shutters. Fresh air rushed in and beams of sunlight brushed over white walls, absorbing and reflecting the upholstered furniture's yellow and blue pigments, turning the wall into a painter's palette of pastels. Ada's palette.

A long couch was angled in front of a stone fireplace in the far corner. She sat down on the couch and noticed a hook in the wall. She wondered why the picture that should have been hanging from it had been taken down and where was it.

After a few moments, Albert jumped off the couch and ran down the hallway. He scratched on a closed door. Sarah picked him up, then turned the brass doorknob and hesitated before entering Ada's bedroom.

Albert jumped up on a four-poster bed and curled up below one of Sarah's own early landscape paintings hanging on the wall. It was painted when she was still influenced by Ada's artistry. It pleased her that Ada had kept it, that she'd found a special place for it in her new home.

Set on top of the dresser was a silver-handled hairbrush and mirror set that had been their mother's. There was a photograph of herself and Ada taken at the Petit Palais in Paris last summer at Ada's exhibition. Sarah recalled the words Ada had used when asked how it felt to be an internationally renowned painter with exhibitions around the world: "Eternal, exquisite happiness."

Sarah sat next to Albert on the bed. He placed his front paws on her lap and looked up at her with the eyes of a wise soul.

"Oh, Albert, if only you could tell me why she killed herself so I could find some peace. What powerful dark force destroyed the 'eternal, exquisite happiness' that she shared with all of us?"

Albert jumped off the bed and scratched at the closet door.

Inside was Ada's large steamer trunk plastered with stickers from different ports of call. Sarah knelt down and brushed her hand over the art deco illustrations. As Ada's fame grew and she traveled by ship to her international exhibitions, the stickers had multiplied until they were pasted on top of one another.

The only time Ada's voyages were curtailed was during the war when the cruise ships were requisitioned for transporting soldiers and war supplies. She remembered Ada restlessly pacing the living room floor in their New York apartment, anxious to travel overseas again. Sarah was silently pleased that her sister had to stay home.

She pushed back the trunk's heavy lid. It was packed with neatly folded dresses, blouses, and women's trousers. A summery wardrobe, the fabrics jersey and linen. "But why was Ada packing for a trip, if she was about to kill herself?" she asked the ever patient Albert sitting by her side. He tilted his head as if wondering the same thing.

The only other piece of furniture in the bedroom was their father's roll-top mahogany desk. Ada, never wanting to part from it, had moved it from their home in Chicago to their New York apartment and now to its final resting place at the Sketch Box. Sarah couldn't imagine how she could take it back to Paris.

She opened the roll top hoping to find anything that might explain Ada's suicide. but its drawers and shelves were depressingly empty.

It had been wishful thinking that she might find her sister's *Book of Quotables*, a leather-bound journal with a square-cut ruby set in its brass clasp and on the bottom right corner, Ada's initials, *ABD*. Ada used to jot down encouraging quotations from her favorite poets and authors and Sarah could've used an encouraging passage right now, but she'd have to settle for one of Rosie's sandwiches.

She left a disappointed Albert in the studio to ward off any uninvited guests and set off across the road. Rosie greeted her at the front door and told her Sirena was home.

At the kitchen table, Sirena was eating a sandwich wearing saffron-dyed coveralls that made her look even younger than she did on the beach.

"Rosie says you're moving into the Sketch Box today," said Sirena before Sarah could even say hello.

"News travels fast around here," said Sarah, choosing a ham sandwich over peanut butter.

She'd hardly taken a first bite when Sirena furrowed her dark brows and asked, "Why don't you use Davenport for your last name?"

Sarah decided to be as candid as the girl was. "Sarah Davenport would always be compared to Ada Belle Davenport. Sarah Cunningham can do whatever she wants."

"Good idea. I wouldn't want my pictures to be compared to anyone else's, especially an artist as famous as your sister. Is your work very different from hers?"

"I think so."

"Can I see it?"

"I'm afraid not. Except for a few recent sketches, everything is in Paris."

"You could invite me to paint with you in Ada's studio. I used to do that with her."

"I doubt if I'll have any time for studio work while I'm here."

Sirena had a face that changed moods like a chameleon changed colors. It would be difficult to paint her portrait with such ever-changing expressions. Right now, it was showing disappointment and, preferring the happy face, Sarah added, "But I'd still like to see your work."

"Okay," said Sirena, immediately brightening. "You know, I'll miss you, Sarah."

"But I only just got here and we're just beginning to know each other."

"I know, but you're going back to Paris soon, aren't you?"

"I hope so. My exhibition is in—"

"You're going to have a show in Paris? Swell. I wonder why Ada never told me that."

"She might not have known," said Sarah, losing her appetite and putting down the sandwich. Could it be that Ada never got her last letter thanking her for all she had done for her and how it had finally paid off with her own exhibition in Paris? And that all was forgiven, and she'd come to Ada's show in Manhattan?

"That would be a shame," said Sirena, as if reading her mind. "That would've made her very happy. Is there anything I can do to help you get back to Paris in time for your exhibit?"

"Yes there is. I need to ship Ada's portraits to New York before I leave, but I couldn't find them in the studio. Rosie thought you might know where Ada stored them?"

"Why would I know?" Sirena said defensively. She picked up her plate and took it over to the sink to wash it, her back to Sarah.

"Because you worked for her."

"So what. That doesn't mean I knew everything." Then she turned to face Sarah and said, "What I do know is if you hadn't stopped writing to Ada, perhaps she might've told you where she was storing the portraits instead of you having to ask her lowly assistant."

*Touché,* thought Sarah, *but why is she is trying to make me feel that I have to justify myself? Is it her way to avoid answering my questions?* Sarah cleared her throat. "Sirena, if you know where the portraits are, please tell me."

"I did tell you. I don't know where they are." The girl returned to her seat and rocked back and forth on the spindly back legs of the chair, like young children do until their mothers say "don't do that," which Sarah said now, and then added more sternly, "I think you do know, Sirena, but I don't know why you won't tell me."

The girl brought the chair's legs down hard on the floor and sat up straight, a certain resolve set in her face. "All right. If it will get you to go back to Paris, there is something I didn't tell Marshal Judd or anyone else. Not even Rosie. It's kind of embarrassing."

"Go on."

"Four days before Ada died, she fired me. It was a total shock to me. We were getting along famously and I thought she was pleased with my work. Those portraits you're looking for? I packed them up in crates and was ready to send them out when she told me to leave. Just about pushed me out the door. So if the crates are gone then I don't know where they are. Maybe she burned the portraits before she killed herself."

"Burned them?" said Sarah, stunned. "Ada never lit anything but coal and that was only to keep warm. After our parents died in a hotel fire she was terribly afraid of flames."

"Oh right. Sorry. I forgot about that."

Sarah had never expected to have such a peculiar conversation with her sister's assistant. A conversation that raised more questions than gave answers. Like, where did this strange girl come from? Ada was known for picking up waifs off the street and giving them money and clothes. Is that where she met Sirena? On the street?

She took some slow sips of water before asking, "Did Ada tell you why she was letting you go so abruptly? I would've thought she'd at least let you ship the crates to New York."

"Nope. Just threw me out. But you know how unpredictable she was. She had a red-headed temper, your sister."

Sirena looked over at the kitchen clock above the refrigerator and stood up, adjusting her coverall straps on her swimmer's shoulders. "Rosie said you might need help shopping for groceries. I could help if we go now. I've got a modeling job later this afternoon and I can't be late or I won't get paid."

# MONDAY, JULY 21

## —5—

The clanging cowbell set off Albert's bark. Sarah opened the front door to see Sirena in her saffron coveralls, a paint-stained sketch box in one hand and a parasol in the other.

"That's Ada's robe," said Sirena, gaping at the silk kimono wrapped around Sarah.

"Yes, it is," she said, tying the loose band around her waist. "Why? Is something wrong with it?"

"It's just kind of spooky. When you opened the door . . . you know . . . I thought you were her." Sirena adjusted the strap on her sketch box. "I'm on my way to Mr. Champlin's class. Aren't you coming?"

"I'll have to meet you there. I overslept." That was only partially true. She'd had fitful dreams of being chased by giant portraits with blank faces and hadn't gotten any sleep until the first morning light.

"Okay. See you on the beach."

"Please tell Mr. Champlin I'll be late," said Sarah, but the girl had run off and was already out of hearing.

When Sarah had hurriedly packed in Paris, she hadn't had time to consider what one wears in a beach town, and she definitely hadn't planned on attending an art class. But, by chance, at the last minute she'd added her painting smock to her valise. And as far as an easel and art supplies, she never went anywhere without her portable art studio—her sketch box.

She put on her only sundress, tied her canvas shoes, and left behind an unhappy Albert. Until she found out who had been using Ada's studio and had the lock on the alley door changed, she needed him to be a guard dog. On her way out of the studio she grabbed a small blank canvas.

When she arrived on the beach, she spotted the students draped in long black smocks, standing like a colony of penguins. Their heads were bobbing up and down under wide-brimmed straw hats as they gazed out at the calm sea and back again at their canvases. Their black parasols, which effectively blocked out the direct sunlight, fluttered in the breeze.

Sarah apologized to Mr. Champlin for being late and hurriedly put on her own smock, which happened to be bright red. He then pointed to a spot on the beach several yards away and said, "Set up over there."

"Is there a particular subject I should paint?" she asked.

"Paint what you see in front of you," he replied.

As she walked over to the ordained spot, she nodded to Sirena and the other students, while taking a moment to glance at their canvases—composed, rather colorless, formations of jagged granite jutting out into the bay, splashed by the silver and white hues of breaking waves. None of their work had the nightmarish theme of the painting that had disappeared from Ada's studio.

She unfolded the three skinny legs that supported her easel and stuck them into the sand. Picking over several tin tubes of oil paint in her sketch-box drawer, she squeezed canary yellow, carmine red, and titanium white onto her palette board. Mixing the familiar pigments gave her a surge of energy and she quickly dipped a wide brush into the oils and made short brushstrokes across the canvas. To get more vivid splashes of color she added cadmium orange. Then with her palette knife she smeared a thick glob of white over the orange.

"I thought you'd studied the basic techniques of plein air pictures under your sister's tutelage," said Champlin severely. Unnoticed he had walked up behind her and was passing judgment over her shoulder.

Without stopping her work, she said, "That was when Ada was teaching at the Art Students League and I was her student. For the past three years I've been studying at the Académie Julian in Paris where I've learned a more modern approach."

"That's very apparent," said Champlin sarcastically. "I hope your sister's teachings weren't wasted on you."

She waited until his sandy bare feet were gone before she wiped the gooey white oil from her fingers and furiously mixed more oils on her palette. Hadn't he told her to paint what she saw? For her, the clouds were not clouds but white sheets drying on a clothesline. And the waves splashing and falling against the coarse, jagged rocks were rain drops in vibrant shades of orange dripping down a crimson wall.

By midday, Sarah felt a headache coming on and sat down on the sand to rest her eyes. She was accustomed to working under studio lights, not glaring sunlight. Sirena saw her discomfort and came over to share her parasol and a thermos of water.

After taking a break under the parasol, Sarah returned to her painting. When she finished her morning work, she had fully expressed van Gogh's belief that a painting should "exaggerate the essential" and "leave the obvious things vague." She was very pleased with her canvas.

"I see you are in need of instruction in color theory, Miss Cunningham," Champlin said as she was putting away her supplies. "I must say your viscous expressions splattered on the canvas are very clever, almost entertaining, but the aesthetic is inappropriate in my class."

She could hear Ada scolding her. *Shame on you, Little Sis. You know he and I both have a limited tolerance for expressionists, but you goad us anyway. Watch out—he doesn't take kindly to whippersnappers.*

A small curl came to Sarah's lips. Ada had often called her a *whippersnapper* when she was trying to teach Sarah how to paint and Sarah wanted to do it her way. But what widened her smile even more was that Ada was talking to her again, even if it was only to scold her.

"Am I amusing you?" Champlin's voice jolted her and she bumped against her easel, its wobbly legs buckled under and her canvas tumbled facedown onto the sand.

The other students turned toward the commotion with various expressions of surprise and concern. Champlin reached down to pick up the canvas but Sarah was quicker.

He turned to speak to his students, "When painting on the beach, you need to position your easel firmly in the sand or accidents like this can happen."

He lowered his voice and leaned closer to Sarah, "Why don't you finish cleaning up and come meet me in my studio. Sirena can give you directions." He climbed up the dune to the Bath House, put on his shoes, and rode off on his bicycle without looking back.

Sarah left her sketch box, her red smock, and the ruined canvas with Sirena, who said she'd drop them off at the cottage. The canvas covered in a million grains of sand would have to be thrown out, but she would hold onto her ideas for the next picture.

The long hot trek to Champlin's house gave her time to remind herself that she only wanted to find out if he knew why Ada killed herself and not to act like a wounded art student being unfairly criticized by her teacher. She should be beyond such behavior by now.

She followed Sirena's directions and turned left on Santa Lucia Avenue. Several minutes later, she found herself on a scenic bluff overlooking another bay, wider than Carmel Bay but with fewer cottages. Down in the river valley on the other side of the beach were two large farmhouses. Farther inland she could see what she later learned was the ruins of the eighteenth-century Carmel Mission bell tower built by the Spanish for the missionary Father Junipero Serra.

She stopped at the front gate of a weathered gray clapboard cottage with LAST CHANCE carved on a shingle nailed to a post.

The flower garden and manicured lawn with grass soft enough to lie down on seemed incongruous; it was difficult to imagine the fastidious Henry Champlin down on his knees tending to such delicate floral beds.

He opened the door and waved her inside with his unlit pipe. Overheated from her walk, she asked where the bathroom was. He pointed across the living room. "Down the hall on the left. I'll be in the kitchen."

Midway across the living room, she was sidetracked by an A.B. Davenport landscape hanging above a riverstone fireplace. Four majestic eucalyptus trees were in the foreground of a golden pasture. The sunlit blue sky brushed lightly with billowing white puffs that seemed to move across the painting. In the background a range of mountains rose in purple splendor.

Ada had captured the fleeting iridescent sunlight with her delicate brushstrokes, making the pastoral scene live and breathe. This iridescent quality was something Sarah had struggled to perfect when she studied plein air, but she'd never succeeded in capturing the sunlight's subtle brilliance like her sister.

In Champlin's bathroom, she splashed water on her face and tried to calm down, but seeing Ada's painting on his wall had shocked her. How did *Eucalyptus Trees* end up on Champlin's wall, when back in January it was hanging over the fireplace in her and Ada's apartment? The last time she saw Ada alive.


*I'd come rushing home after a meeting with the art dealer Peter Merkel, who had been very impressed by my prize-winning painting at the Whitney Studio Club exhibition. I couldn't wait to tell you about his offer to represent me.*

"*Calm down,*" *you said, immediately deflating my excitement.* "*How can you be so naive? Peter says that to all the pretty young artists. It's just a come-on to get you into his bed. I thought you knew better by now, Sarah.*"

*I countered with,* "*You just don't believe anyone would take my work seriously.*"

"*Don't be ridiculous. I just don't want you to get hurt.*"

"*Hurt? That's a laugh. Since when did you care about me getting hurt?*"

"*That's not fair, Sarah. I care very much. That's why I'm telling you not to trust art dealers. They aren't your friends, particularly the likes of Peter Merkel.*"

"*And here I thought you'd be so pleased. With an established art dealer in New York representing my work, I could come back home. We could live together again. Isn't that what you've always wanted?*"

"*Yes, I used to feel that way.*" *You paused and then said,* "*But now I'd prefer you join me in Carmel.*"

"*Carmel? What are you talking about? Why would I want to live out there in the middle of nowhere when I was just offered representation in New York?*"

*You sat down and asked me to do the same, but I remained standing.*

"*It was foolish of me not to tell you at Keens the other night, but we were having such a lovely time. I just put it off.*"

"*Put off what? What are you keeping from me?*"

"*I do wish you'd sit down, Sarah, and stop glowering over me as if I was your worst enemy.*"

*Reluctantly, I sat down next to you.*

"*You see, I've bought land in Carmel and I'm planning to build a cottage on it. I can't afford to keep both places, so I sold our apartment. The new owners are moving in next month. I'm keeping a few mementos of sentimental value, and my paintings, of course.*" *You looked up at* Eucalyptus Trees *hanging above the fireplace, "I'm saving this one for you."*

"I don't care about your damn painting. How could you sell our apartment without asking me?" *My voice faltering.* "This is my apartment too."

"Of course it is, darling, but I'm the one who's been paying the mortgage. If I'd known how strongly you felt about keeping it, I would've asked you, but I thought Paris was your home now, like Carmel is for me."

"My home? A fourth-floor garret with rats scurrying over the leaky roof above my head? That's temporary. I always planned to come back here once I finished my studies."

"I'm sorry, Sarah, but you should've told me that."

*You were right. I should've told you how lonely I was in Paris without you. I should've told you how difficult it was to have a famous artist for a sister. I should've told you how much I loved you. But my pride always got in the way*

*When you put your hand on my shoulder, I brushed it off.*

"Please don't be angry with me, Little Sis. We'll figure something out. You still have the stipend from our parents' trust and if you really want to come back to New York, I'll help pay the rent on a studio apartment."

*When I turned to face you, you looked so sincere, so truly sorry, but I couldn't stop the pent-up resentment I'd felt for too many years.*

"My entire life I've catered to your selfish whims. You've always come first. Stuck while you traveled the world. Never offering to take me with you. Doling out a small allowance to me in Paris that hardly pays for my art supplies while you live in splendor. I even had to wear your hand-me-downs. So now you listen to me. I don't want your painting. I don't want your cottage. I don't want your charity. I want nothing from you. Do you hear? Nothing!"

*I ran to my bedroom, stuffed clothes in my valise, gathered my coat awkwardly around me, and opened the front door to the apartment. Before I left, I looked back at you. You were still seated on the couch, as quiet and as regal as the statuesque eucalyptus trees framed in your painting behind you.*

*From across the room, I yelled, "I'm going back to Paris and I never want to hear from you again. You can find someone else to be your Theo."*

*I slammed the door behind me, stood in the hallway a moment, and waited. You could've come out. Come out and beg me not to leave, tell me you were proud of the prize I'd earned, proud that I now had a New York art dealer, proud that I was your sister. But the door remained closed, the silence of the hallway deafening.*

She was still staring at *Eucalyptus Trees* when Champlin startled her from behind. "It's magnificent, isn't it? I was with Ada when she started painting it. We'd stopped on the side of the road in Carmel Valley to picnic, but she ate very little that afternoon once she had set up her sketch box and started to paint." He reached over to adjust the tilted gold frame and dust it with his handkerchief. "I couldn't afford to buy this now. Her suicide has created an unheard-of demand for her paintings and a significant increase in their value."

"When did you buy it?" asked Sarah, disappointed Ada would've sold the painting she'd promised to her even though she'd said she didn't want it.

"Buy it?" he said, offended. "Ada gave it to me."

Sarah shifted her eyes back to the painting that rightfully belonged to her. But did she deserve to have it after the hateful things she had said to Ada?

She brushed away a stray tear before turning to face Champlin. "I assume Mr. deVrais is the one who has most profited from my sister's death."

"DeVrais is a charlatan." He twisted the right end of his handlebar moustache. "I told her not to get involved with him. He never cared about her work. His only interest is in himself and filling his own coffers. Under what he called his 'creative management skills,' her work actually suffered. All her paintings started to look the same."

Sarah had also encouraged Ada to find a new direction in her work. But now she worried that by encouraging Ada to radically change her canvas was what unhinged her.

He looked fondly at the landscape. "But not this one. This one was an original, pure Ada Davenport, back when she approached her plein air paintings with unadulterated passion."

Seeing how personally attached he was to *Eucalyptus Trees,* she decided not to ask for it back. Ada had wanted her teacher to have it. A farewell gift that he deserved and she didn't.

The living room had a kitchen at one end and an area with a sofa and high-back chairs that looked out on a panoramic view of a white beach below the blue, cloudless sky. As she drew closer to the window, she asked weakly, "Is that where—?"

"Where Ada drowned? Yes it is." He pointed to the other end of the bay. "Over there, where the Carmel River flows into the Pacific, is where Miss McCann found her."

Blood drained from her face and to stop from fainting she pressed her forehead against the cold glass. Champlin took her elbow and guided her over to the sofa where she sank down.

"I'll brew up some coffee. It'll do us both good." He busied himself at the kitchen counter while she took several deep breaths until her heart beat normally. She was composed when he put a mug in front of her and filled it with black coffee. "Cream? Sugar?"

"No thanks."

When he sat down across from her, he held his eyes on her longer than she thought polite.

Finally, he said, "Your eyes express a profound sorrow that wasn't there when Ada painted you as a young woman full of life and hope. Your portrait is an inspiration to anyone who sees it. My favorite in the collection."

The coffee helped get her back on track as to why she was at Champlin's house. She came to find out why he thought Ada killed herself. She told him about Ada's telegram and asked him if he thought the portraits had anything to do with her suicide. He didn't think so.

She asked him when he had last seen the portraits in Ada's studio.

"Two weeks before Ada took her own life. That idiot DeVrais had told her she had no talent with portraits, that she would be ridiculed if she put them on display. It had depressed her and she'd fallen into one of her melancholic moods. Hoping my opinion would cheer her up, she hung all the portraits for my honest assessment."

"And what was your opinion?"

"I told her the truth. The art world would acclaim the portraits as a brilliant new direction for an extraordinary talent. She'd found a way to express the same passion she'd felt when she painted *Eucalyptus Trees*."

"That must have been reassuring to hear that from you."

He shook his head. "She didn't believe me. After deVrais derailed her, she had no confidence in her portraits and went on and on about how the critic Arthur Bye was out to get her and how she couldn't bear to have another bad review. It would destroy her. You women artists shouldn't listen to their chatter. They're never going to give you a good review, however hard you try to please them."

"Easy for the great Henry Champlin to say. Critics are very powerful. We don't have the luxury of ignoring them. Instead, we hide behind our initials when we sign our paintings, so our work gets reviewed and isn't sold for a lot less because we're women."

"My. My. You *are* cut from the same cloth as your sister. She was always getting up on her soapbox about the rights of women artists being abused."

Sarah looked down, surprised at her empty mug, and asked for a refill.

"You gulp down coffee like your sister. She was seated across from me just like you are now when I warned her against drinking too much of it. Bad for her health. She laughed and told me she wasn't planning to live that long. At the time, I thought she was joking."

"Why are you so sure she killed herself? Why couldn't it have been an accident?"

He shook his head. "Your sister could be wild and impulsive, but she wasn't stupid. She knew the ocean's power to kill. She knew she'd be sucked down into the deep underwater canyon twenty yards offshore at low tide."

"But why? I need to know why she would kill herself."

He met her eyes, unblinking. "You really don't know, do you?" He put several spoonfuls of sugar in his coffee and stirred it. "I'd assumed being her sister that—"

"Know what?"

He reached for his pipe, filled it with tobacco, and tamped it down with his forefinger. He put a match to the tobacco and sucked on the pipe until it was red and smoking. "Look, I know it must be painful for you to accept your sister's suicide, but she showed all the familiar signs of an artist with severe neuroses. Exuberant then melancholic. Calm then hysterical. Loving life then wanting it to end."

Here it comes, thought Sarah. Another analysis of female hysteria that men had been spouting ever since Freud published "Dora: The Analysis of an Hysteric." But she let him continue.

"Ada was a thrilling woman to be with, except when she got into one of her dark moods and thought all her years of hard work were meaningless. Her first attempt at suicide was from disgrace."

"You're lying. My sister never tried to kill herself before. I would've known about it."

"I think you and Ada were having some troubles back then. You had moved to Paris and she hadn't heard from you in several months."

There was some truth in what he was saying. Ada hadn't wanted her to go to art school in Paris and it took her awhile to accept Sarah's decision. Sarah asked him to tell her about Ada's attempted suicide.

"She'd had an exhibition of her landscapes at Anderson Galleries in New York. The critics, led by that misogynist Arthur Bye, had organized a campaign against women artists. Ada, the most successful of the group, was Bye's main target. The other critics joined in like the chorus in a Greek tragedy.

"I found her curled up on the floor of her apartment with torn up pieces of his *New York Times* review scattered around her. Bye had said her work was 'Commonplace without redeeming artistic merit.' His review was very effective. None of her paintings were sold.

"When I pulled her off the floor, that lethal pendant she always wore was in her clenched hand. She fought me when I took it away from her. 'Give it to me,' she said. 'There's no point in going on after being humiliated like this. If my work is not appreciated . . . why paint? And if I don't paint then why live?'"

Sarah took her mug to the sink and rinsed it out. Ada had always told her she was very confident about her work, unaffected by the negative critics. But obviously she'd lied. And if she lied about that, what else had she lied about?

Joining Champlin on the sofa, she said, "Is there anything else I should know?"

He struck a match and leaned forward to light her cigarette and relight his pipe. He sucked until the tobacco turned into red hot coals. Its smoke wrapped her in the familiar scent of Paris bistros where men sat smoking on the terraces watching women parading by in the latest fashions as if that was all women ever thought about.

"The day she showed me her portraits she asked me to be a witness to her will. I scoffed at doing it. I told her she was too young to have a will. But she insisted."

"Did you read the will?"

"No. I thought there might be something in it that she didn't want me to know about, because she put a blank page above the signature line. After I signed it, she asked me take down *Eucalyptus Trees* from the wall in her living room."

So that was the painting missing from Ada's cottage, thought Sarah.

"She said I was the only one who had believed in her work from the beginning and to accept it as an expression of her gratitude. She had planned to bequest it to me in her will, but was worried something might happen to it."

"Did she tell you why?"

"She said she was in a nasty legal battle with deVrais. He claimed to own all the copyrights to her artwork and that he had the final say on who bought her work and where it was exhibited, which included *Eucalyptus Trees*."

"Do you think that he was the reason she killed herself?"

He sighed. "No. I lied to you when I said it wasn't the portraits. The truth is I do feel somewhat responsible for what happened. I should never have encouraged her to make such a complete change of subject matter, style, and even color. She just wasn't up to the challenge. I should have known that. Few of us are, including me."

Feeling her own responsibility for Ada's suicide, she crushed her cigarette out in the ashtray.

"Sarah, you might not understand right now, but I'm going to give you some fatherly advice. Ada's death was self-inflicted. She knew what she was doing. Believe me there is nothing you could've done to stop her. Grieve for her and then get on with your own life."

She hurried pass *Eucalyptus Trees* and was already at the gate when Champlin stepped out on the porch and called out, "If there is anything I can do to help you, please let me know."

She turned around and walked back up the steps. "There is something. Do you know where Ada stored the portraits?"

He frowned. "Aren't they in the studio?"

"No, they're not."

"I suggest you ask Paul deVrais. He didn't think the portraits had any value, but that was before Ada's suicide."

## —6—

Sirena had left Sarah's sketch box, her smock, and the ruined painting on the cottage porch. A note from Rosie was taped to the front
door asking her to come to the Lodge right away. As tired and miserable as she felt, Sarah let Albert out and they walked across the road
together.

In the Lodge entryway, she heard Rosie call out, "I'm in the
kitchen."

"Set yourself down, dearie," Rosie said, bringing out a jug from
the ice box. "It's unbearably muggy today so I thought I'd cool off
with a bit of chilled wine. Will you join me?"

Sarah looked suspiciously at the jug Rosie held in her hand.

"It's not contraband, Sarah," said Rosie, putting it on the table. "I
have a prescription, or more accurately a recipe, from Danny at the
pharmacy. I buy a block of pressed grapes and he delivers it. It then
goes into a pot with a gallon of water, ferments in a dark cupboard for
ten days, and then goes in the icebox."

Rosie saw Sarah wasn't interested in how she got around the prohibition laws or her wine recipe and sat down across from her. "Is
something wrong, Sarah? You don't look well."

She forced a smile. "I'm all right." She didn't have the heart to tell
Rosie that Champlin had convinced her of Ada's suicide. And she
hoped foul play wasn't what was on Rosie's mind when she wrote her
note.

Rosie filled their glasses, and meeting Sarah's eyes, said, "Let's
have an Irish toast." They clunked their glasses. "Sláinte." Sarah took

an obligatory sip. It tasted like sour grape juice. She put the glass down.

Rosie perched her round, wire-rimmed glasses on the bridge of her nose and started to read silently from a notepad while she sipped her glass of wine.

"Rosie, was there something you wanted to tell me?" Sarah said, impatiently.

"Hold on, dearie. I've been waiting all day to tell you and I don't want to leave out anything Dr. Lewis told me this morning. Drink your wine while I go over my notes."

The second sip went down easier.

"Who is Dr. Lewis?" asked Sarah, worried there might be an ulterior motive for Rosie giving her a glass of wine. Was Rosie ill?

"Dr. Lewis is my doctor. He's the one who insists I have my heart checked regularly. Of course, I don't believe that malarkey. I'm as fit as a woman half my age." She pulled in her stomach and puffed out her chest. "I know I should eat less scones and get out more often and walk, but—"

"Rosie, what did Dr. Lewis tell you? You're not sick, are you?" Sarah didn't think she could handle any more bad news in one day.

"Of course not." Rosie swallowed a pill with the wine. "In fact, Dr. Lewis told me my heart sounded stronger and to just continue taking these pills to avoid the palpitations. My news is about Ada."

"Ada?" asked Sarah sitting up.

"Yes, Ada. Dr. Lewis told me that she had come to see him with complaints of indigestion and trouble sleeping. She wanted him to give her a prescription of laudanum but he insisted on examining her first.

"I of course asked him if he found anything wrong with her. 'Nothing serious,' he said. 'Her symptoms were only natural.'"

"Natural?" asked Sarah.

Rosie put her hand over Sarah's. "Yes, dearie. He told her to expect her baby in the new year, sometime in February."

"God, no," gasped Sarah. A concerned Albert nuzzled against her legs but she couldn't move to pick him up. "Was he absolutely sure?"

"That's what Ada asked, too. When he finally convinced her, she jumped off the table, startled him with an embrace, and said she'd just about given up on ever becoming a mother."

Rosie looked down at her notes, giving Sarah a few minutes to take in the full meaning of Ada's pregnancy before she said, "Ada asked Dr. Lewis if her age was a problem, but he told her she was in perfect health for a woman of thirty-six and there was nothing to worry about. Then she asked him about traveling by train to Los Angeles. She said she wouldn't go if it would endanger her pregnancy. He told her to have a good time and come see him when she got back.

"Ada told him that wouldn't be until August and that she'd bring the lucky father with her."

Rosie closed her notepad and took off her glasses. "Dr. Lewis wished all of his female patients were as pleased about their pregnancy as Ada was. When he got back after the holidays and heard of her suicide, he just couldn't believe it." She wiped the corner of her eyes with her apron. "Poor, poor Ada."

Sarah didn't know how she managed to get out of the chair or put on Albert's leash, but in a short while she found herself seated on the bench overlooking Carmel Beach.

The bench anchored her to the sand but she'd never felt so adrift.

*Ada, I'm so sorry I ever believed for a moment what other people said about your unbalanced mind. I was so wrapped up in my own guilt that I couldn't see clearly. You were saner than any of us and you would never have killed yourself with or without child.*

Albert pushed his nose under her clenched hands until she picked him up and pressed him against her aching heart.

When Sarah and Albert came back to the lodge, candles were casting a warm light on the lodgers who were eating, talking, and laughing around Rosie's dining room table. Sarah recognized their faces from Champlin's class or from the abalone barbecue. Sirena smiled at her from across the table and a few of the girls shuffled their chairs to one side and made room for her. She had thought to go upstairs, but she was afraid to be alone and took the offered chair.

Rosie introduced her as Ada Davenport's sister and asked the lodgers to introduce themselves. Each girl spoke in turn. Marie and Annie were from San Francisco. Elizabeth, a gorgeous Southern belle, was from Virginia. Two sisters, Hallie and Jeanette, who had a habit of speaking at the same time, were from St. Louis. When it came to Sirena's turn she said Sarah already knew who she was.

Sarah dipped the warm, crusty bread in the beef stew that Rosie put in front of her, but she ate very little of it. The girls talked around her about an upcoming performance of *Pirates of Penzance* at the outdoor Forest Theater in Carmel. Rosie had auditioned and gotten a part in the chorus. The musical director said he couldn't resist her enthusiasm and her strong alto voice.

Sarah made an effort to show interest in some talk about the new shipment of pigments that had just arrived at the art supply store in Monterey, but that was her only contribution. The rest of the time she sat quietly, her emotions in turmoil.

Later, in the parlor, Rosie served gingerbread cake and passed around a tray of sherry. Jeanette sat down at the spinet piano and played a popular Bessie Smith tune, "Baby, Won't You Please Come Home." Her sister Hallie stood next to her and sang the lyrics. Rosie added her harmonic voice and Sarah could see why she got into the chorus of the upcoming play.

Out of the shadows, Ada's ghost-like figure appeared by the piano, her eyes closed, her hands spread over her swollen belly as she sang to Sarah: *I'd give the world, if I could only make you understand,* and then she merged back into the shadows.

*But I do understand, Ada, and I'm not going to let you down this time.*

"Sarah? Are you all right?" Rosie asked, leaning down to give her a handkerchief. "I was hoping the singing would cheer you up."

Sarah dabbed at her eyes, not realizing she'd been crying. "I'm all right, Rosie, it's just that song is so sad."

"C'mon girls," said Rosie. "Let's end the evening with a cheerier tune of Miss Bessie's. And then we should all turn in."

Jeanette played "Nobody in Town Can Bake a Sweet Jelly Roll Like Mine" and Rosie belted out the lyrics, imitating Bessie by swinging her equally wide hips. Albert joined in with an off-tune howl that had everyone, including Sarah, laughing and applauding.

After the lodgers said good night and went to bed, Rosie insisted on walking Sarah back to the Sketch Box. Albert led the way and kept looking back to see what was taking them so long.

Rosie turned on a few lights to dispel the shadows and sat with Sarah for a while in the living room after offering to make tea that Sarah didn't want.

"You can go home, Rosie. I'll be all right. I have Albert to keep me company." Hearing his name, he jumped up on Sarah's lap.

"But before you go, I want to apologize for ever doubting your belief in Ada's murder. You were right. Someone did kill Ada and her unborn child. Will you help me find out who it was?"

"Of course I will," promised Rosie with conviction.

The room took on an ominous silence as the two women considered the weight of their decision.

At the door, Sarah said, "I'd like you to come with me to Monterey tomorrow. There are documents in Ada's safe deposit box at Wells Bank that might help us to get closer to the truth."

"That suits me fine. I have an errand to run in town myself. And after that we should get back to Carmel and see the marshal."

"Don't we have to make an appointment?" asked Sarah.

"No. I think it's better to just pop in on him." Rosie winked. "Take him by surprise to disarm him."

# TUESDAY, JULY 22

## —7—

As they stepped down from the rickety yellow bus at the Monterey Wharf depot, Rosie hooked Sarah's arm and they merged into the flow of pedestrian traffic on Alvarado Street. Two blocks of mostly brick-and-mortar two- and three-story office buildings flanked the busy avenue congested with automobiles, a few horse-drawn carriages, and shoppers bustling in and out of stores.

Ten minutes later, they stood in front of Wells Bank. Rosie was breathless. She pressed her hand against her heart and pointed to a bench under a shady oak. She sat down and told Sarah to go ahead. She'd wait for her. As Sarah walked away, she saw Rosie swallow one of her heart pills.

Inside the high-ceilinged, marble-columned bank, Sarah walked up to a bank teller and told him she was Ada Davenport's sister and wanted to access her safe deposit box. He directed her to take the spiral staircase upstairs to the bank manager's office.

"I've been expecting you," said the portly Mr. Pritchard, waddling around his desk to shake her hand.

"Expecting me?" said Sarah, puzzled.

"Yes, when your sister was assigned her safety deposit box, she asked for extra keys and said that you might come by on your own to collect some papers." He used his belly as a ledge to put his folded hands on and solemnly added, "I hope this isn't inappropriate, but I'd like to speak for my entire staff . . . I can't tell you how distressed we were that such a decent, upright woman as Miss Davenport would ever—" he wrung his hands—"what's the right way to say this, ah yes . . .commit such a desperate act. We have all found forgiveness for her in our Christian hearts and pray for her redemption on the Sabbath." He lowered his head as if expecting her to join him in prayer.

Sarah straightened her shoulders. Until she could prove otherwise, she'd have to tolerate people talking about Ada as if she was a sinner who took her own life. "Thank you, Mr. Pritchard. Now I'd like to open the safe deposit box."

"Of course, but first I must advise you that we haven't received any documentation from the probate office as to the naming of Miss Davenport's executor. Until then, we can't disperse any funds from her depository account." The corners of his mouth curled up into a faux smile.

Did he think she was money grubbing? Coming here to clean out the safe deposit box and claim her sister's assets, so soon after her death? Sarah remained outwardly calm. Until she had the will in hand, there was no point in telling him that she was the executor. "I understand, Mr. Pritchard, but I'm only here today to look in the box and see what it contains, which my sister told you I would do."

"My apologies," he said, wringing his pudgy hands. "And I'm sure any confusion in regard to your sister's bank account will be sorted out by your attorney. Do have him contact us. We really need to clear everything up as soon as possible." She hadn't realized there had been any *confusion*, and hadn't thought she might need an attorney.

Blocking her view as he stood in front of a large walk-in safe, Mr. Pritchard turned the combination knob back and forth until the lock clicked open. He ushered her into a smaller room and pulled the chain hanging from an overhead light bulb, which dimly lit a wall of numbered drawers. A shaft of sunlight from a high window, like a finger, seemed to point to a slim box marked #806, which the banker pulled out. After setting it on a small metal table, he gave Sarah a solemn nod and stood outside the door, leaving it open a crack in case she needed him.

Sarah held her breath and turned the tiny key Ada had placed in her reluctant palm at Keens that snowy January evening in New York. Six months ago, she thought she'd never have to use it.

Clipped to the deVrais Gallery contract was a document written by Mr. Foster M. Giles, Esq. of the New York law firm Giles and Adam, dated June 1, 1924. She didn't need to read the copy of the letter terminating Ada's contract that had been delivered to Paul deVrais. Foster Giles had given her copies of the contract and the letter before she caught the train that brought her to San Francisco and eventually here to this stifling room. She only needed to remember the date of the termination letter.

As Mr. Giles had explained in his office, all copyrights to Ada's artwork reverted back to Ada on July 1, 1924: All inventory stored by deVrais or commissioned to any galleries were to be returned to Ada. DeVrais was allowed to sell any specific, named pieces currently hanging in his Carmel gallery at the usual commission, an outrageous fifty percent, which was unfortunately customary. Ada's fifty percent royalty earned by any paintings he sold were to be accounted for and deposited in her Wells Bank account.

Sarah imagined deVrais's rage when he received this official document, which, of course, he had never mentioned when they met on the Del Monte Express train.

The next document was unexpected. She blinked and reread it several times. It was a deed to the Sketch Box cottage, signed over to Sarah Cunningham-Davenport on July 1, 1924. *Why, Ada? Why would you do this unless you were really frightened by deVrais's threats?*

She turned the box over and let all the papers fall out on the table. Flipping through them, she became more frantic. Where was it? Where was the will? Ada had said it would be here.

Mr. Pritchard cleared his throat and called out from behind the door, "Is something wrong?"

"No, everything seems to be in order," she said, returning the documents to the box. Mr. Pritchard came back into the room and slid drawer #806 back into its slot.

He ushered her back into his office. "Please know, Miss Cunningham, that we look forward to having such a distinguished person as yourself, the sister of the famed artist, Miss Davenport, as our client."

Sarah could see no reason why she would want to become a Wells Bank client, but she needn't tell him that. "Thank you, Mr. Pritchard. You are very kind."

As she crossed the lobby to the high-arched entrance, she was aware of being watched. She glanced over at the bank teller she'd spoken to earlier and he stopped talking to his customer when he saw her looking at him. Had he told everyone she was the sister of the famous artist who had committed suicide? She looked down at her feet and ordered them to march out the door and into the street. Fortunately, they obliged.

Rosie was leaning back on the bench at rest behind heavy lids. Sarah sat down beside her and mulled over what she found and didn't find at Wells Bank. She lit a cigarette and turned her attention to the passersby on Alvarado Street.

Mostly women wearing pastel sundresses like hers, with shawls or jackets covering their bare white arms, probably a precaution for when the inevitable summer fog rolled in and the temperature dropped. For now, their wide-brimmed straw hats shaded their eyes from the bright sun. The men were dressed conservatively in linen suits and Panama or straw boater hats, walking purposely but not in a hurry like they would in Paris or New York.

A large church bell struck once. Rosie woke up and yawned. "Oh my," she exclaimed, seeing Sarah. "I must have drifted off. How did it go at the bank?"

"Not good. The will wasn't there."

"That's odd. Was there anything else of importance?"

"Yes. The deed to the Sketch Box, and it's in my name."

"That's good. Now you don't have to worry about Marshal Judd throwing you out."

"Would he dare?" asked Sarah, shocked that this was even a possibility.

Rosie laughed. "I doubt it. But without the deed he could legally do it if there is no will to prove you're her only beneficiary."

"The bank manager said I needed a lawyer to settle Ada's accounts. Do you know someone?"

"Mr. Peabody. He helped me buy the Lodge. His fees are high, but he earns it. He's trustworthy and thorough. With him, we can't just pop in like with the marshal, we have to have an appointment. Mr. Peabody, like most lawyers, is very particular about his hours."

Rosie pulled herself up and straightened her skirt and looked at her watch. "Now I need to do my errand in *Nihonmachi*."

"Japan Town." said Rosie as an explanation to Sarah's raised brow. "It's just a short walk from here."

They walked arm-in-arm toward the Monterey Wharf, turned onto Washington Street and stopped in front of a plain, blue two-story Victorian building with white trim. Rosie told Sarah that this is where she came to teach English and in return had learned a few words of their language. She translated the larger banner written in calligraphy: "Japanese Association and Language School." They sat down on one of the steps so Rosie could catch her breath.

Sarah watched the Japanese pedestrians cross by in front of her. She was surprised to see them wearing the same stylish clothes worn by white people on Alvarado Street a few blocks away—stylish Western suit jackets, hats, and ties for men and sundresses and hats for women. Back when she lived in New York, she often went to Cantonese restaurants in Chinatown and the Chinese wore traditional Chinese clothes, Mao suits for men and long cheongsam dresses for women, with high cut collars.

The Japanese, in their eagerness to become American citizens, seemed to want to assimilate their previous culture into ours, thought Sarah. The Chinese were not as eager.

Rosie waved to a group of young Japanese women giggling amongst themselves as they entered the temple. "I taught English to several of those girls. They are Nisei, the Japanese term for children who were born in this country and have Japanese-born parents—Issei—who immigrated here. The Issei want their children to learn our language so they'll have more opportunities as birthright citizens. Unfortunately, it hasn't worked out as they had hoped. Their children still face racial segregation at school, and when they graduate, they can only find work in the fields or in Japanese food shops and laundries. It's only going to get worse now that our government is passing stricter laws to stop all Asians from coming here, and some politicians are even trying to take citizenship away from those born here."

"So it's true what I've read about the growing influence of the Ku Klux Klan and other anti-immigration groups in our country?"

"Yes. I'm afraid so. My dear friend, Mr. Kassajara, who we're about to meet, is very worried about the anti-foreign hysteria. His people try not to draw attention, dress like their neighbors, and hope if 'you stay in your place they'll leave you alone,' but white people are just too darn suspicious of all people who don't look like them. Even before the war Asians were demonized as the 'Yellow Peril.'"

Sarah knew of the Yellow Peril from reading the dystopian short story "The Unparalleled Invasion" by Jack London. It was about an Asiatic population taking over its neighbors with the intention of eventually overpowering the entire Earth. She mentioned it to Rosie and asked, "Wasn't Jack London one of the first bohemians to live in Carmel's artist colony?"

"Yes, he was," said Rosie, getting up with Sarah's help. "Goes to show that even artists can be prejudiced."

It was ridiculous to have such fears, but now, standing in front of the Japanese Center, Sarah was beginning to feel the racial tension in Monterey, like the tension she had felt in New York between the whites and the Negroes.

"There's Mr. Kassajara," said Rosie.

An elderly gentleman had come out of the temple entrance. His brown face was lined with wrinkles that came from a long life spent outdoors, his smooth brown head shiny and bald when he removed his hat. But there was nothing worn-out about this solidly built man who Sarah found quite dignified and handsome in his tailored black suit and waistcoat.

He greeted Rosie with a warm, welcoming smile.

"Sarah," said Rosie, "may I present Mr. Shin-ichi Kassajara."

He pressed his hands together and bowed. Sarah had learned from her Asian friends in Paris to return an even deeper bow to show respect. When she straightened up she saw him glancing over her shoulder at someone hurrying past. Sarah saw a flash of saffron and was about to call out Sirena's name, but the girl had disappeared inside.

When Rosie handed Mr. Kassajara a package, he said, "*Arigato*," then bowed again and walked inside, closing the door behind him.

"That was strange," said Sarah. "I could've sworn I saw Sirena go in there."

"Really? I didn't see her," said Rosie, shouldering her shopping bag.

"Can we go in? I'm a huge fan of Japanese woodprint painters and maybe some of their work hangs on the walls."

Rosie put her hand up. "This is not a good time. Mr. Kassajara is the leader of a Japanese cooperative and he is very busy. By trade, he's a fisherman and if he had his choice, I know he'd rather be out in the Bay diving for abalone. But his people are counting on him to find a way to hold on to their fishing businesses now that stricter laws forbid him and other non-citizens from owning property."

Rosie hooked Sarah's arm and pulled her away with a suggestion of lunch.

They stopped at a restaurant near the bus depot with a pleasant terrace overlooking the road that led down to the wharf. They ordered tea and sandwiches, but Rosie was unusually quiet and ate little.

"Is something wrong, Rosie? You said you were hungry."

Rosie looked at the crowded tables and shifted her chair closer to Sarah. "What has Sirena told you about herself?" she said softly.

"Very little. She's a bit of an enigma. I don't even know her last name."

"Well, if she did tell you, she'd say her last name was Silver and that she grew up on a sugarcane farm in Hawaii. She'd say she broke away from her parents to come here to study art." Rosie paused. "A whopper of a story."

"It's not true?" asked Sarah, leaning toward her with curiosity.

Rosie looked out at the blue bay shimmering in the distance and then back to Sarah. "I'm sworn to secrecy, but I think Sirena needs our help, so I'm going to break my promise. What I'm about to tell you could put her in grave danger so you must keep it to yourself."

"What danger could that young girl possibly be in?"

"That was Sirena you saw at the temple."

"Why didn't she say hello?"

"She has her reasons. And they're good ones."

"Go on."

"Sirena's last name is not Silver. It's Kassajara-Silvia. She was visiting her grandfather at the temple."

"Sirena's Japanese!" She'd found the girl exotic, a nymph from the sea, but she'd never have guessed Japanese with her pale wide-set eyes and Mediterranean coloring.

"Not only is she Japanese, but she is an ama."

Sarah looked at her curiously and Rosie explained that *ama* roughly translated to "women of the sea." "Women who were trained from childhood to hold their breath for many minutes so they could dive sixty feet underwater to forage for mollusks. The women in Sirena's family had been amas through many generations. Sirena has carried on the tradition and goes diving at Whalers Cove whenever she can find the time."

"And her father?" asked Sarah.

"Portuguese. Generations past, his family, the Silvias, were whale hunters. They immigrated to Monterey from the Azores. When there was no longer a demand for whale oil, his family started a dairy farm in Point Lobos not far from the Japanese village. He met Sirena's mother, Juniko, at the local Point Lobos school and they grew up playing together at Whalers Cove. Juniko's mother trained her and Salvador to be free-divers and in time they fell in love with diving and each other.

"This all sounds far more exciting than Sirena telling people she grew up on a sugar plantation. I can't see why she wouldn't want everyone to know about her parents. Their story is so romantic."

"Not for Sirena's parents. The miscegenation laws in our country forbid marriages between a white person and someone of another color. If our upright citizens had found out they were married, they could've had them arrested and possibly deported."

Sarah swallowed her tea but not her rising sense of injustice.

"Do Sirena's parents still live in Whalers Cove? I'd love to meet them."

Rosie's face saddened. "I'm afraid that's not possible. When Sirena was eight years old, Mariko and Salvador took their skiff out to dive for abalone off Whalers Cove. Mariko didn't come up from her dive and Salvador dove in after her. Her foot had gotten caught in some thick cords of kelp. He got entangled himself and they both drowned."

Hearing Sirena's story rekindled her own grief at the sudden loss of her parents at a young age. "Did Sirena move in with Mr. Kassajara and his wife?"

Rosie shook her head, no. She explained that Sirena's grandmother couldn't bear to live near where her only child had drowned, and she went back to Japan. After she left, Mr. Kassajara thought Sirena would have better opportunities growing up with the "white" side of her family in San Juan Bautista, which was only an hour by train from here. Sirena still visited him in the summers and continued her training as an abalone diver. Rosie had once asked her why she wanted to dive after what had happened to her parents, and the girl had said she felt their presence when she dived and it relieved her inconsolable grief.

Sarah waited until after the waiter had taken away their plates before asking how Rosie knew so much about the Kassajaras.

"I taught Sirena at the Japanese Association. She was a very determined six-year-old student when she joined my class. Curious and attentive. We became good friends."

Sarah asked again why Sirena had ignored her.

"I'm getting to that," said Rosie. "Last year, Sirena asked me if she could live at the Lodge. She couldn't pay me, but she said she'd help out doing the chores. Of course I wanted to help, but there was one condition that worried me." Rosie lowered her voice and leaned toward Sarah. "She wanted to cross the color line and pass for white. Otherwise she wouldn't be accepted into the Carmel art school."

As a woman artist, Sarah had been turned away by men-only art schools in New York and Paris. Fortunately, Académie Julienne accepted women students, but that was an exception. But she had never had to worry about also being excluded because of the color of her skin.

Rosie added. "If the immigration authorities found out Sirena was passing for white, they would deport her immediately because she is not only bi-racial, which is fraught with its own problems, but she's illegitimate in the eyes of the Court, a child of no one."

Sarah began to feel a deeper sympathy for Sirena and an impulse to protect her. It also made her want to stand up and protest loudly, which was something new to her.

Ada, an early suffragette, had been cross with her when she didn't vote in the first election after women finally gained the right to vote. She wouldn't make that mistake again, though it would be difficult to find any politicians that weren't against immigration.

"Are you the only one that knows Sirena is passing for white?"

"Her grandfather, of course. And Ada knew. She was very sympathetic toward Mr. Kassajara and his community. That's why she hired Sirena to work for her."

"And why do you think Sirena needs our help? She seems to be doing a good job of passing for white on her own. She certainly fooled me."

"Something's bothering her, but when I ask her what it is, she takes the offensive." Sarah had seen her do that when she'd tried to talk to her about Ada. "She's been like that ever since Ada died. I was hoping you could befriend her like Ada did and get her to tell you what's wrong."

Sarah hesitated. She was only going to be in Carmel a short time. But how could she not at least try to help? She might not be able to change the immigration laws, but she could help this one girl who was a victim of them. "I'll do what I can, Rosie."

A single orange-billed tern landed on the terrace railing. Her black eyes gazed into Sarah's, then she flew off, her white-arched wings spanning across the blue sky, her underbelly as white as the clouds she soared toward.

## —8—

Compared to the bustle of commerce in Monterey, Carmel was a quiet retreat. Rosie and Sarah passed by only a few pedestrians as they walked down Ocean Avenue, turned right onto San Carlos, and stopped on the corner of Fifth Avenue. A polished red truck was parked in front of the fire station. Next door, a saddled palomino with a white mane and tail stood hitched to a post outside the police station. Sarah picked up a handful of hay from the ground and fed the mare who snorted her appreciation.

Riley, the officer at the front desk, knew Rosie—everyone seemed to know Rosie—and he told them to wait on the bench in the shabby lobby while he let Marshal Judd know they were there. He returned quickly and said, "The marshal can only see you for a few minutes. He was just on his way out."

A squeaky door opened onto a backroom cramped by an over-sized desk. The only window opened out onto an empty lot. Marshal Judd had a telephone earpiece pressed against his ear and the short stub of a dead cigar clenched between his tobacco-stained teeth. His stocky legs were propped up on the desk, his cowboy boots with their two-inch heels holding down a stack of papers that were flapping under a rotating ceiling fan.

The two women sat down on metal folding chairs. A Zane Grey novel and a magazine entitled *Native Sons and Daughters of the Golden West* lay open on his cluttered desk. Sarah glanced at Rosie, trying not to show her amusement.

He spoke into the receiver, "Gotta go. It appears I have an

unscheduled meeting. I won't be long. No, sugar, I won't forget." He hung up the receiver and put his cigar down in an ashtray crowded with similar dead stogies. The fan gave little relief to the small closed-in space, heavy with the cloying scent of days-old cigar smoke.

Judd stood up, came over to their side of the desk, and closed the book and magazine. He crossed his short arms over his fringed leather vest, just below a shiny six-point badge.

Sarah couldn't stop staring at his getup. It could've been stolen from the wardrobe room of a Hollywood set for a Zane Grey western.

"Well, Miss McCann," the cowboy said in a raspy voice. "I take it that this isn't a neighborly visit. Yours seldom are."

Rosie took no notice of his rudeness and introduced him to Sarah. When he showed no facial recognition, Sarah said, "I'm Ada Davenport's sister."

"Well, Rosie, fancy you springin' Miss Cunnin'ham on me without makin' an appointment."

He returned to his office chair, which made an agonizing creaking noise under his weight as he dropped down in it.

"You caught me at a busy time, Miss Cunnin'ham, but I know you've come all this way from Paris, France, so what can I do for you?"

"The telegram I received from you in Paris said that the cause of my sister's death was unknown and you asked me to be a witness at the coroner's inquest. Unfortunately, the inquest was concluded before I got here. But seeing I came all this way I was hoping you could clear up a few things for me."

"It was pretty much an open and shut case, but I'll help you if I can."

"Seeing you are also the coroner, I'd like to know, Marshal Judd, how you decided upon a verdict of suicide rather than a verdict of accidental death or even murder by person or persons unknown?"

He cleared his throat, sat forward, and put his elbows on the desk.

"First let me apologize for sending you on a fool's mission. Days after I sent that telegram it became apparent that your sister's death was a suicide and I could have saved you a trip."

Sarah raised her hand. "You needn't apologize, marshal, I would still have come to bury my sister. But please do me the courtesy to answer my question. How did you reach that verdict?"

"Okay then, I can see you're a woman who doesn't mince her words, so I'll shoot it to you straight. I interviewed several witnesses who knew Miss Davenport well, and from their testimony we concluded that your sister was rather, well, shall we say, emotionally unstable."

Sarah tamped down her rising anger at his amateur assumptions about Ada's stability, though she had made similar assumptions earlier, and asked, "Was that the professional opinion of a psychiatrist?"

"No. I didn't think that was necessary."

"May I ask why not?"

"It was an obvious suicide." He took out a fresh cigar, bit off the end, and spit it into a brass spittoon next to the desk. Pleased with his good aim, he then took out a small notebook from his vest pocket and flipped through a few pages until he found what he was looking for. "Let's see here. No wounds on a fully dressed body. No signs of struggle, like bruises or scratches. Pockets filled with stones. No suspects with motives, and," he gloated from across the desk, "there was a suicide note addressed to you." He shoved the notebook back in his pocket.

"Is that it, marshal?" Sarah asked.

He reddened. "Isn't that enough? I'm sure this is a most unpleasant situation for you, Miss Cunnin'ham, and you have my sincerest condolences, but there is nothing more I can do. The case is closed, and I make no apologies for that."

Sarah shifted in the hard chair. "If you don't mind, I'd like to see that suicide note and the written testimonies of the witnesses, and of course any notes from your investigation." She kept her expression neutral as she met his beady dark eyes.

Judd stuck the cigar into his mouth and lit it. He shifted his eyes over to Rosie. "Was this your idea?"

"Marshal, Miss Cunningham is only asking for what is her legal right to have."

"Thank you, Miss Rosie, but I don't need a lesson in law." He pointed at a shelf of law books behind his desk. "As you can see, I don't get to be the marshal just because I ride in rodeos. Tell me where you're staying, Miss Cunnin'ham, and I'll have my deputy deliver the files tomorrow morning."

Sarah hadn't expected it to be that easy. "Why thank you, marshal. You can deliver the files to the Sketch Box."

"Where?"

"My sister's cottage on Camino Real."

"I'm not sure her house is legally—"

Rosie interrupted. "The deed to the cottage is in Miss Cunningham's name, marshal. She is now the legal owner. Do you need to see the deed or take our word for it?"

Sarah was about to say she didn't have it with her, when he looked up at the clock and said, "That won't be necessary."

Sarah marveled at Rosie's quick draw on the lazy lawman.

He stood up. "Now if you ladies don't mind, I have to mosey on home."

"One more thing," said Sarah, who had saved this question for the last. "Did you know my sister was pregnant?"

He seemed flustered by her question and took a moment before answering. "Yes, Dr. Lewis did tell me that. I thought it'd be better to keep it out of the newspapers as it wasn't relevant and would just stir things up in the gossip pages. Our village has had enough bad publicity over this case already."

Not relevant, thought Sarah, incredulously. "Didn't you wonder why the father didn't show up at the inquest? Did you make any attempt to find him?"

"Nope. I had enough evidence to reach a verdict without digging further into your sister's personal life."

"But certainly her pregnancy would have been a good enough motive to *not* take her own life?"

"I disagree. I think an unwed mother's burden of shame is all the more reason," said Judd. "You should be thanking me for hushing that up. It wouldn't have done you no good." He stood up. "Now I must be going."

His metal spurs jingled as he walked across the wooden floor to the hat rack. Sarah felt sorry for the palomino waiting outside to take her master home. He reached for an oversized white felt hat with a porcupine quill stuck in the band. If the situation wasn't so terrible, Sarah could've laughed, but instead she sized up her opposition and started to feel up to the task of dealing with a not-so-sharp cowboy marshal.

The metal chairs scraped when Sarah and Rosie stood up.

He turned, pushing the hat down over his small balding head, and said, "I do hope there isn't some other reason you have in wanting to see these files."

"What other reason could there be?" asked Sarah, puzzled.

"I don't know. I just thought you might have some silly notion of trying to reopen the investigation . . . for your own advantage."

"My advantage?"

"Western Life cancelled the death benefit in your sister's life insurance policy because it was a suicide. You're listed as the beneficiary and a tidy sum would've come your way."

Sarah hadn't expected this. "I didn't know there was a life insurance policy."

"That's odd. Mr. Martin from Western Life Insurance in Monterey sent a letter to you in Paris informing you that the policy premium was cancelled. It's called a Moral Hazard clause."

She shook her head. "I never got any letter from Mr. Martin."

He sneered. "No? I'll ask him for another copy."

"Please do," said Sarah.

"Now, ladies, I must be off to the bakery before it closes or I won't get my dinner." He smiled. "You know what fussbudgets wives can be when their menfolk don't come home on time." The two women walked over to the door he held open.

Sarah, a head taller than the marshal, looked down at his gold-capped teeth that glittered when he grinned. "Then again, how could you know, seeing as you're both spinsters." He tipped his hat.

They stepped out onto the porch. Judd mounted his palomino, pulled the reins to the left, gave the horse's belly a hard kick with his spurs, and shouted, "Get a move on, Gertrude." The old mare winced under the kick but obediently trotted toward Ocean Avenue with her bulky passenger bouncing up and down hard in the saddle.

"What a dreadful little man," said Sarah, lighting a cigarette and blowing out the anger she'd been holding in. "Is he a *real* cowboy?"

Rosie swaggered a bit and imitated his raspy voice, "Yep, certified. I grew up on a ranch in Salinas. When I'm not out patrollin' our little community, I ride ol' black bulls in the rodeo shows." Rosie hitched up her skirt. "Well, I used to anyway."

They both laughed, glad to be out of his office and away from his cigar smoke.

"Has he had any experience investigating murder cases?"

"Once, ten years ago. He'd just been elected when an artist from New York, Helena Wood Smith, went missing. Several of her friends, writers and artists in the Carmel artist colony, were furious when he didn't make any real effort to look for her, so they formed their own search party. They found Helena half-buried under a sand dune on Carmel Beach. She'd been strangled. Her friends hunted down George Kodani, a Japanese art–photographer Miss Smith had been living with. When Mr. Kodani finally confessed to the marshal, he was jailed, but an angry crowd gathered outside his cell hungry for a lynching." Rosie paused. "I'm embarrassed to say some of them were my good friends."

"I would've never thought that possible in an artist colony," said Sarah, feeling the horror of such a violent act. "Artists pride themselves on their open-mindedness and justice for all." It was disappointing to know that the racial tension she'd been feeling was as real here as it was in other small towns in America where Negroes had been lynched. She asked, "Did they succeed?"

"Fortunately the marshal does believe in law and order. He and his armed deputies were able to break up the mob."

"At least he's good for something." Sarah looked up Ocean Avenue at Gertrude swishing her white plumed tail as she waited patiently for her master to come out of the bakery. "But that was ten years ago. What has he done since then to keep law and order in Carmel?"

"Mostly he hunts down drunks and cattle thieves and the Canadian rum runners that come down here to deliver whiskey to their distributors along the coastline. Some say he makes a little taste when a shipment gets delivered."

Sarah laughed. "Rum runners? Here in peaceful Carmel? Ada would've loved that. She liked the taste of whiskey sours." She dropped the cigarette on the dirt path and stamped it out under her foot. "Weren't you at all surprised the marshal was willing to hand over his files?"

"He probably thinks that after you read them you'll agree with his verdict, but I think he's a bit nervous about it. The last thing he wants is for you to find any new evidence to reopen the inquest."

"Can I do that?"

"You can if you persuade the District Attorney there's a good chance Ada was murdered."

"And how do I do that, Rosie? Need I remind you that I'm an artist, not a detective."

"By doing just what you're doing. You were very good at holding your own with Marshal Judd. He doesn't know exactly what you're up to, but he knows you're determined to get to the truth, and he doesn't like it."

They walked down Ocean Avenue toward Camino Real. A late afternoon fogbank hovered over the ash-gray Carmel Bay, as if it were deciding whether to come onto shore.

From afar Sarah thought she heard a chorus of keening banshees.

"Rosie, I'd like you to show me where you found Ada. There might be something Marshal Judd missed."

"All right. I'll take you there tomorrow afternoon after I give the girls their lunches. By then you'll have had a chance to look over the marshal's report."

# WEDNESDAY, JULY 23

## —9—

At 8:30 a.m. Albert barked and Sarah opened the front door of the cottage. It was Riley, the deputy from the marshal's office, holding a wooden crate in one arm and a thin brown envelope in the other. He asked her to sign a receipt and left before she had a chance to thank him.

She carried the crate into the kitchen, placed it on the floor, and lay the envelope on the kitchen table, resisting the urge to open either until she had her morning coffee and a clearer mind.

After she gave Albert some of his favorite Spratt's dog biscuits, she percolated coffee and prepared a plate of cheese and bread for herself. She stole several glances at the crate. Whatever was inside, like Pandora's box, it wasn't going to make her happy.

When the coffee was ready, she poured a cup and sat in the banquette. She slit open the brown envelope and pulled out two folders. The first was titled: A.B. DAVENPORT: VICTIM OF SUICIDE, and stamped in red: INQUEST CLOSED. The second folder was titled: A.B. DAVENPORT CRIME REPORT—INVESTIGATOR: ALVIN JUDD, MARSHAL

There was a set of keys in the envelope like the ones Rosie had given her to the cottage, except the alley key to the studio was missing. Something else was stuck in the bottom and she shook the envelope. Ada's "Peace" pendant and chain fell out. The cyanide was still inside. This made her sister's suicide even more unbelievable. If Ada had wanted to kill herself, wouldn't she have swallowed the cyanide and not gone to the trouble of drowning herself?

Albert licked his bowl clean in a few slurps and jumped up next to Sarah. He sniffed the folders, then sat up on his haunches and watched her attentively.

The crime report contained a few pages of Marshal Judd's almost indecipherable writing. She lit a cigarette and prayed for clues to her sister's murder.

Judd had noted that the victim's desk was empty and there was a thick pile of ashes mixed with scraps of paper in the fireplace. He assumed that she had burned her correspondence to prevent anyone from trespassing into her private life after she was gone. A blatant error, thought Sarah, but the marshal wouldn't know Ada was afraid of fires and would never light one. The handwritten suicide note had been found on the kitchen table under a vase of daisies. Sarah looked at the vase still sitting on the table after Rosie had thrown out the dead flowers. She felt creepy inside. Investigating her own sister's murder wouldn't be pleasant.

Sarah puzzled over what she had learned and said to Albert, "The murderer could've cleaned out Ada's desk after he killed her and burned the will and any other evidence, but that doesn't explain the suicide note in Ada's writing." Albert replied by yawning and stretching his front paws on her lap.

She turned to the medical report. A Dr. Rosenthal concluded the victim had died from asphyxiation in saltwater and had been floating adrift until the morning tide had pulled her back onshore. Dr. Rosenthal set the time of death between 10:00 p.m., July 4, and 8:00 a.m. the following morning.

The death certificate was signed by the marshal—"Cause of death: SUICIDE. Manner of death: DROWNING." It seemed indisputable. Fighting off discouragement, she pressed on. Attached was a copy of the one-page letter from Mr. Jonathan Martin of the Western Life

Insurance Company in Monterey. A terse formal letter stating that Sarah was the beneficiary of Miss Davenport's five-thousand-dollar insurance premium, but it had been annulled because of the policy owner's suicide. She jotted down: *Judd rushed the verdict, encouraged by an insurance company that didn't want to pay the premium. Was he compensated?*

Not feeling up to the task in front of her, she stubbed out her cigarette, opened the casement window over the kitchen sink, and listened to the surf rolling onto the shore. To her it sounded like waves of endless grief. She returned to the loose papers ruffling in the sea breeze.

Next was the inquest file. It was dated July 15 to 17, 1924, when she had been on a train reeling across the countryside. The court reporter had neatly transcribed the events with a stenotype machine. The results amounted to four pages of testimony—testimony that stained her sister's character and questioned her sanity.

Paul deVrais testified that he had been Miss Davenport's art dealer for many years. He insisted he'd left for San Francisco the evening of the fourth. Marshal Judd took him at his word and didn't ask for any proof. He said her death was a tragic loss to him and the art world. When asked about Miss Davenport's recent emotional state, he used the words "extremely agitated and irrational."

Henry Champlin was the next witness. He said he had first met Miss Davenport when she was an art student. He stated that several guests were staying with him over the holidays. On July fourth, they watched the fireworks on Carmel Beach and attended the Bath House dance. He had the decency not to mention Ada's previous attempt at suicide, but he did say, when asked by the marshal, that it was true that she suffered from melancholy and at times could become "hysterical."

She read with interest that Elizabeth Peake, one of Rosie's lodgers, was perhaps the last person to see Ada alive. Miss Peake testified that at eight o'clock on the evening of July fourth, she was watering Rosie's front garden when she saw Ada pedal by on her red bicycle. Albert was sitting in the front basket as usual. Miss Peake presumed the victim was going to the beach to paint as she often did at the twilight hour, and called out hello. Ada appeared to be in a great hurry and didn't wave back.

Sarah reviewed the marshal's notes. There was no mention that a red bicycle had been found near Ada's body. She scribbled down, *Important: find Ada's bicycle.* It gave her an unexpected but fleeting thrill to have found a possible clue. Find the bicycle and find where she went that night.

Rosie's testimony in defense of Ada's character and emotional state was reassuring until Judd cut her off and told her to report only what she had seen on the morning of July fifth. "That morning," she said, "an anxious, barking Albert showed up at the front door of the Lodge. He was covered in wet sand. He had gnawed through his leash but half was still clipped to his collar. When I didn't find Miss Davenport at home, I followed Albert to River Beach."

Sarah put Albert on her lap—"You are such a smart dog"—and read the testimony of Miss Davenport's assistant, Sirena Silver. She too saw the fireworks and attended the Bath House dance on the fourth. The last time she saw her employer was on July first at her cottage. Miss Davenport was agitated but this behavior was not unusual. Miss Silver had often seen her like that. And, no, she didn't tell the marshal she'd been fired that same morning.

The last page was the suicide note, Judd's conclusive evidence. Sarah recognized the pale yellow linen paper torn from Ada's *Book of Quotables* and the purple ink she used for writing:

Dearest Little Sis,

I have been at the point of writing this letter for days. My heart has been behaving in such a curious fashion that I can't imagine it means nothing. So as I would hate to leave you unprepared, I'll just try and jot down what comes into my mind. All my art [Sarah put the sheet of paper up to the window but couldn't decipher the word that had been redacted and replaced above with the word art, as if correcting a mistake.] I leave entirely to you to do what you like with. Please destroy all letters you do not wish to keep and all papers. Monies, of course, are all yours. In fact, my dearest dear, I leave everything to you. In spite of everything—how happy we have been!

Forgive me.

Ada Belle

Friday, July 4, 1924

Taking a gulp of now-cold coffee, Sarah ran her finger over the smeared *Dearest Little Sis*. She would have wept, if Ada had actually written this letter to her. Instead, she became furious.

She remembered seeing a book of Katherine Mansfield's published letters in Ada's living room and she carried it back to the kitchen. It was easy to find what she was looking for. Ada had bookmarked Mansfield's dying letter to her husband John Murry.

She compared Katherine's letter to Ada's transcription of that letter, which had been identified by Marshal Judd at the inquest as Ada's suicide note.

She let out a scoffing laugh.

This wasn't Ada's suicide note. It was Ada's transcribed copy of

Katherine's letter to her husband, except someone had blacked out "manuscripts" replacing it with "art," and forged Ada's handwriting to write the salutation and the last three lines at the bottom of the page.

Sarah slammed down her fist and Albert jumped off the banquette. He returned with a leash hanging from his mouth.

"Not now, Albert. We've got to look inside the crate. We'll go out when Rosie gets here." Disappointed, he dropped the leash and stretched out on the floor near the crate. Sarah opened the lid.

A putrid odor of mildew had soaked into Ada's rosebud shawl. Salt had embedded between the silk threads of the embroidered roses. In spite of the smell, Sarah cradled it in her arms. *My impulsive, vibrant sister, how could your wonderful, warm-hearted life have ended so cruelly? Who did this to you?* Albert sniffed the shawl and whimpered.

"Do you know, Albert? Were you with her when she was killed?"

Moments passed before she could lay it aside. She took out jodhpurs, a jersey pullover, a vest, one canvas shoe, and a pair of white socks stained with kelp.

At the bottom of the crate were four polished black stones with 3KG engraved on each one. The stones Judd had mentioned in his crime report. She turned the crate over. Nothing but sand fell out.


Before Rosie took Sarah to see where she had found Ada on the beach, Sarah showed her the forged suicide note torn from Ada's Book of Quotables and Katherine Mansfield's own letter to her husband.

"This is why we needed you here," said Rosie. "You're like Sherlock Holmes. You find clues Marshal Judd is too lazy to see."

Sarah put one of the heavy black stones in Rosie's hand. "Do you know where these come from? What they're used for?"

Rosie turned it over and looked at the 3kg engraving. "Abalone divers. They hang them on their diving belts so they can descend quickly to the ocean floor. Why?"

"Those are the stones the marshal used as evidence to Ada's pre-meditated suicide."

Near Champlin's cottage, they took the stairs down onto River Beach and removed their shoes. Sarah could see Rosie was in no hurry to get to their destination. Sarah reassured her that it was necessary.

They walked on until they reached a swampy lagoon where the Carmel River flowed out into the ocean. Albert dropped down on the sand, trembling, and Rosie said, "This is where Albert brought me."

Rosie described Ada staring straight up at the sky. "I closed her eyelids and unwound her rosebud shawl, which was tangled around her neck." Her voice faltered. "Albert was whimpering just like he is now."

Sarah picked him up to soothe him and tightened her grip on her own rosebud shawl billowing in the wind.

"The morning tide was coming in over her legs," continued Rosie. "I was afraid she'd be pulled back out to sea like driftwood, but I couldn't move her on my own, so I ran back to Carmel Point for help. Mr. Jeffers doesn't have a phone but his neighbors, the Kusters, were home. I used their phone to call the marshal. Then I rushed back and waited with Albert until he came with Dr. Rosenthal and they carried her above the tideline."

Sarah let Albert down and put her arm around Rosie, who was pressing her hand against her heart. "You were very brave to bring me here, Rosie. I know how hard this must be for you. We don't have to stay here any longer. I've seen what I needed to see."

They were walking back along the shore when they saw a man in a navy blue knit cap jump out of a fishing boat and pull it up on the beach with a rope.

"Let's go ask him if he was out fishing that night," said Sarah. "Maybe he saw something."

As they drew nearer, he took out a large bucket full of shiny flailing fish. At first Albert barked, then curiosity triumphed and he ran up to take a sniff.

The young fisherman was wearing rubber overalls over a frayed work shirt and smelled of sea kelp.

"That's quite a catch," said Sarah. He grinned proudly, showing a chipped front tooth.

"Yes ma'am. Mid-tide is the best time to catch rockfish because they're fishing themselves while the sea's calm."

Albert sniffed the wild-eyed fish and growled when their bodies flapped.

"Does the tide always come in at this hour?" asked Sarah.

"Depends on the moon. I always check my tide calendar before I go out." He pulled a small worn datebook out of his shirt pocket.

"Do you keep records of all your fishing days?"

"Yep, and how many fish I catch. I got plenty today."

"Were you fishing here on the Fourth of July?"

"Sure was. I don't have to look that one up. It was a full moon that night. The following morning I heard they found that poor woman washed up on shore."

"Did you see her on the beach the night before?"

"No. But out in my skiff I got to see the sky burst wide open with fireworks on both sides of me. Carmel and Monterey had their own display to the north, and to the south I watched those Japs out on Point Lobos shoot off their 'works." He crouched down and petted Albert. "It still gives me the willies when I think that drowned woman might have been floating dead near my skiff and I was so excited by the fireworks I didn't see her."

He stood up and pulled off his stocking cap. A thatch of brownish hair stood up on ends, stiff from dried salt water. "Why do you ask? Did you know her?"

"Yes, we did," said Sarah. "We're trying to understand what

happened . . . We thought maybe it was an accident . . . that she got pulled out by a wave when her back was to the sea."

"It's possible. Some tourists don't know about these rogue waves. That'll yank you out to sea and suck you under fast." He scratched his head. "Your friend must have been dragged back to shore by the early morning tide." He scratched his head again. "Though that don't make much sense."

"Why is that?" asked Sarah.

"There's a deep underwater canyon out there. It'd be like throwing yourself off the Grand Canyon but instead of hitting rock you'd be sucked down under the kelp. If she washed ashore, it would have been farther south where the canyon doesn't come so close to shore."

He pulled his stocking cap down over his forehead and started to walk back toward his skiff. "Excuse me, ladies, it's nice talking to you but I got my catch to bring home and clean while it's fresh."

They watched him drag his skiff farther up on the beach. He tied it to a rusty ring in a rocky outcrop and walked up to the road as his heavy, full bucket swung by his side.

"These fishermen understand the coastal seas. It's their livelihood," said Rosie. She sat down to rest on a large boulder. Sarah joined her and Albert stretched out on the sand nearby.

"Do you see what this means?" said Sarah, excited. "Ada couldn't have drowned at River Beach as Judd presumed. The current would have either pulled her out into the underwater canyon and the divers' weights would have dropped her down even deeper or, as the fisherman said, the current would've washed her ashore farther south. So someone must've brought her here after she was dead."

"And that someone must've put the diving weights in her pockets to make it look like a suicide," said Rosie, picking up where Sarah left off. "And there's something else that isn't right. When I found Ada, her clothes were drenched in seawater. But her hands weren't wrinkled as they would've been if she'd been submerged in water for any length of time.

"I read about a case like this in 'The Mask.' Any forensic expert would have noticed the discrepancy, but when I mentioned it to the marshal he dismissed it as unimportant."

"So if what we're saying is that she didn't drown," Sarah said hopefully, "and her suicide note is fake, and the diving weights were planted on her *after* she was already dead, don't we have enough evidence to get the inquest reopened?"

Rosie shook her head. "No. They'd say it's all circumstantial evidence. We need actual proof and we need a suspect." She saw Sarah's disappointment and added, "But it's a good beginning."

Seagulls began cawing relentlessly over their heads. Sarah tried to light a cigarette but the wind had started blowing in from the ocean and she burned herself.

"I told you those coffin nails are no good for you," said Rosie.

Sarah half smiled, and after cupping her hand she got it lit and took a deep drag.

Albert barked and they both turned to look up at a tall, lanky man standing on top of a rock tower. Behind him was a stone cottage that seemed to be barely holding on to the edge of a rocky outcrop.

"Why there's Mr. Jeffers, our local poet." Rosie waved at him, but he didn't respond.

"That tower is a gift to his wife, Una, and their two young children. He's been building it on his own for three years. He carries the granite boulders up from the beach all by himself."

"A poet who builds a tower with his own hands while making a world out of words. That's someone I'd like to know. Have you read his poetry?"

"It's too disturbing for my taste. But Ada admired his work and often visited him. You'll find his books in her cottage."

"I wonder why he wasn't a witness at the inquest?" said Sarah. "He has a clear view of River Beach and he might have seen Ada there on the fourth. Let's go ask him."

Rosie looked at her watch and shook her head. "Not now. It's only three o'clock. He keeps to a very strict writing schedule. Or I should say his wife Una does. She only allows visitors to see him after four o'clock."

# FRIDAY, JULY 25

## —10—

Sirena stopped so abruptly that Sarah bumped into her. "Why are you stopping at Mr. Champlin's cottage?" she asked. "Aren't we painting on the beach like we did on Monday?"

"He wants us to work inside this morning," said Sirena. "We're going to make more copies of his seascape paintings. Boring! Hopefully we'll get to paint on the beach in the afternoon."

Sarah had decided to attend Champlin's class again, hoping to discover who was painting in Ada's studio when she first arrived or anything else she could learn about Ada's last days alive. She wanted to get back to Paris in time for her exhibit, but she had to find Ada's killer first or at least get the inquest reopened.

"There's something I want to ask you before we go in," said Sirena.

"Sure, if you think we have time."

"This will only take a minute. Want a smoke?"

Sirena deftly hand-rolled two cigarettes (something Sarah had been trying to do for years without success), lit both, and handed one to Sarah.

The younger painter took a long draw and said in her now-familiar curt manner, "Aren't you going to have a memorial service for your sister? Everyone is expecting one."

Sarah was embarrassed. She should have thought of that herself. Rosie had offered to take her to the mortuary where Ada's ashes were being held, but first she wanted the insidious word SUICIDE deleted from the death certificate so she could give Ada a decent burial in a cemetery.

"Sarah?" asked Sirena after a long silence.

"Sorry, yes, you're right, and thank you for mentioning it. I've just been so wrapped up in my own grief that I haven't considered how other people who knew Ada must be feeling. Of course we should have a service."

"I hoped you'd feel that way," said Sirena. "Ada's death was so unexpected and none of us had a chance to say goodbye or give her a proper send-off."

"I'll need your help," said Sarah. "You were her assistant, so you must know her friends in Carmel and Monterey, even San Francisco. Would you make me a list?"

"Sure I can do that. You can also announce the date and time in our local paper, the *Pine Cone*."

"All right. But first we'll have to decide on a date, time, and place."

Mr. Champlin was standing at the doorway to his studio.

"We better get going," said Sirena. She threw down her cigarette and stomped it out next to Sarah's, then picked up the butts and dropped them in the deep pocket of her saffron coveralls.

Sarah would've never thought the girl to be particularly neat and asked her why she did it.

Sirena shrugged. "It's just something Ada taught me. She believed you should never leave any messes behind when you leave your camping grounds. I thought it was good advice to follow and now it's a habit.

"She read it to me out of her *Book of Quotables*, but I don't know who said it."

*Poor Ada, she did leave a mess behind*, thought Sarah, *but I'm going to clean it up for her. Even if it means canceling my exhibition. I owe it to her.*

She was about to tell Sirena that the quote was from one of her favorite writers, Katherine Mansfield, but Sirena had gone inside.

Champlin's studio looked like a garage from the outside, but inside it was as elegant as his wardrobe. The subtle light filtering through expansive windows on the northern wall made the small space look larger than it was. Edwardian couches and chairs where a model might languish in seductive poses to please the artist took up one corner.

Eight students were seated on benches around an easel displaying one of Champlin's iconic tonal seascapes. Champlin stood as stiff as his waxed moustache next to the easel. Hallie and her sister Jeanette turned and waved at Sarah. She and Sirena took the last available bench in the back.

Champlin tapped a stick on the side of his easel and started a lecture on tonal color theory, using his own work as an example. "Anyone can see the relation to this . . ." His voice droned like the fly buzzing overhead while Sirena doodled and Sarah visualized the last painting to be made for her exhibit.

Champlin finished his lecture and said, "This afternoon on the beach I want you to use these ideas on your own canvases. You should apply a refined, controlled palette." He looked directly at Sarah.

In spite of his jab, she spent an enjoyable morning drawing, erasing, and changing the lines and spaces until her sketches took on a formal style similar to Champlin's. It freed her from having to produce an original composition and allowed her instead to concentrate on interpretation. In Paris and in New York, she often went to the museums to copy the masters and get away from her own work. Copying Champlin's painting also freed her from thinking about Ada, if only for a short while.

When he dismissed the class, he said he'd join them on River Beach after lunch. Sirena stopped Sarah outside and let the other women pass by. "Before we go down there, I think you should know—"

Sarah stopped her. "Rosie already showed me where Ada's body washed to shore. I know we'll be painting nearby, but thank you for your concern."

They walked for a few minutes and then took the steep, rickety staircase down to the beach where the other students were seated in a circle eating from their lunch boxes. Rosie had given Sirena an extra lunch for Sarah. Ham and cheese on a roll dripping with mayonnaise. Not exactly a fresh baguette with jambon-beurre, but she was hungry and very grateful. With everything she had on her mind, she'd forgotten to add eating to her to-do list.

Elizabeth passed around a box of homemade MoonPies her mother had sent from Charlottesville, Virginia—marshmallows squashed between graham crackers dipped in chocolate. She said they were her mother's peace offering after their fight. Elizabeth wanted to stay in Carmel to continue her studies through the rest of the year. Her mother wanted her to come back home. There was a beau waiting for her in Charlottesville and, with Elizabeth's twenty-second birthday around the corner, her mother thought he was her daughter's last chance for marriage. Elizabeth didn't want to give up her career as an artist and didn't mind the idea of spinsterhood if it would allow her to paint.

The close circle of women shared stories of their families who did or didn't support their wishes to be artists. Most families didn't. This was a conversation Sarah might have had with her girlfriends in Paris, but it would have taken place in a dank, airless studio. She was beginning to understand why Ada chose Carmel for her home. The salty breeze, the sun on her back, the open space, the reassuring rhythm of the surf, the rumble of the small rocks tumbling over one another as the waves tossed them about.

Sirena had been unusually silent, but now she "shushed" her friends, "Quiet! Sarah has something she wants to ask you about." But Sarah was just about to bite into a MoonPie and it took her a moment to realize Sirena was talking about the memorial service.

"What is it, Sarah?" said Hallie and Jeanette in tandem.

Embarrassed, Sarah put down the MoonPie. "I'm planning a

memorial service for my sister and I'm looking for suggestions as to where it should take place."

The unfurling waves brushing against the sand filled in the silence.

Annie, a stunning blonde from San Francisco, spoke first. "That's a wonderful idea. We all miss Ada and I'm sure the entire artist colony would come to pay their respects. If you want a church service, I could ask Father Joseph at St. Agnes to officiate."

"Annie," Sirena said sternly, "a Christian service is never allowed if someone took their own life." The women turned their eyes away from Sarah and stared at their half-eaten MoonPies.

Sirena was right. As long as Ada's death was considered a suicide, there could be no religious service, not that Ada would've wanted one anyway. But what would she have wanted? wondered Sarah.

Sirena gave her the answer. An answer that could've come from Ada. "Hey, c'mon, who wants a god-fearing priest speaking about Ada anyway? He never knew her like we did. We can have our own service, and instead of a burial we'll scatter her ashes."

"I agree," said Elizabeth, "and I know the perfect location—Whalers Cove." She pointed to the granite outcrop projecting into the Pacific like a giant finger. "There's a marvelous view of the sea from its summit."

"A terrible idea," said Sirena. "What does the Japanese village have to do with Ada? She never went to Whalers Cove to paint. Why not have it right here on the beach where Ada used to paint?"

Now that Sarah knew Sirena was from that Japanese village, she marveled at how the girl maneuvered the conversation away from her home and her true identity. Sarah felt an obligation to shield her. "I agree with Sirena not to have it at Whalers Cove, but I don't think I want to have the memorial so near where Ada was found. Any other ideas?"

"Uh-oh," said Jeanette and Hallie, "here he comes."

Champlin was looking down at them from the top step of the wooden staircase.

Sarah gave a cursory look at his students hurriedly opening their sketch boxes and propping up their easels. Their oil-stained palettes were mostly tonal and none had the black and purple pigments of the dreadful painting that had disappeared from Ada's studio.

Sirena's palette was stained in black, but Sarah had seen her applying bold calligraphic lines on the borders of her landscapes with a narrow brush. The students at Académie Julian used a similar technique when copying the Japanese wood-block stamps. If only she could speak honestly with Sirena, she would ask her if she had been taught this technique by someone in her village. The Japonaiserie style that had influenced van Gogh's paintings was all the rage in Paris, and as far as she knew it wasn't taught anywhere in the States.

Sarah opened her sketch box, propped up the easel, and daubed titanium white on her palette, but when she went to add cobalt blue, the tube was empty.

There was a whole trove of paints in Ada's studio, but since her futile search for the portraits and the disappearance of the scary canvas, Sarah had locked up the studio and hesitated to go back in. Besides, those were Ada's paints, Ada's palette. There might not be a church who would glorify Ada but her studio was sacred to Sarah.

Sirena had put her easel next to hers and seeing Sarah's disappointment, shared her own tube. "Thanks. I only brought a few oils from Paris in my sketch box."

"If you like, I'll take you to Oliver's art supply store in Monterey tomorrow."

Sarah had planned to see Paul deVrais in the morning but she had also promised Rosie to be Sirena's friend. "Can we go in the afternoon?"

"Sure. It's open all day."

Out of the corner of her eye, Sarah saw that Champlin had walked over to the tide's edge and set his gaze on the Carmel River outlet.

*A perfect subject*, thought Sarah, blending a few pigments on her palette until she had a muddy brown she liked. She brushed quick strokes on to her canvas that defined his angular profile from the Panama hat down to his bare feet, which she exaggerated.

She stepped back and looked from the canvas to her subject several times. Yes, she'd captured the dark tension his body emanated.

What was her subject thinking about? She looked up at his house that was barely visible from her angle. Was he really watching fireworks the night Ada died? Could he be the father of Ada's child? Highly unlikely.

He turned around to face her. Was that a flash of anger at her watching him or just the glaring sunlight bouncing off his white Panama?

He started walking toward her but then seemed to change his mind and stopped to speak to a few of his other students. By the time he reached her easel, Sarah had covered his figure with thick gray strokes and created a jagged rock rising up out of a red boiling sea. Similar in style to the painting she'd found in Ada's studio. She didn't think it was Champlin who had painted it, but she wanted to see if he recognized the style.

He stood behind her and squinted at her canvas through his monocle.

"Do any of your other students paint like this?" she asked.

"Certainly not."

He walked over to Elizabeth's easel. "Good work," he said, loud enough for Sarah to hear. "You have followed my instructions."

An hour later, Hallie and Jeanette came up to Sarah while she was putting away her supplies and invited her to go with them to the Mission Tea House.

"We all meet there at the end of the day for a cup of tea," said Jeanette, flashing a conspiratorial grin toward her sister.

"I have to send a telegram," replied Sarah. She needed to let Eric Crocker know that she was still tracking down the portraits and to please be patient. She should have telephoned him, but he would have wanted an explanation and she didn't have one.

"If you tell me where to find the Tea House, I'll join you later."

Hallie and Jeanette pointed inland. "Just beyond the cow pasture you'll see the old mission's crumbling bell tower. The Tea House is down the hill in an orchard surrounded by an adobe wall."

"Is it all right if I bring Albert?"

"Sure. Dogs are allowed everywhere in Carmel. It's the law."

A herd of cows raised their bulky heads to watch Sarah and Albert trespassing on their field. Chewing their cuds was far more interesting and they dropped their heads back down. Albert pulled her in the right direction and they made their way to the mission. Sarah heard voices interspersed with laughter spilling over a chipped wall. Several bicycles were propped up against it. None were red. She passed through an opening into a courtyard bordered by beds of flowers in the spectrum of a rainbow.

Crimson geraniums in large terra cotta planters hung in front of the windows of an ancient one-story adobe. A summery pastoral scene.

Rustic picnic tables were arranged on the grass patio under the shade of fragrant fruit trees. The seats were taken by young men and women who sipped from teacups, smoked cigarettes, and bantered loudly across the tables. The men wore white boater hats with black or red striped bands and beige linen suits or sweaters with open collars. The women art students from Champlin's class had shed their black paint smocks, revealing pastel summer dresses or slacks with loose blouses under embroidered Spanish vests. Most of them wore wide-brimmed straw hats. Sarah wished she was wearing one. Even with the shade of the orchard, the sun was glaring.

Sarah stood in the center of the courtyard breathing in the

fragrances when she heard Ada say, *See, Sarah, didn't I tell you how dazzling Carmel is?*

*There you are,* thought Sarah, happy to have her sister's company, though her voice seemed to have faded since she last spoke. *Please don't leave me, Ada.*

*Why would I? I have nowhere else to go.*

"You found us!" said Sirena, grabbing Sarah's hand and pulling her over to a long table. Sarah bent down and unclipped Albert's leash. He wagged his way from table to table and was rewarded with pats on the head and savory snacks.

Sirena had been saving a space for Sarah. When she sat down, the conversations stopped and everyone turned to look at her. The young man who'd given her abalone on the beach, Tony Mac Ginnis, was seated across from her and greeted her with a warm smile. He was hardly recognizable in a white linen suit, black bow tie, and boater hat.

Sirena leaned toward Sarah. "Hope you don't mind," she whispered. "News travels fast in our colony and everyone knows now that you're Ada's sister. They asked me to say something nice about her."

Before Sarah could stop her, Sirena stood up. Everyone else at the table stood up. Teacups were raised toward Sarah.

"I'd like to make a toast to Ada Belle Davenport," said Sirena. "She was a very special person, well-loved and respected by our colony, which is why we are so very pleased to have her sister, Sarah, with us today."

Sarah was touched by their sympathetic faces and Sirena's kind words. She stood up and chinked her cup against Sirena's and acknowledged the raised cups of the rest of the party. "Please know that I really appreciate this warm welcome." The unexpected taste of wine loosened her tongue. This must be the "cup of tea" Hallie and Jeanette had mentioned.

She raised her cup again, and in a stronger voice said, "To my sister, Ada. May she rest in peace."

Everyone had sat down and resumed their animated conversations when two more guests joined their table. A very attractive couple, thought Sarah, admiring the girl's skilled application of makeup, her painted red lips and perfectly manicured hands.

The girl's kohl-penciled eyes were keeping a territorial watch over her escort and Sarah could see why. He was remarkably handsome in a linen suit and straw trilby hat pushed back from his face. He could've been a Hollywood film star.

People squeezed together to make room for the newcomers on the crowded bench. Sarah ended up between the tall, dark stranger and Elizabeth.

Elizabeth whispered in her ear that the stranger was Robert Pierce, a popular Hollywood photographer for the cinema beauties. His companion was Louise Brooks, an up-and-coming Hollywood starlet who had come to Carmel to perform in *Pirates of Penzance*, the same musical in which Rosie was a member of the chorus.

"Why, she can't be much older than Sirena!" said Sarah.

Elizabeth raised her brow. "Yes, I think you're right, but she's already been around the block a few times, if you know what I mean."

Sarah unintentionally bumped shoulders with Robert Pierce. She apologized but he was quick to say, "Don't apologize! I like it when pretty women bump into me." He winked and tipped his trilby at her.

What a ridiculous flirt, she thought, trying to deny the feeling of pleasure that ran through her when she looked into his sea-gray eyes shaded under thick black lashes.

She reached for her teacup. He saw that it was empty and poured from the pitcher. She was already starting to feel a bit tipsy, but didn't stop him.

Tony came around the table and patted Robert on the back. "Hello, old man, good to see you're back in Carmel." Without waiting for Robert to reply, he said, "I don't think you knew Ada Davenport, but this is her sister Sarah, an artist from Paris."

Robert gave Sarah his condolences and lowered his voice, "I know how painful it is to lose a sibling to suicide. I lost my younger brother not so long ago."

Sarah was eager to move on to a lighter subject. "What brings you to Carmel?" she asked.

"I'm a photographer and when I'm not shooting in Hollywood, I come here to get away and photograph nature. Sea otters are less troublesome and a lot cuter than starlets." He looked over at Louise Brooks, who was laughing loudly at something Tony said.

Robert turned back to Sarah. "Have you been here before?"

"No, this is my first time."

"I could show you around if you'd like. Carmel has extraordinary scenic views." Sarah shifted on the bench. His offer was tempting. Ada would've said yes. But Sarah wasn't Ada. "I'm only here another week. I need to get back to Paris."

"I wish I had that excuse," he said. "What is it like living in Paris? I've always wanted to go there."

As they discussed the Parisian art world, she heard a change in his tone that seemed far more sincere than his earlier flirtatious banter. He had a quick wit and a sympathetic ear when she spoke of the difficulties she faced being a woman artist living alone in Paris. He told her about his photography and how dissatisfying it was working with actresses in Hollywood. Whenever he could, he escaped to Carmel to hike and shoot outdoor pictures. Nature asked nothing more of him other than to respect her beauty and tread lightly across her lands.

Immersed in their conversation, she lost all sense of time until Sirena tapped on her shoulder. "Sarah, it's late. We have to get back to the Lodge for dinner or Rosie will be cross." She and the other girls had gathered up their sketch boxes and smocks and were ready to leave.

Sarah was unsteady when she stood up. Unintentionally, she put her hand on Robert's shoulder and leaned toward him. "Are you all right?" he asked, reaching out to stop her from falling in his lap.

"I think so. I'm just not used to so much sunshine and tea."

He stood up and took her arm firmly. "I have a car. Let me take you home."

"That's all right, Robert," said Sirena, coming between them. "We'll take her home."

Before letting go of her arm, he said, "I'd like to see you again. How do I find you?"

"I'm staying at my sister's cottage on Camino Real."

Sirena led her away, but Sarah managed to look back and say, "Across from McCann's Lodge."

Outside the adobe wall, Sarah leaned against Elizabeth and grinned foolishly. "I drank too much wine, didn't I?"

"We all know what that's like, don't we, girls?" said Elizabeth.

Sirena had clipped on Albert's leash and was pulling him toward the cow pasture. Annie and Elizabeth flanked Sarah, helping her walk, and Hallie and Jeanette brought up the rear.

The cows stopped chewing when they heard the girls mooing. Unimpressed, they returned to munching but a massive black bull showed far more interest. With his horns raised he started walking toward the mooing "cows." The girls hushed up and escaped over the fence to the other side of the field.

After taking the rickety stairs up to St. Lucia Road, they all stopped to shake out their shoes and catch their breath.

"My, oh my, honey," said Elizabeth in her slow Virginian drawl, "you certainly made an impression on Mr. Robert Pierce. Louise was hopping mad. He ignored her and spent the entire time talking to you."

"Watch out, Sarah," said Annie. "Robert is a ladies' man. A lot of girls are stuck on him already in the colony."

"Oh, don't worry about me," said Sarah, still feeling tipsy. "I know his kind." Her face showed more distaste than she felt. "Even if he *is* woefully gorgeous, I know a flirt when I see one. I bet I never hear from him again."

Sirena had walked on ahead with Albert. He kept looking back to make sure Sarah was close behind.

# SATURDAY, JULY 26
## —11—

S arah walked up Ocean Avenue to May Laundry where she dropped off Ada's mildewed clothes for cleaning and her red Chanel suit for pressing in preparation for her return to Paris in the near future.

She sat down at a table in the Blue Bird Tea Room where she had a clear view of the deVrais Gallery. While she waited for the art dealer to arrive, she thankfully sipped real tea from a cup. She'd awoken that morning with a splitting headache but managed to get herself up and dressed for the dreaded meeting with Paul deVrais.

She recognized the gray pinstripe suit deVrais had been wearing on the train. This morning he was wearing a maroon tie rather than the gaudy pink ascot. An elegantly dressed woman arrived as he unlocked the front door and they both went inside. He flipped the sign on the door from CLOSED to OPEN.

Sarah paid for her tea and made her away across the dirt road, holding up her mid-calf hem to keep it from getting mud-splattered. A seascape painting titled *Sunrise at Carmel Beach,* signed "A.B. Davenport," was in the storefront window. Even with a wall of thick plate glass separating her from the canvas, Sarah felt like she could step onto the pristine beach and dig her bare feet into the warm sand. A sea breeze danced with her skirt, the early morning sun warmed her face.

Her brief escape from her worries was interrupted when deVrais's diamond-studded, white-cuffed arm appeared over the painting. He placed a SOLD sign on the edge of the gilded frame. She was sorry it was sold, but then remembered she owned all the other Davenport paintings in deVrais's gallery.

She was about to enter the gallery and claim her ownership when she saw a small poster taped to the glass door that stopped her. *A.B Davenport, Portraitures, Hotel Del Monte Art Gallery, September 27–30, 1924,* was written under Ada's portrait of Katherine Mansfield.

Ada had told her that Mansfield had been the first portrait she'd made for the collection and how it had inspired her to make the others. "I was drawn to painting women. Not just famous women like Katherine, but others who live more common but noble lives. Cézanne once said that the goal of all art is to paint the face. I think he was right."

*Mr. Crocker, I have found the portraits,* Sarah whispered, hardly able to control her excitement at seeing the first, if only a facsimile, from the missing collection of portraits her sister had painted.

The overhead doorbell jangled as she pushed open the door. Paul deVrais glanced over, but the lady who had just bought *Sunrise at Carmel Beach* required his attention. She was complaining about its elevated price.

A collector, thought Sarah, casting a side glance at the woman's tailored jacket and ermine collar. Her silver-streaked hair was tightly pulled back into a round bun, her red polished fingers weighted down with jewels that sparkled under the overhead gallery lights. "I've met your type at the 291 gallery in New York," Sarah said under her breath, "more of an investor in art than an aficionado." She was equally disgusted to hear deVrais telling the buyer that Ada's painting was a bargain considering the demand for her work after her suicide.

She wandered over to the other side of the gallery and began to examine the paintings displayed on the walls. She focused on several small California landscapes that were hung together. The artists' names were familiar from her student days at the Art League in New

York. Back then, she'd admired their work and tried to duplicate it, but since her time in Paris, she now found them quite conventional and drab. A flat, tonal representation. No emotional tension.

Across from one of the walls was a painting propped on an easel. When she stepped around to look at it, she slapped her hand over her mouth to muffle an involuntary cry. It was the painting she'd found in Ada's studio. The plaque below read: A BLEAK MORNING: A.B. DAVENPORT (1886–1924). If that wasn't obvious enough, a black mourning band was draped underneath the frame.

It was a forgery. Done at the behest of an art dealer who wouldn't hesitate to exploit an artist's death for profit. A buyer for this morbid painting would not be someone who loved art. It would be someone who thought a desperate artist had lashed out with her paintbrush to express her darkest emotions before destroying herself. DeVrais might as well have entitled it *The Suicide*.

Sarah wanted it off the easel, even if she had to take it down herself. She raised out her arms.

"Don't touch!"

She twisted around and faced Paul deVrais's eyes aimed at her like bullets. She'd been so consumed by her outrage that she hadn't heard the jangling doorbell and she hadn't heard him coming up behind her after his client had left.

"Oh, it's you, Miss Cunningham. Excuse me, I thought you were a tourist who didn't know how to behave properly in a gallery."

Sarah gave him a calm, even smile and tried to appear in control of her emotions.

"What brings you to my gallery on this bright, sunny day?"

"You invited me."

"Yes, I remember, but," he showed his pearly teeth, "you weren't exactly gracious on the train. I was planning to seek you out at Miss McCann's lodge but I was detained in San Francisco on business. As you know, we have serious matters to discuss."

She felt him hovering over her as she bent closer to inspect Ada's forged signature in the bottom right corner. She clasped her hands behind her back and pretended to show good behavior while her mind went on a rampage. How could she prove that Ada didn't paint *A Bleak Morning*? It would be his word, a reputable dealer, against hers, the grieving sister of a suicider.

"I do worry about the canvas getting damaged," he said. "It's one of your sister's last paintings, and as you can see the oil is still wet. It takes a very long time to dry thoroughly. Being an artist, of course, you would already know that." He went on. "The demand for that painting has been incredible. Several dealers and art collectors have already made lucrative offers."

"But why? It isn't her style. It's not anything like the painting you just sold."

"I'm a dealer, Miss Cunningham. It doesn't have to look like her work to be profitable. What matters is she painted it on River Beach where she later took her life. This painting represents her last moments. Her darkest thoughts." Sarah imagined him telling this to a potential buyer with the same pitiful eyes he was now steadying on her.

"Ada never used black pigments in her paintings," she said, flatly. "Even her shadows were brushed on in blues, greens, and reds. Never completely black like this."

"As *black* as you might find it,"—irritation seeped into his mild manner—"Ada painted it, and, as I said, I've had several offers."

He smoothed out his tie and the strident tone in his voice.

"Miss Cunningham, why are we standing here discussing Ada's painting when there are urgent matters to discuss?" He walked to the front door and flipped the sign to Closed. "Let's sit down." She followed him to his desk at the back of the gallery.

He opened the doors of a finely crafted antique breakfront. Inside was a liquor cabinet filled with glasses and bottles of wine and spirits.

He saw her surprise. "It's a Prohibition bar," he said. "Can I offer you something to drink?"

"Just water, thank you." She sat down across from his desk. He leaned forward to light her cigarette with an inlaid mother-of-pearl lighter like the one he'd given Ada. Sarah now recognized its rich colors as abalone shell. She took a drag from her cigarette. Did Ada give him back the lighter? Or did he take it back after she was dead?

He poured her a glass of water and set the pitcher down next to a stack of posters advertising Ada's exhibition. She picked one up.

"Did Ada tell you about the Del Monte Gallery?"

*Yes,* she thought, *it's the gallery where Ada didn't want her portraits exhibited.*

"When we had our last exhibit there, all of Ada's California landscapes on display sold. An unheard of success for a female artist."

She took a sip of water. He leaned his hips against the desk, his arms crossed, watching her.

"That's why Ada decided to exhibit her portraits at the Del Monte." He held up the poster. "I see no reason to cancel it," he said, adding solemnly, "It's what Ada would've wanted."

"Au contraire! That's not what she told me."

He glared at her. "What are you talking about? Ada wanted this exhibit. It was her idea."

"Yes, she did want an exhibit, but not at the Del Monte."

"Who told you that?"

"Mr. deVrais, my sister and I were very close. She confided in me when I saw her this past January in New York. I know of the tension between the two of you. And I know she wanted to have the portraits exhibited in New York. You needn't suggest otherwise."

He picked up a ship-in-a-bottle paperweight on his desk and rocked it back and forth in his hands. "That was a stupid idea. If she'd only listened to me, she'd still be alive." He slammed down the paperweight and narrowed his eyes at Sarah just like a bull before he lances the matador. "I believe you were the one who suggested she experiment with portraits. It's what drove her mad."

She ignored his accusation and looked over his shoulder at a closed door. "If you don't mind, Mr. deVrais, I'd like to see those portraits that you say drove her mad."

If looks could kill, I'd be dead, thought Sarah. He was a formidable enemy.

"I don't know what game you're playing, Miss Cunningham, but I don't have the portraits. The last time I saw them was in Ada's studio a few days before she died. Her assistant was packing them into crates. I would've arranged to pick them up sooner, but when the marshal told me you were coming I thought to wait until you got here. You can give me the key to the studio's alley door and I'll have them picked up."

She could've easily lashed out at his appalling brashness but chose to take her time and mull over the fact that Sirena had been telling the truth when she said she packed the paintings, but why hadn't she told Sarah that deVrais had been there too?

She took another cigarette from her packet and lit it herself, taking her time. She too could pace herself in the bull ring.

"I'm sorry to disappoint you, Mr. deVrais, but the portraits are not in the studio."

"But I saw them there. I would've picked them up myself, but decided to wait until you got here."

"I have no reason to lie to you. Sirena seems to think Ada might have burned them."

"Burned them? Ridiculous! She was too obsessed with those portraits to ever destroy them, and she was afraid of fire."

"Then perhaps they were stolen."

"Equally ridiculous. Why do you say that?"

"When I first arrived at Ada's cottage, I found the alley door to the studio unlocked. I think someone was using her studio. Perhaps that same person stole the portraits. Perhaps someone you know."

DeVrais started pacing back and forth nervously. "If that is true, I will immediately report the theft to Marshal Judd and move all of Ada's artwork out of the cottage to my storage vault where they'll be safe."

His arrogance was becoming increasingly intolerable. Sarah straightened her spine and said calmly, "Let me speak plainly, Mr. deVrais. I am Ada's executor and I forbid you to touch any of her artwork. If anyone is going to report the portraits as stolen, it will be me, the owner, not you."

He stopped pacing and glared down at her. His mask of politeness completely gone. His face hard and bitter.

"I made Ada Davenport who she is. Her work would be worth nothing without me. Do you hear me? Nothing! Ada understood that. That's why she entrusted me with her legacy. Not her sister who abandoned her three years ago to live in Paris."

Sarah hurled back. "Need I remind you, Mr. deVrais, that your contract expired on July first of this year? Four days before my sister's death." She rearranged her rosebud shawl and imagined Ada close by, willing her to be strong.

DeVrais clenched his jaw, walked back behind the desk, and pulled out a folder from the bottom drawer. "That's not what it says here. Only if Ada legally gave notice that she was terminating our agreement would it expire. Otherwise the contract remains in effect. Here, look for yourself." He thrust the contract toward her.

She pretended to read the document she already knew well. It gave her time to consider her next move. Slowly, she opened her satchel and took out her copy of Ada's termination letter. "Then tell me what this is?"

He snatched the letter from her hand as if to tear it up and she let him know there were other copies and there was also certification from the post office that he'd received the letter and signed for it, so it was fruitless to deny it.

"Mr. Giles will be contacting you in regard to turning over all of Ada's paintings to me."

His face drained of color. No more the suave dealer who thought he could bluff and manipulate to get what he wanted. In a dry business-like tone, he said, "I don't care what you say, I never received this letter."

She stood up, picked up the stack of posters for the Del Monte exhibit, and dropped them in his wastebasket. "I must ask that you remove all advertisements for this event and inform the Del Monte Gallery that there will be no exhibition. When found, the portraits will be exhibited at Eric Crocker's gallery in Manhattan." She mimicked him, "It's what Ada would've wanted."

DeVrais stared at her, slack-jawed. His cigarette had nearly burned down to his manicured fingers and he stubbed it out.

"Before I go, I'd like to make you an offer," she said, putting out her own cigarette and boldly facing him. "*A Bleak Morning* in exchange for my fifty percent share of the painting you just sold." His menacing stare was unnerving, but she held her ground. "I don't want this picture ending up in some gallery where a critic might judge it as the final artistic moment of my sister's life."

DeVrais seemed to be at a loss for words. Only his clenching jaw moved. Sarah continued, gaining confidence.

"And I also think you should know that I'm presenting new evidence to Monterey's District Attorney in my petition to reopen the inquest. If you continue to deny receipt of the termination letter, I will find it necessary to put it in evidence as a motive for my sister's murder. When she terminated your contract and you couldn't convince her otherwise, you killed her. You may be indicted."

"Murder? Are you out of your mind? Ada killed herself."

She walked away from him and gave one last look at the forged painting before reaching the front door. "Please deliver that travesty to Ada's cottage. And be forewarned, if you try to sell it, I will insist on it being authenticated."

He threw back his head and laughed, regaining his former swagger. He approached her. "If you think that's a forgery, you're blind. Maybe it's not her *best* work, but it certainly is a true expression of the fundamental darkness that destroyed her. If you continue to threaten me with these false accusations, I will destroy whatever's left of Ada's reputation and take you down with her."

Sarah ripped the poster advertising the Del Monte exhibition off the door, dropped it in her satchel, and turning to face him, smiled. "It's been a pleasure, Mr. deVruis. No need to show me out." The hanging bell reverberated through the gallery as she jerked open the door, stepped outside, and firmly closed it.

She started walking rapidly up Ocean Avenue with an unfamiliar boldness to her steps. Her black rose-embroidered shawl blew behind her in the breeze—a flag of courage.

When she reached Dolores Street, she stopped to catch her breath. *Oh Ada, aren't you proud of me. I stood up to him just like you would've done.*

Her exuberance was tempered when she heard her sister's disapproval. *Little Sis, there's no telling what this weasel might do now that you've threatened to expose him. You have to be more careful.*

# —12—

Sirena was waiting at the bus stop when Sarah arrived and they got on the rickety yellow bus together. As it slowly groaned its way to the top of Carmel Hill in low gear, Sarah turned to Sirena, "Do you know Paul deVrais very well?"

"Are you kidding? Mr. deVrais never pays much attention to us students. He's too busy managing Ada and his other famous artists to have any time for the likes of me."

"Did he often come to Ada's cottage when you were working there?"

"Not much. She didn't seem to like having him in the studio. I don't know why. I wish I could get that kind of attention from a major art dealer. I'd do anything to have deVrais show my work. Why do you ask?"

"I was just at his gallery and he told me that he was in the studio when you were packing the portraits in crates."

"Well, he's mistaken. Maybe he came after I left."

Sarah looked out at the passing pines as the bus descended the steep hill toward Monterey, her thoughts on Sirena. If only she could get her to tell the truth about herself maybe they could be real friends. Until then, she couldn't trust her.

She turned to face Sirena. "Where are you from?"

"Hawaii. Have you been there?"

"No. I've seen pictures. A tropical paradise. Were you born there?"

"Yes. I grew up on my dad's sugar plantation."

"You must have had a very unusual childhood."

"Not really. It's pretty boring standing between rows of sugar cane for entertainment. It's not like you can talk to the sugar cane or make friends with them. I'd much rather have grown up in a big city like you did."

Sarah was amazed by how easily Sirena could lie. "Perhaps we all want what we don't have. You must miss your family."

"Not so much," Sirena said dismissively. "They shipped me out to San Francisco to study nursing and then they were disappointed when I quit and came here to study art. They stopped my allowance soon after that. That was a year ago. We haven't spoken since."

*Mon dieux*, thought Sarah, but said, "I'm sorry to hear that. It's hard enough to succeed as a woman artist let alone have parents who oppose it."

Sirena shrugged. "Lots of the girls I know are in similar situations."

Sarah didn't think there were many girls in Sirena's situation.

The bus screeched to a stop at the depot next to the Monterey Wharf and the passengers crowded into the aisle to get off.

As they disembarked, Sarah pointed through the towering pines to the bell tower of Hotel Del Monte. "Ada and I stayed there with my parents."

"My, my, aren't you the cat's meow," exclaimed Sirena, fluttering her eyes.

"Not really. I was only four years old," Sarah said, defensively. "Life is quite different for me now. But I remember riding in a horse-drawn carriage, and we had a picnic high up on a cliff overlooking the sea."

Just then a bright red, open-air sedan car driven by a uniformed chauffeur sped by. Four children and their parents were all holding onto their hats. Sirena waved and the carefree, laughing children waved back as if they were in a parade.

"I'm afraid your horse-drawn carriage ride has been replaced by touring cars like that," said Sirena.

"I hope the Del Monte hasn't changed. It was a gorgeous hotel. Why don't we have tea there after our shopping?"

Sirena dug into the pocket of her saffron coveralls, which were splotched with paint and pulled out a dime, and said, "Sorry. This is just enough to take the bus back to Carmel."

"Don't worry," said Sarah. "It'll be my treat. I sold a painting before I left Paris so I can certainly afford to take you to tea."

Sirena stretched out her coveralls like a skirt and curtsied. "Then I graciously accept your invitation." She dropped the dime back into her pocket.

"How do you manage the cost of art supplies, lessons, and renting a room at Rosie's lodge?" asked Sarah.

Sirena puffed out her round cheeks, took a cigarette from behind her ear, stuck it between her lips, and strutted around Sarah. "I'm a man of many trades," she said gruffly from the other side of her mouth. "For a price, I can do just about anything." Then she took off laughing and skipping down Alvarado Street.


In Oliver's Mission Art and Curio Store, Sarah felt like one of the faithful entering a church. She stood very still in the center aisle, closed her eyes, and breathed in the heavy fragrance of pigments, linseed oil, and solvents, which brought back childhood memories of shopping with Ada in Chicago.

Even back then, Ada stood out, not only as one of the prettiest, but as one of the very few women shopping in an art supplies store. The other students and professional painters in Chicago were mostly men wearing dark suits and bowler hats. The few female customers wore corsets under heavy skirts down to their ankles, and wrapped their long hair in braids and hid it under bonnets with ribbons tied in bows under their chins. Not Ada. Her flaming red tresses cascaded down her back unrestrained. And, having sworn off the corset, she wore loose, flowing dresses like one might see in a Middle Eastern bazaar.

Now, at Oliver's in California, six years after the war, the majority of customers were young women wearing trousers or mid-calf pleated skirts and, like Sarah, they wore their hair cropped.

Sarah stood spellbound in front of the display case of metallic tubes of oil paint wondering which ones to choose. They were all delicious, like a box of chocolate.

An attractive young salesman wearing a French beret and an apron with Gus stitched on the front asked if he could be of service. He laid her selected tubes out on the counter, a cobalt blue, a Paris green mixed with arsenic to create its brilliant emerald hue, Monterey azure, lupine violet, and kelp ochre. The last three would never be available at Sennelier's art supply store in Paris, she thought, rationalizing such an extravagant purchase. If truth be told, her transatlantic journey had depleted her savings, the money she'd made on the painting was almost gone, and she didn't know when Ada's estate would be settled.

Gus cleared his throat, patiently waiting for her to make up her mind.

"There you are!" She heard Sirena's bright voice. "And isn't it just like Gus to find the prettiest girl in the store to help."

"Hi, Sirena," said Gus. "You two know each other?"

"Best friends," said Sirena proudly, linking Sarah's arm with hers. "Sarah's taking me to the Del Monte for tea this afternoon." Sirena's attention was diverted by a group of girls her age waving her over and she left as abruptly as she'd arrived.

"What else can I help you with?" asked Gus.

Sarah hesitated in front of a row of paintbrushes organized by size in Mason jars. She'd never had the same mind for tidiness as Ada, who was always keeping after her to clean her brushes.

"Take your time," Gus said as he was pulled away by an impatient customer. Sarah was eager to indulge on her own. She tried several brushes feeling their weight and balance in her hand. Her final choice was a narrow sable brush.

Gus returned and added up the cost of her purchases at a cash register. After she paid him, he said, "Excuse me for asking, but are you Ada Davenport's sister?"

"Yes I am. What gave me away?"

He smiled. "Certainly not your choice of pigments. She would never have chosen the Paris green you bought today. She only bought the 'natural' colors."

She laughed. "You're so right about that. Then how did you know?"

"I saw your portrait in her studio a short time ago."

It seemed that everyone in Monterey had seen her portrait but herself.

"Ada and I go way back. I took classes from her at the Art Students League when I lived in New York. After the war, I moved here to Monterey. Sometimes she invited me to paint with her and Sirena on the beach."

Just then Sirena's laughter crossed the room. They both turned to watch her modeling a parasol to a circle of customers. "She's quite a live wire, that Sirena," said Gus. "Nothing ever seems to faze her."

He shut the cash drawer and handed her the change. "Your sister was very good to me. If I can ever be of any help—"

"Do you believe she killed herself?"

He paused and then waved over another salesman and said, "Let's talk outside."

Sarah looked around for Sirena and saw she was now posing for a young fellow who was drawing her on his sketch pad. She admired the girl's nerve. If she had been trying to hide her racial identity, she wouldn't be showing off, let alone let her face be drawn, even though she looked white.

Gus brought her to a quiet bench under the canopy of a giant oak in a park next to the store. Blue patches of sky filled in the spaces between the oak's branches.

"To answer your question, no, I don't believe Ada killed herself, but I was worried about her. When we last painted together on Carmel Beach, she was very anxious and kept looking over her shoulder. When I asked what was wrong, she said someone had been following her."

"Do you have any idea who it might have been?" asked Sarah, feeling goose bumps on her arms though it was a hot summer day.

"No, but I can tell you this. Ada was not the desperate woman the marshal portrayed her as. She was very excited about her portraits and the upcoming exhibition. I wanted to testify at the inquest, but Judd said there were enough character witnesses already. What a laugh. It was only Rosie who was allowed to speak in her defense."

He looked toward Sirena who was coming out of Oliver's and turned back to Sarah. "Be careful. There are some powerful people in this town who just want the whole thing to be over with. It's not been good publicity for the Del Monte Gallery having one of their most famous artists commit suicide."

He stood up. "I've got to get back to work."

"Thanks, Gus. You've been really helpful. If you think of anything else, I'm staying at Ada's cottage."

She saw Sirena stop him at the door and they exchanged a few words.

"Isn't he the nicest guy? And so cute," said Sirena plopping down on the bench.

"Let's go have that tea I promised you," said Sarah.

Sarah and Sirena walked down the seaside boardwalk that led to Hotel Del Monte, crossed the train tracks of its private train depot, and turned up a long driveway bordered with Monterey pines and coastal oaks. As the impressive gothic-style chateau came into view, Sarah looked up to admire its gabled roofs and four-story tower.

"When I was here before, I imagined a princess locked in the tower throwing down her long braid to Prince Charming," said Sarah.

Sirena laughed and said, "I wish I was that princess. I'd do anything to escape from here."

"I thought you liked Carmel."

"Oh, don't get me wrong. It's just sometimes I dream of living in Paris, like you do, away from conservative teachers like old Mr. Champlin. My hand just wants me to do something different. And so does my heart."

"When am I going to see your work?

"You were serious?"

"Of course I was serious. I can't make any promises but maybe I can help you to get a scholarship at the Académie Julian in Paris. That's how I got in."

Sirena's face fell. "They'd never give someone like me a scholarship."

"You could at least apply."

Sirena looked away, but not before Sarah had seen the shadow of hopelessness in her young face.

As they climbed a short staircase leading up to a wide, covered veranda, a cool ocean breeze swept through the open archways bringing with it the sweet fragrance of blooming white roses.

At pale pink table-clothed tables, women were wearing pastel linen dresses and straw hats adorned with bouquets of paper flowers. The fashionable men were wearing expensive, tailored suits. The tables were adorned with tempting pastries and baskets of red and yellow fruit that reminded Sarah of a Pierre Bonnard still life.

A maître d' dressed in a black tuxedo looked down at Sirena's paint-splattered coveralls and Sarah's hatless head and ushered the two women down to the end of one veranda away from the other hotel guests.

Sarah demanded they be moved to a better table.

"It's all right," said Sirena, seemingly unaffected by the maître d's blatant rudeness. Sarah quickly realized that the last thing Sirena would want was to make a scene in an uppity place like the Del Monte where she wouldn't be allowed entrance if she wasn't passing for white.

Sirena plopped down in a chair and Sarah joined her. "Look." She pointed across a slanted lawn to a very large swimming pool crowded with lounging guests both in and out of the pool. "Look at those skimpy bathing suits. Isn't it wonderful that we no longer have to wear dresses down to our knees when we swim and we can show off our legs?"

Soon after they ordered, a waiter appeared with a copper teapot, delicate porcelain floral cups and saucers, Devon cream, strawberry confiture, and a plate of still-warm muffins. He noticed Sirena's napkin was still on the table and laid it across her lap.

"This is too gorgeous," exclaimed Sirena, moistening her lips and rubbing her hands together. She loaded her plate and ate while watching the swimmers take high dives. "Look at that fellow's somersault! Not even a splash"

"Did you ever come swimming here with Ada?"

Sirena put down her butter knife and squinted at Sarah. "I hope you didn't bring me here to talk about Ada."

"No. Of course not. It's just . . ." She took a sip of her tea. "Do you mind so much talking about her?"

Sirena bit into a peach. "She never brought me here."

"Then could you tell me about your morning swims with her on Carmel Bay? Wasn't the water freezing?"

Sirena took another bite of her peach. "You don't think about it. If you did, you'd never go in the water."

"What *do* you think about?"

"You don't think at all. You feel how exhilarating it will be to get your blood surging and after your swim you hurry back to your studio to paint. Ada knew about things like that."

After the waiter had cleared their plates, Sarah brought out a package and handed it to Sirena. "You've been so good to me, taking me around and introducing me to everyone, I wanted to give you a little gift from Oliver's."

Sirena quickly tore off the tissue, opened the package, and gasped when she saw the sable paintbrush. She stroked the brush back and forth in her palm. Sarah noticed her calloused hands. She didn't get those from painting. She remembered Rosie telling her that Sirena was an abalone diver.

"This is really generous of you, Sarah. I've always wanted a sable brush."

"And this is a replacement for the tube I borrowed," said Sarah, holding up a tube of cobalt blue.

The grandfather clock in the lobby of the hotel chimed five times.

"Got to go," said Sirena, jumping up. "I need to catch the next bus to Carmel." The waiter looked sternly at Sirena who was shoving muffins in her pocket. She grinned back at him.

"But why the hurry?" asked Sarah, as she asked the waiter for the check. "I was hoping to take a walk in the Arizona Gardens where Ada and I played among the exotic plants when we were children."

"Next time," said Sirena as they hurried down the path away from the Del Monte. "Robert Pierce has hired me to model for him. I prefer posing for painters, but he pays more."

"That good-looking fellow I met at the Mission Tea House yesterday?"

"Yes, that's him. He's a protégé of the photographer Johan Hagemeyer. Hagemeyer lets him stay at his Carmel cabin while he's in Europe."

"I met Hagemeyer when I was working in New York as a receptionist for Alfred Stieglitz."

Sirena stopped walking and turned to Sarah. "You worked for Alfred Stieglitz at 291! That gallery is famous. What other artists did you meet?"

"Georgia O'Keeffe was one of my favorites."

"No!" exclaimed Sirena. Several strolling hotel guests turned to look. Sirena whispered, "Did she talk to you?"

Sarah nodded. "She was most generous with her time. She encouraged me to go to Paris to broaden my approach. And she was so right. And now I'd like to encourage you, Sirena, if you let me."

Sirena took off without answering but she looked more hopeful than when Sarah mentioned it earlier.

# —13—

After a silent bus ride back to Carmel, Sirena was about to leave Sarah on Ocean Avenue when she said, "I almost forgot to tell you. Una and Robinson Jeffers are having a garden party tomorrow afternoon. They were very good friends of Ada's and they asked me to invite you."

"I'd love to come." It would give her a chance to talk to Mr. Jeffers and find out if he saw Ada on the beach the night of the fourth.

She stopped at May Laundry to check on the clothes she'd left that morning and was impressed that they were ready to be picked up. When she paid, the Japanese woman behind the counter gave her an envelope and said they'd found something in the side pocket of the vest.

Outside under the sunlight, she opened the envelope and a gold wedding band slipped out into her hand. FOREVER YOURS was engraved in tiny letters on the inside.

Albert was eagerly awaiting her return with his leash loosely hanging from his mouth. He'd been cooped up all day and deserved an outing. Albert chose to leave his mark below a Monterey sapling, not caring that it was also in front of a hacienda-style three-level establishment perched on a hillside overlooking the bay with lots of people passing by.

A sign hung from the stone-arched entrance: HOTEL LA PLAYA, LARGE ROOMS, PRIVATE BATHS, VIEW OF OCEAN. A path bordered with geranium flowerbeds led up to the inviting entrance.

Jovial people were strolling in and out of the lobby, some stopping to exchange greetings with their friends. A young couple bent down to pet an enthusiastic tail-wagging Albert and Sarah asked them about the hotel. They told her there was a lounge where people gathered and no, she didn't need an escort.

She was missing Ada, and being around people sounded like a better way to spend her evening than sitting in the cottage. She decided to take Albert for a walk on the beach then go home and come back on her own.

She and Ada had always shared their clothes, so she didn't hesitate to put on the black trousers and jersey hanging in the closet, which went well with her rosebud shawl. She studied her reflection in the bathroom mirror and colored her lips red, adding a trace of rouge.

The La Playa Hotel doorman directed her down the hall. She knocked on the locked door and a single human eye looked her over through a peephole. She must've passed inspection because the door opened and she stepped inside without a word spoken.

She could've been in a speakeasy in New York—it was just as sultry and seductive. Red leather booths were lit by yellow votive candles flickering on black tablecloths, their occupants cast in shadows. A chandelier shown down on a mahogany bar with brass fixtures. There were casual-chic men and women propped up on bar stools, sipping from martini glasses like models in an Edward Hopper painting.

To one side, a Negro in a black tuxedo was seated at an upright piano playing the blues. Behind him was a wall of photographs of popular blues and jazz singers and musicians. Bessie Smith was there along with Ma Rainey, Louis Armstrong, and Duke Ellington.

In spite of the obscure lighting and the jaunty notes being played, Sarah felt awkward standing there alone. She was about to leave when she heard Sirena's voice coming from a dark booth in the back of the room. As she started to walk toward her, she saw Robert Pierce sitting across from her. They seemed to be having a heated argument so she quickly changed course, and seeing Mac holding court at the bar, joined him. Happy to see her, he introduced her to his friends, another man and two young women, about Sarah's age.

"Let me buy you a drink," he insisted. "What's your poison?"

"What are you having?"

"A whiskey sour."

"Okay. I'll have the same."

The bartender shook the ingredients in a silver cocktail shaker and poured the amber concoction into a coupe glass, topping it off with a ruby-red cherry pierced on a stick and a thin slice of orange balanced on the rim. Sarah admired his artistic palette, remembering the fun nights Ada and she had spent in their favorite jazz bar drinking this very cocktail. Feeling her sister's profound absence, she lifted her glass and whispered, "To you, my dear sister, I miss you so much."

"Hey! Don't toast alone, I'm here," said Tony, clinking her glass. Sarah chatted for a few minutes with him, then excused herself and carried her drink out onto the terrace to watch the approaching sunset.

She had just lit a cigarette when she felt a soft tap on her shoulder and spun around to find Robert Pierce's sea-gray eyes gazing into hers. "Gorgeous, isn't it?"

She felt an undeniable tremor of pleasure ripple through her body and blamed it on the whiskey sour.

"How good to see you again so soon," he said, looking around the deserted terrace. "Are you here with someone?"

"No, just me."

She turned toward the horizon, away from his lingering gaze.

"It's an alluring sunset. I'd like to paint it."

"Funny you should say that. I was wishing I'd brought my camera."

"I would think photographing sunsets must be rather boring after snapping pictures of Hollywood femme fatales," she said, trying to say something witty, but his wide smile faded into a frown.

"I can assure you I'd rather be taking photographs of sunsets than laboring under hot light bulbs trying to make some up-and-coming starlet look radiant under heavy makeup."

At least it pays well, thought Sarah, noting the diamond pinned on his silver silk tie and quickly said, "I didn't mean to insult you. I think you're very fortunate to be able to make a good living as an artist. Not many of us can do that."

She sipped her drink trying to find a less objectionable subject. She found it in her hand. "Am I safe drinking this cocktail?" she asked. "Is there any chance I might be arrested?"

"Not with me here," he said, his smile returning. "I know Louie, the owner of La Playa. He'd warn me if we have to make a run for it and I know the back way out of here."

"Are you serious?"

He winked. "No. The marshal would only arrest you if you were causing trouble." He leaned toward her, "Do you cause trouble, Miss Cunningham?"

"Sometimes," she replied, surprised at her coyness. It wasn't like her to be flirtatious like her sister.

"How does the La Playa manage to stock a full liquor bar when it's against the law?"

"It's a licensed private club. The rum runners are more than willing to keep Louis's basement well stocked."

"So it's true about the rum runners docking in this bay." She picked up her drink and swallowed the last drop. "It does seem pretty silly that there are laws against drinking in America, the land of the free."

"It's more than silly," he said with a rush of anger. "I spent two years fighting the damn Krauts and I don't think any suffragette or Washington politician, including President Coolidge himself, has the right to tell me how to live my life. A life I might have lost while he and his cronies sat at home getting smashed on whiskey."

It disturbed her that he spoke of Germans as "Krauts," and she felt equally disturbed by him comparing women fighting for equal rights to unscrupulous Washington politicians, and she had been so enjoying his company up until now. He in turn stared out at the bay for so long that she started back to the bar.

"Don't go," he said, reaching for her arm. "I shouldn't have spoken to you like that. It's just hard to not feel anger and resentment after what happened. I lost a lot of friends in the war."

Her heart softened toward him. She too had lost friends. Her boyfriend was only twenty-two when he got killed and she still wore his St. Christopher. After he died, she had dedicated herself to making art and had done her best to avoid flirtatious, handsome men up until now.

"Please stay. There's a good chance we might see the green flash tonight. The conditions are just right." He drew her back to the railing and she didn't resist.

"My sister told me about that phenomena, but I've never been lucky enough to see one."

"Concentrate on the horizon as the flash only lasts a couple of seconds."

His body leaned into hers from behind and she held very still while they watched the upper half of the sun be swallowed by the vast Pacific until only a strip of bright gold remained.

He said softly, "'. . . it will be green, but a most wonderful green, a green which no artist could ever obtain on his palette, a green of which neither the varied tints of vegetation nor the shades of the most limpid sea could ever produce the like! If there be green in Paradise, it cannot but be of this shade, which most surely is the true green of Hope.'"

"That's so beautiful. Did you write that?"

He laughed. "I wish. It's a quote from my favorite novelist, Jules Verne."

She kept her hands on the railing and her eyes on the edge of the world until the last golden sliver turned the sky into a crimson flame that then went out leaving the sky without light until a half-moon appeared and the constellations relit the sky.

He gently turned her around and his sea-gray eyes gazed into hers. "I was really hoping you'd see your first green flash with me here."

"Me too," said Sarah, suddenly overcome by sadness. Her voice faltered. "My sister said she saw it for the first time in Carmel. Maybe she was standing right here."

He kissed the tear falling down her cheek.

"I see Robert found you," said Sirena, intruding out of nowhere.

Embarrassed, Sarah pulled away from him.

"I thought you'd gone home," he said harshly.

"I guess you were wrong," said Sirena, who was equally unpleasant.

Sarah wrapped her rose-embroidered shawl over her shoulders, and said to both of them, "It's rather chilly, isn't it?" And then to Sirena she smiled and said, "Why didn't you tell me Carmel had a speakeasy a few blocks from Ada's cottage?"

"I'm surprised she didn't tell you. She was a regular customer," said Sirena, still glaring at Robert.

"Sirena, be a sweetheart and ask the waiter to bring us two whiskey sours. Have one yourself at the bar and add it to my tab."

Sarah didn't like the way Robert spoke down to Sirena and took the girl's arm in a gesture of female support, "Why don't we all go inside and have that drink together?"

He followed them back inside where they joined Mac and his friends. Robert insisted Sarah sit on the barstool next to him. She found it impossible to say no.

He pulled out his wallet and paid the bartender for their next round of drinks from a thick wad of bills and included a generous tip. He saw the curious look on Sarah's face and said, "My wallet isn't always so padded. I just got paid by *Cosmopolitan* for a fashion layout."

She listened to Robert and Tony talk about a battleship docked at the wharf that they'd both admired. Robert seemed to know a lot about the ship's war history and Tony, who had been too young to go to war, listened attentively. Sarah felt Robert's arm press against hers. It sent a tingling sensation up her arm that she found way too pleasant.

This has got to stop, she said to herself, moving her arm away. She looked around for Sirena but she was gone, her drink left on the bar.

A few couples were on the dance floor, dancing cheek to cheek while the piano player sang Ma Rainey's "See See Rider." Sarah tapped her feet to the bluesy beat, trying to ignore the guilt she felt for enjoying the music Ada had loved and would never hear again.

"Would you like to dance?" asked Robert.

Moments later, he had her moving smoothly across the floor, guiding her with his hand pressed firmly on her back. Earlier she had noticed a slight limp when he walked, but it was unnoticeable on the dance floor.

He had a fabulous two-step and he twirled her around until she felt like a professional ballroom dancer. He even knew the Charleston. After "Lady Luck Blues," Sarah was laughing and fanning her flushed face with her hand.

"I think we could use some air," said Robert. He grabbed his jacket and her shawl from the bar and, taking her hand, led her back onto the terrace.

The half-moon's reflection was undulating on the rippling water. The brisk sea air made Sarah shiver. Robert draped his leather jacket over her shoulders. She felt cozy inside it, the fur collar warming her neck.

Her boyfriend, Joe, had returned to New York wearing a similar jacket when he was on furlough. The last time she saw him alive. "Is this a commissioned naval jacket?" she asked.

"Yeah. I was wearing it the night our ship was bombed and I caught a bullet in my right leg."

"I'm sorry you were wounded."

"Don't be. I was lucky. It got me sent home. Many of my shipmates didn't make it back."

A few hundred feet from shore a loud powerboat crossed in front of them in the moonlight.

"I'd like to give you a ride in one of those. It's wild fun. They go really fast."

Her fear was visible.

"Hold on," he said, squeezing her hand. "I wasn't suggesting we go out now. But what about in the daylight?"

"I don't think so," said Sarah. "I'd be too afraid."

"Why? You'd be safe with me and if you don't know how to swim there are life jackets."

"That's not the reason. I grew up swimming in Lake Michigan, but now the ocean frightens me because of what happened to my sister."

"Of course, how stupid of me not to realize," said Robert. "After my brother died, I didn't want to be anywhere near San Francisco."

Sarah turned to face him. "When was that?"

Robert spoke softly, avoiding her eyes. "Just last year. Jake had failed his classes at Berkeley and started drinking and running with a bad crowd. I tried to get him to stop and go back to school, but he wouldn't listen to me. He told me he didn't care what I thought and to leave him alone. The day before his birthday I called him up to say I was in San Francisco and I'd like to take him out for dinner. He sounded much better, said he'd stopped drinking and had registered for fall classes. The last thing I expected when I got there was to find him hanging from a rafter in his apartment."

Sarah gasped. "How awful for you to find him like that."

"The worst part of it is I can never shake the feeling that it was somehow my fault. I should've done more to keep him safe." He

turned to her. "I don't ever talk about it, but I thought you'd understand, because of what happened to your sister. Do you know why she
killed herself?"

"She didn't," said Sarah, pulling away from him.

"But I understood from the newspapers and from Sirena—"

"She's wrong! They're all very wrong!"

Just then Sirena stepped into their circle of moonlight on the terrace and hooked her arm in Sarah's. "It's getting late. We should be
getting back home."

Sarah handed Robert his jacket and said good night.

"I'm not giving up on that powerboat ride," he called out as the
two girls walked away.

Because there were no streetlights in Carmel they barely saw their
feet or each other's faces on their silent walk home.

"Why don't you like Robert?" asked Sarah when they reached the
Sketch Box gate.

"Who said I didn't like him?"

"You certainly don't act like it. You were arguing with him when
I came into the lounge and you kept throwing daggers at him all evening. He seems like such a nice guy. He's been through so much, what
with the war and his brother."

"Do you believe all that stuff?"

"What do you mean by that? Robert has no reason to lie to me.
Look, Sirena, if there is something going on between you two, please
tell me, and if it upsets you I won't see him again. I promise."

"He's not my boyfriend if that's what you're worried about. I'm
just his model. That's all."

"Then what were you arguing about?"

"Money. What else? He's loaded and he should pay me more for
my hours."

"But you told me he did pay you well."

"That's why we were arguing. He was backing off on his original offer."

"I'm sorry to hear that," said Sarah, lifting the gate latch. "He didn't seem tight with money."

Sirena stopped her from opening the gate. "Look, I'm sorry. I shouldn't take my anger with Robert out on you. Will you still come with me to the Jeffers' party tomorrow?"

"Why wouldn't I?"

"I don't know, I thought you wouldn't want to go with me now that you have Robert to take you around."

"Sirena, you can't be serious. I hardly know him."

"Just be careful. Annie meant it when she said he was a ladies' man."

Sirena took off across the road, her footsteps echoing in the night air.

# SUNDAY, JULY 27
## —14—

Sarah woke in a sunny, warm bed and breathed in the gentle breeze coming through the open bay window. Ada would've been more than pleased that Sarah had moved into the upstairs bedroom that had been designed especially for her. And if things were the way they should be, Ada would be in the kitchen making coffee, she thought sadly.

Her attention fell on the easel Ada had placed in front of the window knowing Sarah would want it there. The sudden impulse to paint made her sit up. She'd been in Carmel a whole week and, except for the two days in Champlin's class, she hadn't held a paintbrush.

But how could she paint knowing the portraits were still missing and she wasn't any closer to finding out who murdered Ada? She slapped her palms down on the quilt in frustration. Albert jumped up on the bed and rolled over, demanding his morning tummy rub. She obliged while her thoughts went once again to the missing portraits.

Eric Crocker would have received her telegram. He'd be furious. She had to tell him something. But what? The truth was unbearable. A lie was far worse.

She took a brisk walk with Albert and returned to the Sketch Box wondering what to do with herself until the Jeffers's garden party. There was a row of poetry books on Ada's living room bookshelf and she brought out Robinson Jeffers's *Tamar and Other Poems*. Inside the cover was an inscription: *Before there was any water there were tides of fire, both our tones flow from the older fountain. With admiration and affection, Robin.*

She brought the slim book, a pack of cigarettes, and a glass of lemonade onto the fenced-in back patio. Stretched out on a lounge chair, she read and slowly turned the pages, attracted and repulsed by the visceral scenes in *Tamar*, Jeffers's epic poem. That Jeffers had published it himself was understandable. It would have been difficult to find a publisher willing to publish a story based without censure on the incestuous love affair between a brother and sister living in a mountain village in Big Sur.

She must have fallen asleep because she was startled awake when Sirena called her name, her head popping over the backyard fence. "Wake up, Sarah. It's two o'clock. We're going to be late. You must hurry."

Slipping into her sundress in the upstairs bedroom, she realized she'd forgotten to purchase a wide-brimmed hat in Monterey to protect her eyes from the California sun's glare, plus it wasn't really acceptable to be hatless at a social event. She ran down to Ada's bedroom remembering there was a wide-brimmed teal-blue straw hat hanging on the closet door. The quill of a big and colorful eye-of-the-peacock feather was pinned to its band. The feather's oculus of bright and iridescent indigo, green and gold looked skyward.

The eye-of-the-peacock seemed to be daring her to wear it. *Oh why not?* she thought as she tamped it down on her obstinate hair that she didn't have time to press into submission.

When she came into the living room, Sirena gaped at her like she did when Sarah had worn Ada's bathrobe.

"Is something wrong?" asked Sarah.

"Sorry," said Sirena, quickly recovering. "You look so like Ada. She always caused a stir when she wore that sun hat."

Sarah took it off. "Maybe I shouldn't wear it. Mr. Jeffers might think I was being disrespectful to my sister's memory."

"Not at all. He'd say it looks swell on you." Sirena grinned and reached for it, "Or if you're too uncomfortable, I'll wear it."

Sarah laughed. "Oh no, you don't. You look very vivant already with your string of red beads and carmine red lips. I'll wear my sister's hat."

"C'mon, we're late," Sirena said, hurrying out the door.

As they walked down Camino Real, Sirena spoke of the famous writer, Mary Austin. Like Jack London, Austin was an original member of Carmel's artist colony. She now lived in Santa Fe, New Mexico, and was a guest at the Jeffers home.

"She was quite a firecracker in her day and I hear she still is," laughed Sirena.

Sarah asked if Mr. Champlin would be there.

"Probably not. He's not one to mingle with the locals. Friday was his last class and he'll be leaving soon to go back to New York."

"I wish I was leaving too," confided Sarah. "I'll have to cancel my exhibition if I don't get back soon."

"Oh no, Sarah, you shouldn't do that! After Ada's memorial, you should go. Rosie and I can take care of Albert and the cottage until you can come back and sort things out."

"Thanks, Sirena. But it's not just the cottage and Albert that are keeping me here."

They walked on in silence until they reached the Jeffers's stone cottage. TOR HOUSE was written on the gate.

On the beach with Rosie, Sarah hadn't had as clear a view. Now, from this angle, she immediately recognized the cottage perched on a wild, unprotected outcrop of boulders, its foundation a stronghold against the many squalls and blustery waves thrown up against it. The hues of yellows, oranges, whites, and blues against the gray granite walls of the cottage were as breathtaking as when Ada had painted it.

The guests were sitting on limestone benches on the stone patio or milling about in the garden of herbs and bushes, weeds and wild-flowers. Sirena urged her forward through the gate, but Sarah told her to go on ahead. She wanted to take a few moments to enjoy the beauty surrounding her. She was wondering where Ada's painting of Tor House might be, when pounding steps on the stone walkway approached her from behind.

"Where have you been, Miss Cunningham?" said Paul deVrais with a menacing voice. "My lawyer has been trying to reach you, but Ada's telephone is disconnected. As I told you, I'm very worried about Ada's paintings. And as you don't seem to realize their value, they must be removed from the cottage immediately and placed in my vault."

Sarah looked straight into his eyes. There was something less intimidating about a man who was her exact height. "I told you yesterday, Mr. deVrais, you no longer have any rights to Ada Davenport's artwork."

"You're not taking me seriously, Miss Cunningham. That's a mistake. Be forewarned. Ada's paintings are legally mine, including the portraits. My lawyer, Mr. L.G. Hubbard, will track you down and make that clear." He flung open the gate and stomped inside.

"He's two hoops and a holler," said Sirena, returning. "What was that all about?"

"He wants me to believe he has power over me, but he doesn't. I won't cower to his threats."

Sarah tilted Ada's wide-brimmed hat down to shade her eyes. The ever-watchful eye-of-the-peacock looked straight ahead. "Do I look all right?"

"Sensational," Sirena said, hooking her arm through Sarah's. "Shall we make our grand entrance?"

Sarah heard a few murmurs as she approached the guests and then a buzzing of whispers like hummingbird wings, making her wish she'd left Ada's hat at home. Nothing to be done about it now.

She tossed her shawl over one shoulder, raised her chin and stepped onto the flagstone patio.

An attractive woman with lustrous auburn hair loosely pinned back off a robust Irish face, with round cheeks and wide, intelligent eyes, came over and gave her a hearty handshake. "Hello. I'm Una Jeffers. We were hoping you would come." Before Sarah could respond, "You needn't introduce yourself. I know Ada's hat. It becomes you."

"It's a pleasure to meet a good friend of my sister's," said Sarah, taking an immediate liking to her lovely hostess.

Una turned to Sirena, "Thank you for bringing her. If you'll excuse us, I'd like to have her to myself for a few minutes." Sirena shrugged and joined the other guests.

Una picked up a drink from a dozen of the same on a side table and handed it to Sarah. "Please have a glass of my homemade Coine-Eairngorm wine. A recipe from the Scottish Highlands. It's made from oranges, raisins, and rice and promises to put you at ease. I know this might be a rather awkward situation for you."

"If I had known the attention I'd get . . ." She reached up to take off Ada's plumed hat.

"No. Wear it. Proudly."

Though of small stature, Una had the poise of a very confident woman who was accustomed to people doing as she bid. Sarah took a sip of the wine and told Una it was delicious, which it was. Just the right amount of fruits and spices and wine.

Her hostess led her to a corner of the garden, presumably to show off her yellow rose geraniums and purple lavender but when they were alone she dropped her voice.

"The circumstances surrounding Ada's suicide were very strange and frankly beyond belief. We knew Ada very well and Robin and I both want you to know that we do not believe your sister killed herself. Marshal Judd was not at all thorough and we think the insurance company pressed him for a quick verdict in their favor."

Sarah inhaled quickly and breathed out. "Thank you for telling me that. It's encouraging to know that at least a few people in Carmel feel the same as I do."

"We'll help you anyway we can in your search for the truth."

"When did you last see Ada?"

"The day before the fireworks. She stopped by here with Albert. She was very excited about something, but when I asked her what it was, she said she wanted you to be the first to know and was sending you a letter. Did she?"

"No. But I think I know what it was." Sarah was about to tell Una about Ada's pregnancy, hoping she might know the father, but before she could confide in her, they were interrupted by two boisterous women joining them.

The conversation immediately turned to the upcoming local play. "It's unfortunate," said Una, "that *Pirates of Penzance* was scheduled to be the last play in the outdoor theater this summer. Even now it can be chilly in the evenings, but we'll have a few bonfires to keep everyone warm and Alain Delacroix, who's playing the role of Frederic the Pirate, is known to light a few fires himself." At this she gave a little shoulder shimmy. The two women smiled in agreement and nodded their heads. Una turned to Sarah, "Have you seen Alain perform on Broadway? He's simply marvelous."

"No, I haven't," said Sarah, slightly irritated. She could care less about this actor and wanted to resume their private conversation.

"Then come meet him and my husband," said Una. She took Sarah's hand and drew her away from the other guests over to a low ornate metal gate on the other side of the garden that fronted the Pacific. Two men were slowly climbing up a steep wooden staircase from the rocky coast below.

"There they are." The gaunt man leading the way up heard Una call out "Robin" and he raised his long arm and waved. His prominent nose, arched cheeks, and square chin appeared to be sculpted from the granite boulders below.

A savage pirate followed behind him, or so it seemed from Sarah's first impression. Thick black hair fell down to his shoulders and a bushy beard and thick brows covered most of his face. He was a well-built, muscular man like Robin, but smaller in stature. He looked up at the two women and tripped on a step. Robin quickly gripped his arm to keep him from falling off the steep ledge.

"Alain!" said Una, when they reached the top step. "Have you been dipping into my Irish whiskey again?" The pirate turned and squinted at the horizon. He seemed to be looking for a boat to rescue him.

Robin Jeffers, the poet of *Tamar,* was just as Sarah had imagined him: a commanding figure, who was now holding her hand in an iron grip, his alert eyes probing hers.

"Miss Cunningham. What a pleasure to finally meet you, though I wish it were under better circumstances. I was deeply fond of Ada. Her death was a terrible shock. I can't even begin to imagine how difficult it must be for you, her sister."

Alain Delacroix showed no interest in their talk of Ada. When he finally did turn to face Sarah, his swarthy complexion was barely visible. A pointed moustache curled on its ends as if in cheerful rebellion against the brooding face it was attached to.

"Alain is our pirate-in-residence," said Robin, smiling down at his companion on the step below.

"That's why we forgive him the hirsute mask," added Una. "It's impossible to see right now, but there is a gentle poetic soul lurking underneath this pirate of Penzance. Lucky for us, when the other Frederic got sick, we were able to convince him to take a break from shooting a film in Hollywood to take over the role."

Delacroix, clearly uncomfortable with the attention, looked at the eye-of-the-peacock waving in the breeze and turned away.

"Alain, don't shirk!" said Una. "It's not like Sarah wants your autograph. A pleasant hello will do."

He did as he was asked and turned away again.

"Excuse us, Sarah," said Una, "but our guests are anxious to meet Alain—though I can see he'd rather be somewhere else. He seems to have forgotten that he was the one who volunteered to play Frederic."

Robin and Sarah watched Alain and Una join the guests on the patio. Robin stayed behind long enough to say, "I'd like to talk to you privately, Miss Cunningham. Can you meet me at the tower in thirty minutes?"

Sarah looked over at the unfinished pile of stones. "Don't worry," he said. "It's safe. I built it with my own hands and I can assure you it's a solid structure." He looked amused. "And you don't have to scale it. There's an interior staircase that will take you to the top." Una called for him, and he left Sarah on her own.

She heard a voice behind her—"Sarah!"—and spun around to see a stocky, elderly woman in baggy trousers and a long cape. Her face was shaded under a wide-brimmed bolero hat and a snow-white braided pigtail fell down over her right shoulder.

She came up to Sarah, stuck out her hand and brusquely said, "I'm Mary Austin. I was a good friend of your sister's. So glad to finally meet you. Will you join me over here on this bench?"

This was the author that Sirena had mentioned, a bohemian member of Carmel's artist colony before the war. The bench she suggested was on a ledge hanging over the turbulent waves. The strong current gushed through a forest of ochre sea kelp rooted to the seafloor.

After they sat down, Miss Austin struck a match and cupped her hand to protect the flame. She sucked on a corncob pipe until she got it lit. "Ada told me you've been studying art in Paris for the past three years," she said, puffing out a cloud of smoke. "Was it worth it?"

Sarah paused. She hadn't expected such a candid question. "Yes, I think so. I'm going to have a one-woman show there at Nouy Gallery. That is, if I can get home soon enough to finish preparing for it."

"I've heard of that gallery. It would be a feather in your cap. What's keeping you here?"

Sirena could have taken lessons from Mary in asking abrupt personal questions.

"My sister's death. She's been falsely accused of suicide and to clear her name I have to find out what really happened to her."

"Good. I was hoping that was what you would say."

They watched as a fisherman in a boat anchored close to the shore suddenly yanked on a bent, wobbling fishing rod. A salmon struggled against the hook in his mouth as he was dragged across the water's surface. The fisherman grabbed the fish by its tail and whacked it hard against the side of the boat until it was dead.

"A damn shame what happened. Ada was an extraordinary individual and a brilliant painter until a monster came up from the sea and stole her from us. A damn tragedy."

"So you too think she was murdered?"

"Well, she certainly didn't kill herself, did she? That woman was exploding with plans for her future. Death was not on her list."

"Do you know who that *monster* is?"

Mary puffed on her pipe for what seemed like forever before answering.

"No. But I received a letter from Ada at my home in New Mexico postmarked several days before her death. She told me about her upcoming exhibit and how anxious she was about Paul deVrais's recent behavior. He had been in a rage ever since she ended their contract and was threatening to take her to court. She knew what I had gone though as a female artist in this cutthroat man's world and she wanted my advice."

She clamped down on the pipe in the side of her mouth. "Art dealers are greedy and unscrupulous. Book publishers, too. Middle-men who can't make art but think they deserve to control, even own what isn't really theirs, particularly when it involves women artists who have no recourse." She took a few puffs and added, "But I have to say, though deVrais is certainly a bully, I doubt he would have the courage to actually kill someone, even if the reward was a very valuable art collection. Down deep he's a bit of a wimp, don't you think? Most bullies are."

Sarah asked Mary to please send her the letter. She might need it as evidence.

"Before you go off accusing deVrais, you should know he wasn't the only man mentioned in her letter."

"What?"

"Last summer, when Ada and I were sitting out here on this very bench, she told me she'd fallen in love with a dashing adventurer who would take her to his hideaway and make love to her. I'm sure you know how your sister loved romantic interludes. She knew he was trouble. I think it was the sex she didn't want to give up."

Sarah was too curious to be offended by Mary's insinuation that her sister was promiscuous. Nor could she argue. Ada often had affairs with the wrong kind of men. Sarah had often bailed her out of sticky situations. So had she misread Ada's telegram? Was this the "mess" Ada had gotten herself into, which had nothing to do with deVrais or the portraits?

"Apparently he traveled a lot so they only met on the spur of the moment," added Mary. "In her letter, she told me she had finally met someone who even you would approve of and she wanted to end the sordid affair."

A sudden squall brought Mary to her feet. She wrapped her cape tightly around her shoulders. "I'm going to catch a chill if I don't go inside."

Sarah jumped up. "Wait. Don't leave me without telling me their names."

"Sorry, but Ada never told me their names." She hugged Sarah. "I'm so glad we had a chance to talk before I go back to Santa Fe." She handed Sarah her calling card. "I'll send you that letter as soon as I get home, and you let me know when you find out who killed Ada."

Sarah was too agitated to stay still. She paced the rocky ledge in front of the bench, turning this unexpected information over in her head until she saw Robinson Jeffers at the entrance to the tower, motioning her to join him.

He bent his head under an arch and entered without a word. The stairway was very narrow, almost claustrophobic, and the limestone stairs were slippery and difficult to climb. When she finally reached the rooftop, a gust of wind would have knocked off her hat if she hadn't quickly grabbed the eye-of-the-peacock.

She sat down next to Jeffers sitting on a stone bench carved into the citadel, and unable to keep her hat on, let the wind snap at her hair. The poet stared off in the distance as if she wasn't there. His unlit clay pipe cupped in his hand. His jaw clenched.

"Mr. Jeffers," said Sarah finally losing patience, "what was it you wanted to tell me?"

When he turned his eyes on her, the wind seemed to hold its breath waiting for him to speak. "On the Fourth of July, Ada was not painting on River Beach. I would have seen her on my twilight walk or she would've stopped by to see me, as was her habit."

"But Marshal Judd claims that's where she drowned."

"Marshal Judd is an ass," he said harshly. "He has no understanding of the sea's temperament or of Ada's."

Sarah leaned toward the poet to hear him better over the wind. "Around midnight, after the fireworks were long over, I came up here for a smoke. It was a clear night and the full moon illuminated the wide stretch of white sand until I was almost fooled into believing it was daylight."

He handed her the binoculars that had been hanging around his neck. "Here, see for yourself. Look southward toward the Carmel River outlet." She'd never looked through binoculars before and was startled to see how close the beach appeared through the magnified lenses.

"I heard a fisherman motoring to shore the night of the fourth. With my binoculars I could see his boat was weighed down and he was having trouble bringing it in. When he finally got it beached, he pulled out a bulky sack that looked like it might be full of rockfish, or maybe salmon. It was only later, after I heard about Ada being found near the river stream, that I wondered if he was the one who brought her to shore."

In a mix of excitement and horror, Sarah almost dropped the binoculars over the edge of the tower. "But none of this is in Marshal Judd's report. Why didn't you come forward as a witness at the inquest?"

"I would have, but Judd thought I was too far away to see anything. It's not the first time he didn't believe me. Ask Mary Austin. She was living here when Helena Wood Smith was murdered ten years ago. Judd didn't listen to me then and he almost let that killer get away, too."

Rosie had told her a similar story, but Jeffers didn't mention Smith's Japanese killer was almost lynched. She didn't imagine the poet would have joined that racialist mob. His darker emotions burned from within and were channeled through his provocative poetry. He kneaded his callused hands, hands strong enough to build a tower out of boulders and sensitive enough to hold a pencil and write poems about illicit yearning and desire.

"Judd didn't want to waste his time searching for an unknown fisherman when he was certain it was a suicide. I thought you might be more interested in what I saw."

"Thank you," said Sarah with gratitude. "Thank you very much." But she wished he'd been more insistent with the marshal or gone to the District Attorney. "Would you testify to what you witnessed if the inquest is reopened?"

"Yes." He stood up at the portal arch, ready to go down the stairs, indicating that their conversation was over.

Sarah also stood. "Is there anything else you can think of that might help me find the fisherman you saw that night?"

He looked down the coast and then back to Sarah, his brows coming together like a hawk. "Sometimes I would see Ada at twilight riding her bicycle toward Point Lobos when I was carrying stones up to here. Sometimes I would see her pedaling back at dawn the next morning.

"Ada's temper flared when Una asked her where she went in Point Lobos and why she stayed late into the night. Told Una it was none of her business. Una never asked again."

He got up and looked down over the granite balustrade. "I have to go down. Una will be cross if I don't rescue her from our guests soon. See, there she is now waving up at us."

It was a mistake for Sarah to look down. She hadn't realized how high up they were. Swaths of color encircled the shingled roof of the Tor House, which was now the size of a dollhouse. Dizzy, she sat back down on the bench. "I'll stay here for a minute," she said. "You go ahead."

"Watch out," said Jeffers as he looked up from the stairwell's black shadows. "These stairs are slippery."

She was in awe of this reclusive poet who had built this indestructible stone edifice with his own hands. He'd found a way to immortalize his life. Hawk Tower and Tor House would still be standing long after he was gone, even if his poetry was forgotten, though she doubted it would be.

The dark shaft felt even narrower going down than coming up and Sarah had to squeeze her arms to pass through it. She envied the agile man who had descended so quickly. She took timid steps like a blind person and used her hands to feel her way. She was very grateful when she got to the bottom and felt the ground beneath her feet.

As she walked into the courtyard looking around for Sirena, several of the guests crowded around her and introduced themselves. She'd come to be known as the sister in the peacocked hat and everyone wanted to meet her and talk about Ada.

"She was a great artist."

"A terrible loss to our artist colony."

"Helped many young painters. Encouraged them in their work."

"Donated paintings to support local art clubs."

"Volunteered to build sets for the theater productions."

No . . . No one had seen her on the fourth, but that was to be expected. It was generally known from previous summers that the fireworks frightened Ada and she never came to the beach to watch.

The sun had slipped behind the horizon and turned the sky a deep orange, deeper than the blooming geraniums in the Tor House garden. She looked around for Sirena, but she must've gone home. When Sarah went to say goodbye to her hosts, Una gave her a bottle of Coine-Eairngorm wine to take with her and told her to come back soon.

She walked quickly under a row of young cypress and eucalyptus trees that would in time grow higher than Hawk Tower, but she hardly noticed them. After what the Jeffers and Mary had told her, she was blind to anything but her own scary thoughts.

When she reached the cottage gate and looked through the dark windows into the bleak empty rooms within, she hesitated going inside. Over at Rosie's Lodge, lights were on in the parlor and she heard faint notes coming from the spinet piano. She considered joining them, but then she heard Albert's frantic bark behind the front door. She walked up the steps and opened the door to a welcoming yelp as he jumped into her open arms.

She carried him into the kitchen and gave him a well-deserved treat. While he gnawed on a beef shank, she drank a glass of Una's ambrosial wine between bites of bread and cheese. She had no appetite for anything else.

An hour later, after writing down what the Jeffers and Mary Austin had told her, she put away her drawing pad and gathered up the inquest paperwork that was spread out on the table into a neat pile. Then she picked up Albert and went upstairs to bed, exhausted.

# MONDAY, JULY 28
## —15—

Sarah and Rosie stood in front of a white two-story adobe building at the corner of Alvarado and Franklin Streets. An engraved brass plaque on the front door read: ELMER PEABODY, ESQ., ATTORNEY AT LAW. BY APPOINTMENT ONLY.

The only other law office Sarah had ever visited was the elegant, art deco office of Mr. Foster M. Giles in New York. She met with him before she boarded the train to San Francisco. He'd given her a quick course in estate law and spoken crossly about Ada choosing to write her own will. If he had written it, he'd have given Sarah, the executor of Ada's estate, a copy.

The two women mounted the stairs to Mr. Peabody's office and opened the glass-paneled door. There was no secretary in the outer office to greet them but the desk was neat and orderly.

Rosie knocked on the inner office door.

A very skinny sixtyish human scarecrow opened the door. He was dressed as a Victorian gentleman in a three-piece suit with a gold pince-nez perched on the bridge of a prominent nose. He stretched his long, thin neck outward and looked down at Rosie. "Miss McCann, you're five minutes late."

Rosie apologized and quickly introduced Sarah. The ladies were then ushered over to two Queen Anne chairs. Mr. Peabody, surprisingly quick for a man of his age and height, sat down in a massive black leather chair behind his desk. He scrunched his hooked nose and the pince-nez fell down and swung from a gold chain attached to a button hole in his lapel, ready when needed.

"Tell me now, Miss McCann, what is so important that you insisted on an appointment during my lunch hour?"

Sarah hadn't expected him to be so severe, but she sat up straight, met his eyes, and spoke before Rosie could: "I need representation in the settlement of an estate for which I am the executor and the sole beneficiary."

"I see," he said, retrieving his pince-nez and perching it back on his nose. "May I see the decedent's will?"

Sarah explained that she didn't have the will in her possession, but expected to have it soon. She hurried on before he could object. "How long does it normally take to settle an estate?"

"It's difficult to say without reading the will, but if it clearly states you are the only beneficiary then it will be fairly simple." He raised a long forefinger. "However, if another party contests your authority then it would have to be settled in probate court. That is a much more arduous and expensive process."

He sensed Sarah's anxiousness and added, "Is there someone who will contest the will, Miss Cunningham?"

"Not that I know of," she lied.

"Well then . . ." he tapped the same finger on the plunger of a shiny black metal timer clock sitting on the side of his desk. The shrill bell made the ladies jump. "Then by all means, let's proceed." He dipped a black Sheaffer fountain pen into the inkwell and the slurping sound of the thirsty pen held everyone's attention.

Once filled, he held the pen's gold nib over a yellow legal pad similar to the one Mr. Giles had used. "May I have the name of the deceased?"

"Ada Belle Davenport."

He cleared his throat and squinted at her over his pince-nez. "The famous artist who drowned recently on our shores?"

"Yes. Did you know her?"

"And your relationship?" he asked, ignoring her question.

"She was my sister," Sarah said and asked again insistently, "Did you know her?"

The scarecrow lawyer screwed the top onto his pen and studied her for a long moment, long enough to make her shift in her chair and re-cross her legs.

"Considering Miss Davenport is deceased and you, her sister, are the one asking, I can legally tell you that Miss Davenport *was* briefly my client. I had one meeting with them, that was all."

"She was with someone?" asked Rosie.

"Yes. These matters always involve two people."

"And can you tell me who she was with?" Sarah asked when she found her voice.

He frowned and with one finger on his temple, he rolled his eyes upward as if the answer was on the ceiling. "Right now his name escapes me. I have many clients that I only meet once. I can hardly be expected to remember all their names. I rely on my secretary to keep accurate notes of my meetings. If Miss Honeysuckle were here she could tell you, but she's on holiday right now."

"Could you tell us what the document contained?" asked Rosie, as stunned as Sarah.

"It was a nuptial agreement."

"Nuptial agreement?" said Sarah and Rosie in unison.

"Yes. I too was taken aback. It's a highly unusual request here on the Monterey Peninsula. But after Miss Davenport explained her situation and her fiancé had no objection—"

"Fiancé?" said Sarah, looking down at the gold band that she was wearing on her right finger for safe-keeping.

"Miss Cunningham, how could you not know of your sister's impending marriage?"

"I live in France, Mr. Peabody," she said, defensively. "I haven't seen my sister since January. She never mentioned a fiancé in her letters. I guess she was planning to surprise me. She's like that."

"She didn't tell me either," added Rosie, "and we were very good friends. Had they been engaged very long?"

He threw up his hands. "Ladies, I have no idea about such matters. All they said was that they were getting married and wanted a nuptial agreement drawn up immediately. I said it would be an imposition because of the upcoming Fourth of July holiday."

"When was that meeting?" asked Sarah, trying to take in the full implications of what he was telling her without appearing even more dumbfounded.

Mr. Peabody opened his appointment book and flipped back several pages. "Ah! Here it is. July second at four o'clock, near closing hours. Your sister had expected me to write the document while they waited. Obviously she was unaware of what she was asking. I suggested we meet again the following week to sign the agreement, but her fiancé said they would be away and would schedule another meeting when they returned."

"May we see a copy?" asked Rosie.

"No."

"No?" exclaimed Sarah. "Why not? You said you were free to discuss—"

"There isn't one. I never drafted it. When I returned to my office after the holidays prepared to draw up the papers, Miss Honeysuckle informed me that Miss Davenport was deceased."

"Are you certain you don't remember his name? Or at least what he looked like?" asked Rosie, seemingly concerned over Mr. Peabody's mental capacity if he met the fiancé less than a month ago.

"As I said, Miss Honeysuckle is the one to ask. I do remember she was quite taken by the fellow."

"When will she be back?" asked Sarah.

"Wednesday." He folded his hands and looked at Sarah suspiciously.

"I must say, Miss Cunningham, I am curious to know why you didn't know about the nuptial agreement when you were the reason for it."

"I was?"

"She was?"

Sarah and Rosie said in unison.

"Yes. Her fiancé was to inherit nothing from your sister if she was to die before him. Her estate was to go to you. Most of my male clients are very interested in their wives' assets, especially one of such proportion as your sister's, but he didn't seem to care.

"And Miss Davenport did appear to have her senses about her. She was a bit overeager about her betrothal, but women are like that. That's why her suicide was—"

"My sister did not kill herself, Mr. Peabody," interrupted Sarah.

"What?" he said, his pince-nez falling off his nose. "Then pray tell, what did happen to her?"

"My sister was murdered. And, if you agree to represent me, I will ask you to petition the District Attorney's office to reopen the inquest based on new evidence."

"Oh. I see." Mr. Peabody said without offering an argument. He looked over at the ticking timer. Rosie reached out for Sarah's hand and gave it a reassuring squeeze.

The lawyer stiffly leaned forward from his swivel chair. "If you're asking me to represent you in a legal case of this magnitude, Miss Cunningham, I must advise you that the District Attorney would only consider reopening an inquest if there were substantially new, reliable evidence and, most important," he raised his forefinger, "if there was a suspect or suspects who had a serious motive and no verifiable alibi. Otherwise, you're wasting your money and my time. Do you have any suspects?"

"Yes, I do," said Sarah, with much more confidence than she felt. Rosie squinted at Sarah but said nothing.

"And who might that be?" he said, unscrewing the top of his pen.

"I can't say. I need more time to prove my theory before I accuse anyone."

"Theories do not hold up in court, Miss Cunningham." He screwed the top back on and put it down. "May I suggest you use your time more wisely by first searching for the will rather than investigating your murder theories." He reached down and brought up a straw basket. "Now, ladies, it's time for my lunch." He reached his hand toward the clock.

"I haven't finished," said Sarah.

He sighed and reclined back in his chair. "Miss Cunningham, I am not a philanthropist. Time is money."

"You needn't worry about that, Mr. Peabody. I will pay you for your valuable time and I see that you are already counting the minutes with your timer."

He shifted his eyes over to Rosie who gave him an encouraging smile.

"Go on then, I'm listening."

"My sister's artwork was represented by Mr. Paul deVrais, an art dealer in Carmel," said Sarah.

"I'm very aware of Mr. deVrais and his standing in our community."

"Mr. deVrais told me his lawyer, Mr. L.G. Hubbard, will be contacting me about taking possession of my sister's artwork stored at her cottage."

"Didn't you just tell me that no one would contest the will?"

"I did. And I assure you he has no legitimate right to my sister's artwork." Sarah reached into her satchel, took out the termination letter and Ada's contract with deVrais and handed the documents over to him.

The clock ticked as Mr. Peabody put back on his pince-nez, read, scribbled on his legal pad, and read again.

Minutes later he looked up and said, "Did Mr. deVrais receive this letter?"

"He claims he didn't, but my sister's lawyer did send it to him and we have a certification from the post office that deVrais signed. I also have a witness who received a letter from Ada stating that Mr.

deVrais was threatening to take her to court after she terminated their contract."

Peabody put down his pen. "All very interesting, Miss Cunningham, but if there is no will, the estate must be settled in the probate court. And Mr. deVrais is not one to give up easily. If this goes to probate, he'll fight you all the way."

She thought of the long days and probably weeks in court and the cancelling of her exhibition in five weeks if she didn't get back in time. "I will bring you the will," she said firmly.

"Excellent. The wisest course of action. And until then I'll make sure L.G. holds off serving you with any papers. We're playing golf tomorrow at the Del Monte Club." He hovered his finger over the timer. "Now, ladies, I would very much like to have my lunch."

"There is one more thing," said Sarah. "Mr. Pritchard at Wells Bank asked that I have my lawyer contact him. He said there was some confusion over my sister's depository account. Can you look into that, also? That is, of course, if you are going to represent me."

He scribbled a few more notes and screwed the top back on his pen. He crossed his hands and said, "I must admit your case does intrigue me, Miss Cunningham. You ladies should get on your way, so I can get to work on it."

"You mean you'll take me on?"

"Didn't I just say that? I'll have Miss Honeysuckle draw up a client agreement and if you call her in the next few days she'll schedule our next appointment. I'll expect a retainer from you at our next meeting."

He hit the bell, the ticker stopped, and he turned his attention to the lunch basket.


When they walked out into the open air, they both sighed in relief, and after basking a bit in their successful meeting, Sarah said she needed to renew Ada's telephone service. Rosie pointed out the Pacific Telephone building down the street. They made plans to meet in front of the Customs House overlooking the wharf.

Pacific Telephone was housed in an imposing brick building. All customer business was transacted in a spacious room on the first floor. The executive offices were upstairs. There was a poster on the wall advertising employment opportunities for "Happy Girl" telephone exchange operators.

A perky young receptionist greeted Sarah at the front desk. She listened to Sarah's request, asked her to sit down, and said a clerk would be with her right away.

Several other young female employees were seated at a row of typewriters in the middle of the room.

Sarah had a friend in New York who was employed as a Happy Girl. She would meet Sarah for cocktails after work still wearing her uniform, but Sarah found it a bit off-putting to be in a roomful of Happy Girls. They were all neatly dressed in white button-down silk shirts tucked into tight mid-calf skirts and they wore stockings and hi-heeled shoes. The only spark of individuality in their uniforms were the multi-colored cravats tied around their bare necks that might lead one to think that they were actually having fun.

The long telephone exchange was attached to the wall on one side of the room. The Happy Girl phone operators wore the same attire, but they also wore headphones and spoke into black conche-like shells strapped around their necks. Their polite voices chirped "What number please?" as they skillfully plugged in and pulled out the jumble of cords in front of them.

Sarah wondered how they could possibly keep from crossing the wires and connecting their customers to the wrong person. A male supervisor paced up and down the aisle watching over the girls to make sure those mistakes didn't happen.

"Miss Cunningham?" said a Happy Girl adjusting her cravat. Sarah nodded. "Please come with me."

When they sat down opposite each other at her desk the Happy Girl smiled at Sarah and asked, "And who was the previous subscriber?"

Sarah adjusted her legs under the cold metal chair. "Miss Ada Belle Davenport. I am her sister."

The girl began to say something else, but the supervisor was watching her. She went through a metal box of labeled subscription cards, pulled out one, and studied it. "The last time I saw Miss Davenport she couldn't have been more pleasant," she said softly. "Such a cheerful disposition. And then just days later . . . I guess you never know, do you, what these famous people are really thinking?"

"No, you don't," Sarah said, duplicating the girl's grin.

The girl looked down at the card again. "Miss Davenport was thrilled to be going on holiday. She said she'd be back in August and would reconnect her phone then."

Sarah's heart quickened. This was the kind of real evidence she needed to build her case for the D.A. If Ada was about to kill herself why would she plan a holiday?

The girl handed her a subscription form to fill out and was then called away by her supervisor. While Sarah filled out the form, she slipped Ada's subscription card into her satchel.

When the supervisor came over, Sarah was afraid she'd seen her take the card, but she only asked if Sarah would be home tomorrow afternoon for the service man to come and reconnect the line.

"Yes. I can be there," Sarah said, smiling. "Thank you. You've all been most helpful."

Mr. Kassajara was sitting beside Rosie on a bench outside the Custom House. He stood up and bowed. "I'm very happy to see you again, Miss Cunningham. When we first met, I didn't get a chance to tell you how sorry I was about Miss Ada's unexpected death. I will always remember her kindness toward me."

She thanked him and asked him how he knew her sister.

"She sometimes painted on the wharf and we would talk. Always very respectful toward me and the other abalone divers."

He looked at his pocket watch, let out a deep sigh, and turned to Rosie. "It's time to go to that meeting I told you about." He bowed to the two women and hurried off before Sarah could ask him if he knew where she could find diving weights similar to the ones found in Ada's pockets.

"He seems to be carrying a heavy burden," said Sarah. "Is he worried about his granddaughter?"

"He often is, but today it's for another reason. He has a meeting with Monterey's town council. They want to put a quota on how many abalone and salmon the Japanese can catch in the bay."

"Can they do that?"

"They'll do anything to stop the Japanese from competing against them with their own fisheries. You'd think there would be enough fish in Monterey Bay for everyone but the council doesn't feel that way. They think the Japanese are poaching their fish supply and the foreigners should be sent back to Japan. Our government has agreed to write new laws that will take away the legal rights of all Asian immigrants who have found a home on our shores.

# TUESDAY, JULY 29
## —16—

Seated on his haunches, Albert studied Sarah with his attentive black-button eyes. When he didn't get her attention, he jumped up on her lap and nuzzled his cold nose under her hand but she continued reading.

Albert rolled over and finally Sarah stopped rereading Judd's investigation file long enough to scratch his belly. "Okay, my friend, I get the hint. Let's go for a walk and then I'll treat you to a gourmet breakfast."

Sarah's mind meandered as she strolled along Camino Real. Albert's mind meandered too, sniffing every paw track and tree root as if he were Sherlock Holmes. That's what I should be doing, she thought, "Leaving no stone unturned." But she wasn't a detective. She was a painter who made pictures. How could she solve her sister's death with a paintbrush?

As they circled back to the Sketch Box, Albert barked at the delivery boy standing on the porch. A parcel wrapped in brown paper was leaning against the wall. One peak under the wrapping and she knew it was *A Bleak Morning*.

She hadn't really expected deVrais to deliver it. Was it a bribe? Was he still hoping they could work out an "arrangement," thinking if he showed good faith, she would let him represent Ada's legacy after all? If so, he was going to be sorely disappointed.

The art dealer had just given her the leverage she needed to disarm him. He wouldn't contest her legitimacy to Ada's estate if she could prove he was a forger and destroy his reputation as a reputable art dealer. As soon as the telephone was connected, she'd call an authenticator in San Francisco and have *A Bleak Morning* examined.

After filling Albert's doggie bowl with leftover beef from last night's stew, she took a mug of coffee into Ada's studio. Since she wasn't getting anywhere using logic, why not do what Sherlock Holmes did when he couldn't solve a mystery and activate the creative side of her brain to help her find Ada's will and portraits?

With that thought, she propped a blank canvas on the easel, and then arranged a vase of violet-blue lupines and yellow wildflowers she'd picked on her walk with Albert. She started to paint using the complementary pigments in the wildflowers to create an abstract painting. She was layering the brilliant oils when the front door cowbell clanged. Albert started barking and the Paris green on her brush splattered across the canvas.

"Damn!"

It was the service man from the telephone company. The line connection didn't take long and she'd just gotten back to the canvas, excited to be working and liking the accidental spray of Paris green, when Sirena burst through the alley door. She was reminded of how irritated Ada would get when she would burst into her studio unannounced. "I'm not disturbing you, am I?" Sirena didn't wait for an answer and walked over to the easel. She looked at Sarah's palette board on the table next to it.

Oblivious to Sarah's frown, she then studied the brushwork on the canvas. "Love that green, but isn't that the one that's toxic to work with?"

Sarah was losing patience. "Sirena, is there a reason for your visit? If not, I'd like to get back to work."

"I have a message from Rosie. She'd like you to come over at four o'clock for tea. She says there's someone she wants you to meet."

Sarah sighed at the thought of yet another interruption. But maybe by four o'clock she'd have something to show for her first day back at work.

Sirena was walking around aimlessly.

"Is there something else?" Sarah asked.

The girl shrugged. "No, just looking around."

"Then if you don't mind I'd like to get back to work."

"I thought you might look at some samples of my artwork this afternoon. Remember, you promised."

Sirena's plea reminded her of herself when she'd try to get Ada to pay attention to her work and said, "Sure. Give me a couple of hours to finish some ideas I want to get down on the canvas and then I'd love to take a look."

Sirena's half-moon brows lifted. "Really?" she said, scrunching her small nose up like a kitten.

"Yes, really."

Two hours later Sirena returned carrying a portfolio case under her arm. Sarah asked her to spread out her samples on the worktable.

When Sarah saw the sophisticated technique used in the brush-strokes, the precise black calligraphy lines and the application of such well-conceived colors right down to the simple green blades of grass, she was speechless. How could this precise, disciplined work come from the hand of this impulsive, misbehaved girl-child?

She finally said, "Sirena, these are beautiful. Van Gogh used a similar technique after studying the work of Japanese artists and it's caught on in Paris though he died over thirty years ago. Where did you learn to do this?"

"Oh," said Sirena, with a shrug, "I just copy things."

She looked through Sirena's work again and said, "I think you have an excellent chance of getting accepted into the Académie Julian. May I take a few samples back to Paris?"

"You would do that for me?" said Sirena, raising her bushy brows in disbelief.

"Of course I would."

"Swell," said Sirena.

The sunlight streaming down from the skylight shone on her violet eyes, which were the same pigments as the lupine wildflowers but iridescent. Sarah had just been trying to capture that color on her canvas. Impulsively, Sarah asked Sirena if she would model for her.

"Okay," said Sirena. "And I won't even charge you my usual fee."

Sarah wanted to ask if she was still working for Robert, but didn't want to spoil this new camaraderie between them. Maybe they could be friends.

Sirena put her samples back into her portfolio and left through the alley door.

Sarah was working on magnified impressions of the wildflowers when she noticed the time. She washed up quickly and a few minutes after four o'clock she was seated in Rosie's parlor when Rosie came in from the kitchen.

"I'm sorry I'm such a mess. I was painting."

Rosie was pleased. "That's good to hear. I can see that by the color in your cheeks."

"Sirena said you wanted me to meet someone," said Sarah, rubbing off some of the blue and red pigments that had stained her hands violet.

Rosie removed her spectacles and rubbed her nose. "Abigail Cutcliffe is coming for tea. The Cutcliffes are my dear neighbors. They don't enjoy our summer fog like I do and their dog Buster is frightened by the annual fireworks, so every year, like clockwork, on the Fourth of July before the fireworks start they go to their cabin in the Sierras. They just got back yesterday."

"And . . ." said Sarah.

"Patience, my dear," said Rosie. "The Cutcliffes have been isolated in their cabin and they only just heard the terrible news about Ada from me. Can you imagine wanting to live that remotely?"

Before Sarah could ask what any of this had to with her, there was a tap at the front door and Albert went to see who it was. The guest paused briefly in the entryway to say hello to Albert who instead of barking led the guest into the parlor.

Miss Cutcliffe was an elderly, athletic woman with a boyish haircut and a tan, weathered face. She was dressed in overalls and a red flannel lumberjack shirt as if she had just come in from cutting wood.

Her hand was out to meet Sarah's before her swift feet had crossed the parlor rug. "Sorry I'm late," she said, and introduced herself.

Sarah stood up and shook the firm, callused hand. Abigail sat on the edge of a chair facing Sarah and Albert jumped into her lap.

"He smells our dog Buster, a close friend of his." She patted Albert's head. "You must be miserable without your Ada."

She looked up at Sarah. "I'm so sorry. You're way too young to be faced with the loss of your sister."

A respectful silence followed while Rosie poured the tea.

"Abigail, please tell Sarah what you told me," said Rosie.

"Ada and I would often chat when we saw each other in front of our neighboring cottages, but on the evening of the fourth, she was in a terrible hurry. She was about to take off on her bicycle. Albert seated up in the front basket as usual.

"Something changed her mind and she came over to me and said she'd been running late all day and was in a terrible rush. She looked up and down the street as if expecting someone and then unstrapped her sketch box from the back of her bike and said, 'Will you keep this for me?'"

Abigail stopped to take a sip of tea. "The poor dear looked so worried I would've done anything for her at that moment. I told her we were leaving on our holiday but I would put the box in the coat closet and leave a key for her under the doormat. She thanked me, jumped on her bike, and pedaled off."

Abigail shook her head. "To think that was the last time I saw my dear friend—her flaming red hair blowing in the wind and Albert in the basket, his nose up in the air, as proud as he could be."

"And the sketch box?" asked Sarah anxiously.

Abigail, seemingly embarrassed, looked over at Rosie. "I'd forgotten all about it until this morning when I went to the closet to put away our suitcases. It was right where I'd left it on the fourth. I was walking over to her cottage to return it when I saw Rosie in her garden and heard the sad news."

Sarah was on her feet. "Where is it now?"

"In the entryway."

Sarah recognized the box immediately by the ABD engraved plaque. Albert was sniffing around the box and growled at Sarah when she reached for it. "It's all right, Albert," she said, picking him up and carrying the box into the parlor.

Abigail stood up, her mission accomplished. "I must be off."

Sarah put Albert down, placed the sketch box on the coffee table, and dropped down on the couch in front of it. She held her breath in anticipation and felt for the dent. Both women jumped when the secret drawer sprang open. Albert barked.

"Jiminy Cricket!" exclaimed Rosie. "How did you possibly know to do that!"

Sarah quickly explained that she had the sketch box especially made for Ada and had the secret drawer added. In the drawer was a folded sheet of Ada's pale blue stationary and a sealed white envelope.

Her hand shaking, she unfolded the delicate paper and read out loud:

July 4, 1924

Dearest Little Sis,

My life has taken such a bizarre turn since I last saw you in New York, but I couldn't be happier than I am at this moment. I just found out that I'm going to have a baby and I'm going to get married. Yes, me! Your big sister. You know how independent I am, but the father of my child is someone I really love, so I'm leaving tomorrow morning to join him in Los Angeles. He loves me, Sarah, and not because I'm famous, but because of me. Imagine that. Isn't it glorious? You two will get along famously.

We thought of getting married right away in Carmel, but when I got your letter confirming you would come to New York in October for my exhibition . . . we decided to wait so you could be the maid of honor. Don't worry, I won't wear white and it'll be a loose-fitting gown so I won't embarrass you.

Oh, Little Sis, I'm so excited about your one-woman show in Paris. You so deserve it after all your hard work. Isn't life wonderful. So full of fabulous surprises!

Ada must've been interrupted, because the next paragraph was written so fast that it was almost illegible and the tone was no longer one of joy and hope.

I've just received an unexpected message from someone who could destroy my happiness. I don't want to meet him tonight at Whalers Cove but I have no choice. If I'm successful, I'll be released from a promise I foolishly made. If I fail my past indiscretions might end up being the cause of my ruin.

I'm putting my will in this secret drawer where you'll know to find it. The safe deposit box wasn't safe.

If you're reading this now, my darling Little Sis, be brave, be careful, and trust no one.

Your loving sister, Ada Belle

Sarah felt her body crash against a wall of sorrow and regret. This was the *mess* Ada had written about in her telegram, the telegram that she had heartlessly ignored. The one saving grace was that she now knew for sure that Ada had received her last letter.

Just then the two sisters, Hallie and Jeanette, came into the entryway giggling. Rosie went out and asked them to hush. After they retreated up the stairs to their rooms, she returned to the parlor and did her best to console Sarah.

Sarah asked Rosie to open the envelope. Folded inside was another blue sheet in Ada's handwriting. Sarah, still reeling from her sister's letter, asked Rosie to read it.

I name my sister, Sarah Cunningham-Davenport, to be the Executor and sole Beneficiary of my Estate. An inventory of my work, including all unsold artwork in Paul deVrais's possession, is attached. It is my wish that Paul deVrais desist from selling or representing my work as stated in my contract termination letter to him, dated July 1, 1924, and that he transfer all listed artwork to my Executor.

As to my other assets, bonds, shares and any depository bank balance, it is my wish that all these assets, including the Sketch Box cottage and all that it contains, be transferred over to the Executor of my Estate.

My last request is that my dear sister take responsibility for the care of my loyal, loving canine companion, Albert Davenport.

It was signed *Ada Belle Davenport* and dated July 1, 1924. Two witnesses had signed underneath:

Henry Champlin
Sirena Silver

Night had fallen when Sarah woke up on Rosie's parlor couch with Albert cuddling at her side, the parlor dimly lit by one lamp. Woozy and unsteady, she picked up Ada's sketch box and stepped out into the dark with Albert leading the way.

# WEDNESDAY, JULY 30
## —17—

Sarah screaming in frustration sent Albert under the kitchen table. She was seated at Ada's kitchen nook having just read through Ada's list of paintings and was feeling the magnitude of her sister's legacy that she was now responsible for.

But it was the sixteen missing portraits listed separately under "Crocker Exhibition" and marked for shipment to New York that made her scream. Who or what prevented Ada from sending them? And where were they?

She frowned at Sirena's signature on the bottom page of the will before placing the documents back in Ada's sketch box drawer and hiding the box in Ada's closet. She told Albert she needed to talk to Sirena and would be back soon.

Elizabeth answered the door and told her that Sirena had gone to Salinas to visit a sick friend for several days and wouldn't be back until Friday. Sarah was disappointed but took the opportunity to ask Elizabeth about her testimony at the inquest.

"Oh yes, I'm definitely sure that I saw Ada take off on her bicycle at eight o'clock on the evening of the fourth."

"How did you remember the exact time?" asked Sarah.

"I was worried that I'd get my watch wet while I was watering Rosie's garden and I had just looked at the time before taking it off. That's when Ada passed by on her red bicycle with Albert in the front basket."

Sarah returned to the cottage feeling a bit less frustrated having confirmed the hour Ada was last seen alive.

With a working phone, she had no further excuse not to place a call to Eric Crocker. It was a relief when his secretary answered and said he was out of the office. Sarah gave her phone number, Carmel 4155, and asked him to call. Her next call was to Mr. Peabody's secretary, Miss Honeysuckle. Sarah made arrangements to drop off the will tomorrow morning.

Sarah felt there was nothing more she could do, and seeing it was a damp, dreary morning, she made a fire using some logs and kindling she found on the side of the cottage.

Soothed by the warmth of the crackling wood, she curled up on the living room couch. A burning log falling off the grate interrupted her reading of Jefferson's *Tamar*. She picked up a poker and crouched down to push the log farther back into the fireplace when something red glimmered in the far corner.

With the help of the fireplace trowel and iron tongs, she pulled out the ruby from Ada's *Book of Quotables* still glued to the last scrap of her burned leather journal. Sarah was so excited to find it she almost burned her hand grasping it.

In her mind, there was no doubt now that someone had burned Ada's journal after tearing out her excerpt from Katherine's letter to John Murry. She was certain that whoever Ada went to meet at Whalers Cover that night had sat where she sat now and burned Ada's journal to cover his tracks. Tracks that she would now follow.

She put the iron screen back in front of the fireplace, went into the kitchen, and hurriedly packed a lunch for herself and dog biscuits for Albert. Into her knapsack she added his orange rubber ball, her drawing pad, and the framed photograph of Ada and herself that she'd found on Ada's dresser.

She and Albert set off walking south on Camino Real, climbed down the staircase to the wide, sandy shore of River Beach, and continued southward. The sun had broken through the fog and painted the sky in cobalt blue.

At the far end of the beach, she put her shoes back on, climbed up the granite boulders, and stepped over and around shallow tide pools drained by the morning tide. They took a trail winding along the coast, with Albert running ahead to chase rabbits and squirrels.

Half an hour later they reached an attractive white, shingled, two-story house surrounded by several smaller cottages situated on a promontory jutting out into the Pacific. Across the wide cove below her, she could see a huge warehouse next to a dock. PT. LOBOS CANNING COMPANY was painted in red above the entrance.

On the promontory, many Japanese women were wearing black rubber aprons to protect their clothes as they laid the shucked mollusks out on wooden racks to sun-dry. Albert showed no interest in the pungent abalone and kept his sensitive nose to the ground, sniffing more important trails that only he could detect.

As Sarah drew nearer, the women made side-glances at her, and between shy giggles, spoke to one another in their own language. Sarah nodded her head in deference and followed Albert down a path to the cove where men and women carrying heavy wooden crates scuttled back and forth between the Point Lobos Cannery and the dock where boats were waiting to be filled.

Up from the beach was a weathered board-and-batten cabin where several men sat eating at a rustic picnic table. A man greeted Albert in Japanese and patted his head. When Albert spun around on his hind legs some of the men laughed and rewarded him with scraps from their lunches. Albert didn't have a language problem to get what he wanted, but Sarah wondered how she could ask them if they knew Ada when she didn't speak any Japanese?

Unsure what to do next, she sat down on a flat rock on the beach. A spot where she felt least conspicuous, if that was possible, but near enough to the tideline where the sea air pushed back the fishy odor of the drying abalone.

Children came down on the beach to play. They called to Albert, tossed his ball in the air, and rewarded him with a pat on the head each time he fetched it. If Albert was so well known here, Sarah thought hopefully, then so was Ada.

Though Albert and the children played without a care, Sarah felt like an unwanted gatecrasher. She knew suspicious eyes were watching her, but when she turned around to look, the villagers turned back to their work.

After she ate her sandwich, she took out her drawing pad and started making sketches of the fishing boats bumping against one another in the crowded harbor. She then shifted her gaze to a three-masted schooner anchored farther out in deeper water. An interesting subject but difficult to draw as it bobbed up and down in the rolling swells.

The horizontal glare of the sun's slow descent started to sting her eyes. The workers at the cannery began to finish up their work packing boxes of abalone. Several were climbing up the hill toward their village. The children were no longer playing on the beach.

It's now or never, she decided, and packed up her knapsack.

In front of the old cabin, she approached a few older men and some boys standing under the canopy of a weather-beaten old cedar. White skullcaps on their heads. White baggy shorts. White cloth wrapped around their feet. Even white goggles around their necks. Rosie had said the traditional abalone divers wear white to ward off the sharks and to bring good fortune.

She saw fishnets hanging from their waists and stone weights like the ones found in Ada's pockets tied to their belts. The tools of abalone divers. Her heart sped up.

One of the boys smiled at her, and feeling encouraged, she introduced herself. He said his name was Tajuro and, yes, he lived here at Whalers Cove.

"Here?" she asked pointing at the old cabin behind them.

He laughed. "That's where we keep our diving equipment. I live up there." He pointed upward to the village and asked if she was lost.

"Not exactly," she said, impressed by his perfect English.

She brought out the photograph and showed it to him, trying not to appear anxious. "Did you ever see this lady on the beach?"

"Nice lady," said Tajuro. "I still have the sketch she drew of me and Albert playing catch on the beach."

"She used to meet—" Before the boy could continue, one of the men standing nearby, who had been glancing sideways at the photograph, put his hand on the boy's shoulder and spoke to him in Japanese.

Tajuro said goodbye and began walking toward the shoreline where several divers had already boarded their skiffs.

Sarah realized Albert was no longer chasing birds on the beach. "Did you see where Albert went?" she called out to Tajuro.

"He ran off behind the cabin around ten minutes ago. He was chasing a squirrel."

Sarah hurried down the trail behind the cabin. After crossing through a grass meadow blanketed with orange and purple wildflowers, she reached a narrow country road and thought she recognized Albert's insistent bark somewhere in the dense pine forest on the other side. She held back, afraid to enter the deep, shadowy maze. When his barking became more frantic she forgot her fear and sprinted into the darkness.

She found Albert standing in a dwindling patch of late afternoon sunlight. He was panting heavily and his pink tongue was hanging from his mouth. His eyes were wild. She was about to scold him when he took off again farther into the woods. When she finally caught up to him, his white tail was pointing straight up to the sky and with one foot bent, his nose pointed at his prey—a red Schwinn bicycle on the ground, half buried under brown pine needles.

Albert sniffed its rear-rack panniers, one of which held a canvas knapsack. Sarah pulled out the mildewed sack and sat down on the soft ground beneath the tree, gripping the sack in her hands. Hands that shook as she fumbled with the leather straps. Inside there was a drawing pad, its front cover damp and warped from being outdoors. She recognized the quick shorthand pencil lines and detailed images. Studies that Ada might have painted later in her studio, if there had been a *later*.

Albert jumped up and put his paws on her shoulders. She patted his head, consolingly. "You were with Ada when she came here on her hike, weren't you, Albert? No one saw her that night at River Beach because she wasn't there. At least, not alive. She came to meet someone here at Whalers Cove." He yapped twice, hopped off her lap. "Oh Albert, you are the smartest hunting dog in the world!"

She stood up and brushed pine needles off herself and her canine companion. After placing both hers and Ada's knapsacks in the two rear panniers, she walked the bike out of the forest.

She felt an urgency to get back to the cottage. The straight dirt road looked like a faster route back to Carmel with the bicycle. With Albert in the front basket, she raised her right leg over the center bar and put her feet on the pedals. Remembering the determination on the faces of the bicyclists in the Tour de France as they raced toward the Parc des Princes in Paris, she imagined herself on a similar course and took off under the growing shadows.

To her distress the road curved eastward after several hundred yards when she wanted to go north. Albert jumped out of the basket and she carried the bicycle to the other side of River Beach and up the wooden staircase. It seemed to get heavier with every step she climbed.

When she finally reached Camino Real, the road was blanketed in a fog. She put Albert back in the basket and, imagining she was near the finish line, let loose a second spurt of adrenaline and plunged into the gray vapor.

She almost missed the cottage's picket fence and was just dis-
mounting when she heard an anxious voice calling out, "Sarah? Is
that you?"

A yellow lantern appeared in the fog and then she heard quick
footsteps. Albert started barking and she had to grab his collar to
stop him from leaping out of the basket.

A white collar and then Robert Pierce's handsome face shone in
the yellow haze.

"Sarah, thank god, I found you."

"I didn't know I was lost!" she said, out of breath but very happy to
have won the race and to see a friendly face, though surprised it was
Robert's. "What are you doing here?"

"I was going to meet some friends at La Playa and I thought I'd
invite you to join us. I found your neighbor Miss McCann standing
on your porch. She was worried that something awful had happened
to you. I said I'd go out looking for you."

He frowned at the muddy red two-wheeler. "Where did this come
from?"

"I found it in the woods and rode it back," she said proudly. "Or
I should say, my super-hunting dog found it." She patted Albert on
the head. He waved his tail and jumped out of the basket and, after
sniffing Robert's shoes, went under his favorite tree to relieve himself.

"I don't know how you did it. These tires are almost shot," said
Robert, shining the lantern down on the bicycle wheels.

Sarah was too exhausted to immediately deal with the implication
of finding Ada's bike near Whalers Cove, and wanting to celebrate
her successful outing, she said, "If that invitation is still open, I could
sure use a hot toddy right now."

"Atta girl. Where do you want me to put the bike?"

Sarah suggested the studio and Robert was reaching for the handlebars when Albert growled and she had to quiet him down.

"Sorry," she said to Robert. "He's just being protective."

"Good man," said Robert. "A pretty girl like you needs protection."

Under the studio's electric light, Robert studied the half-deflated tires.

"Do you know anything about bikes?" she asked.

"Just how to ride. My photography teacher, Johan Hagemeyer, lets me use his bike when I stay at his cabin. But you don't need to know about bikes to know this one needs fixing."

"Sirena told me you were his protégé. I knew him briefly when I worked at a gallery in New York that showed his work. I really liked what I saw. Very modern."

"Small world," he said, seemingly unimpressed, his attention on testing the brake levers. "If you'd let me, I'd like to take this back to Johan's and tighten the brakes and put some air in the tires." He propped it up on its kickstand.

"That's very kind of you to offer," said Sarah.

"I must admit that I have a hidden motive." A wide smile crossed his face.

"Oh?"

"Johan tells me the Del Monte forest has stunning views along its bike paths. I haven't had a chance to see for myself, but he says there are some great locations for taking photographs. In return for fixing the bike, how about riding with me this Sunday?"

"That's hard to refuse," said Sarah, flattered.

"Then it's a date." He took hold of the handlebars. "I'll put this in the car and bring it back Sunday morning in tip-top shape for our ride."

"Wait." It didn't feel right giving up her sister's bike just after she'd found it. "I can't explain everything right now, but this bike means a lot to me. It might be my sister's."

He saw her hand tightening on the handlebar. "Trust me, Sarah. I'll take very good care of it. I promise. You can't ride it like this."

When Sarah let go, it felt as if she were letting go of her sister's hand and she immediately put her hand back on the handlebar. "Sorry, Robert, but would you mind tuning it up on Sunday before our picnic?

He released the handle. "Sure. I understand. There are things of my brother's that I still haven't been able to get rid of."

"I visited Point Lobos today," said Sarah steering the conversation away from her sister.

"That's a coincidence. I was at Point Lobos today too. I took some photographs at Cypress Grove. A shame I didn't see you there, but Point Lobos has many trails. Which one were you on?"

"Whalers Cove."

"Why would you want to go to that smelly place? Certainly you don't know any of those aliens."

"They're not *aliens*," said Sarah, shocked and disappointed he felt that way.

"Well whatever you want to call them, you shouldn't go there again on your own," he said in a tone Sarah found off-putting. She didn't like anyone telling her what to do. "You can never tell what they're up to. The sooner we send them packing back to the jungle they came from, the safer we'll all be."

"I'm sorry you feel that way. I think they have as much right to live here as we do," said Sarah.

He turned away from her to untie the straps of Ada's knapsack in the pannier.

"Stop!" Her voice was louder than intended.

He twisted back around and said, "What's wrong? Don't you want this off the bike?"

"Sorry. It's just that my drawing pad is in there and I'm rather sensitive about anyone touching it."

He raised his empty hands. "Sorry. I was just trying to help. Here, you do it."

She struggled with the straps. From behind her, he reached over and put his hands on hers to help. In spite of what he'd just said about the Japanese, she felt her body betraying her as it did the other night on the balcony at La Playa. She knew she should push him away but felt weak in the knees overtaken by her desire that was stronger than her will.

The watchful little dog growled.

"Albert. Where are your manners?" she said, crouching down and hushing him, glad to have an excuse to move away from Robert.

He finished untying the knapsacks and was carrying them over to the work table when he saw the studies she'd made of Sirena's eyes. She hadn't meant to leave it out.

"You're a very good colorist. I like how you captured the light in Sirena's cat-like eyes. I wish I could get that iridescent effect, but with black-and-white film I have to use special techniques in the darkroom and the results are never as natural as this."

He looked at the canvases leaning up against the wall. "Sirena mentioned that your sister was working on a series of portraits. Can I see them? I could use some new ideas for photographing my Hollywood models."

"I'd love to show them to you, but I've been unable to find them." She suddenly felt very tired, not sure it was from the bike ride or just trying to fend off her strong feelings for Robert.

He reached for her hand and put it up to his lips. "Now how about that hot toddy at La Playa?"

She pulled her hand away. "Can I take a rain check? Today was pretty exhausting."

He shrugged. "Okay. It won't be easy, but I'll just have to wait until Sunday."

All this time Albert had been watching them. "It might be better if he stays at home when we go on our picnic. I don't think I can handle the competition."

"He won't like that, but you're right." she smiled down at Albert. "It won't do having two dates at the same time."

At the alleyway door, Robert tossed his black curls off his forehead and gazed into her eyes. "Are you sure you won't come? I'd love to dance with you again." She felt herself leaning toward him, but managed to pull away before he kissed her. Missing his mark, he laughed and gave her a kiss on the forehead. "See you Sunday. I'll come by earlier to fix the bike."

After he left, she locked the studio doors and before turning off the lights made a quick call to Rosie to let her know she'd made it back to the cottage and would come over tomorrow to tell her what she'd found.

She brought Ada's knapsack upstairs to her bedroom. Her loyal dog followed behind.

Seated at the small desk, she took out the warped drawing pad and turned back the pages under the lamplight. The front pages were rippled and the pencil sketches were stained from being out in the elements, but in the middle of the pad, the pages were drier, the sketches precise. Jagged rocks. Abalone shells. Twisted tree trunks. And one detailed sketch of the schooner that she had also drawn at Whalers Cove that afternoon, but Sarah hadn't seen the name of the schooner, *Ocean Queen*, painted on its black stern.

Another page was filled with several studies of masculine facial features. Arched cheekbones. Square chins. Crooked hawkish noses.

The last page made her gasp. Evil, hollow eyes stared out at her from a human skull. A black gaping hole for a nose and a mouth of jagged teeth. Below the skull were two crossbones and below the crossbones Ada had written in thick black letters: *THE PIRATE.*

Frightened, she called to Albert who jumped up into her lap.

She hung Ada's drawing pad on the easel to dry out, changed into her nightgown, and leaving on the light, nestled up to her silent companion warming her bed.

As tired as she was sleep did not come easily. When she did close her eyes she saw floating pieces of a disassembled face. She struggled to assemble them, only to have the face shatter like cracked glass that woke her from her dream.

Albert jumped off the bed and started barking and scratching on the closed bedroom door. For a few long seconds, fear strapped her to the bed as she listened to muffled sounds coming from somewhere downstairs. She looked around the room for a weapon to defend herself but came up empty-handed. She finally summoned her courage, opened the door, and followed Albert downstairs.

He barked and scratched at the studio door in the kitchen. Her nerves shattered, it took several tries to turn the lock. When she finally got it open, a shaft of moonlight coming through the skylight lit the studio floor. It was strewn with paintings, like a hurricane had passed through. A human one.

Albert ran to the alley door, barking. The extra padlock she'd hooked on the door clasp had been jimmied off and the door was banging in the wind. She wedged a chair against the splintered door to keep it closed and gathered up the canvases. Up in the storage loft, paintings had been pulled out of the shelves and left in heaps.

What were they looking for? A professional art thief would've known to take the valuable pieces but none were missing. Nor was Ada's bike.

Too full of worries to go back to bed, she rewarded Albert's bravery with a mutton bone she'd been keeping in the icebox and rewarded herself with a glass of Una's wine. Seated at the banquette, she opened her drawing pad and did the only thing that would ease her mind—she sketched a plan of action: *Install strong new lock on alley door. Change front door lock. Report the break-in to Marshal Judd???* And then crossed it out. There was no point in getting him involved. Nothing had been stolen and for now she was working on her own investigation into her sister's murder. A murder that the marshal didn't believe had even happened.

# THURSDAY, JULY 31
## —18—

Sarah burst into Rosie's kitchen. "The studio was broken into last night!"

"What did you say?" Rosie said as she shut off the running water, her hands in a sink of sudsy dishes.

"Someone broke into the studio last night," said Sarah, stopping to breathe.

Rosie turned around, water dripping onto the floor. "Blimey!" She dried her hands on her apron. "Are you all right? Was anything taken?"

"I checked the studio inventory list. Nothing was missing. Except the portraits, of course, but they're already missing. I think the thief was looking for something in particular and ransacked the studio to find it. It's a miracle none of the pictures were damaged."

Rosie pressed her hand against her heart and sat down.

"I'm sorry. I didn't mean to shock you," said Sarah.

"Never you mind. I'll be okay. My heart can take more abuse than you think, and if not, I have this." She held up a silver pillbox.

Sarah brought her a glass of water and stood by while Rosie took her heart medicine. "Stop hovering over me, child. I'm fine. Now tell me everything."

Sarah sat across from Rosie and started from when she woke to Albert's barking to finding the pictures on the floor to finding the alley door open, the extra padlock she'd put on it jimmied.

"Mother of Jesus!" Rosie said, her hand still pressed to her heart. "I'm so relieved that you weren't hurt, but where's Albert?"

"I left him to guard the studio. The alley door is splintered and won't lock."

"I'll ask our local carpenter to install a new lock today."

"He can do it that soon?"

Rosie smiled. "Charlie's a good friend of mine and once he knows the urgency, he'll find the time. He can change the locks on the front door at the same time."

"Thank you, Rosie. I don't know how I'd manage without you."

She patted Sarah's knee. "You'd do just fine. But two people do shorten the road."

Sarah filled Rosie in on finding Ada's bicycle in the woods near Whalers Cove and showed her the pirate sketch in Ada's drawing pad. And how it all fit in with Mary Austin and the Jeffers telling her that Ada was having an affair with someone.

She could see the older woman's mind considering the new evidence and she gave her time to think it out.

"You've got some good evidence," Rosie said finally, "but it's still circumstantial. Was it Ada who hid her bike in the forest? And if so why? Or did someone else steal it and abandon it there to go back and get it later? Or did the person who murdered her hide it there after he killed her? And who was the nefarious stranger she was meeting at Point Lobos?"

"I don't know. But there is no doubt that this is Ada's drawing pad."

"That's not enough. We need to know who buried the bicycle in the woods," said Rosie, warming to the topic. "And there is a way to find out."

"How?" asked Sarah, feeling deflated.

"I read a story about how a murderer was identified by his fingerprints found on the glass of sherry he'd given his victim. I don't know if Marshal Judd is aware of this newfangled fingerprint equipment, but let's ask him to check for fingerprints on the bicycle."

Sarah paled. "I'm afraid it's too late. The bicycle is now covered with my prints—and Robert's."

"Robert? The gentleman I saw last night? It's lucky he showed up. I was ready to form a search party." Rosie knitted her brows and set her concerned blue eyes on Sarah. "Promise me you won't go back to Whalers Cove on your own."

"But I have to go back, Rosie," Sarah exclaimed. "I showed Ada's photograph to one of the villagers and he'd seen her several times at the Cove. Now I need to find out if any of the villagers actually saw her that evening."

"Then ask Robert to go with you," said Rosie. "He seems like a sensible man to have around in a dangerous situation. What does he do when he's not looking for lost girls?"

"Rosie, I wasn't lost," said Sarah with a bit of irritation, "and your knight-in-shining-armor shoots starlets in Hollywood."

Rosie frowned. "That's disappointing. Where did you meet him?"

"At the Mission Tea House. And then, by chance, I saw him again at La Playa. When he has time away from Hollywood, he stays at Johan Hagemeyer's studio here in Carmel and works on his own pictorial photography. He's Hagemeyer's protégé."

"Then I guess the fellow must be talented because Hagemeyer wouldn't take him on otherwise," said Rosie. "Too bad he's wasting his talent in Hollywood."

"Rosie! He has to make a living, and I think he makes a very good one."

A buzzer went off. "Oh my, that's my shepherd's pie. I need to get it out of the oven before the potato topping burns to a crisp."

As soon as Rosie settled back down in her chair. Sarah said, "I telephoned Miss Honeysuckle. She said I could drop off the will this morning and she'd give it to Mr. Peabody."

"I'll go with you. But first let's stop at Charlie's and make arrangements to have a new door and locks installed. Then after we drop off the will, we can get lunch at Pop's on the wharf. Just thinking about his abalone chowder makes my mouth water."

"All right," said Sarah. "I'll go get the will and come back for you."

As she stepped outside, Sarah heard Albert barking in Ada's studio. A lanky man hunched over in a flaming-orange jacket and stocking cap came running out of the alleyway. She called to him but he ignored her and made a sharp turn at the corner and was gone.

Sarah rushed up the alleyway to see if he had broken into the studio but the chair she had jammed against the door was still holding it closed. She called out to Albert who was still barking in the studio and she ran around to the front door to let him out.

After Sarah had quieted Albert down, Rosie said, "That man was dressed like one of those Portuguese fishermen you see down at the wharf." She folded her arms and shook her head. "There are way too many peculiar things happening at Ada's cottage. What with the portraits missing, the break-in, and now this fisherman lurking about."

"And don't forget someone painting in Ada's studio when I first got here," said Sarah.

While Sarah got the will and inquest files to give to Mr. Peabody, Albert held his leash in his mouth. She felt badly not taking him with her, but she needed him to continue watching the studio in case the fisherman came back. A lamb shank from Rosie's shepherd's pie was an acceptable bribe.

A wooden sign, CHARLES MURPHY CARPENTRY, hung over the entrance of an old barn. The lofty space was filled with pieces of furniture that had been fixed or were waiting to be fixed. Charles, a white-haired older man, was bent over his workbench. The tools of his trade were hung neatly on the wall in front of him.

His full attention was concentrated on fitting together the complicated parts of a table leg joint. It wasn't until the two women were casting shadows on his work that he realized someone was there and looked up with irritation until he saw it was Rosie. He raked back his thick hair and greeted her with a pleasant smile.

"What a pleasant surprise," he said, wiping his hands on a rag. "Why Rosie, you're as pretty as the day we met. How do you manage to stay so young while the rest of us fade away?"

"Ah, Charlie, always a flirt," she said, though obviously pleased.

He turned to Sarah. "And who might this young lady be?"

Sarah introduced herself and told him she was Ada Davenport's sister.

He offered his condolences.

Getting down to business, Rosie said, "Sarah's been staying at the Sketch Box and the studio was broken into last night."

"I'm sorry to hear that," said Charlie. "What with all those tourists crowding into our village on weekends, it's just not as safe as it used to be."

"The thief jimmied the alley door," said Rosie quickly. She knew well how the locals felt about the tourists, and to avoid a long discussion said, "We were hoping you could replace the lock while we did our errands in Monterey."

"That should be easy enough. I installed that alley door for Miss Ada when I built the Sketch Box with my son."

"You built the Sketch Box?" asked Sarah. "That's certainly something to be very proud of." Knowing now that he was a superior craftsman, she felt embarrassed when she asked him if he could also change the lock on the front door.

"Don't you worry, Miss Sarah, I'll take care of it right away."

Sarah remembered Albert, but Charlie said Albert was a good friend of his and there'd be no problem.

He turned to Rosie, "If I finish before you return, shall I leave the new keys in the usual hiding place in your rose garden?"

Rosie blushed and said, "So you haven't forgotten?"

"Forgotten what?" asked Sarah.

"Never you mind, Sarah," said Rosie. "Now let's leave the man alone so he can do his work. As my Da used to say, 'Lose an hour in the morning, and you'll be looking for it all day.'"

The carpenter said again how good it was to see Rosie in his shop and that she should visit more often.

"Thank you, Mr. Murphy, for helping me out," said Sarah.

"No need to be formal, Miss Sarah. You can call me Charlie. Like your sister did." He walked them outside. "Grief has a way of working itself out, Miss Sarah. It just takes time. If you're as strong of character as your sister was, you'll get through this just fine."

When they climbed the stairs to Mr. Peabody's office and opened the door, Miss Honeysuckle was there to greet them. She apologized for Mr. Peabody's absence and said he was playing golf.

Rosie looked again at Mr. Peabody's secretary. Finally she said, "Don't I know you, Miss Honeysuckle?"

The secretary's round face brightened. "I wasn't sure if you'd remember me. I was your student at the Japanese Association. If I hadn't taken your courses in English, I never would have gotten into secretarial school."

"Why Saint's alive. You're Machiko!" exclaimed Rosie as she gave the secretary a warm hug and exchanged greetings in Japanese. "How good it is to see you after all this time. Why just look at you. You were just a wee thing in pigtails when I last saw you and now you're a sophisticated young lady.

"But why are you now called Miss Honeysuckle? Wasn't your family name Inaoka?"

The secretary suddenly became shy and shuffled some papers on her desk before answering. "I knew I'd have a better chance of getting work if I used an Occidental name. I'm afraid Machiko Inaoka on a resume would have put me at the bottom of the stack or in the wastebasket."

Both Sarah and Rosie told her that they wished things weren't like that.

"I quite like your adopted name," said Rosie, "but might we still call you Machiko?"

"Of course. Now let me see that will and I'll make you a copy."

Machiko opened a closet door onto an enormous black mimeograph machine. "This new invention has made my life a lot easier," she said. "I wouldn't want to copy every document that comes through Mr. Peabody's office by hand."

Sarah handed her the will, the inventory of Ada's paintings, and the inquest files. "Can you please copy these too?"

Thirty minutes later, Sarah had all the copies and the originals were in Mr. Peabody's locked desk.

It was then that Sarah asked, "Machiko, do you remember the name of the man who came here with my sister?"

"Didn't Mr. Peabody tell you?"

"He said to ask you," said Rosie. "He seems to be quite dependent on you to remember things for him."

Miss Honeysuckle smiled. "I'm afraid his memory is not that good when it comes to names. But he is a very smart lawyer. You're in good hands with Mr. Peabody." She frowned. "Though it is rather embarrassing that he forgot Alain Delacroix's name. After all, he is a famous actor."

Sarah dropped down into a nearby chair. Never would she have considered the dark, swarthy man she met at the Jeffers's to be Ada's fiancé. But then again she and Ada had very different taste in men.

"Are you all right, Miss Cunningham?" asked the secretary.

Sarah said faintly, "Are you absolutely certain it was Mr. Delacroix?"

"Oh yes, no doubt about it. I was very excited to meet him in person."

"When will Mr. Peabody be back?" asked Rosie. "We must see him as soon as possible."

Machiko looked at her appointment book. "We could squeeze you in at two o'clock? He should've finished his golf game by then."


"I still can't believe it's him!" exclaimed Sarah, pointing to a Forest Theater playbill in a shop window with the actor's face prominently featured.

Now that she knew, it seemed like *Pirates of Penzance* playbills were displayed in every window on Alvarado Street. And walking down to the Monterey wharf, she felt his eyes stalking her.

His face was in Pop Ernst's Abalone and Sea Food Restaurant window as well. Sarah picked up a copy of the poster at the counter before a waitress ushered them through the busy restaurant to a corner table overlooking the wharf.

"Thank you, Molly," said Rosie.

"The usual?" asked Molly.

"Yes, please. And the same for my friend."

Molly left and Sarah pointed to the playbill, still stunned. "I was introduced to him as Ada's sister at the Jeffers' party, so he had to know who I was, but he ignored me. He was even rude. Why not tell me he was Ada's fiancé? And why keep it from their mutual friends, the Jeffers?"

Rosie waved at a group of elderly ladies who shuffled into Pop's like a brood of swans.

"Did you ever see Ada with him?" she asked Rosie.

"No. Never. I'm just as shocked as you are. The first time I laid eyes on Alain Delacroix was at yesterday's rehearsal at the Forest Theater."

"I need to speak to him, Rosie."

"Of course you do, my dear, and so you shall. On Sunday night, after the last performance, there's going to be a cast party. You can come as my guest."

"Rosie, you're a miracle."

Large abalone shells filled to the brim with steaming chowder were placed in front of them by Molly.

Rosie stuffed a napkin into her collar and dipped her spoon into the bowl. Minutes later she looked up at Sarah, "Now wasn't this worth waiting for?"

Sarah nodded yes and wiped the creamy white sauce off her chin before pointing to Alain Delacroix's face on the playbill. "I'll take this poster back to Whalers Cove and ask the Japanese villagers if they saw him there with Ada."

"I don't know if that's wise, Sarah. A.M. Allan is a rancher who owns all the land at Point Lobos, including the property the village is built on, and except for his family who live nearby, the villagers are suspicious of white people coming into their cove. I don't think they would tell you even if they did recognize him."

"It's still worth a try."

Rosie sopped up bits of chowder with a piece of crusty sourdough bread. "All I'm saying is I don't want you to get into trouble. If any of the villagers are somehow involved in Ada's murder, it could be dangerous. Let me ask Mr. Kassajara."

It had been a long time since Sarah had been mothered by Ada and while she found it slightly annoying, it was a comfort to know that someone other than Ada cared for her, and she didn't have to fight all her battles alone.

Sarah showed Rosie the telephone subscription card.

"What's this?"

"It's a record of Ada's subscription. It accidentally fell into my satchel while I was at the telephone company the other day." Rosie laughed. "It shows that she ordered her phone to be disconnected until her return on August 1st." Sarah pointed to the dates on the card. "If she was planning to kill herself why would she do that?"

"My oh my, Miss Holmes. Well worth the snatch!"

"Why thank you, Miss Poirot."

After generous portions of apple crumble pie à la mode, the two self-appointed detectives topped-off their lunches sipping coffee and observing the other diners who, like them, were white.

"I can't believe I'm asking this, but don't you find it surprising that Mr. Peabody hired Miss Honeysuckle?" asked Sarah. "I would think in this race-based town she'd be excluded from having such a trusted position in a law firm."

"Mr. Peabody is an intelligent man. Miss Honeysuckle is very qualified. He knows what he's doing. If only there were more people like him in Monterey who had the courage to step over the racial line."

"I wish there were more people like him everywhere," said Sarah. "I've been away for three years and though I've read how common racism had become in my own country, particularly after the war, I didn't really believe it. Why even Robert, who's a really nice guy, was calling the Japanese people *aliens*. And when I think Sirena has to pass for white to be accepted into art school, I am embarrassed for my race."

Molly brought the bill and Sarah insisted on paying.


They were chatting with Machiko in the outer office around two o'clock when Mr. Peabody came out from his office. He was dressed in a red and black diamond-patterned argyle sweater and baggy plus-four golf slacks gathered below his knees with matching calf-length socks. Otherwise, he was wearing the same blue and white polka-dot bowtie and a starched white shirt. Of course, at the club he would have to substitute his wing-tipped brogues for his spiked golf shoes.

He ushered them into his office and sat down at his desk. They'd hardly settled in their seats when his finger hit the time clock, which resounded with a shrill whang.

Sarah held up the Forest Theater playbill.

"Yes, I know," said Mr. Peabody, shifting in his high-backed chair. "I must admit I'm rather embarrassed that I didn't remember his name. Thank goodness I have Miss Honeysuckle to keep me on the straight and narrow.

"At any rate you should be proud of yourselves, ladies. You have found a crucial player in this case. I would talk to Mr. Delacroix to see what you can find out, but be very cautious. My first impression of him was of an upright gentleman. But seeing he did not come forward at the inquest to acknowledge the deceased as his fiancé makes him a questionable character and a possible murder suspect."

"I'm hoping that's not true," said Sarah. She didn't want to believe the father of Ada's child could be a murderer.

Mr. Peabody held up the will. "I happened to stop by my office just after you left this. I delayed my golf game to look it over and it's in good order. There should be no problems with the probate court. I will also give them a copy of the inventory of your sister's paintings currently in Mr. deVrais's possession. Your sister's estate will be resolved shortly, in spite of Mr. deVrais's claims."

Sarah smiled. Now they were getting somewhere. "Thank you, Mr. Peabody, that makes me feel a lot better."

She asked if he'd read the inquest files, particularly the suicide note.

He clipped his pince-nez on his permanently dented nose and shuffled through his papers until he found it. Looking up at Sarah, he asked, "Didn't the handwriting expert confirm that this was Miss Davenport's handwriting?"

"It is Ada's handwriting, but let me explain." She came around his desk and put the bookmarked page next to the suicide note and pointed out the redactions.

He looked back and forth at the pages. "Hmm. Most curious."

Sarah put the ruby attached to a scrap of burnt leather on the desk beside the note. "I found this in my sister's fireplace. Someone burned her journal, and this is all that remains."

He twitched his nose like a rabbit smelling a carrot and the pince-nez dislodged and swung from its chain, but he waved the suicide note in the air. "It's still circumstantial evidence, nothing can be proven, Miss Cunningham, and I'm afraid it's inadmissible. I sympathize with your situation, but if you want the District Attorney to reopen your sister's inquest you'll have to come up with something more concrete, or better still, a suspect without an alibi. Let's see what Mr. Delacroix has to say."

He held his forefinger over the black box, "If there's nothing else, I have delayed my golf game long enough."

As if in collusion, neither woman budged from their seats.

"Did you read *all* the inquest files?" asked Sarah.

He shifted his tall frame slightly. "In the little time I had, yes, I did."

"Didn't you find it noteworthy that my sister was last seen riding her bicycle, but that the marshal never tried to find it?"

"Yes, I agree, there was negligence on his part."

"I found that bicycle yesterday, Mr. Peabody. It was in the woods behind Whalers Cove." She rushed on, "And I have two witnesses who didn't see Ada on River Beach the evening of July fourth."

"And who might these witnesses be?" asked Mr. Peabody, picking up his fountain pen again and clipping his pince-nez back on his nose.

"A young fisherman who was out fishing that evening." She paused.

"His name?" asked Mr. Peabody.

Sarah looked over at Rosie who turned up her empty hands. "I don't know but I'll find out."

"And your other witness?"

"Robinson Jeffers."

"Are you talking about the poet?"

"Why yes. Have you read his poetry?" Sarah asked, surprised a lawyer read anything besides legal briefs.

"I certainly have," he said rather proudly. "He's a fine writer. I'm sure we'll be hearing much more from this talented young man. But he's rather eccentric and is not very popular within our community because he is a known pacifist who didn't enlist during the war. Judd might not consider him a reliable witness."

"Balderdash," said Rosie. "He'd be an ideal witness."

"Perhaps," said Mr. Peabody. "But as I said before, we still need a suspect before I can request a hearing. Let's see what you can find out from Mr. Delacroix."

Sarah and Rosie tried not to show their disappointment.

"One more thing, Mr. Peabody, please," said Sarah. "Did you speak to Mr. Pritchard about the confusion at the bank regarding my sister's depository account?"

"Ah, yes." He cleared his throat. "It appears Mr. deVrais is a signatory on Miss Davenport's depository account and one of the bank tellers allowed him to make a withdrawal."

"That's outrageous!" said Sarah, slamming her hand down on his desk. "That teller should be fired and deVrais arrested. You're my lawyer. Isn't there something that can be done about this kind of behavior? Certainly deVrais's breaking the law."

Mr. Peabody ignored her outburst and said calmly, "This happened the day before you came to the bank. Mr. Pritchard was very confused as to who was the rightful beneficiary to Miss Davenport's estate, you or Mr. deVrais. I told him to expect instructions from the probate court and until then not to allow Mr. deVrais to make any more withdrawals."

"Mr. deVrais's having delusions of grandeur if he thinks he has any right to my sister's assets."

"I think you have a good point there. Be assured that I am taking care of this by following the rules of law. I have advised Mr. deVrais's lawyer, Mr. Hubbard, that the will has been located and that you are the executor and the sole beneficiary of Miss Davenport's estate. You needn't worry about any more withdrawals."

# FRIDAY, AUGUST 1
## —19—

Sarah had been irritated by the minutes clicking by on the kitchen's wall clock reminding her of what little time she had left to return to Paris for her exhibition and stopped winding it up. But now she rotated both hands to ten and let the ticking commence. A harsh but necessary reminder to keep her going in spite of the hurdles she faced.

She hoped to learn more from Alain Delacroix on Sunday. And as far as the portraits, she'd spoken to Eric Crocker and he'd given her another week to find them before he cancelled Ada's exhibition. She still wanted to ask Sirena about how she came to be Ada's witness on her will, but she wasn't due back at the Lodge until that evening.

As promised, Charlie had put a new lock on the front door and installed a burglar-proof Segal deadbolt on the new alley door, which made her feel much safer.

She went into the studio where she hoped to find some rest from her racing mind.

After putting on her red smock, she walked over to several blank white canvases leaning against the wall. It was unusual that Ada had stretched so many of them, but Sarah blocked out any further thoughts of her sister and propped one of them up on the easel, taking down the one Robert had seen of Sirena.

She wanted to paint the girl's portrait again. Sirena's exotic cat-like eyes would be the essence of the painting. Her other facial features vague, almost flat like a mask. A pale blue sea would complement the pigments of her violet eyes.

She squeezed a pure red and a Monterey azure onto her palette and added a generous amount of pearl white at the bottom. With her fingers dipped in linseed oil, she smudged the oils onto the canvas with circular strokes and then continued with brushstrokes and bold swaths with her palette knife adding the white until she got the colors she wanted. It was her way of using the canvas as a palette for blending hues.

After a few hours of concentrated work, she was pleased with the results. It was only then that she became aware of Albert sitting patiently below the easel with his leash hanging from his mouth. She wondered if he had learned such patience by waiting for Ada to take a break from her work.

"Okay, Albert, I understand that you want to take us away from these poisonous fumes and breathe in the good stuff—pure blue air."

They were just on their way out the front door when Sirena came bounding across the street in her saffron coveralls over a bathing suit with a towel draped around her neck. She was fanning her face. "Can you believe how miserably hot it is? I came by to see if you'd like to join me for a swim."

Sarah had been working on the color of Sirena's eyes and was irritated to look into the actual eyes of her model and know she still hadn't captured the correct palette. Sirena's irises were the color of the wild lupines growing in the Point Lobos fields, but capturing their iridescence was like trying to capture fireflies glowing in the night air.

"I don't know," she said. "I was about to take a walk with Albert."

"He can come along. C'mon, you said you used to swim in Lake Michigan. It's not any colder. Go get your bathing suit. You can change at the bathhouse."

Sarah hesitated. Even though she now knew Ada hadn't drowned and there were far more dangerous things on land than in the sea, she was still afraid to go swimming. But maybe this was just the right moment to get past that fear.

"All right." She looked down at Albert pulling on the leash. "Would you take him with you while I find a bathing suit?"

Sirena took the leash and rushed off before Albert had a chance to say no.

When Sarah got to the bathhouse, Sirena was down on the beach and sitting beside her was a man in street clothes. Sarah couldn't see his face, but the hat looked similar to the trilby that Robert had been wearing at the Tea House. Albert came running up the sandy slope, his leash dragging behind. She unclipped it from his collar and told him to wait for her.

She quickly wriggled into the one-piece bathing suit she'd found in Ada's closet, yanked it up over her bare breasts, and slid her arms through the straps. She shoved her clothes into her knapsack, slung it over her shoulder and stepped back into the warm sunlight. With Albert leading the way, she ran down the dune to the beach below.

She dug her bare feet into the warm sand while looking up and down the shore. There was no sign of Robert, if it had even been Robert, and Sirena was already swimming out past the crashing waves. Beachcombers were scattered here and there. A few painters had set up their easels. Sandpipers pranced and pecked for food along the shore, leaving their forked footprints in the damp sand. An optimistic Albert ran off to try to catch one.

Sirena had left her towel near the tideline and there were two indentations where she and the stranger had been sitting. A game of tic-tac-toe, X'd out in the sand, was now being erased by the incoming tide. The towel would soon be soaked. Sarah dragged it to higher ground.

She saw Sirena's head bobbing up and down and waved but her friend was too far out to get her attention. Bracing herself, she ran out into the water and banged into what felt like a turquoise wall of ice. Its force crashed against her, pushing her back on the shore. She stood there stunned. She'd had no idea how powerful the Pacific could be, but she could be powerful too. After several underwater somersaults, she managed to dive deep enough and emerge on the other side of a giant wave.

Sirena saw her and waved her over. Sarah began a breaststroke and swam toward her. Her arm and leg muscles welcomed the physical exertion that warmed her body. Her recent fear of swimming in the ocean was soon forgotten.

Sirena disappeared behind another surge of rough unfurling waves. Sarah dived again and resurfaced in calmer waters, then flipped over to lie on her back. The sun heated her face and the tension from the past two weeks went out of her body as she let the natural buoyancy and rhythm of the sea soothe her.

It wasn't until she sat up to dogpaddle that she realized the current had pulled her way out. Albert was now only a brown dot on the beach.

A sudden massive wave crashed over her and its turbulence pulled her down under. Before she could regain control of her body, she was caught in a succession of waves that tossed her about like she was a Raggedy Ann doll. She thrust out her legs, pushed with her arms, and surfaced, gasping for breath, only to be dragged down again.

A break in the waves gave her a chance to swim to shore, but the strong current kept pulling her back three feet for every one foot she gained. She thought she heard Ada shout: *Hold on. I'm coming* and tried to swim toward her.

An icy hand clamped onto her wrist like a vice and pulled her back. She panicked and tried to shake free, but it was much stronger than she was. An arm hooked around her chest, flipped her on her back, and held her in its grip. The sky blackened and she went limp.


When Sarah regained consciousness, she was lying on the beach, but it wasn't Ada hovering over her.

"I'm sorry, Sarah. I'm so sorry," Sirena cried out. "When I saw the current dragging you farther out, I swam after you. I finally caught up and reached out for you, but you fought me and went under. I dived after you, grabbed hold of you, and pulled you to shore."

Sarah tried to sit up but fell back down. The girl helped her up and she began to cough up saltwater. Sirena wiped the sand off her face and Albert jumped up on her lap. She hugged the wet, trembling dog. Sirena said he had tried to swim out to her but the waves tossed him back on the shore.

Sirena kept blaming herself and apologizing. Sarah kept thanking her for saving her life. Minutes later, realizing the danger was over, they began laughing and hugging each other and Albert was yapping and running in a circle around them.

They walked back up the beach and stretched out on their towels, depleted.

After a while, Sarah turned to Sirena. "Was Robert here earlier? I thought I recognized his hat."

"No. That was just a local beachcomber."

They walked up to the bathhouse and changed into their dry clothes and then all three walked together up to the Sketch Box gate. Sirena was turning to go to the lodge when Sarah invited her to come in. She shrugged okay.

Sarah piled some kindling in the fireplace, put a log over it, lit it and stoked the flames until the wood cackled.

Sirena lit their cigarettes and they lay back on the rug and blew out smoke rings that floated over them and dissolved into the air just like their earlier panic had dissolved.

"I feel so much better now," said Sarah, consoled by the warmth of the fire after nearly drowning.

"When are you leaving for Paris?" asked Sirena as if they'd just been talking about Sarah's return trip.

Sarah rolled over on her side to face Sirena. "Not until I find out how Ada died. And I still have to find the portraits."

Sirena sat up on her knees. "Don't cancel your show, Sarah. Go home. That's what Ada would want you to do. That's what I want you to do," Her luminous eyes pleaded as she begged, "Please go."

"Then tell me the truth, Sirena. Tell me what really happened between you and deVrais in Ada's studio. Were you planning to steal the portraits?"

"Of course not," said Sirena indignantly. She jumped up and put another log on the already brisk fire.

"Then why didn't you tell me that deVrais came to the studio? What are you hiding from me?"

Sirena took a long drag from her cigarette, tossed it in the fire and turned to face Sarah. Her eyes now cold, the warmth gone.

"As I told you before, Ada asked me to crate the portraits and arrange for them to be shipped to the Crocker Gallery in New York. But you're right that isn't all that happened. Ada went for a walk with Albert while I was packing—" She hesitated.

"Is that when deVrais showed up?"

"Yes. He swaggered into the studio as if he owned it. I told him he shouldn't be there while Ada was out, but he ignored me. And when he saw the New York shipping address on the crate I was packing, he flew into a rage. He ordered me to stop crating the portraits and said he would manage Ada when she came back."

"So deVrais was at the studio when Ada fired you. But why lie?"

"Because I was afraid you'd be angry with me."

"Why? What have you done that would make me angry?"

Sarah could see she was frightening the girl and she needed to take it easy or she'd learn nothing. She stood up and invited Sirena to join her on the couch where they'd be more comfortable, but Sirena returned to her kneeling position on the rug and cradled her head in her hands.

"Did you do as he asked?"

"No. At least not right away. I told him I worked for Ada and she would have to tell me to stop the shipment, not him. That's when he told me he was very worried about Ada's recent behavior. She had gotten this crazy idea in her head that he was no longer her dealer, which wasn't true. And she'd be in a lot of trouble legally if the portraits were sent to another gallery owner. He could even have her arrested."

"But you had signed Ada's will. It stated very clearly that he was no longer her dealer."

"So you know about that, too. She only showed me where to sign. I never read it. And like I told you before, Ada *had* been acting very strange. Even hysterical at times. So what he was saying seemed quite possible, especially after what happened later."

Sarah found it hard to accept Sirena's obstinate belief in Ada's suicide but it was more important now to find out about the portraits than argue with her over Ada's sanity.

She asked Sirena to continue. And the girl now seemed more than willing, almost supplicant. As if it was a relief to finally confess.

"Ada had given me permission to work in her studio and I'd hung a few of my paintings on the wall to dry. Finally, he stopped complaining about Ada and walked over to look at my work. That was when he offered me a show in his gallery. I thought he was really interested, until he asked me for a favor in return." Sirena joined Sarah on the couch. "You know what it's like. I would've done anything at that moment to have a show in his gallery."

Sarah did understand. Hadn't she done just about anything to get a dealer interested in her work? But she'd also suffered for it later. She handed Sirena a cigarette and after lighting it, said, "What was the bargain he made?"

"Change the shipping order to his gallery/address. I was just telling him I would if it would help Ada when she burst into the studio. She'd heard everything from the kitchen and was furious. She fired me on the spot and told us both to get out of her studio."

"Do you remember the date?" asked Sarah.

"How could I forget such a miserable day Ada and I had been such good friends and in an instant she hated me. It was the first of July."

"Did you ever see the portraits again?"

"No. After I learned Ada was dead, I went back to the studio to remove my paintings. The crates were gone and so were the portraits. I thought Ada had shipped them and was surprised when you said they never arrived in New York."

"Did deVrais still offer you a show?"

She nodded yes. "He invited me to his gallery and showed me where my paintings would hang, but said there was still something I needed to do for him. I was afraid he'd ask me to deliver the portraits and I'd have to tell him they were no longer in the studio."

Sarah was relieved that deVrais had been telling her the truth and that he believed the portraits were still in the studio. But if he didn't have them, who did?

"So if not the portraits, what did he ask you to do?"

Sirena looked down at her half-smoked cigarette and snuffed it out in the ashtray. "He commissioned me to paint a violent seascape. Like someone suicidal might paint. He showed me a picture of Dante's Inferno and told me to use those same pigments on my palette."

Sarah had suspected Sirena but still hoping she was wrong, she asked, "That was you in the studio?"

The girl lowered her head. "I'm sorry, Sarah. I didn't mean to scare you."

Sarah got up and paced in front of the fireplace for several minutes until she felt calm enough to approach Sirena.

She pointed her finger down at the girl. "It was you who painted *A Bleak Morning* and put Ada's name on it."

"He didn't tell me Ada's signature would be added later." Sirena started crying.

Sarah didn't know whether to throw the girl out or take pity on her. She decided on sympathy. She knew personally what an artist would do to have her work shown in a gallery. DeVrais had taken advantage of Sirena and the girl had suffered enough. She returned to the couch and enfolded Sirena in her arms. "Don't cry. Your secret is safe with me. I bought *A Bleak Morning.*"

"Why would you do that?" sniffled Sirena.

"I couldn't have people thinking it was Ada's last work. DeVrais had it delivered here a few days ago. It's in the studio." She paused for a moment, then said, "Sirena, the work I've seen of yours is far better than that disgusting painting. Promise me you will never do anything like that again."

"I promise," she said solemnly and then asked in a whisper, "Are you going to have me arrested?"

"Arrested? Sirena, you just saved my life. Why would I do that? It's Paul deVrais who should be arrested. Not you."

The dark cloud over Sirena's face was chased away by a wide smile. "Really?"

"Really."

Sirena got up and slung her towel over her shoulder. "I've got to go. I promised to help set up the Del Monte Gallery for tomorrow night's invitation-only opening. I get a bit of pocket money helping out. I mustn't be late."

"Who are the artists?"

"You don't know? Everyone's talking about the William Ritschel and Armin Hansen exhibition. It's going to be a sensation. You must come."

"I haven't been invited."

"That's no problem." She winked. "I have connections. Meet me tomorrow at the entrance of Hotel Del Monte at six. There'll be quite a crowd, but you can slip in the back way with me."

Before she could reply, Sirena was gone. Sarah remained seated by the fireplace and thought long and hard as she held the poker and drew Sirena's name and a big question mark in the cinders.

# SATURDAY, AUGUST 2
## —20—

Ada's extravagant teal-blue hat shaded Sarah's eyes from the late afternoon sunlight as she walked along the wooden boardwalk parallel to Monterey Bay's shoreline. She paused to admire the foam-crested waves spreading across the sand like a brush of titanium silver. She turned inland toward the Hotel Del Monte.

There were a few clusters of people standing near the hotel's arched entrance. She was early so rather than wait there for Sirena, she followed a sign pointing toward the Maze where she and Ada had gotten lost in its deceptively simple pathways leading to its center.

At the arched entrance, dense cypress hedges carved into bishop and knight chess pieces still peered down on her as they had when she was a small child, but they didn't seem as frightening now, or as tall. The last time she was here Ada had to take her hand before she'd even enter, and Ada was the one who found the center of the Maze.

Inside, between the tall chessmen, Sarah became less and less confident in her sense of direction as she kept reaching dead ends, until she felt completely lost. Panic set in and she cried out for help. Her cry only to be muffled by the tall hedges.

"Stop being a child," she said to herself. Then heard Ada say, *You will find your way. Just keep going.*

Just then a shaft of sunlight shone down between the shadows of the knights and bishops and with newfound courage she started walking again. Minutes later she reached the center of the Maze.

Very pleased with herself, she sat down cross-legged like she and Ada had done for an afternoon tea party on this tapestry of smooth river stones. At the same time their mother had been frantically looking for them on the hotel grounds. Their giggles from behind the hedges had finally brought her to the center of the Maze.

Mother had been so relieved to find them safe she plopped down between them in all her finery, took the imaginary teacup offered by Sarah to her lips, and drank the elixir that Sarah now raised to her own lips.

She took a moment to say a silent prayer for her mother and father and Ada, who had all died brutally before their time.

When Sarah returned to the Del Monte entrance, the queue stretched down the front lawn. As she found a place at the rear of the well-dressed art aficionados, she noticed curious glances from people mingling around her, who quickly looked away when she stared back. It took her a moment to realize it was Ada's eye-of-the-peacock sun hat that was drawing their attention and not the plain sundress she'd inappropriately worn to a society event at the Del Monte.

A gentleman in front of her had the broad shoulders of Robert Pierce. She was about to tap his shoulder when he tipped his trilby hat to a friend joining him. She looked away, disappointed it wasn't Robert.

She spotted Sirena coming toward her in saffron striped black bolero trousers, a stand-up-collar tux shirt, and a silky yellow bow tie. She took Sarah by the hand, pulled her out of line, and swiftly led her under the porte-cochère side entrance and into the hotel.

At the end of a long corridor, Sirena pushed open a wide door and they entered an elegant ballroom with walls papered in crimson suede. Burnished mahogany columns supported the high, vaulted ceiling and dozens of gilded amber globes hung down from crystal chandeliers. "How glorious," whispered Sarah to Sirena. "I feel like I'm in a church."

The ballroom seemed an odd venue for an art gallery, Sarah thought. The Nouy Gallery in Paris was far less pretentious, although it had shown the earlier work of some of her favorite fauvists, André Derain and Maurice de Vlaminck, and it was a major coup to get a one-woman show there. Standing now in the center of this gallery, she yearned to get back to Paris and finish the last piece for her own show.

The doors to the exhibit would soon open onto the waiting crowd, so she took the opportunity to study the paintings without being crushed. She wasn't alone for long. From over her shoulder she heard a husky voice with a German accent. "What do you think?"

She was studying a pastoral landscape with a cattle ranch in the foreground. "I'm not a very good judge of California landscapes but these are some of the best I've seen." Without looking at her inter-loper, she added, "Well-executed representational work."

The interloper followed her to the next canvas, a dramatic sea-scape of Point Lobos. Tension. Disharmony of nature. Frightening but compelling. She was imagining herself falling over the edge of the precipice into the agitated waves and being smashed against the impenetrable rocks when she heard a voice from behind and turned around to find Sirena saying, "So, you two found each other."

"Not yet," said the interloper. Sarah met the jovial eyes of someone who appeared to be an elderly statesman dressed in a formal black suit and a rather stiff white collar that propped up his long neck. His bushy dark brows met above a distinguished nose. His barrel moustache was dark like his brows, but his thinning hair and grayish beard made him look older.

"Then I'll introduce you. Sarah Cunningham, may I present William Ritschel."

Sarah blushed as she shook his hand. "I'm sorry. I didn't know . . ."

"That's quite all right, Miss Cunningham. I have the advantage. Sirena told me you had arrived recently from Paris and I recognized your sister's plumage." He lowered his voice. "Please let me express my sincere condolences. Ada was a shining star amongst us. It's a tragedy to the art world to lose her."

"Did you know her well?"

"I knew her by sight and of course by reputation but we never spent much time together. My studio is in Carmel Highlands and occasionally I'd take walks on River Beach where she painted, but I never disturbed her. She was a very disciplined artist and, like myself, not one for idle conversation when she was working." He laughed. "I actually knew her little dog better than the woman herself. He would run up and give me a stick to throw in the ocean for him to fetch."

The doors opened and the aficionados began walking in noisily, stopping in front of the pictures to discuss them and look at their prices. *A familiar gallery scene*, thought Sarah.

A young man waved frantically from across the room, trying to get Ritschel's attention. "Excuse me," said Ritschel, "it looks like I'm being summoned. I hope art dealers in Paris are less blatant than mine and I hope they know something about art other than how to sell it."

"No," said Sarah, "I'm afraid most dealers are the same everywhere."

"Humph," said Ritschel, stroking his beard. "Well, it was lovely to meet you, Miss Cunningham." He tipped his hat and walked away.

Sirena took Sarah's arm and led her over to another Ritschel painting, *Incoming Tide*. Sarah studied the stormy, deep blue hues of the surf, powerfully expressed with swirling green and blue brushstrokes that seemed to rise up and hold their positions like warriors while their comrades ahead attacked the granite rocks.

Ritschel's impassioned brushstrokes captured the conflict she tried to express in her own work. If she had the time, she could spend days studying his work.

Sirena had moved to another of his marine paintings. She turned to Sarah. "I wish I could paint like this!"

It was a much calmer piece, illuminated with mellow pigments that expressed a mood of joy and peace. The same feeling Sarah got looking at *les estampes japonaises*, and the artwork Sirena had shown her the other day.

She'd just said to Sirena, "But you do paint like that," when a waiter came up to them with an irresistible tray of champagne-filled flutes. She smiled to herself wondering if anyone in Monterey respected the Prohibition laws? Apparently not at the Del Monte.

They both took a glass and Sirena lifted hers to Sarah's and quoted what Ritschel had written on the wall above his paintings. "Live, breathe, eat, and paint!"

"Yes," said Sarah, clinking Sirena's glass, "what better life could we ask for?"

They crossed to the opposite side of the room with their champagne glasses in hand and stood in front of an Armin Hansen painting, *Nino*. One fisherman, as bold as the red shirt he wore, stood alone in a skiff, confronting the turbulent sea that filled the background.

"His complementary palette reminds me of one of my favorite artists, André Derain," said Sarah. "But the comparison ends there. Derain focused on beautiful but somewhat stark and barren landscapes, mostly without human figures. I can see that Hansen is more interested in the powerful narratives of the plights of fishermen. His subjects have such a strong sense of self. It seems like they're fighting against the fundamental darkness in all of us. And yet his brush strokes are in such vibrant colors."

"Really, Sarah, you should be a curator. I don't see it that way at all," said Sirena. "I just love his intense yet simple palette of blues and reds."

They moved on to the next painting. Two fishermen on a ridge overlooking the bay in the early morning light, ominous gray clouds in the distance like a towering wave. A young man was carrying two thick wooden oars over his shoulder. He was accompanied by a lanky older man with shoulders hunched over from years of hard work on the sea.

When she moved closer to the painting, she froze. It was the same orange fisherman's jacket that was on the man running away from Ada's cottage.

"Have you ever seen this man in Carmel, Sirena?" she asked, pointing to the older fisherman. "Or someone dressed like him?"

"No," said Sirena, with a notable edge in her voice. "Why would I know any Portuguese fishermen? There are dozens of them dressed like that down at the wharf."

Sarah was amazed by how easily Sirena denied her own Portuguese heritage. A necessary subterfuge that she's learned to do so well, but at what cost?

"You know, Hansen's a fisherman himself," said Sirena, effortlessly switching topics. "He goes out with the Sicilian sardine fishermen. That's what makes his marine paintings so realistic. There he is now," she added, pointing toward a hefty-set man gesturing dramatically with his hands as he spoke to a group of admirers. His sunbaked face was clean shaven except for an unruly moustache above a wide mouth, tilted upward in a perennial smile that dwarfed the small pipe he held in the corner of his lips. Like the robust fishermen he painted, he was a man who lived outdoors. His open tweed jacket, pullover sweater, and Scottish-tweed cap confirmed that fact. His clothes and looks were in sharp contrast to the fashionable suits with stiff shirt collars standing around him and looking at him as if he was Poseidon, the god of the sea.

Sarah felt as if a refreshing blast of salty air were coming from his direction in an otherwise stuffy room.

"C'mon. He told me he wanted to meet you." Sirena took Sarah by the arm, positioned her in front of the artist, and interrupted his conversation.

"Hi, Mr. Hansen, here she is."

He turned to look at Sarah. Their eyes exchanged equal curiosity.

"It's a pleasure to meet you, Miss Cunningham," he said, giving her his full attention. "Your sister was a dear friend of mine. We often painted together on the wharf. This might not be the most appropriate time to say this, but I was deeply saddened by her death." Sarah was relieved there was no mention of suicide and thanked him for his condolences.

Their conversation turned to a discussion about the colorists they knew and respected. When Hansen said he had to leave, he asked her if she wanted to join his class on Monday. "I think you'd enjoy painting on the wharf," he said, "and it would give us a chance to continue our discussion."

*At least until I'm free to return to Paris*, she said in an argument with herself. *And being down on the wharf I might recognize that Portuguese fisherman and find out why he ran away when I called out to him.*

She glanced over at Sirena who was starting to help with the cleanup after the show. "Can Sirena come too?"

Hansen lit his pipe. "I don't see why not." His eyes glanced up at Sarah's hat and grinned. "But please don't wear that peacock feather. It would be a distraction not only for me, but the other students as well."

Sarah blushed. Was Armin Hansen flirting with her? If so, she rather liked it.

# SUNDAY, AUGUST 3
## —21—

Sarah had offered to make sandwiches for her picnic with Robert and walked up to Leidig's on Ocean Avenue with Albert. It was disappointing. No Parisian foie gras, Camembert, or fresh baguettes. Just blocks of orange cheese, salami, and the new spongy Wonder Bread that even Albert turned his nose up at. She impulsively added fresh-baked strawberry tarts to her basket and hurried home.

And now what to wear. She put on a white linen blouse, slipped into a pair of Ada's brown jodhpurs, and for spice added a red plaid silk vest and matching bow tie. Why not? The boyish look was fashionable and the jodhpurs would be far better for biking than her mid-calf sundress.

She looked at herself in the mirror from all sides and topped her chic sporty outfit with a tweed cap. She tilted it to one side and winked at herself.

The cowbell clanged and she opened the door.

Robert's startled look was not what she'd expected.

"Is something wrong?" she asked, adjusting her bow tie.

He smiled. "No. Not at all. I was just taken aback by what a lovely girl you are even if you are dressed like a boy." He handed her a bouquet of yellow daffodils he must have picked on the roadside. There were no flower shops in Carmel.

"That was thoughtful, Robert, thank you. Let me go put them in a vase before they wilt." *And you see me blushing like a schoolgirl!*

"No hurry." He held up a bike pump. "I have some work to do."

She'd already put Ada's bicycle out on the front porch.

When she came out again, Ada's red bicycle was leaning against the fence, gleaming and polished like it was new. She looked at Robert, stunned. "Can that be the same bike?"

"I just cleaned it up a bit, oiled the brakes, and pumped up the tires so it'd be safe to ride."

He swung a black bicycle out of the rumble seat of a swanky white Ford coupe with an open-top and turned to Sarah, "I hope the fog burns off soon."

She stopped staring at the Ford and straddled Ada's Schwinn. "So where are we going?"

"I thought we'd head north through part of the Del Monte forest, then pedal along the shoreline and picnic near Cypress Point. After lunch we could go on to the Monterey wharf and then take the bus back to Carmel. But maybe a twelve-mile trek is too exhausting for a Parisian girl," he added, teasingly.

"Oh please! I get plenty of exercise walking the streets of Paris."

"There are lots of challenging hills in the forest."

"Really, Robert. Do I look that frail?"

"No. But you are shaped like a willow and you might be blown out to sea at Cypress Point."

In response, Sarah stepped on the pedals and took off. She hadn't had any light-hearted fun like this in quite a while and it felt so good. She was reminded her of the rides through Central Park she used to take with Joe Donaldson before he was killed in the war.

"I can see I'll have to keep a watch on you," said Robert, as he caught up to her and they stopped to rest. "You might take a fall speeding like that."

"It might surprise you to know, Robert, that this *willow,* as you say, is very athletic. I even broke through my recent fear of the water by taking a swim in the ocean."

"That wasn't very smart, Sarah. There are strong currents offshore. I hope you didn't go swimming on your own."

"Of course not. Sirena was with me. She turned out to be a very good lifeguard."

"I'm sure she is. She has those well-built swimmer's shoulders."

"Have you gone swimming with her?"

He laughed. "With Sirena? She's a bit too young for me, don't you think? Besides, I don't like to swim in the ocean when I can sail over it. Remember, I'm a naval man."

"Do you swim at all?"

"Not really. Though I've been near water all my life, my father had me working on the docks at such a young age I never had time to learn."

They pedaled across Ocean Avenue and passed through the Carmel gate onto the inland forest road. The fog had lifted and sunshine filled the air. With a burst of speed she triumphantly caught up to an astonished Robert on an uphill stretch through the pine trees.

"I'll race you to Cypress Point," she yelled as she flew by laughing.

An hour later they reached the Point, gasping for breath. Sarah jumped off her bike and ran out to tag the famous lone cypress rooted to a steep precipice.

"I won, I won!" she shouted back to Robert who was just getting off his bike.

She leaned over the rocky ledge, which dropped abruptly to the churning surf below.

"Get back!" shouted Robert as he came up and gripped her waist and pulled her back.

He snapped several photographs as she laughed, hugged, and kissed the silver trunk of the ancient tree. They then rode their bikes up to Point Joe and stopped to rest. Nearby Sarah saw a sign wedged between two rocks: ROCKS AND FOG SPELL DISASTER.

"That sign marks where the *Celia* was shipwrecked," said Robert. "It was the same time as the 1906 earthquake in San Francisco."

"Did anyone drown?"

"Only a cargo of lumber was lost."

"I guess you know a lot about ships after working on the docks and being in the war."

"Kind of," he said, as if he didn't want to talk about it. He strapped his heavy camera case over his shoulder. "Let's go down on the beach. We can have our picnic there."

"This is so gorgeous!" said Sarah, plopping down on the sand and pulling off her shoes and socks. She found a flat area to spread out the red-checkered tablecloth she'd brought in her knapsack. They were both disappointed that the salami and cheese sandwiches had gotten crushed and the white bread was damp and stained yellow from the oozing mustard.

"Sorry," said Sarah. "Shopping at Leidig's isn't like Paris."

"No worries. Next time I'll bring something gourmet from a Hollywood delicatessen."

Sarah liked him saying "next time."

They soon forgot about the miserable sandwiches when Sarah brought out the strawberry tarts. Robert ate three.

After she put away the paper plates and the tablecloth, she pulled out her drawing pad. She looked at Robert and started to sketch. She tried to draw his handsome features, deep-set wide eyes and square chin, but he kept moving around and she ended up with a lot of squiggles. "Hey, I let you photograph me."

"Sorry, but I don't like to be drawn. It's just a silly superstition I have about someone capturing my soul."

Sarah put down her pencil. "That's certainly hypocritical, Robert. You take pictures of me and other people all the time."

He jumped up. "Look!" A family of sea otters was floating on their backs on top of the sea kelp, clutching their abalone shells to their chests with their tiny hands. "I'm going to go take some pictures," he said. "Do you want to come?" he asked.

"You go ahead. I'd rather stay here and sketch." As much as she was liking his company, it would be pleasant to have some time on her own.

He picked up his camera. "Okay. I'll be back in an hour."

After she made some sketches of the frothy waves splashing against the rocks, she moved under the canopy of a bent cypress. The bike ride had been more tiring than she realized and she soon fell asleep.

She woke up when she heard, "You're going to get wet, Sarah. The tide's coming in." Disoriented, she sat up and rubbed her eyes. Robert was kneeling over her. "Have I been asleep long?" she asked, looking around her, distressed not to see the drawing pad that had her sketches.

"Here, is this what you're looking for?" He handed her the drawing pad, then pulled her up. He was putting his arms around her when an unexpected wave crashed nearby and splashed them. He bent down to save his camera and strapped it over his shoulder. "C'mon, my sea-maiden," he said, gallantly.

He firmly took her hand and they walked up the beach and got back on their bicycles.

A fog was coming into shore when they were pedaling down to the Monterey Wharf.

Sitting on a bench, Sarah leaned back and closed her eyes. She listened to the halyards slapping against the wooden masts of scarcely visible fishing boats that rose and fell at anchor on the lapping waves. The natural rhythm gave her a precious second of tranquility from her worries.

"Sarah!" shouted Robert. She stared wide-eyed into the lens of his camera just as he clicked a photograph of her.

"Robert, please don't do that again." She made room for him on the bench. "You're right about souls being captured, but by drawing pads as well as cameras. Let's make a bargain. I promise not to draw your portrait without your permission and you do the same for me with your camera."

"Okay," he said. "It's just I can't resist taking pictures of you. You could be a model, you know? After I develop the images I took of you today, I'd like to show them to you. I don't think you realize how photographic you are."

Embarrassed, she turned away to take out her drawing pad and pencil. "If you don't mind, I'm going to make a few quick studies of the mist-covered boats to take back to Paris where I can put them on canvas in my studio."

Robert leaned back on the bench and watched her sketch. "Paris? Are you leaving soon?" he asked with a tone of undisguised disappointment.

"I do hope so, but I have unfinished business here." She put down her pencil. "I can't leave until I reopen my sister's inquest."

"Reopen the inquest? Can you do that? I thought the case was closed after the verdict of suicide."

She returned to her drawing. "I thought so too until Rosie told me that if I can find enough evidence to prove Ada didn't commit suicide, the District Attorney will listen to my appeal. I think I've almost gathered enough evidence, but I still need a suspect and a motive."

"Sarah, don't you think you should stop this foolishness?" said Robert sternly.

She closed her drawing pad and turned to him. "It's not foolishness, Robert. If you'd known my sister, you would know the inquest verdict was wrong."

"But even if you found your killer, it wouldn't bring your sister back. Trust me, I know what you're going through, but the sooner you stop blaming yourself for what happened—"

"That's not what this is about, Robert!" she said with a burst of anger and stood up. "I know I can't bring Ada back. But someone killed her and I can't let them get away with it."

She picked up the pad that had fallen on the ground and shoved it in her knapsack. Up until now it had been a perfect day with Robert. Why did Ada have to come up? Always Ada.

The loud thud of a fishing boat hitting the wharf made them both jump.

"We should get back." He checked his wristwatch. "The next bus is leaving in fifteen minutes."

He stood up, took her hands, and pulled her up from the bench. But their eyes did not meet this time and he didn't hold her in his arms. She wished she hadn't been so outspoken. She was so enjoying their flirtation.

There was a cold silence between them as they walked to the bus stop. Robert tied their bicycles to the rack on the back. The bus was crowded and they had to squeeze together on the bench.

The bus reached the top of Carmel Hill and while it crawled slowly down Ocean Avenue, Robert put his arm around her shoulders. "I'm sorry, Sarah. You have every right to investigate your sister's death. It's just that I don't want you to get hurt. If you're right and someone did kill your sister and you find out who that was, your life could be at risk. If you're willing to forgive me for what I said, I'd like to help you any way I can."

"Really, Robert?"

"It was wrong of me to compare your sister's death to my brother's. Your situation is quite different. I had no reason to doubt his suicide. So tell me how I can help you."

"Come with me tonight to see *Pirates of Penzance* at the Forest Theater." The truth was, though she'd never admit it to anyone, she was afraid to confront Alain Delacroix alone with what she knew. Having Robert nearby, as Rosie had suggested, would make her feel safer and a bit braver.

He gave her a puzzled look. "I don't see how I can help you by taking you to a play, though I'd certainly be happy to do so. The lead actress is a friend of mine—I think you two met at the Tea House."

Remembering the gorgeous Louise Brooks, Sarah suddenly wished she could rescind the invitation. "Yes, I met her," she said flatly.

"So why the play? It seems an odd place to find a possible suspect? Who is it?"

"I'd rather not mention any names until I have more information, but it's one of the performers."

"All right." He lightly squeezed her shoulder. "But please don't keep me in suspense too long, Mademoiselle Sleuth." Sarah wasn't amused by him making a joke of her investigation, but she forced a smile.

"We can go to the cast party afterward, too. Rosie got me an invitation."

"Do you know where the party will be?" he asked, as they stepped off the bus at Ocean Avenue.

She shook her head no.

"I'll ask Louise," he said.

*Great,* thought Sarah. *Not only do I have to confront Alain Delalcroix, but I'll also have to worry about Robert being distracted by a gorgeous woman when I might need his help.*

After they pedaled back to the cottage, Robert placed his bike in the back of the Ford. He was starting to get in the driver's seat when he looked up at Sarah and said, "This is none of my business, but now that you told me that your suspect is in the play tonight, I was wondering if it might be Alain Delacroix?"

Sarah was surprised. "Why would you think that?"

He shrugged. "I don't know. It's just a wild guess."

Sarah told him he was right and asked him not to tell anyone. When he didn't start the Ford, she asked, "Is there something else you want to tell me?"

"Look, I don't know Delacroix personally, but he doesn't have a great reputation in Hollywood. He's known to not always be a gentleman because of his wild temper on and off film sets. Why do you suspect him?"

She paused. "Alain was my sister's fiancé. I want to talk to him tonight about why he didn't appear at the inquest or make any effort to contact me."

"Whoa. Fiancé? He certainly doesn't act like one when he's working on a Hollywood set with his female co-stars. I'm glad you told me, Sarah, and I'm glad you asked me to come with you tonight. You shouldn't see him on your own. If he knows you're onto him, with that temper of his, he could be dangerous."

Robert told Sarah he'd be back at six to pick her up and drove off. She walked Ada's bike down the alleyway and locked it in the studio.

She had a couple of hours to get ready and took a deep soak in Ada's claw-footed tub to clear her head and relax her strained muscles. She wasn't that fit despite her bragging to Robert. And now that she was away from him, she wondered if he really could be helpful? But hadn't he already helped by telling her about Alain's salacious reputation in Hollywood?

# —22—

I t looked like the entire community of Monterey had come to see the play at Forest Theater. Robert had to park several blocks away and then they joined the queue of playgoers climbing up the steep hill. They passed through the ticket gate at the top of a hillside arena sheltered by lofty pines backlit by the shimmering blue Pacific.

Several families were enjoying their picnics on the theater's grounds. Robert took Sarah's arm to support her as they descended the wooden stairs toward the stage. Tiers of rustic benches were already filled.

Their seats were in the center, two rows back from the stage. Sirena was Rosie's other guest. She was seated directly behind them.

She rambled on about how excited she was to go to the cast party at the James House. "You know, Mr. James is a fabulously rich tycoon. He wanted a getaway where he could write novels, so he hired the famous architect Charles Greene to build his stone house on a cliff overhanging the ocean. I've only seen it from the beach below, but I bet it's swanky inside." Sirena shifted her eyes to Robert's back and whispered, "Are you bringing him?"

Sarah glanced at Robert. He was reading the theater program.

"Why, do you mind?" whispered Sarah.

"Not at all. Just curious. I thought he might be Louise's date."

Just then, floodlights lit up the stage. The thrill of anticipation hushed the theater.

The merriment of the chorus in the opening scene gave Sarah a moment to relax and enjoy the comic opera. Their seats were so close that she could see Rosie. She had the urge to wave at her, but she didn't want to draw any more attention to herself. When she had chosen Ada's metallic silver ensemble to wear, she hadn't realized how much it would sparkle under the moonlight or how she resembled Joan of Arc armored for war.

Alain Delacroix made his entrance dressed all in black as Frederic, the Pirate Apprentice. His imposing figure swaggered back and forth across the stage singing "Oh, False One You Have Deceiv'd Me" in a resonant tenor voice and the audience responded with a generous applause.

Robert and Sarah stayed in their seats during intermission while Sirena left to get something to drink.

When they were alone, Robert took Sarah's hand in his. "I'm so glad you're here with me," he whispered in her ear. It had been a long time since anyone had said that to her, if ever, and she put her head on his shoulder and closed her eyes.

The second act was even more boisterous and silly than the first. The finale featured the entire cast along with the chorus and everyone stood up to clap and shout, "Bravo. Bravo." The actors returned several times to take their bows and when they finally exited, Delacroix came out alone and strutted to the rim of the stage. He swept off his black plumed pirate hat and bowed.

During the thunderous applause that followed, he looked out into the audience and spotted Sarah. The recognition between them was brief, but explicit. Robert must have felt it too, because he put his arm around Sarah and whispered, "You didn't tell me that you actually knew him."

"I don't. I met him last week at a garden party, but only briefly."

The stage went dark, the applause faded. "You're shivering," said Robert, as he helped her put on her coat and ushered her up the crowded aisle as the audience spilled out into the chilly, black night.

Sarah offered Sirena a ride to the cast party and before they all piled into Robert's Ford, Sirena insisted that Robert put the top down, despite the moist air. He looked at Sarah who nodded in agreement. He tucked a blanket around her and tossed one to Sirena in the rumble seat. Sarah tried to ignore it, but there was a chill between her two friends that had nothing to do with the weather. She somehow felt responsible for it.

They followed a caravan of cars for several minutes as they drove down an unlit, bumpy road along the coast. Silent anticipation prevailed in the coupe until they saw flaming torches lighting up the front of a stone castle. "There it is!" called out Sirena from the backseat.

They joined the other guests and walked down precarious, dimly lit flagstone steps until they came to a sharp turn that led to the carved-redwood entry door of the storybook castle.

Sarah stepped into the high-ceilinged living room filled with massive mahogany furniture, plush Oriental rugs, and a roaring fire that could roast two pigs. This was far removed from the humble furnishings of her garret. Through wide-arched windows, she saw moonlit waves rise and fall in the Pacific.

She was introduced to several people but after a short while the crowd of faces seemed overwhelming, and she felt the need to be alone. She saw a moment to escape and slipped outside through a side door onto a wide terrace bordered by an iron railing. The breaking surf flailed against the granite boulders below and the earth shook under her feet. Not exactly the peaceful moment she was hoping for.

She heard Robert's voice from the doorway, "Sarah! I've been looking for you. What are you doing out here?" He reached out for her hand and drew her back inside and over to the blazing fire. "Are you all right?" he asked.

"Yes, I'm fine," she lied.

Rosie came over and started introducing them to more guests,

mostly local writers and artists and the actors from the play. Then
Louise Brooks came over, ignored Sarah and spoke privately to
Robert.

Sarah was moving away when Mary Austin stopped her and
immediately started a tedious critique of the musical's composers,
W.S. Gilbert and Arthur Sullivan. After a while Mary paused. "Very
overrated fluff. Don't you agree, Sarah?"

"What's that?" Sarah replied, finding it increasingly difficult to
pay attention.

"Sarah, honey," said Mary, "if you have something better to do
than talk to me, I'll say good night."

"I'm sorry, Mary. It's just . . . have you seen Alain Delacroix?"

"No, but I'd like to tell him he's wasting his talent in such a silly,
pompous play. I'm sure he only did it because Ted Kuster is his good
friend—he's the producer, you know and—"

Sarah cut her off. "Can you tell me where the powder room is?"
Mary pointed to a corridor on the far side of the room. Sarah excused
herself, squeezed her way through the party, and closed the door
behind her.

The mirror was lit by a single flickering candle and her reflection
in it was pale. She pulled back the silvery headscarf draped over her
forehead, combed her fingers through her hair and painted her lips.
Joan of Arc looked out at her and said sternly, *You've got to go find
him.*

As she stepped back into the hall, someone took her by the arm
and pulled her into a dimly lit room. An overhead light was flipped
on and Sarah stood face to face with Alain Delacroix.

She saw no way out of the small servant's quarters except the door
that he was now leaning against. She was scared but managed to say,
"What do you want?" in a surprisingly strong voice.

"The Jeffers's told me you're investigating Ada's suicide. I want to
know why. Or are you just as crazy as your sister?"

"Fine words coming from a grieving fiancé," she retaliated.

"Fiancé! How do you know that? Nobody knows that. Not even the Jeffers."

"Remember Mr. Peabody? You came to his office with Ada and asked him to draw up a nuptial agreement."

He didn't deny it. She felt her advantage and said, "You're the one who has some explaining to do."

He sank down on the edge of the narrow bed and stared at the stone floor. She sat down in the only chair.

He mumbled, "What do you want to know?"

"For a start, where were you the night Ada died?"

"Arriving at the Los Angeles train station. But why does it matter? I don't need an alibi. The woman killed herself."

"Really?" said Sarah trying to hold back her anger. "Then please enlighten me as to why you think she would do that?"

"I told you. She was crazy. You don't need my word. There was an inquest and that was the verdict. What else am I supposed to think?"

"Did you know she was pregnant?"

He walked over to the arched window and looked out. "Yes, she told me."

"Weren't you happy about it?"

He twisted around. "Are you kidding? Happy? I was thrilled. I rushed out to buy her a wedding band and had it engraved.

"I was starting production on a new film and had to get back to Hollywood. I wanted her to leave with me, but she insisted on staying an extra night. She said she needed the time alone to crate the portraits and send them out to her New York dealer.

"When I went to meet her train she wasn't on it. I tried to telephone her, but the line was disconnected. At first, I didn't think much of it. If anything was wrong she'd have called me or sent a telegram. I figured she got delayed packing the portraits.

"I was on my way to the train station to pick her up the following day when I got a call from my agent telling me Ada had drowned. It was a terrible blow. Then I heard there would be an inquest."

"Why didn't you call Marshal Judd? Help him with the investigation? Or at least come back for the inquest?"

"I wasn't thinking straight. I kind of went off the deep end for several days. Then I spoke to my agent and he said I should wait until after the inquest to see if my suspicions were justified—that she had really killed herself.

"And after I read the verdict in the *L.A. Times*, all I wanted to do was forget her. And here you are stirring up things that are better forgotten."

"You should've told the truth about your relationship with Ada to the marshal."

He sat back down on the bed. He glared at her. "The truth? You think I should've told the marshal the *truth*? That Ada chose death rather than become my wife and the mother of our child. Oh sure, the paparazzi would have loved to have served that on everyone's breakfast table."

"I see," said Sarah, unmoved by his self-pity. "It wouldn't have been good for your career."

"My career? You don't know what you're talking about. I didn't care about that." He lit a cigarette.

"Did you ever consider for a moment that it wasn't a suicide. That someone might have killed Ada?"

"No. I'm afraid Ada's only enemy was herself. She was too wrapped up in her *art*. Stressed about the new exhibition and how that critic Bye and his cronies might ruin her. Wearing that stupid pendant, like it was all the rage, and bragging that she could kill herself at any moment like some of her friends had already done if life got too difficult."

"You are pathetically wrong about Ada. She didn't kill herself." Sarah stood up. "Somebody killed her and made it look like a suicide."

He raised his voice. "What are you talking about? There was a suicide note."

"The suicide note is a fake!" She was fed up with his ridiculous insinuations. "How do I know it wasn't you who faked it and signed her name to it, seeing that you've been hiding out and taking no responsibility for what happened?"

"Christ almighty, woman. I loved Ada. Why would I kill her?" He snuffed out his cigarette.

He was either a damn good actor or he was a deluded man. But hadn't she also thought Ada killed herself when Champlin had said she'd attempted suicide before? She stopped to consider her options and took a few deep breaths. In spite of what Robert had told her about Alain, she didn't think he killed Ada. His feelings were too raw to be false.

She sat down beside him on the bed. Her anger spent. She took the gold band off her finger and put it in his hand. It gleamed like hope even in the dreary light.

He held it between his fingers and looked at the engraving. "This was supposed to mark the beginning of our life together." He closed his hand over it. "Where did you find it?"

"It was in her pocket."

He gave out a short moan like a wounded animal. He tried to give it back to her, his cheeks moist.

"You keep it. Ada would've wanted you to have it."

Her own eyes welled up and she went over to the window to give them each a private moment with their grief.

When she returned and sat down, she saw that he was gripping Ada's ring. His knuckles white.

There was an insistent wrap at the door. Then another, louder. "Sarah, are you in there?"

She cursed. It was Robert looking for her.

The knob jiggled, but Alain had fortunately locked the door. Sarah put her finger to her lips. They waited a few minutes until it was quiet again. The banging at the door had stopped. Then she whispered, "Come to Ada's cottage tomorrow where we can talk."

"I can be there around nine o'clock."

"I've got to go," said Sarah. "Tomorrow you'll know everything and then you'll have to believe me."

# MONDAY, AUGUST 4

## —23—

Standing at the stove, waiting for the water to boil, Sarah's troubled thoughts turned back to the night before.

After she left Alain, she found an ill-tempered Robert waiting for her in the living room. Only a few guests remained. She'd wanted to tell him about what she'd learned from Alain, but he was furious with her for asking for his help and then disappearing. "I made a fool of myself searching for you."

"Sorry. I didn't think you would miss me. You seemed very occupied with Louise."

He ignored her sarcasm. "Where were you? Did you talk to Delacroix?"

"Yes, but I'd rather not talk about it."

On the ride back to the cottage, no woolen navy jacket was offered, no soft blankets placed over her knees. When they pulled up to the Sketch Box, he didn't get out or even say good night.

She sat down in the banquette and, sipping her brewed coffee, watched the sky transition from gray to blue. Robert was right to be angry with her. After all, she'd asked for his help and then saw Alain on her own. She hoped he would give her a chance to apologize.

Albert finished his breakfast and jumped up next to her. Seated on his haunches, he kept his keen eyes on her, his head tilted as if asking a question. Sarah scratched behind his floppy brown ears. "You're right, Albert. Why am I worried about Robert when I should be taking you for a walk?"

She finished her coffee and Albert ran to get his leash.

Even after a long walk on the beach, Albert didn't like being pulled away from his friends, but Sarah needed to get back before nine. She left Albert with Rosie, thinking he might bark at Alain, and she didn't want to broadcast their meeting.

Biding her time in the studio, she sat on a stool and was making some sketches when she heard three hard knocks on the alley door. She let Alain in and locked the new deadbolt behind him.

"I needed to take precautions," she said when he looked questioningly at the shiny new lock. "There was a break-in a few nights ago."

He looked around the studio. "Where's Albert? He's usually a pretty good watchdog."

"He certainly is. He's the one who chased away the burglar."

Alain was disappointed when she told him that she'd left Albert at Rosie's. He looked at Ada's paintings covering the wall and turned back to Sarah. "And speaking of 'sorry,' I want to apologize about last night. I wasn't myself. Since Ada died I've been drinking a bit too much."

She accepted his apology and they went through the studio into the kitchen where the inquest folder lay on the table.

She felt her own grief reflected in Alain's haggard face. He raked his long, silky hair behind his ears, then walked over to the kitchen sink and looked out at the seascape through the open window.

"Ada loved this view. Painted it all hours of the day. Loved the incoming fogbanks. 'Never the same lighting,' she'd say." He turned toward her and she saw Ada's gold band hanging from a short chain around his neck.

"Don't you find it sad to stay here?" he asked, rubbing the band. "I feel like I'm trespassing on her spirit."

"Sometimes. But I also feel she's here with me and it's consoling."
She walked over to the stove. "Would you like some coffee?"

"Please."

As she opened the cabinet to the right of the sink, he noticed a
bottle of whiskey she hadn't seen before. "I was told rum runners sail
down the coast from Canada and deliver crates of that stuff at night
to avoid the coast guard. The coast guard tries to enforce Prohibition
laws at sea, but if Ada has a bottle of that in her cupboard, I don't
think the coast guard is doing its job."

Uninterested in the provenance of Ada's whiskey, Sarah heated
the coffee and asked, "How did you and Ada meet?"

"It was a few years ago, in New York. I was working in a Broadway
play. One night some friends invited me to a gallery opening. It happened to be your sister's. Her career was just taking off and so was
mine. We liked each other right away but we were both so occupied
with our work that we only saw each other in short spurts." His lips
curved in a winsome smile. "But when we did the sparks were flying."
His joy was fleeting and she felt his grief return. Yet in that brief
moment she could imagine how good it must have been between Ada
and him.

She handed him a mug of coffee and poured one for herself.

"Later, I got an offer to go to Hollywood and star in a motion
picture and I moved to California. We stayed in touch, and after she
moved to Carmel she started to come down to Los Angeles on the
train whenever she had time. I came up here occasionally, but it was
a bit awkward. I was getting too well-known in Hollywood. I had to
stay at the La Playa to avoid the paparazzi."

"Was that really necessary?"

"We were being hounded by one guy in particular from *Photoplay*
magazine. He was prowling around looking for juicy stories and if
the journalists found out I was spending time here, with an equally
famous artist, it would have made our lives miserable." He scratched

his beard. "I have enough trouble with the gossip in Hollywood about the affairs I'm *not* having."

"Is that why you didn't tell the Jeffers?"

"Yes. And in hindsight I wished we had. It's been very awkward staying at their home without telling them the truth."

"I apologize if this sounds blunt, Alain, but you might have some information that will help me, or should I say help you and me, to find out who killed her."

"Okay. Go ahead."

"Did you come here for any other reason than to substitute for the original Pirate?"

He scratched his beard. "The truth is I've had a bad time of it since Ada's been gone. I've tried to blame her for what happened but it never made much sense—her killing herself. The Jeffers were good friends of Ada's and I wanted to know if they knew any reason for her suicide without letting them know we were engaged. When they told me how pleased they were that you were investigating her death, I was stunned. And quite honestly, I was worried if you found out I was her fiancé you might suspect me."

She took out the suicide note from the inquest folder. "You should look at this."

Alain read it and looked up at her curiously. "They reached a verdict of suicide based on this letter Katherine Mansfield wrote to her husband?"

"You know this quote?" asked Sarah, feeling a familial bond growing between them.

"Sure, I know it. Ada and I spoke about it. She was furious that Katherine's dying instructions were disregarded by her husband. John Murry went ahead and published everything. That's why she asked me to agree to a nuptial agreement. You were the only one she trusted to be the executor of her estate and quite honestly, I didn't think that was something I could handle or something I was interested in." He smiled, shyly. "I think she liked that about me. I was more interested in her than her paintings."

Sarah brought out her cigarettes and passed one to Alain, who lit hers first and then his own.

He got up and began quickly pacing back and forth across the kitchen floor as he did on the stage the night before, but there was far less room. Sarah asked him to sit back down, he was making her nervous.

She laid out her other evidence: The garnet stone from the burned journal; finding Ada's bicycle at Whalers Cove; Jeffers's eyewitness account; the planted weights in Ada's pockets; the cyanide-filled pendant that Ada would've swallowed if she had wanted to take her life, though Sarah would never use it as evidence.

"What a fool I've been," he said, "to ever think Ada would kill herself." He looked up at her, his face wrenched in pain. He laid his head on his arms.

Sarah waited a few minutes before she nudged him and he raised his head.

She picked up her pencil and opened her drawing pad to a blank page. "I know this is painful for you, but I need you to tell me everything that happened those last days you were with Ada."

"All right. If you think it'll help."

"First off, did you see her portraits while you were here?"

"Yes, the night before I left."

She wrote down *1–July 3: Alain last person to see portraits*

"I must confess at times I thought Ada loved her portraits more than me. She talked about them morning and night. Then the last night we were together, she put on that gorgeous silver-sequined gown. She said it was a dress rehearsal as she intended to wear it for the opening night of her gallery show in New York.

"You were wearing it last night. You scared the hell out of me when I saw you from the stage. For a moment, I thought you were her."

"I'm sorry. I didn't know."

"There's no reason why you would've." His face brightened as he told Sarah about his last evening with Ada. "We had much to celebrate. Our coming marriage. Our child. Her exhibition. I don't know much about art, but those paintings were terrific. I knew they were going to be a big hit for her. Have you seen them?"

"I wish. They're not here," said Sarah. "I think they might've been stolen."

"Do you think that's why she was killed? For the portraits?"

"That's one possibility. But there might be another motive."

Sarah took a deep breath and chose her words carefully thinking of the letter Ada had left for her in the sketch box, especially the final paragraph . . . *my past indiscretions might end up being the cause of my ruin.*

"I think Ada was involved with someone else before you. She had tried to end it. But he wouldn't hear of it. He insisted on seeing her the night of the fourth. He might have been the one who killed her."

His eyes flashed. "Why didn't she tell me? I would have understood. She didn't have to meet him on her own. I would've taken care of him."

That's probably why she didn't tell you, thought Sarah, remembering what Robert had said about Alain's bad temper.

"Before you left on the fourth was Ada acting strange?"

He scratched his beard again. "Not at first. After an early breakfast she said she wanted to write to you, tell you our wedding plans, and she went into the bedroom."

Sarah scribbled a second note. *2–Ada writes letter to me and hides it in her sketch box.*

"I stayed in the living room studying my role as Captain Hook in *Peter Pan.* As I said, we were going to begin production."

"Did anyone come by?"

He thought a moment. "Why yes. Her assistant, Sirena. I was

rather surprised to see her because Ada had told me she'd let her go after some kind of altercation with her and Paul deVrais.

"She let herself in with a key while I was rehearsing in the living room. She was holding an envelope and went right in to see Ada. It was only a few seconds later that she came back out and left without speaking to me. She seemed to be in a great hurry."

Sarah felt a sharp pain in her heart remembering the moment when the joyous tone in Ada's letter changed to dread. Gripping the pencil, she wrote *3–Sirena messenger of Ada's fate!!!*

Alain noticed her distress and asked if he had said something that upset her. She told him it was nothing and asked him to continue.

"Right after that, I felt Ada was trying to push me out the door. I figured she was just nervous about her own departure the next day and was worried about having enough time to send off the portraits to Crocker's gallery. I left soon after."

"What time was that?"

"It had to be around nine for me to get to Salinas in time to make my connection on the *Daylight* train to Los Angeles."

*4—Alain leaves in morning. Ada packs portraits before meeting former lover.*

He lit another cigarette and blew smoke out the open kitchen window. He then turned and looked up at the ticking wall clock. He glanced at Sarah with a worried look.

"I don't think I should go back to Los Angeles today. You're not safe here. Whoever killed Ada might come after you."

"I've considered that. But if Ada's killer was spying on her, he knows who you are. If he should see us together, he might feel threatened and leave town before we have enough evidence to arrest him. You should take that train."

"I don't know, Sarah."

"Don't worry," she attempted a smile. "Albert will let me know if I'm in danger."

He looked as unconvinced as she felt.

"I'll need you to come back and give your testimony when the inquest is reopened," she added. "It won't be pleasant. It'll probably come out that Ada was pregnant and that you were the father. If the press finds out, it could damage your career. You might even be a suspect."

"I don't care about that. I know that sounds hypocritical now, since it's the reason I didn't come back in the first place. But I'll do anything I can to help put her killer in the electric chair. Whoever he is, he deserves nothing less."

He looked up at the kitchen clock again. Then he scribbled a number down on her drawing pad. "This is the telephone number at the Beverly Hills Hotel where I'm staying. I'll give the hotel instructions to get hold of me on the film set if I'm not there when you call."

Sarah walked him through the studio to the alley door thinking it was better if he wasn't seen leaving the cottage. "I'm very happy to have met the man my sister was going to marry." Her sadness was palatable. "I only wish we'd met at your wedding." She reached out her hand, but he embraced her in a loving hug.

"Take care, Sarah. Call me if you need me and I'll take the next train out of Los Angeles. I promise."

She snapped the deadbolt shut as soon as he left. She should have felt safe knowing there were now two men very concerned for her safety. But Robert might never talk to her again and she'd just let Alain go.

# —24—

Feeling a strong urge to get out of the cottage and paint, Sarah tied a blank canvas to her sketch box and strapped the box on her back. She walked the red bicycle up to the top of Carmel Hill and coasted down on the main road to the Monterey Wharf. The fresh, salty air blended with the woodsy pines plus the speed of her swift descent gave her a much needed shot of pure bliss. If only it could last longer than a few seconds.

As she walked out onto the wharf, the sunshine sparkled like diamonds on the crystal blue bay. Japanese abalone divers were diving off their black and white skiffs into icy water.

Hansen's students sat on stools or stood painting at their easels, their smocks billowing in the coastal breeze. Sarah scanned the group for Sirena, wanting to ask her about the letter she delivered to Ada, but she didn't see her saffron coveralls. When she went down to the wharf hoping to find her at Hansen's class and didn't see her saffron coveralls, she felt an uneasiness as she looked out at the sea.

As calm as the bay's surface was today, Sarah was aware of the danger that lurked underneath. She felt the dark spirits waiting to yank her down under if she leaned too close.

She brought out tubes of paint and brushes and set up her sketch box on its tripod, propped a canvas on the easel and put her thumb up through the hole in the wooden palette to get a secure grip before blending any pigments.

Many of the abalone divers wore dark woolen jumpsuits and had brass diving helmets over their heads with air hoses attached to their mouths. The other divers she had seen at Whalers Cove were easily recognizable in their white cotton outerwear offering little protection against the numbing water. Sarah raised her brush to the canvas.

Hansen shouted encouragement, "Just paint. And don't stop." Responding to his command, Sarah threw her body into her paintbrush and covered the canvas with thick, short strokes, her head flitting back and forth from the diver to the canvas, as if she were watching a tennis match. This way she forgot everything but her canvas.

The oldest diver was standing up in the helm of his boat supervising the others. Sarah set her painterly eye upon him, but her abstract conception made the details of his figure almost indistinguishable. She swept her palette knife back and forth on the canvas, piling up layers of pigmented oils with as much determination as the divers bringing up abalone from down under and tossing their catch into waiting fishnets before diving back down again and again.

The communal whoops shouted by the divers every time they brought up an abalone from the sea cheered her on until she too felt satisfied with the results of her labors.

She was putting away her brushes when Hansen came over. He stood shoulder to shoulder with her and looked at her painting. "I see you've found your subject. Mr. Kassajara and his diving crew are an excellent choice."

Sarah laughed. "You weren't supposed to know it was Mr. Kassajara. I was being abstract."

He smiled. "And you are. Good work. I like the energy."

Hansen talked for a few minutes about the modernist movement in Paris and mentioned how it had affected his own work as a colorist. She asked if he knew why Sirena hadn't come to class. Had he heard from her? No.

He then asked Sarah if she'd ever seen Sirena's paintings.

"Yes I have. I was surprised how good they were."

"Me too. Her pictures portray a floating world all her own. Very personal. I don't know who's been teaching her, but her paintings are deceptively simple. They remind me a bit of Hiroshige and Hokusai's woodprints, but still her ideas are original. She will go far if she continues her studies."

Sarah told Hansen she hoped to paint with him again and was walking up the wharf, swinging her sketch box, carefully holding the wet canvas with her other hand, when she heard a voice over her right shoulder. "That's a beautiful box." She stopped, turned around, and saw Mr. Kassajara beaming at her.

"Hello, Mr. Kassajara. Nice to see you again."

"I often see painters' sketch boxes on the wharf," he continued, "but I've only seen one made of burled wood like that."

"Then you must have seen my sister's," said Sarah. "They were both made by the same French craftsman. Would you like to take a closer look?"

He sat down on a bench and set the sketch box on his lap. He pulled open the drawer and studied the brushes. "Miss Ada had brushes like this, too." He stroked his palm with a brush. His muscular, weathered hands reminded Sarah of Sirena's—callused from foraging for abalone in the underwater canyon.

She stopped herself from asking Mr. Kassajara if he knew where Sirena was. Instead she asked, "Do you paint?"

He grinned and shook his head no. "Your sister made a picture of me on this bench."

So Ada too had found synergy in this aristocratic man with gold-capped teeth and soulful eyes.

"Miss Ada saw beauty in all faces. All different kinds of beauty," he said as if he'd heard her thoughts.

She wondered where Ada had stored Mr. Kassajara's portrait. She hadn't seen it in the studio. Or had it too been stolen?

While they walked together toward her bike, Sarah thought what a shame it was she could not speak to Mr. Kassajara about his talented granddaughter. She wanted him to know she was going to help Sirena get a scholarship to an art school in Paris. She wanted him to know how sorry she was that his people were not treated fairly because of narrow-minded people's unwillingness to see the humanity in those who are different from them.

"Can we give you a lift?" asked Mr. Kassajara, pointing toward a truck at the end of the wharf. "We can pass through Carmel on our way home."

She let his crew put the bike and her sketch box in the back of the truck and wedged herself and the canvas between the driver and Mr. Kassajara on the bench in the front cab.

After dropping off her things at the cottage, she walked over to the lodge to pick up Albert, but as she reached for the knocker, the door swung open.

"I was just coming to get you," said Sirena, with a stricken look on her face.

"Why? What happened?"

"It's Rosie. I found her curled up on the parlor floor. I got Dr. Lewis to come and he revived her with smelling salts and gave her a tincture of laudanum and helped me get her into bed. I stayed with her and tried to get her to relax, but she wouldn't settle down until I promised to go and get you." She stopped to catch her breath. "Dr. Lewis will be back to check on her this evening. He's very worried about her weak heart and gave me instructions to not let *anyone* excite her. Promise me you won't talk about Ada." Sirena flashed a reproachful look at Sarah.

"You needn't worry about that," said Sarah as she squeezed past Sirena into the entry way. "I care about Rosie as much as you do. I'll stay with her until Dr. Lewis comes back and then you and I need to talk."

In Rosie's bedroom, several books of poetry were stacked on a side table next to an armchair. There was also a *Silver Sheet* pulp magazine with a melodramatic cover illustration of a desperate man holding an expiring woman in his arms. It was advertising a new motion picture, *Scars of Jealousy*. Not something Sarah would want to see.

Rosie lay sleeping, her glasses still perched on her nose. A book of Emily Dickinson's poetry still in her hand draped over the bed. Rosie's literary taste was such a contradiction, thought Sarah, taking the book before it fell on the floor.

Rosie groaned and half opened her eyes.

"Sarah, is that you?" she said, hoarsely.

"Yes, it's me, Rosie." She took her friend's hand and gently squeezed it. "Sirena told me you fainted. Are you feeling better?"

"Most embarrassing. I was looking out the window at the Sketch Box and . . ." Her eyes closed again.

"Rest, Rosie. We can talk later."

Her blue eyes opened wide and she pulled herself up on the pillows. "No, this can't wait. Your life is in danger."

"Dr. Lewis said you need to rest. Do you want me to ask him to come back?"

"No, I don't! He'll just give me another dose of that stuff he gives hysterical women, which I'm not."

Sarah put her hand on Rosie's forehead only to have it brushed away.

Rosie asked for water and cleared her throat. "This afternoon I was cleaning the bay window in the parlor when I felt a dark omen pass over me like a shadow. I looked out the window and saw the same fisherman in the brown stocking cap and orange jacket who ran away from your cottage earlier."

Her flushed face and nervous excitement worried Sarah. She started to get up to call the doctor when Rosie grabbed her hand.

"Stop looking at me like I've gone off the deep end and listen to what I have to say." Sarah sat down reluctantly. "He was the same fisherman I saw perched on a high rock when Albert led me to Ada's body on the beach. Albert started barking at him and I leaned down to quiet him. When I looked up again the fisherman was gone."

"Why didn't you tell me this before? Or the marshal?"

"I did tell him. He said if there had been such a man he would've seen him when he was walking toward me. I was in such a state at the time that I believed him and forgot about it. But today, when that ominous cloud crossed over me what I had seen came flooding back. I rushed to the door to go after the fisherman and fell over in a faint."

"Do you think it was Paul deVrais masquerading as a fisherman?"

"I don't know. His back was to me. But he was tall and broad-shouldered like him."

"And like hundreds of other men," said Sarah.

"But most men don't wear Portuguese fishing jackets. Nor do they disappear into thin air like that man on the beach. It was as if he flew away."

Now it was Sarah's turn to be excited. "Wait a minute, Rosie. You might have something. What if he had a powerboat tied behind the rocks? What if he wanted Ada to be found so it would look like a suicide, but was worried the tide would come in and drag her out so he let Albert go and waited behind the rock to be sure she was found? Then as soon as you and Albert arrived, he jumped into his powerboat and got away."

"By Jove, you're right. Good deduction work, Sarah." Rosie gave her a satisfied smile and folded her arms over her heaving chest. "We both deserve a wee glass of sherry. Don't you agree?"

"I don't think Dr. Lewis would agree. He'd tell you that what you need is a good night's sleep."

"Balderdash! Sherry is a far better potion than any doctor's tincture. Now do be a dear girl. You'll find the decanter in the cabinet on top of my wardrobe closet."

Sarah switched on Rosie's bed light and poured the sherry into thimble glasses.

"My, how that warms the cockles of my heart," said Rosie, after taking a sip. "Now I want to know about Alain Delacroix."

Rosie listened keenly to Sarah's account of her meeting with Alain, stopping her only once to ask her to pour another sherry.

When she was finished, Rosie said, "So that's why I never met him. La Playa was their hideaway."

Sarah then told her about Sirena delivering a message to Ada, which made her a suspect in Ada's murder.

"That poor lassie. If what you say is true, she's in more trouble than I ever imagined."

"I know," said Sarah, feeling as miserable.

The sherry did seem to be the perfect medicine for Rosie as she now settled down in her bed and closed her eyes. Sarah was just getting up to leave when she sat up again and clutched her heart.

"What is it?" said Sarah, alarmed.

"I know how he did it!"

"Rosie, don't you think you should get some rest?"

"No. This is too important. Just this morning I was reading a modern crime story. The detective used forensic evidence to prove the victim was strangled."

"I don't see what this has to do with Ada."

"When I found her on the beach, her shawl was wrapped around her neck. In the story I read, the murderer strangled his victim with a scarf and then submerged her body in a bathtub so it would look like she'd drowned herself. The detective solved the case when he learned from a forensic expert that it was possible to strangle someone with a soft cloth that leaves no marks. They eventually got a confession from the victim's boyfriend."

Ada's shawl used as a murder weapon was a grim possibility and Sarah sank back down in the chair, nervously kneading her own shawl between her fingers. It was one thing to solve murders while reading a mystery novel that had nothing to do with you personally, and quite another to actually take on the "burden of proof" when the victim is your sister.

Several agonizing minutes passed before she could let go of her shawl and smooth out its wrinkles. When she looked up, Rosie was asleep. Sarah took the empty glass from her limp hand, put it down on the bedside table, and slipped out.

Sarah was standing at Rosie's parlor window when Albert ran in with Sirena behind him. Sirena demanded to know why Sarah wasn't with Rosie.

"She's all right, Sirena. She's asleep."

Sirena slumped down on the couch and Sarah sat down next to her. "I missed you at Hansen's class today."

"I got a modeling job," she replied. "Besides, classes are too expensive. And what's the point? I'll never become a successful artist. I've got too many things going against me, so I might as well make money instead."

"I'm not sure Hansen was going to charge us anything or I would've loaned you the money."

"I don't need your charity, Sarah," she snapped. "I was doing very well before you came here and somehow I'll be doing very well after you're gone."

Sarah was stung by the girl's sudden venom and walked over to the window. She had hoped they could talk things over and find a solution but that didn't seem possible with Sirena slithering in and out of personalities like an actress forever recasting her role. She had gotten a lot of practice always pretending to be someone she wasn't so she wouldn't be caught for passing as white.

*You're going about this all wrong. Stop feeling sorry for the girl. There's no more time for being nice,* she heard Ada say as if she was standing beside her.

Sarah returned to the couch and sat on the edge with her eyes on Sirena. "I thought we were good friends, but good friends don't keep things from one another."

"I told you everything," said Sirena, almost hissing.

"No you haven't," said Sarah, her own anger rising. "But you're going to tell me now or I'll turn you over to the marshal and let him get the truth out of you."

Sirena was shocked but managed to snap back. "Sarah, I think you should go to the cottage, pack your things, and return to Paris."

"All right. I will."

"Really?"

"Yes. Once you tell me who gave you the message that you delivered to Ada on July fourth."

Sirena jumped up and glared down at Sarah like a tiger staring into the gun of a hunter. "Whoever told you that is a liar," she snarled. "The last time I saw Ada was on the first of July when she threw me out of her studio. You already know that. Why don't you believe me now?"

"Alain Delacroix was at the cottage when you came to see Ada. I want to know what was in that message and who wrote it."

Sirena started toward the door. Sarah grabbed her hand, pulled her back onto the couch, and stood over her, blocking her escape.

"Did you know my sister was pregnant?"

Sirena's face drained of color. Her eyes wildly looking for a way out. She leaped away from Sarah, ran to a corner and slid down its wall, wrapping her hands around her knees, her head down, moaning.

Sarah kneeled down in front of her. "You have to trust me, Sirena. You've gotten yourself in a load of trouble, but I can't help you unless you tell me who you're protecting and why."

"I can't do that," Sirena cried out. Her fear palpable. "I might not be able to save you the next time. Please, Sarah. Go back to Paris where you'll be safe."

Sarah was about to ask what she meant about not being able to save her the next time when the brass knocker followed by Albert's bark interrupted her. She rushed to the entryway to prevent Albert's barking from waking Rosie. It was Dr. Lewis. She asked him to come into the parlor and help her to calm Sirena with the excuse that she was overwrought about Rosie's illness and needed a sedative.

"Why, she was just here," said Sarah looking around the empty parlor the girl had escaped from.

The doctor was much more interested in seeing his real patient and headed down the hallway.

After examining Rosie, he whispered to Sarah, "Thank goodness her heartbeat is normal and so is her pulse. She's on the mend." He put his stethoscope back in his medical bag, clicked it shut, and turned off the bedside light. They tiptoed out.

In the entryway, Sarah said, "Thank you, Dr. Lewis, for taking such good care of her."

"She's a stubborn woman, but I'm quite fond of her just the same. Just don't tell her that." Dr. Lewis smiled, tipped his fedora, and left.

Worried about Sirena, Sarah ran upstairs to her bedroom but she wasn't there.

Sarah scribbled a note: *I'm sorry I upset you, but whoever you are protecting must be stopped. Together we can do it, but you have to trust me. Come to me, Sirena, let me help you.*

# TUESDAY, AUGUST 5
## —25—

Albert scratched at the kitchen door. Sarah let him in and he rewarded her with a thin rolled-up newspaper at her feet.

"You smart little dog. Was it Ada who taught you to fetch the paper or was it something you learned on your own?" It was the second time that he'd brought her the weekly *Pine Cone* newspaper.

Albert wagged his tail and Sarah gave him a milk bone.

She sat down in the nook with a plate of biscuits and jam and a mug of hot coffee. The newspaper had only six pages and they were mostly dedicated to goings-on about town—local art committee meetings, advertisements for the Pine Inn, the Hotel la Playa, Leidig's Market, and other small commercial enterprises. As she flipped through the pages she was drawn to an article about a new collection of Edith Wharton novellas that had just arrived at the Carmel Library. Next to it was an advertisement for a movie *A Woman of Paris,* directed and written by the comic actor Charles Chaplin, which was going to open at the local theater the following week.

On the following page she read about a photo exhibition of the famous photographer Edward Weston. The opening was tomorrow night. Her heart skipped a beat. Maybe she'd see Robert there. She immediately chastened herself for thinking about Robert when it was Sirena she should be worrying about.

Earlier she had telephoned the lodge only to be told the girl had gone out and didn't say when she'd be back. Sarah reached for her drawing pad to make a few quick sketches of the silhouetted pine trees in the morning mist and then went into the studio.

She was at her easel blending titanium white and cobalt blue on her palette when there was a knock. Albert barked and ran over to the alley door. Sarah hoped it was Sirena, but after she unbolted the door and pulled it open she saw it was Marshal Judd, bent down, inspecting the new deadlock. He lost his balance and stumbled inside. Albert sniffed his cowboy boots but found nothing of interest and returned to his nap under the easel.

To regain his dignity, he adjusted his cowboy hat, a bit oversized for such a short man, and stood up straight. "Charlie Murphy did an excellent job," he began. "No one will break through this door." There are no secrets in Carmel, thought Sarah.

"Is there a particular reason for your visit, marshal?"

He reached in his pocket, pulled out a folded sheet of paper and opened it. "I heard about your break-in and brought you a crime report to fill out. We're more accustomed to cattle rustlers than house thieves here in Carmel, so I'd like to lasso this vermin before he gets to burglarizing any more homes."

Sarah looked at the form. She had her suspicions that Sirena had something to do with the break-in, but she wasn't ready to hand her over to the law when she still hoped the girl would come to her with the truth. And whatever she was guilty of, Sirena wasn't *vermin*. She handed the form back. "Thank you, marshal, for coming by. It's true that the studio was broken into, but nothing was stolen and as you can see I've changed the door and the locks."

Ignoring the artwork leaning against the walls, he approached Ada's red bicycle. "Good lookin' bike. Surprised the thief didn't take that. Is it yours?"

Sarah considered her options and decided it would make more sense to befriend the marshal rather than alienate him by telling him to leave. If Sirena arrived, she could send him on his way.

"No. It's not mine. But come into the kitchen. I'll make some coffee and tell you whose bicycle it is."

Calculating the sitting space in the nook as too narrow for his girth, he brought over a stool and straddled it, putting his hands on the table as if he was riding his mare, Gertrude.

Sarah sat across from him while the coffee percolated.

"So, tell me," he said, "whose bike is it?"

"It was Ada's." Judd continued staring out the window as if he found the view far more interesting than the owner of a bicycle.

She hid her irritation and told him where she'd found it. With still no reaction, she said, "Don't you think it's a tiny bit interesting that my sister's bicycle was in the woods behind Whalers Cove when her body was found on River Beach?"

He shrugged. "How do you know she rode it that evening?"

"Remember your witness, Elizabeth Peake? She stated at the inquest that she saw Ada pedal by at eight o'clock on the evening of the fourth. Since then, another witness has come forward, Mrs. Cutcliffe. She actually spoke to Ada just before Elizabeth saw her ride off."

The marshal cleared his throat and took out his small notebook and stubby pencil from his fringed vest pocket. "Why didn't Mrs. Cutcliffe come forward with this information?"

"She left that same evening to go to the High Sierras with her husband. She didn't hear about Ada's death until she got back home a few days ago."

He looked at her, suspiciously. "Why have you been keeping this to yourself? Since you have this crazy idea that your sister was murdered, I'd think you'd have told me this right away."

"I was waiting until I gathered enough evidence to present my case to the District Attorney's office."

"Your case?" He scoffed. "Are you a detective now, Miss Cunnin'ham? Need I remind you there was a thorough investigation into the cause of your sister's death and the verdict was suicide. The inquest won't be reopened, in spite of any evidence you might have, unless I decide it should be, not the DA." He pointed at his badge. "So it's me you should talk to if there are any new developments."

Fortunately, the percolating coffee gave her an excuse to step away and collect herself before she said something she might regret.

She poured the coffee into two mugs and sat back down.

"Honestly, I didn't think you'd be interested in what I've learned about my sister's death, and it appears I'm right."

He heaped sugar in his coffee and gulped it down. "Anything that happens within my jurisdiction is of my interest, Miss Cunnin'ham." He turned to his notebook again. "So what else have you got?"

"Mr. Robinson Jeffers told me that on the fourth he saw through his binoculars a fisherman hauling in what he first thought was a heavy sack of fish, which seemed odd so late at night."

He took a pinch of snuff out of a small tin and sniffed it up each nostril. "I wouldn't believe anything that un-American pacifist says. And you shouldn't either. He's a very unreliable witness."

Sarah continued, undeterred. "Maybe her killer dumped the bike in the woods and then brought her body over to River Beach to make it look like a suicide?"

"I'd say you and Miss McCann have been reading too many crime magazines. Did anyone actually see her in Whalers Cove that night? And who is this *killer* you've concocted out of thin air? Let's stick to the facts, shall we? What we do know is your sister's body washed ashore on River Beach with weights in her pockets and she wrote a suicide note.

"If you have any *facts* to add to that, then I'm all ears." Sarah said nothing. "No? Well then, maybe we should ask Albert for his testimony seeing as he was with your sister that evening and is your only real witness."

Sarah saw she wasn't getting anywhere discussing her case, but she had one more card she wanted to play, if only to get a knee-jerk reaction.

"Marshal, as you already know, my sister was pregnant."

"And?"

"I've since learned that she was engaged to be married and I was able to track down her fiancé."

"And who would that be?"

"Alain Delacroix."

"What? You can't be serious. The famous actor?"

"Yes, that's him," she replied, casually, enjoying his astonishment. "I'd like to talk to him."

"But why?" she said, innocently. "As you said, the case is closed."

He stuffed his notebook in his vest pocket and stood up. "I'm the marshal here, Miss Cunnin'ham, and if Mr. Delacroix has any information concerning Miss Davenport's death, although I doubt it, my job is to know about it. Tell me where I can find him?"

"He's in Hollywood. He left yesterday. He had to get back to finish a motion picture."

His face turned the color of his bandana, scarlet. "You let him go without talking to me?"

"You were never interested in finding out who the father was. Why now?"

Sarah lit a cigarette and sat back in the nook, letting him stew before she said, "Mr. Delacroix promised to come back if there is a reopening of the inquest. I do not think he's a suspect. He has a legitimate alibi and why would he kill the woman who was carrying his child?" She took a drag from her cigarette before adding, "It's deVrais's alibi you should be checking on. Or what about finding the fisherman Miss McCann saw up on the rocks when she found Ada's body?"

"Miss McCann was hysterical at the time and Mr. deVrais has a solid alibi. He was on a train to San Francisco." He reached for his

ten-gallon hat and pushed it down on his forehead. "A final warning to you, Miss Cunnin'ham. If you find out anything else in your
so-called *investigation*, you tell me and not the D.A. And now I've got
important business to attend to."

Sarah poured the remnants of his coffee down the drain and
washed it. She took hers into the studio to work on Sirena's portrait.

# WEDNESDAY, AUGUST 6
## —26—

Rosie called to say that Sirena had telephoned the lodge. She didn't want Rosie to worry but she had been visiting her sick grandmother in San Juan Bautista. Sarah was relieved to know the girl was all right. She'd spent yesterday and today worrying about her and not even her work in the studio had helped the time go faster.

Albert watched Sarah get dressed for the Weston gallery opening, but then he realized he wasn't going with her and dropped his leash and curled up on his pillow with his back to her.

"I know I haven't been paying much attention to you, Albert. Walks too short. Tummy rubs too quick. I'll make it up to you, I promise. Once this is all over."

The road was barely visible in the approaching fogbank and she switched on her flashlight as she stumbled and cursed tripping over another knuckled oak root.

She reached Ninth Avenue and hastened her steps when she saw a petite figure moving through the mist wearing saffron-striped gypsy pants shining like tiger stripes in her flashlight's beam.

"Sirena!" she called out, running up to her.

The girl spun around. "Stop following me, Sarah!"

Sarah was not to be put off and grabbed Sirena's hand. "Come and sit down over here," she commanded and pulled the unwilling girl over to a bench half hidden under the canopy of a twisted cypress. "You can't run away from your troubles. You have too much to answer for. And if you're not going to be honest with me then I will have to turn you over to Marshal Judd. Is that what you want?"

Even in the dusky light, Sarah could see the fear in Sirena's eyes. She wanted to put her arms around her and protect her but she needed to know the truth. "Is your grandmother feeling better?"

Sirena stiffened. "So Rosie told you about my Portuguese grandmother and you probably know who my Japanese grandfather is too. I should've known not to trust her. Or Ada. Or any of you whites."

"That's not fair, Sirena. It's you we can't trust."

"So what do you think of this yellow monkey hanging on a limb." She held up her arms and scratched under her arms.

"Stop it, Sirena. I don't think of you that way. I too know what it's like to be different."

"Really?" she said with heavy sarcasm. "I don't think so. How could *you* possibly know how that feels? Oh yes, you suffer for being a woman striving to be accepted as an artist, but you don't have to suffer for being from a different race. You've never been confronted by someone telling you that you're not wanted because of your color? That you're only chance of succeeding as an artist is to risk passing for white?"

She started to get up and Sarah reached for her hand and pulled her back down.

"You're right, Sirena. I don't know how that feels, but I still want to help you."

"Would you really tell the marshal?"

"Of course not. Your secret is safe with me." Sarah brought out her cigarettes and offered one to Sirena.

"I'm a pretty good actress, aren't I?" said Sirena blowing a few smoke rings. "My people call it Asian power when you expend physical effort, sweat, and hard work to achieve something that is easily in reach if you have white privilege."

Sarah nodded and lit their cigarettes. "But it must be exhausting to always pretend you're someone you're not. To have to deny your grandfather when you see him in the street. And look at the trouble you're in because of it."

The tip of Sirena's cigarette turned fiery red as she took a deep drag. "I'm not in any trouble as long as you keep quiet."

"Oh c'mon, Sirena, why don't you give up this racial masquerade?"

Sirena stood up and glared down at her. "You can't be serious. Do you have any idea what would've happened to me if that snooty waiter at the Del Monte had known I was of a mixed race and was passing for white?"

"He would have asked you to leave?"

"No. He would have called the marshal and had me arrested right there in front of all of you pure white folk, and the immigration authorities would've had me deported to Japan where, I've never lived. That's the law in the land of the free. Ha!"

She retreated back into the shadows when two men passed by and politely tipped their hats.

After they were gone, Sarah reached out her hand and touched Sirena's arm. She was encouraged when the girl didn't pull away. "Please listen to me, Sirena. You're not to blame for trying to succeed as an artist by crossing the colored line. It's the bigoted people that exclude you that should be punished.

"Let me take you away from here, Sirena. Come back with me to Paris where you'll be free to be the artist you deserve to be."

Sirena slumped down on the bench, all the bravado gone. She looked at Sarah in disbelief. "Why would you do that?"

Sarah was actually as shocked as Sirena by her impulsive offer. But now that she'd made it, it didn't seem like such a bad idea. She was certain Sirena never meant to bring harm to Ada and if the girl told her who Ada's murderer was she could forgive her for her deceit.

They sat smoking in silence, their thoughts shrouded in the misty fog.

Sirena slipped her hand into Sarah's. Her voice weak. "I've done bad things, Sarah, much worse things than passing for white. I don't deserve your friendship or your generous offer."

"Believe me when I tell you that everything is going to be all right, but you have to trust me. Tell me who killed Ada and I'll have him arrested. I'll keep you out of it and then when I leave for Paris, you'll be on the train with me. I promise."

Sirena was about to say something when they heard, "Paris?" It was the two sisters, Hallie and Jeanette, appearing out of the mist. "Who's going to Paris? Can we go too?"

"Hello, girls," said Sarah. "No one's going to Paris right now. I was just telling Sirena how much I love living there."

She was suddenly aware of how many people were passing by on their way to the Edward Weston exhibit. Bits of conversations and laughter carried easily in the night air, even hushed conversations. She was certain Sirena would've told her the name of the murderer, if the sisters hadn't shown up, but now, as much as she wanted to know, it wasn't safe. She'd have to wait until they were alone.

She stood up and pulled a reluctant Sirena along with her. "Stay near me," she whispered.

With the sisters behind them, they turned the dark corner onto Monte Verde and the electric lights coming from the Art and Crafts Club cut through the fog. As they squeezed their way into the crowded foyer, they were separated.

Sarah was looking for Sirena when she bumped into Robert. An easy smile spread across his face when he saw her. He took her by the hand and drew her over to a corner of the room.

"I'm so glad you're here. I've been wanting to apologize for my behavior at the cast party, I—"

"No, Robert," said Sarah, "it's I who should apologize. It was rude of me to ask you to come and then run off."

"You said you spoke to Delacroix? Did you learn anything?"

"Yes. I was wrong about him. I know now that he loved my sister. He would never have hurt her."

"I wouldn't be so sure. Just because someone loves someone doesn't mean they're beyond hurting them. Even if by accident. I don't think you should see him again without me there."

"That won't be hard. He's gone back to Hollywood."

"Oh. Well that's even better. Is there anyone else you.suspect?"

"Ada's art dealer, but he has an alibi."

"Then what's next?"

She was about to tell him there might be a new suspect when Mac bumped into them. Robert put his arm around Sarah's shoulders and said, "Hello Mac, are you enjoying the show?"

"I'm thrilled to see Weston's photographs. His show is a smashing success."

As Robert ushered Sirena farther into the gallery he began speaking enthusiastically about Weston's photography, but an argument broke out between two photographers standing nearby. One was saying that Johan Hagemeyer's manipulated photographs weren't as honest as the natural photography of Edward Weston. Robert stepped in to defend his teacher's modern methods.

Sarah took the opportunity to slip away to find Sirena.

In a smaller gallery, Weston's earlier, less-known photographs were displayed. Sarah froze when she saw that the only other person in the room was Paul deVrais. His back was to her as he stood in front of a photograph of Whalers Cove.

She thought to leave but then decided it couldn't have been a better time to settle accounts. "I was just there the other day," she said, coming up behind him.

He turned around and said with displeasure. "It seems you've been rather busy in our little village, Miss Cunningham. Judd came to see me this afternoon about some new evidence. He felt obliged to ask me for the punched ticket the conductor gave me after I boarded the train to San Francisco. Unfortunately, I'd thrown it out, but I assured him the conductor would remember me, as I often take the evening train."

Sarah was pleased Judd had taken her investigation seriously. Probably her mention of the District Attorney getting involved kicked a spur in his side.

"I've also heard from my lawyer," continued deVrais. "He tells me the preliminary findings of the probate court show that you are, in fact, the sole beneficiary of Ada's estate and her executor. That's a serious responsibility for a young inexperienced woman like yourself, Miss Cunningham. You're lucky to have me to represent Ada's work and make the right decisions. In return, I will offer you the same fifty percent share that I gave Ada for any paintings sold. Under my expertise, you will become a very wealthy woman. You can live like a queen in Paris."

Sarah put her hands on her waist. "I'm sorry, Mr. deVrais, but I have my own plans for Ada's legacy and I won't be needing your services. In fact, it's very opportune that I saw you here tonight so I could tell you before you hear it from Mr. Peabody."

"Hear what?"

"You are to return all of Ada's artwork to me, including any paintings out on consignment."

"That's ridiculous. As I told you before, I never received a termination letter from Ada and therefore the contract is still valid. And it's valid in perpetuity, I might add."

Sarah leveled her eyes on her adversary. "Mr. deVrais, let me make this perfectly clear. If you insist on pursuing these false claims, I will have to resort to less pleasant ways to force you into compliance."

"My oh my, such strong language from such a pretty young lady." His grin faded. "Have you lost all sense of propriety? Women are not made to handle such matters. Let the men take care of this. I'll have L.G. talk to Peabody about any misunderstandings you might have." He turned to leave.

"Before you go, Mr. deVrais, I want to thank you for delivering *A Bleak Morning.* I had an authenticator in San Francisco verify its provenance." In truth the painting was actually still hidden in the loft above Ada's studio.

"He confirmed my suspicions. The painting is a forgery and so is the signature. You commissioned someone to paint *A Bleak Morning* and then you forged Ada's signature and tried to sell it."

He fidgeted with his shiny pink ascot. "You can't prove that. Sirena was the one who delivered the painting to me and she said it was Ada's. If Sirena forged the painting, she should be prosecuted, not me." Sarah blocked his path.

"Did you know that Ada kept a complete list of all the artwork given to you?" His eyes flashed like silver bullets, his hands tightened into fists as if he was ready to punch her, but she didn't wince.

"You may have burned other documents that might have incriminated you—I'll leave that up to the marshal to find out—but the inventory list was hidden in a safe place."

She didn't give him any time to think about her accusation.

"It's a detailed list, Mr. deVrais. It accounts for all the paintings in your vault and elsewhere. You've been rather busy since Ada's death. Several art collectors have recently bought her paintings. Others are hanging in galleries on consignment. In fact, I'm told there is a second painting of Ada's about to be hung at the Metropolitan."

"There's nothing unusual about that. It just shows I've done a very good job representing her work. All the more reason for you and I to forget our silly spats and work together to our mutual benefit."

"We have no future, Mr. deVrais. You have been selling these valuable works without sharing the profits with your artist. I'm told that's a criminal offense and can result in a jail sentence."

"You're crazy like your sister. What proof do you have?"

Sarah pulled proof out of thin air. Proof that could blow up in her face if she was wrong, but Ada had told her deVrais needed to get out of debt and might be exploiting her, so she took the chance.

"Ada's bank statements show that no deposits have been made to her account this year. Yet paintings have been sold during that time. It seems you were mishandling her affairs even before she died. But no worries, Mr. deVrais." She smiled. "We can sort this out *to our mutual benefit.*"

He glared at her, but she stood her ground and didn't flinch.

His slow clapping hands echoed in the small hollow room. "Congratulations, Miss Cunningham," he said with a mocking laugh. "I can see you're close to putting a noose around my neck." He paused. "What are your terms?"

"I want you to pay Ada's estate for any paintings you've sold. I want you to acknowledge the termination of your contract as Ada's dealer, and . . ." She paused. "I want you to leave Sirena alone."

His grin was malicious. "I'll give your offer serious consideration, Miss Cunningham. But don't think I'm going to make this easy for you. Your sister learned the hard way. I don't take well to being on the wrong end of the stick."

"Then I will see you in court, Mr. deVrais."

He stomped out of the gallery.

Sarah went to the ladies' room and splashed water on her over heated face. It was truly incredible that he didn't even try to deny her accusations. It had only been a hunch, but now she knew he actually had been embezzling money from Ada.

*Well done, Little Sis. I couldn't have done it better myself.* Sarah smiled into the mirror and painted her lips red.

Walking back into the main gallery, she saw Sirena at the exit and rushed over to her. "Don't go yet. We need to talk."

"Mr. deVrais just left," Sirena said nervously. "He was in quite a temper."

"Did he say anything to you?"

"Only that I'd better keep my mouth shut about *A Bleak Morning*. Does he know I told you?"

"No." She put her arm around Sirena. "You have nothing to worry about now. Mr. deVrais can't threaten you in Paris."

"So you're serious about taking me with you?"

"Very serious."

Sarah looked around the crowded gallery. "Did you see Robert? He was here a minute ago." She took Sirena's hand. "C'mon, let's go find him and tell him the good news."

Sirena let go of Sarah's hand. "I can't right now. Grandfather is picking me up at the lodge. I promised to stay with him tonight." She leaned toward Sarah. "Meet me at the Cove tomorrow morning at nine and I'll tell you everything. Make sure you're not followed."

Sirena was gone before Sarah could stop her.

"There you are," said Robert, showing up at her side. "I've been looking for you. If you're ready to go, I could give you a ride."

As he drove down the hill to the cottage, she leaned her head against his shoulder and felt a very welcome sense of peace knowing that tomorrow she'd know who had killed her sister and with a clear conscience could return to Paris in time for her exhibition.

When they got to the Sketch Box he came around to the passenger side to let her out and walked with her up onto the porch. She remembered the Canadian Club whiskey and invited him in for a nightcap. He said he'd love to but he had to catch the night train to San Francisco. A gallery had shown interest in exhibiting a series of his nature photographs and he was meeting with them in the morning.

"That's wonderful news, Robert," she said, hiding her own disappointment. "Will you be gone long?"

"Just a few days."

"I'd love to see your photographs when you come back."

"Then why don't you ride your bicycle over to Johan's studio

Sunday morning. We could look at my pictures and then take that boat ride I promised you."

"I'd love that," she said. "Where is Johan's cabin?"

He gave her directions, brushed a loose strand of hair off her forehead and ran his fingers down her face, stopping at her lips. She felt herself melting into him as his lips covered hers.

A very tender kiss was followed by a deeper, sensual one. She wrapped her arms around him under his jacket and drew herself into the heat of his body. When he finally let her go and said, "See you Sunday," his voice was raspy, his face flushed like hers.

# THURSDAY, AUGUST 7
## —27—

At eight o'clock the next morning Sarah was pedaling toward Whalers Cove. She remembered Sirena's warning and kept looking back to make sure no one was following her. Albert wanted to go with her, but it was an hour-long ride, and his weight would slow her down.

When she arrived at Whalers Cove, she saw a group of Japanese villagers huddled together on the shoreline. No one was working at the cannery. Judd's mare, Gertrude, was tied to a post by the cabin. Something was very wrong. She dropped the bicycle on the sand and ran toward the shore.

Marshal Judd was trying to get the villagers to leave, but no one was paying any attention to him, or they didn't understand him, as he was yelling at them in English. He looked at Sarah as she approached. "What are you doing here?"

"I came to meet—" she stopped. "What happened? Why is everyone here?"

"Bad business. The girl was already a goner when I got here. Shot through the chest and the bullet went straight through her heart. This old man seems to know her."

As she looked through an opening between the silent villagers, she saw Mr. Kassajara kneeling in the sand beside a crumpled body in a white diving suit. He turned and looked straight at her and nodded, his face ashen.

"The old man said she was an abalone diver," said Judd. "Though I can't imagine why a white girl would be out here at the Jap village diving for abalone."

"Oh no!" said Sarah as she dropped to her knees. A cry of rage and pain rose up from deep within and she pressed her hands over her mouth to stifle her scream. A small sob escaped.

He crouched down next to her. "Did you know her?"

She heard herself say, "She's my friend. Sirena Silver. She lives at Miss McCann's lodge."

"I'd like you to go tell Miss McCann what's happened and find out the girl's next of kin. We need to get in touch with her family right away. I'll come to the lodge and take down the details as soon as I can get away from here."

"But—" Sarah stopped herself and glanced at Mr. Kassajara tucking the blanket around his granddaughter's body. He should be the one to tell the marshal.

Sarah pedaled back to Carmel blinking away the stinging tears to see the road in front of her.

All of the lodgers were out when she got there, but Rosie was in the kitchen. Sarah choked when she said Sirena's name, but she managed to tell Rosie.

"Why that's impossible," said Rosie. "Her grandfather picked her up here last night. I'm sure she's with him. She can't be—dead?"

Sarah bit her bottom lip. "The marshal told me we should wait here until he comes to get the information on her next of kin. By then, I'm sure Mr. Kassajara will have told him the truth."

They sat in the parlor to wait. After a while, Sarah got up and offered to make a pot of tea, but Rosie said, "Let me do it. I need to keep busy or I'll burst out crying." She went into the kitchen and Sarah heard the water running as she filled the kettle.

When Judd finally arrived, Rosie took him upstairs to show him Sirena's room. Sarah went into the kitchen, put the teapot on the tray with cups and saucers and brought it into the parlor. She set it down on the coffee table and walked over to the open window to take in some air as she was feeling faint, her mind and body filled with terror. Had she caused Sirena's death?

When they came back downstairs, Rosie was out of breath. Sarah helped her sit down and gave her a heart pill with a glass of water. She could use one herself, her heart was beating so fast.

"I just can't get over that she grew up out *there*," said the marshal standing over them. "She doesn't look like one of them, though the old man, Kassajara, says he's her grandfather. He was the one who told me her parents both died in a diving accident and she moved to San Juan Bautista to live with her dad's parents. She came back here to study art and that's when she started passing for white. Why would she want to do a dumb thing like that? Why didn't she stay with her own kind and work in the cannery, or something like that, and keep out of trouble?"

*Because of people like you*, thought Sarah. *People who don't realize that Sirena and "her kind" should have the same rights and opportunities as you have.*

"Mr. Kassajara must be beside himself with the loss of his granddaughter," said Rosie.

Judd frowned. "So I'm not telling you anything you don't already know. And you still allowed her to live here with the other girls?"

Rosie looked him straight in the eye and said, "Yes I did, marshal, and I don't regret it."

He looked at her sternly and jotted down a note in his little book. "The old man said his daughter, Juniko, married a neighboring Portuguese boy by the name of Salvador Silvia. His parents were dairy farmers. The Silvias with a bunch of other aliens originally came over here from—" He flipped through his notebook.

"The Azores," interjected Rosie. "Their families settled here in the late eighteen-hundreds to hunt whales. That's why it's called Whalers

Cove. You can still see whale bones near the cabin, which they built to store their harpoons and sailing equipment. When the use of whale oil for heating became unpopular many of the Portuguese turned to dairy farming."

"Is that so?" he said, finally sitting down. Rosie poured the tea.

"Why would anyone want to kill that sweet child?"

"I think I have a pretty good idea."

Rosie knitted her brow and looked at him curiously.

"The rum runners. I'm almost sure they use the Cove to smuggle in their whiskey. I've suspected that for a long time and I think the Japs probably help them. Or they're paid off to keep quiet. I know there's a lot of shady things going on out there, but I've never been able to catch anyone.

"Let's say the girl needed money and put the screws on the smugglers and she threatened to tell all, unless they paid *her* off?"

Both women looked at each other as if to say, *Did he just say that? Is he out of his mind?*

"Are there any other possible motives, marshal?" asked Sarah. "I only knew Sirena a short while, but she didn't seem like the kind of girl you're suggesting."

"Then it was one of those yellow boys in her village," he said. "A jealous boyfriend maybe. The girl rejected him and he shot her."

Another incredulous look between the two women.

"Marshal, do the villagers even have guns?" she asked.

"I don't know," he said. "But you can be sure I'm gonna find out. We found a shell casing a short distance from where the girl was shot. The bullet that killed her was from a Colt .45 revolver. That shouldn't be too hard to find. I'll form a posse and search the village."

Sarah was shocked at his lack of empathy as he offhandedly described the weapon that killed Sirena and his ridiculous plan in one breath. It took her a moment before she said, "Isn't that rather rash? Don't you think that would upset Mr. Kassajara and the villagers?"

"I've got to find the killer, don't I?" he said, gulping down the rest of his tea. He slammed the cup down on the table. It was a miracle he didn't break it.

"Now, Miss Cunnin'ham, why don't you tell me what *you* were doin' out at Whalers Cove this morning?"

Sarah took a deep breath and let it out slowly, allowing herself time to consider her words carefully. "I saw Sirena last night at the Edward Weston exhibition and she invited me to come to the Cove this morning so she could show me how she dives for abalone." Sarah and Rosie's eyes met briefly and Rosie nodded and put her hand over Sarah's.

"I think you should know that Paul deVrais threatened Sirena last night at the gallery."

"And why would Mr. deVrais do that?" he said, reopening his notebook.

"You'll have to ask him."

"And you, Miss McCann," he said, pointing his stubby finger accusingly at Rosie. "You're in a bit of trouble here. You consider yourself an expert on immigration so you must know the laws about harboring a non-citizen. You should have reported that mixed breed to the immigration authorities rather than letting her pass as one of us."

Judd closed his notebook, stood up, and stuffed it in his vest pocket just below his six-pointed badge. "But I'll have to deal with you later. Right now, I've got to get back to the Cove and find the thug who shot her."

He tipped his cowboy hat, "Good day, ladies."

After hearing the front door slam shut, Rosie stopped rubbing her pearls and folded her arms over her chest. "What an insufferable man. Did Sirena tell you who wrote the letter she delivered to Ada?"

"No," said Sarah. "She was going to tell me this morning but someone stopped her before I got there."

Rosie pushed away her teacup. "Well, we're not going to figure out who that was by sipping tea. We've got work to do, Sarah. And right now Marshal Judd is our biggest problem."

"Why do you say that?"

"You heard him. He's going to send a search party into the Japanese village to find Sirena's killer. Think what that might trigger, if word gets out that a murderer might be hiding out at Whalers Cove. The white folks could get into a frenzy and turn into a wild mob."

Sarah started for the door. "You're right, Rosie. Let's go."

"Okay, but where?"

"We've got to speak to Mr Peabody."

# FRIDAY, AUGUST 8
## —28—

M r. Peabody had done as they'd asked and convinced the District
Attorney to stop the marshal from searching or arresting anyone
in Whalers Cove without a warrant. He also ordered him to keep
quiet about his investigation.

Sarah and Rosie were sitting solemnly at the banquette in Ada's
kitchen when the cowbell clanged and a startled look passed between
them.

Sarah went to the door and brought back into the kitchen Tajuro
Watanabe, the young diver she met at Whalers Cove. He'd come with
an invitation from Mr. Kassajara to attend Sirena's funeral service
that afternoon at the Japanese temple in Monterey.

Sarah told him they would certainly come and she asked after
Mr. Kassajara. "He's doing his best," said Tajuro. "Making plans for
Sirena's wake and funeral has kept away his sadness. Last night, his
family and their friends sat *tsuya* for Sirena—"

They gave him a questioning look.

"It's a vigil, passing the night watching over her body lit by only
one candle to keep the bad spirits from finding her. The Silvias came
from San Juan Bautista to join in the vigil.

"This afternoon's funeral is the Buddhist ceremony of departure,"
Tajuro explained. "Sirena will be given a new name, Shizuko, to prevent her spirit's return from the afterlife when her name is spoken
by the living. Seven days after the funeral, there will be a *shonanoka*

celebration, a celebration of Shizuko's future life in the land of the dead. We say *Namu amida butsu*—thank you to the Buddha— because Sirena's departure helps us to appreciate and honor our own lives here in the present. Her ashes are spread and then carried by the wind to the afterlife." He paused. "It's a happy moment we all share."

Tajuro bowed and when he looked up his eyes met theirs. He had spoken with little emotion but the sadness in his eyes expressed his unspoken grief.

"Do you know where our temple is in Monterey?" he asked.

"Yes, I do," said Rosie. The young man bowed again and left.

Rosie told Sarah that Tajuro had attended her English classes with Sirena and she often saw them playing together as young children.

Now she understood why Sirena thought a memorial service for Ada was so important. Sirena wanted Ada to have a happy afterlife.

Sarah was very moved by the spiritual concepts behind the Japanese rites of passage, and as much as she was grieving the loss of her friend, she found comfort in chanting *Namu amida butsu* to herself.

That afternoon, Rosie and Sarah took the bus to Monterey, walked to the Japanese Association, and waited at the steps with the other mourners. As they entered, they were given white gardenias, the traditional color of sorrow. The austere room was decorated with symbolic Japanese flags and calligraphy scrolls. The Japanese from Whalers Cove and other Japanese communities filled the rows of folding chairs in front of a raised stage.

After a while they began filing out of their rows, one row at a time, and walking down the center aisle to place the gardenias in Sirena's open casket. When Sarah's turn came, she hesitated. She didn't want to see her beautiful young friend lying there cold and motionless. But Rosie whispered that it would be disrespectful not to participate.

As she reached the casket she drew in her breath and stifled an involuntary cry. Sirena was dressed in a white kimono, very different attire from her usual saffron coveralls or gypsy pants. A garland of white lilies around her head and shoulders. Her face powdered white. Her lips painted carmine red.

A sable paintbrush, the one she'd given her as a present, was in her right hand, an abalone shell was in her left hand. Favorite possessions to take with her into the afterlife.

Sarah felt her legs collapsing and her hand shaking as she placed her bouquet near Sirena's silent heart. Rosie was next to her and took her arm to steady her as they stepped back. The other mourners shifted to make room for them as they walked back down the center aisle to their seats. As they sat down, Sarah bowed her head and took the handkerchief Rosie offered her.

Wearing a black silk jacket, Mr. Kassajara then led the ceremony. As he chanted a Sutra prayer over the casket the sound of his voice soothed Sarah and a sense of peace flowed through her wounded soul. A stick of sweet-smelling incense was handed to her and she prayed for Sirena.

At the end of the ceremony, they followed the casket out of the temple and stood by as it was lifted by Tajuro and the other pall-bearers into the back of a horse-drawn wagon and Sirena began her journey to the crematorium and the afterlife.

Sarah thought about what Tajuro had said—the second service for the dead was given to help those who were left behind. It was given to help them continue on their own journeys through life. Sarah felt that Sirena's crossing into the afterlife was like an awakening of her own spirituality on Earth.

An idea formed in her mind and she looked for Mr. Kassajara. She spotted him on the lawn. A line of mourners were stopping to say a few words, bowing, and then moving on.

Sarah joined the queue and when it was her turn, he thanked her for coming and then lowered his head for several moments as she spoke quietly to him. When she was finished, he met her eyes and they both smiled.

"I like your idea very much," he said. "And yes, we will honor both Ada and Sirena at the *shonanoka* celebration."


Rosie and Sarah climbed the stairs to Sirena's bedroom to gather her belongings to give to her grandfather.

Quietly and carefully, they folded Sirena's few pieces of clothing and laid them in a box.

When they were finished, Sarah looked around and asked, "Where is her sketch box? And where are her paintings? She's been studying for a year but there are no paintings here and no drawings either."

"I remember she asked me once if she could use the attic," said Rosie. "Maybe she kept them up there."

They opened a door at the end of the hallway and climbed the narrow wooden stairs.

There was a tiny garret just large enough for a stool, an easel and a worktable. "Saints alive!" said Rosie. Sirena's paint-stained sketch box was on the worktable beside an oil lamp and several drawings. A circular window under the peaked gable of the roof offered a bird's-eye view of the ocean and the only natural light.

"Sirena must have been up here painting by the light of that lamp when everyone else was sleeping," said Rosie. "And I never knew it."

Sarah held up a Japanese woodprint and a copy that Sirena had made on canvas. "There aren't any teachers here in Monterey who could teach her how to paint like this. She had to have taught herself. She hid her work because she was afraid that painting in the Japanese style would expose her racial identity."

"She was so alone in this world," said Rosie. "I bet no one is excluded in the afterlife because of their color."

"She wasn't alone," said Sarah, looking at the woodprints lining the wall of traditionally dressed women and children walking on bridges or having picnics by a lake or looking up into a starry sky. "She created her own community up here, closer to the sky."

Sarah sat on the stool and studied the painting that was on the easel. "Armin Hansen was right," she said.

"Right about what?" asked Rosie.

"He told me Sirena created a floating world all her own, a very personal world. Look how she's used the view from her window as her subject. She cropped it to show gnarled, black tree branches crossing her canvas, with the spaces in-between filled with the indigo blue of the sea. It's flat without shadowing or perspective. Simple but profound.

"I felt the same sense of peace and serenity when Mr. Kassajara was chanting today at the service."

"Sarah, come look at this," said Rosie, standing next to a painting on the wall near the far corner. "Isn't this Mr. Kassajara?"

"Yes it is. And my sister painted it." No, she would not cry, not now. She took it off the wall. "Ada and Sirena would both want Mr. Kassajara to have it."

They left the garret and went down the squeaky stairs. At the entryway, Sarah wrapped her arms around Rosie and gave her a heartfelt hug.

Albert was anxiously waiting for her at the Sketch Box. She curled up on the couch and sobbed for the loss of her sister and now Sirena. Albert nuzzled against her, comforting her through her spasms of grief until they were spent.

# SATURDAY, AUGUST 9

## —29—

Sarah felt the gentleness of Robert's hand on her face and pressed against its warmth, but all she got was the touch of Albert's cold nose. She woke up and a disenchanted Albert jumped off the bed.

It wasn't just Robert's kiss she was wanting. It was his reassurance that Sirena's death wasn't her fault. She couldn't stop thinking that Ada's killer somehow found out Sirena was going to betray him and that's why he killed her before Sarah got to Whalers Cove.

She took Albert for a long walk on the beach and didn't return until late afternoon. It gave her time to go over the last days leading up to Sirena's murder. She decided that if she was in any way responsible it was failing to find Ada's killer before he killed Sirena.

Ada's voice spoke to her as it had when she was lost in the Maze at the Del Monte. *You will find your way. Just keep going.*

Sarah returned to the studio, hoping to escape her sadness, but she only felt worse looking through the few studies she'd made of Sirena's portrait. The first one was the most representational, a portrait of a young girl with opalescent eyes. She would give this painting to Mr. Kassajara.

She wasn't satisfied with the other studies and wanted to try something completely new. An abstract improvisation, or as Armin Hansen instructed his students, "Just paint."

There were several similarly sized blank canvases stacked against the wall and she pulled out one from the back for good luck. As she began to prep the canvas with a coat of white primer, the surface rippled. *How curious.* Ada was always so careful. She always stretched her canvases flat.

Sarah examined the surface from all angles. There were several more ripples. Puzzled, she turned it over to check that the nails gripping the stretched canvas were secure in their frame. Looking closer, she saw that there were actually two overlapping canvases.

Using a small claw hammer, she slowly pried out all the nails on the four sides of the frame that held down the outer canvas. Then she turned the frame over and carefully peeled off the outer canvas to see what was underneath.

The sea-gray eyes of Robert Pierce were as startled as she was.

He was posing in the stern of an anchored schooner in Whalers Cove. *Ocean Queen* was painted in red on the stern. She looked at the bottom right corner. It was signed *A.B. Davenport.*

The initial shock was immediately replaced with confusion. Ada knew Robert? And she knew him well enough to paint his portrait? But then . . . Robert knew Ada. And he knew her well enough to pose for her. On their picnic, when Sarah had tried to sketch his face he had turned away and said he didn't want her to "capture his soul." Well, Ada had succeeded where Sarah had failed.

Her face reddened as her confusion changed to rage. She'd fallen for him like a silly schoolgirl. "You have a lot to answer for, Mr. Pierce." She couldn't bear to look at him and dropped his portrait face down onto the floor.

She pulled off her smock, scooped up Albert, and grabbed the bike. Minutes later she was pedaling up Eighth Avenue with Albert in the front basket. It wasn't until she turned right on Mountain View and pedaled for a few more minutes that she saw a rough sign and put on the brakes. Hagemeyer's name was carved into a shingle nailed to a tree trunk. Above his name was a black arrow pointing down a trail leading into a dense pine forest.

She jumped off and strode down the trail with the bike, Albert still in the basket. The tall pines blocked out most of the daylight but she wasn't going to let her fear of the dark stop her from confronting Robert.

A rustic redwood cabin came into view. She took Albert out of the basket and put him on the ground but he whined and cowered. She bent down and patted his head reassuringly, "It's all right Albert. This won't take long." She put him down on the porch and tied his leash around a post.

"Robert?" she called out. No answer. The door was unlocked and she stepped inside. There were a few pieces of roughly made furniture and a stone fireplace. She hardly noticed. It was the eight-by-ten-inch black-and-white photographs pinned to the wall across the room that pulled her forward.

Her eyes were first drawn to several photographs of herself kissing the tree at Cypress Point. Then later at the wharf when she asked Robert to stop. She'd teased him about capturing her soul and he'd done just that. *What a stupid fool I've been.*

Next to the photographs of her was a series of photographs of Sirena modeling in front of the Whalers Cove cabin. Sirena alive. Sarah could hear her laughter as she flirted with the eye of the camera. Robert's eye.

Farther down the wall hung a white sheet. She yanked it off. Underneath was a large glossy pin-up of her sister lounging in a low-cut bathing suit on the *Ocean Queen*. Her lips puckering at the unseen photographer.

Albert's high-pitch howl made her rush to the door where she bumped into Robert coming in. "What happened to Albert?" she cried out. "Where is he?"

"Calm down, Sarah. He broke his leash and I was afraid he'd run off so I put him in the toolshed."

Sarah stared at the handsome face that Ada had rendered so

perfectly with the strokes of a paintbrush. The portrait came forward to embrace her but she pushed Robert away. He looked surprised, even hurt. "What's wrong, Sarah?"

"I saw Ada's portrait of you."

"So that's why you're here." He seemed unaffected by her discovery. "I thought it was because you couldn't wait until tomorrow to see me. Where did you find it? I looked everywhere."

"Ada hid it under a blank canvas," she said, gulping down the rising panic in her voice. She'd felt so smug, so smart and confident when she told Rosie that it would be so like Ada to make a mistake with a handsome, charismatic man. And here she'd done the exact same thing. And with all the evidence in front of her she was still hoping for some kind of explanation that would prove him innocent.

"Such a very clever woman your sister was." He glanced over her shoulder at the pin-up. "And so incredibly beautiful." He turned back to Sarah and touched her face. She backed against the wall. "You're so like her. I thought she'd come back from the dead when I saw you wearing that ridiculous peacock hat."

"Where did you see me wearing her hat?"

"You wore it to the Jeffers party and then again at the Del Monte Gallery. I had to keep a watch on you. Make sure you didn't cause any trouble." His voice was smooth, flawless, without emotion.

Her heart thumped wildly when he closed the door and locked it.

"Please, Robert, let me go."

"Why the hurry, Sarah? I was just developing some pictures to show you tomorrow. But why wait?"

He gripped her hand and pulled her across the living room and into a darkroom, a room barely large enough for two people. The only light was a reddish-brown bulb hanging over the sink. The stench of vinegar burned her nose and made her nauseous.

Three headshots of Ada, Sirena, and herself had been clipped to a metal wire and hung up to dry. Their unblinking eyes were frozen in time. He had taken their lives and she was next.

Robert's breath was hot on her neck as he put his hands on her shoulders and pushed her toward the sink. "I'm a good photographer, don't you think?" he said in a soft, droning voice. She was so close to the images they looked blurred. She breathed in the vinegar dripping from their glossy surfaces. Her eyes burned.

"I tried to convince you that Hollywood pansy Alain Delacroix killed her but instead he charmed you, just like he charmed your sister."

A beaker labeled Acetic Acid over a skull-and-crossbones was on the edge of the sink. If she could just distract him long enough to get hold of it. She forced herself to turn around and face him. "How did you get Ada to come to Whalers Cove that night?"

"I told her if she didn't bring me my portrait I'd tell her *fiancé* that she and I were still lovers and the child she was carrying was mine. Not his."

Sarah felt bile rising up from her stomach and swallowed it down. She fumbled behind her for the beaker, but she only pushed it farther out of reach.

"Like old times, she motored out with me to the *Ocean Queen*. I waited until we were aboard before I asked her why she hadn't brought the portrait. She pleaded with me to let her keep it until after her damn exhibition. And when I insisted that we'd have to go back and get it, she got angry."

"Why would you care if she showed it?"

"The coast guard knows the *Ocean Queen* is a Canadian schooner transporting crates of liquor. My liquor. They've been looking for it, but we've managed to keep them out of Whalers Cove by greasing a few pockets, like that marshal of yours. But if someone in the coast guard saw a painting of me onboard the *Ocean Queen*, my cover would be blown."

The reddish-brown glow of the overhead light bulb made the rum runner's face grotesque, a sickly orange. A monster.

Behind her back, she stretched her fingers and barely touched the beaker. While she inched it forward, she heard Ada. *Be patient, Little Sis, you'll only have one chance.*

"Is that why you killed her? Because of your portrait?"

"I told you, Sarah, it was an accident. She came at me like a bear-cat, flailing her arms, clawing me and screaming. The coast guard patrols at night. They would've heard her.

"When she ran to the stern I chased after her, but before I could reach her, she tripped on a cable and fell overboard. I dived in after her and got hold of her shawl and tried to muffle her screams. I didn't mean to hurt her, Sarah. You believe me, don't you?"

"Then why not report it as an accident? Why take her body to River Beach?" she asked, finally getting her hand around the beaker.

"I couldn't take that chance. If I was arrested they'd find out I was a rum runner with a long record and hang me. But if they found her body on River Beach no one would come snooping around Whalers Cove and bust my operation. I left her on River Beach and motored over to Carmel Bay.

"I used her key to get into the cottage and set up the suicide note. Don't you think the vase of flowers was a nice touch? Something Ada would've done if she'd really planned to kill herself." He sneered. "It certainly convinced that dressed-up cowboy, Judd. But you're smarter than him, aren't you Sarah?"

She didn't answer.

"If only I'd found that damn portrait before you did, you would've never known it was me. When I came back later to look again, you'd moved in and that mutt ran me off. A shame you found it. I was so enjoying our romance."

She gripped the beaker. "And Sirena? How did she get involved?"

"She knew about Ada and me. And when she heard Ada was dead, she confronted me. I told her it was an accident, but she said I had to turn myself in. She kept insisting until I told her if I was arrested, I'd lie to the coast guard and say her grandfather and those other yellow monkeys distributed my whiskey and they killed Ada when she threatened to expose them to the coast guard. When I told her I put their diving stones in Ada's pockets so the marshal would believe my story, she promised to keep her mouth shut.

"That is until you showed up and started snooping around. I told Sirena to convince you that Ada killed herself, and when that didn't work I told her to arrange your drowning. And then what does that fool do? She saves you! I watched the whole circus. The two of you laughing on the beach like you were the best of friends."

"But why kill her?"

"You didn't see me, but I was behind an easel displaying a Weston photograph when Sirena asked you to meet her at Whalers Cove. After I dropped you off, I drove out there. Her white diving suit was an easy target at night."

Sarah swung her arm around and threw the acid in his face. He screamed in pain and grabbed a rag to wipe it off. She opened the darkroom door and ran across the living room. He stumbled after her, squinting and rubbing his eyes. She was struggling to get the door unlocked when he came up from behind and dragged her back into the darkroom. He twisted her arm and pressed a wet cloth over her mouth. She felt herself dropping into the abyss.


When she woke up, she was groggy and her head was throbbing. In the moonlight she saw that she was in the hull of a powerboat, water lapping against its wooden sides. She struggled to stand up but her hands were tied behind her back. Her mouth gagged and taped. The face of the full moon looked down upon her without pity.

She propped herself up against the engine and saw that the boat was beached under the rocky promontory at Whalers Cove. The golden lights of the cottages looked down on her but the villagers were too far away to hear her muffled cries for help. She struggled to get up again.

"Here let me—" said Robert, jumping into the boat. He leaned down and pulled her up to an awkward sitting position. He was wearing an orange fisherman's jacket.

"You're shaking," he said, seemingly concerned. He tucked a blanket over her legs as he had done in his Ford coupe. It gave her little warmth or comfort.

"Sorry you had to wait so long. I had to clean out the cabin and prepare the *Ocean Queen* for my long voyage back to Canada." She winced. "Don't worry. You're still going to have that boat ride I promised you."

She struggled to pull her hands out of the rope but the knots were too tight and they cut into her skin.

Suddenly she heard Albert's bark over running footsteps. A torch lit the face of Mr. Kassajara. "Let her go," he shouted as he drew nearer.

Robert jumped out of the boat with his revolver raised. Albert clamped his teeth on his leg. Robert yelled and dropped the gun. Mr. Kassajara locked his arms around Robert. They scuffled. Albert went after his leg again, but Robert kicked him and he yelped and fell down.

Robert punched the face of the older man. He collapsed on the sand next to Albert. Neither got up. Robert returned to the boat and started pushing it out into the cove.

From over Robert's shoulder, she saw Mr. Kassajara come after Robert from behind. His arms raised in the air and wailed like a banshee. A giant abalone shell gleamed in the moonlight before it came down with a dull thud on Robert's head. He groaned and fell over in the water.

Mr. Kassajara lifted the shell to strike him again, but stopped when he saw the current was pulling the boat out to sea with Sarah banging and kicking against its hull. He dropped his weapon, dove into the water, and pulled the boat back to shore.

He was starting to untie Sarah's arms when Robert came up from behind him and cracked Mr. Kassajara over the head with the butt of his revolver. Robert climbed back into the boat, revved up the motor, and headed for the *Ocean Queen*.

When they reached the schooner, Robert cut the motor, untied the rope around her wrists and ordered her to climb up the ladder. Onboard, he quickly tied her hands and her feet and sat her down on the deck next to the pilot house that he went inside. She could hear him calling his crew on the radio. They were to wait for him beyond the International line where they were safe from the coast guard. He would be joining them soon.

In his hurry, her ropes were loosely tied and she was able to squeeze one hand free and then the other. She untied her feet, tore the gag from her mouth and crept up the steps of the pilot house. The blue sheen of his revolver was sticking out of the holster he'd hung on a hook.

Her rage against this man who had killed her sister and who had probably used this very gun to kill Sirena and who had left Mr. Kassajara and Albert wounded or dead on the beach made her reckless. She pulled the gun out of its holster "Raise your hands or I'll shoot," she said, sticking the gun in his back.

He laughed. "C'mon Sarah, I don't have time to play now. Put that gun down."

Off in the distance the engine of a powerboat could be heard.

Robert cursed, "Damn, it's the coast guard."

Sarah ran out on the deck to call out to them and Robert chased after her. They struggled with the revolver. It went off and the explosion burst into the sky. The gun fell, clattered down on the deck, and slid out of reach.

Robert rushed for her again but his eyes were still blurred from the acid and he tripped on the anchor line, fell forward, and hit his head. He staggered up, blood dripping from a cut on his forehead.

She ran to the bow. A painted wooden sculpture of a woman gleamed in the moonlight. She crawled out onto the figurehead and hung over the waves lapping against the ship's hull.

Her hands began to slip on the damp wood and she hugged her arms around the woman's neck and tightened her legs around her torso. If she could just hold on until the coast guard got there.

Robert called from the deck. "C'mon Sarah, stop playing hide and seek with me. Where are you?"

The noise of racing engines became louder and suddenly search-lights lit up the *Ocean Queen*. It panned over Sarah's body clinging to the figurehead. Robert saw her in the lights and began to crawl toward her. She pulled herself farther out and gripped her hands on the long tresses. Robert aimed his revolver at Sarah and pulled the trigger but the bullet missed her.

Several more gunshots were fired from the coast guard's boat. Robert's head snapped back and he fell overboard. Sarah hung on to the figurehead and watched as the orange jacket sank, dragging him down under.

Sarah crawled off the figurehead just as the searchlights were pan-ning across the *Ocean Queen*. Afraid of getting shot, she ran to the stern just as Mr. Kassajara was climbing up the ladder onto the deck.

Her teeth were chattering and her voice was hoarse. "Is Albert all right?"

"Yes. He's waiting for you on the beach."

Mr. Kassajara took her hand and helped her over the stern and down the ladder into his waiting skiff below.

They had just reached the shore when Marshal Judd rushed up and shined his flashlight in their eyes. With his other hand, he pointed his gun at Mr. Kassajara. "Freeze!"

Albert snarled and Sarah cried out, "Put that down. He's not the one you want."

Judd dropped his arm. Sarah picked up Albert and held him tightly.

"What's going on here? Someone reported a rum runner. Where is he?"

"Out there," said Mr. Kassajara. More boats had arrived and Robert's schooner was ablaze under the searchlights. Uniformed men were climbing aboard like black spiders.

"Who called the coast guard?" said Judd. "This is my jurisdiction."

Without answering, Mr. Kassajara put an arm around Sarah's waist and walked her up the beach to his truck parked next to the old cabin. Judd stood by, bewildered and speechless.

A black police wagon with the gold U.S. Coast Guard emblem on the door pulled up and several men jumped out and rushed down to the shore. They ignored the tall, young woman holding a small, scruffy dog in one arm, her other arm around a short, old man.

# —30—

Rosie was waiting for them at the lodge. She put her arm around Sarah and brought her to the couch. Mr. Kassajara knelt in front of the fireplace and started stoking it.

Once Rosie was certain Sarah wasn't hurt, she looked back and forth from one to the other. "Well, don't keep me in suspense, what happened?"

Mr. Kassajara told her about the fight on the beach and that Robert had been killed by the coast guard. While he was talking, Sarah felt her eyes closing. They didn't open again until she heard Rosie exclaim, "Bejeezus. It's a miracle you're both alive."

Still chilled, Sarah sat on the footstool by the now-roaring fire. Her throat stung from the ether Robert had drugged her with. Rosie poured her a glass of water from a pitcher. Mr. Kassajara sat on the footstool across from her.

Albert put his paws on Sarah's knee, cocked his head, and looked at her until she picked him up.

She turned to Mr. Kassajara. "How did you know where to find me?"

"I came to the Sketch Box earlier this evening," said Mr. Kassajara. "I wanted to tell you it was the rum runner who killed my granddaughter and probably your sister, too. I wanted you to go with me to the marshal with what I knew. The front door of the cottage was wide open. I called out but no answer. I looked inside for you and then I went into the studio. I turned over the canvas on the floor and was startled to see the rum runner's portrait."

"So all this time you knew about Robert?" asked Rosie.

He nodded. "He kept his schooner anchored in our cove. That's how Sirena met him. She often dived at night for abalone and he saw her out diving and asked her to model for him. Said he would pay her good money."

He took a sip of tea from the cup Rosie offered him and put it down. "I dropped Sirena off several times at the cabin to model for him. I knew he was not a decent man, but she would not listen to me. She said she needed the money to pay for her classes."

He paused and looked down at his hands. This was not easy for him and Rosie and Sarah waited patiently for him to continue. "The night before my granddaughter died she told me about delivering the rum runner's message to Miss Ada." He looked up at Sarah. "She did not know what he'd written. She was going to tell you that when you met.

"After I saw the portrait, I knew you were in danger and drove to the Hagemeyer cabin. Miss Ada's red bicycle was outside. The cabin was empty. I saw the photos of you and Miss Ada and Sirena on the wall. I ran out the door to look for you and heard barking in the tool house. Albert was inside."

Albert got up when his name was called and Sarah cupped his face. "I'm so sorry, Albert. You tried to warn me about Robert several times, but I didn't listen. And then I put your life in danger when I went to confront him with what I'd learned. Will you ever forgive me?"

The little dog yapped once and turned over for a belly rub. They all smiled, a reprieve from the sorrow and regret they all shared.

Mr. Kassajara looked over at Rosie. "I brought Albert with me to Miss Rosie hoping you'd be here."

Rosie leaned forward in her armchair eager to tell her part. "After Mr. Kassajara told me Robert was a rum runner and he might be holding you hostage, I telephoned the coast guard. I told them there was a smuggler's schooner anchored in Whalers Cove and they'd better hurry out there if they wanted to catch the ringleader. I called Marshal Judd and told him the same thing."

"That was quick thinking, Rosie," said Sarah. "I wish I had been as smart. I never questioned whether Robert really was a successful Hollywood photographer, or a wounded soldier, or a nice guy." She realized that even the story about his brother's suicide was probably made up to gain her trust and sympathy.

"Was he even in the navy?"

"Oh yes, he fought in the war," said Mr. Kassajara, "but for the Royal Canadians. After the war he returned home to Vancouver and went into the distillery business with his father. Prohibition offered them an opportunity to make lots of money. His father is known as the Rum Baron and their fleet of ships sail from Vancouver to Los Angeles distributing whiskey. His son was second-in-command."

"I even suggested he should help you find Ada's killer," said Rosie. "And I thought I was a smart detective."

Sarah turned to Mr. Kassajara. "Do you know how he met my sister?"

"Miss Ada often came to paint in the Cove, and after they met he started taking her out on his schooner."

Sarah imagined Ada at the helm, sailing out into perilous waters with Robert by her side, and loving the adventure.

Rosie served more tea. Mr. Kassajara thanked her and took a few sips before putting it down and looking directly at Sarah.

"I will always remember the light of hope in my grandchild's face when she told me you had invited her to go back with you to Paris and go to art school. I had not seen this hope in her eyes since her parents died and I had sent her away."

His voice broke and she reached for his hand that was so like Sirena's.

"Yes, I also saw the light of hope in her face when I made my offer and that's how I will remember her."

"May both Sirena and Ada find peace in the afterlife," said Mr. Kassajara. He started chanting *Namu amida butsu* and Sarah and Rosie joined him.

After Mr. Kassajara left, Sarah returned to the Sketch Box with Albert. It was two in the morning and she was exhausted, but she wouldn't sleep this night. There was too much work to be done.

She entered Ada's studio and picked up Robert's portrait off the ground and placed it back on the easel.

One by one she took the blank canvases leaning against the wall and pulled out the nails from the backs of their frames and peeled off the outer layers. It took until dawn to carefully liberate thirteen of the portraits hidden underneath. Each one was thrilling to see uncovered.

While she worked, she wondered what Ada's state of mind had been like when she spent all day alone painstakingly hiding the portraits under the blank canvases so deVrais wouldn't find them, knowing when she was finished she'd have to meet Robert at Whalers Cove . . . *my past indiscretions might end up being the cause of my ruin.*

Sarah loved the painting of Katherine Mansfield, but the last one she uncovered took her breath away. It was a portrait of Sarah that Ada started back in January at their apartment before their fight. Ada had her pose in an upright chair in front of an amber curtain to emphasize the golden flecks in her deep green eyes. Her cheeks were flushed from sitting next to the coal stove. Her chin rested on her open hand as she stared out of the canvas, as if challenging the viewer to capture her inner thoughts and feelings in a fleeting moment.

*Poised radiance* came to Sarah's mind. She had never thought of herself that way and was surprised and very pleased by the understated beauty of her sister's artistic impression of her. She was glad she had listened when Ada had said: "Sarah. Be still and look at me. Open those gorgeous eyes wide so I can make you immortal."

As the morning light streaming through the northern window lit the portraits she had lined up against the wall, she considered the significance of the series. Each portrait had an individual life of its own, strong personalities expressed in a palette of rich colors and smooth strokes by the painterly hand of a great artist.

It was up in the loft that she found the last hidden portrait—a larger canvas than the others. It was a self-portrait of Ada. Long red hair fell loosely over her bare shoulders. Her left hand spread over her slightly swollen stomach under a painter's smock. Alain's gold band glimmered on her left ring finger. She must have added the ring at the last moment; it was still moist from her brushstroke.

A joyous bride and mother-to-be, thought Sarah, with an aching heart.

*I can't bring you back, but I will build a bridge between you and your paintings. Your legacy will live on. I promise you that my dearest sister Ada Belle.*

When she stood up and looked down from the loft, she saw Robert's sea-gray eyes staring at her from the easel and knew the first decision she would make as Ada's executor.

She climbed down the ladder and stood in front of him. "No! Robert. You will not be in Ada's exhibition. I have much more suitable plans for you."

Palette knife in hand, she felt Ada guiding her hand as she roughly scraped the paint off the canvas until there were only splotches on a raw surface. She picked up a wide paintbrush and brushed over the remaining splotches with titanium white until Robert disappeared. Completely.

In her mind, she saw what she would paint over him—a full figure of Sirena wearing her white diving suit.

And how perfect to bury Robert underneath her. She was certain Ada would've wanted this.

As she layered short brushstrokes, Sirena's large violet eyes came into being through a spectrum of blue and red pigments. She imagined the painting on display at the Nouy gallery on opening night: *Ama—Ode to a Sea Maiden.*

She continued working throughout the morning fueled by Una's Coine-Eairngorm wine.

When she finally took a break, she telephoned Eric Crocker. He was very pleased to hear the portraits had been found and that she would immediately arrange for them to be crated and sent to his gallery in New York. She told him that one of the portraits had been permanently destroyed but there were still fifteen pictures for the exhibit. Her only request was that the two portraits, the portrait of herself and Ada's self-portrait, could be displayed, but were not for sale.

# SUNDAY, AUGUST 17
## —31—

O n the afternoon of the memorial service in Point Lobos, Rosie, Sarah, and Albert met Alain at the Monterey train depot in a hired car. He looked much healthier than he had ten days ago. His expression was solemn but his dark brown eyes were clear. He stared at the porcelain urn on Sarah's lap. She asked him if he would like to hold it. He hesitated, then agreed and folded his hands around it protectively.

As their car headed south along the coastline, Sarah looked out at the silver-blue bay. Ada's life had ended on its shore, but her passion for eternal beauty would live on, expressed in her work and in the hearts of those she left behind.

News had traveled fast through the art world, and as executor of Ada's estate she'd already received several requests from museums that wanted to acquire an Ada Belle Davenport painting for their permanent collections.

Albert stuck his head out the back window of the Ford sedan to feel the wind against his face. His ears pressed back. Sarah joined him.

She had announced in the *Pine Cone* that the memorial service would be held that day at Whalers Cove at sunset and, as they got closer, people were already on the road walking or driving in the fading light to the designated spot.

Alain, Rosie, Sarah, and Albert stepped out of the car in front of the abalone cannery, merged into the procession, and took the wooden steps up the hill to the summit overlooking Carmel Bay.

Sarah was wearing a black silk kimono Mr. Kassajara had given her for the celebration. He'd told her it was the traditional costume worn at a *shonanoka* service to celebrate the crossing of the dead into the afterlife. She draped the black shawl with the embroidered crimson roses that Ada had given her over her shoulders. Folded over her arm was Ada's matching shawl.

She recognized several people she had met during her short stay in Carmel. Gus Gay from Oliver's art supply store, Mr. Peabody with Machiko Inaoka, Armin Hansen, William Ritschel, and Una and Robinson Jeffers. Henry Champlin, who was in San Francisco at the time, had taken the train down to Monterey.

Marshal Judd was not there. He had taken a sudden leave-of-absence from his job after the coast guard found papers on the *Ocean Queen* connecting him to the smuggling operation at Whalers Cove. He was on their payroll.

Paul deVrais was also away, but he had given his accountant instructions to attend to any *confusion* in regard to monies he owed to Ada's estate. Mr. Peabody with Machiko's help had sent letters to all the collectors and dealers holding Ada's paintings that they were to deal from now on with Sarah directly.

Tajuro Watanabe, the young nisei that Sarah had met in Whalers Cove, introduced her to several relatives from the Silvia family. Sirena's Portuguese grandmother had recovered from her illness and walked beside Sarah with a determined stride so like her granddaughter's. Sarah reached out and took her arm, Rosie on her other side.

The procession formed a semicircle around Mr. Kassajara who was waiting for them on the rim of the summit. On each side of him, as Sarah had requested, two easels displayed Ada's self-portrait and Sarah's new painting of Sirena, which she had finished in a flurry of painterly concentration in four days.

As the sun slowly sank in the west, Sarah and Mr. Kassajara dipped into the two urns with their white gloves and, handful by handful, flung Ada and Sirena's ashes over the precipice. While Mr. Kassajara quoted from the *Sutra*, the ashes swirled like silver pigments brushed onto a brilliant orange canvas and fell into the azure waves below.

Sarah dropped Ada's shawl over the precipice and a gust of off-shore wind sailed it above the waves until it was out of sight.


Several days later, as Sarah locked the front door of the Sketch Box, she made a promise to return. It had been a sad parting with Rosie, but her dear friend had promised to visit her in Paris the following winter when her lodge was empty of art students.

Sarah boarded the Del Monte Express to San Francisco and took the Overland Express #23 for the long journey to New York, retracing the route she had taken a month earlier.

Rolled-up canvases of Sirena's work were safely packed away in Ada's steamer trunk. Sarah had decided her first gallery exhibition would be a two-woman collaboration between herself and Sirena Kassajara-Silvia. She'd have just enough time to frame Sirena's canvases before the gallery opening.

Albert was sitting next to her on the train. He resented being carried in an open carpetbag and often sniffed and snorted to make his discomfort known. When possible, she took him out and held him in her lap and once in a while she let him run up and down the aisles and stretch his short legs. None of the passengers seemed to mind and, as always, he made several friends. And to Sarah's relief, no one paid any attention to the lady in the red Chanel suit.


When the RMS *Majestic* pulled away from the Hudson River Piers on New York's West Side, she and Albert were strolling across the ship's deck. She picked him up when they got to the stern, worried he might slip overboard.

She held him close and looked down at the churning ocean as the ship's massive propellers cut through the water with a deafening noise. She looked up and watched as her native country slowly receded into the distance. As the ocean widened, she felt an overwhelming sadness as she thought about the people she was leaving behind.

She imagined Rosie in the kitchen making dinner for her girls who were out making art on the beach; Mr. Kassajara would be down at the wharf with his divers celebrating their abalone catch; Armin Hansen might be heard shouting to his students at their easels, "Just paint!"

Sarah breathed in the blue air and closed her eyes. When she opened them, a white-plumed tern with slender legs was perched on the railing in front of her. Brilliant black eyes gazed into Sarah's and she knew this was Ada coming to say goodbye. Her own heart soared when the elegant tern hovered above her and spread white-arched wings over her like a shawl. Kree-aaahh, kree-aaahh she called out to Sarah before soaring into the cobalt sky and disappearing beyond the horizon.

# AFTERWORD

A month later, Rosie sent a letter to Sarah in Paris. Enclosed was Ada's revised death certificate signed by Monterey's District Attorney—"Profession: Artist. Cause of death: Strangulation. Manner of death: Homicide." Rosie also included an August 10, 1924, clipping from the *San Francisco Examiner*'s front page: *Famous Rum Runner Captured: Robert Pierce died from wounds suffered in gun battle with the coast guard in Monterey Bay.* There was, of course, no mention of Sarah or Mr. Kassajara's involvement in his capture.

After the very disgruntled Western Insurance Company received the revised death certificate, Sarah received the cash proceeds of Ada's life insurance policy. She then contributed the funds to create the Davenport Art Association of Carmel, stipulating that a grant be given each year in the name of *Sirena Kassajara-Silvia* to a worthy art student. All races would be considered and would be eligible for membership in the Association.

Eighteen years later in 1942, during the Second World War, hundreds of Japanese immigrants (issei) who had come to the United States in pursuit of the *American Dream*, and their American-born descendants (nisei), like Machiko Inaoka and Tajuro Watanabe, were rounded-up from their homes in Monterey and sent to a detention center on the Salinas rodeo grounds. Several months later, they were transported to an internment camp in Topaz, Utah, where they lived for three years, enduring inhumane living conditions. When they were allowed to return home after the war, they found their village in Whalers Cove destroyed and Japan Town mostly razed. Nothing was left. Not even a plaque to mark their moment in history. Mr. Kassajara died before the Second World War and fortunately never spent any time in the internment camps, nor did he witness the destruction of his village.

# OF HIJTORICAL NOTE

I n February 1942, after Pearl Harbor was attacked, President Franklin D. Roosevelt issued Executive Order 9066, which empowered the military to remove any persons from any area in the country where national security was at risk. Even though the executive order did not mention the Japanese by name, it was effectively designed to contain Japanese Americans in California, Oregon, and Washington State.

These states enforced curfews that required Japanese Americans to stay inside their homes between 8:00 p.m. and 6:00 a.m. The Federal Bureau of Investigation (FBI) went to work arresting suspicious "enemy aliens" who might be leaders in the Japanese community, such as Shinto and Buddhist priests, businesspeople, teachers, and professionals. California fired all state employees of Japanese ancestry without reason or constitution.

Executive Order 9066 displaced some 120,000 Japanese Americans from their homes; about 70,000 of this group were U.S. citizens. They were sent to detention centers. Several months later, they were transported to internment camps across the country.

After the war, more than 440 people in Monterey—including novelist John Steinbeck, photographer Edward Weston, and poet Robinson Jeffers and his wife Una—signed a petition calling for residents of Monterey to "insure the democratic way of life" of those of Japanese ancestry who would be returning to their homes on the Monterey Peninsula in the months ahead. It was published in the *Monterey Peninsula Herald* on May 11, 1945.

# ACKNOWLEDGMENTS

All my creative writing starts from within me, but no way would my words ever make it to paper if I didn't have the support of my extended family, my amazing circle of supportive friends, and the professionals who saw this through to publication. Unfortunately I only have room to mention a few, but I will carry you all in my heart forever.

Thank you to my husband, Jim, who critically reviews my work and encourages me to never give up. Thank you to my children, Amie and Sam, who put up with me when the going gets rough and help me to laugh at myself.

Thank you to Heather Lazare, editor extraordinaire, who helped me turn my mystery into a sweeping historical novel. To Steve Lewis and Randi Feldman, who read through several rough drafts and made it so much better. To Sasha Tropp, a smart copyeditor, who caught some embarrassing whoppers. To Brooke Warner at SWP, who gave me the "green light," and to my project manager, Shannon Green, who kept the light green.

Thank you to Caitlin Hamilton Summie, an exceptionally dedicated publicist, who is always there when I need her, and to my agent, Beth Davies, who never stopped telling me how much she loved my book. Thank you to my taskmaster, Andrea Pirrotti, for being my social media guru. Thank you to Marjo Bryant and Aurelia Nichols for being elegant readers who left no word unturned. Thank you to Kat Martinez who knows how to handle social media far better than me.

Thank you to the good citizens of Carmel-by-the-Sea for pre-serving the hundred-year-old historical landmarks that revved my imagination. Thank you to the legendary Carmel Art Association formed on August 8, 1927, by a small group of artists who gathered at "Gray Gables," the modest home/studio of Josephine Culbertson and Ida Johnson at the corner of Seventh and Lincoln in Carmel-by-the-Sea to listen to my great-aunt Ada Belle Champlin, a member of the Laguna Beach Art Association, talk about the merits of establishing an association for "the advancement of art and cooperation among artists." And a special thanks to Belinda Vidor Holliday who is an ever-present inspiration and the third artist-in-residence to inhabit The Sketch Box studio.

# A NOTE ON SOURCES

Mary Austin, Louise Brooks, August "Gus" Gay, Armin Hansen, Una and Robinson Jeffers, and William Ritschel appear as fictional characters in this book, but I have tried to render respectfully the outward particulars of their lives.

For my research, I depended upon a number of newspaper archives, especially Carmel's own *Pine Cone* archives from 1924. The Images of America series, Arcadia Press, was extremely helpful. A special kudos to Monica Hudson's publications in that series: *Carmel-by-the-Sea* and *Point Lobos*, with Suzanne Wood. It was a thrill to have Monica give me a guided tour of Point Lobos in the middle of a squall; I got soaked, but I also came up with a few plot points while standing in a downpour in front of Whalers Cabin.

Tim Thomas gave me a guided tour of Monterey Wharf and the Japanese American Citizens League museum—an incredibly rich resource of Monterey's Japanese history and culture. Monterey Museum of Art is where I viewed the brilliant Armin Hansen retrospective exhibit. Other location resources were: Robinson Jeffers Tor House Foundation, which give tours of Tor House and Hawk Tower; Herbert Heron's Forest Theater, an historic amphitheater where plays are still performed; the La Playa Hotel lounge, which I converted into a speakeasy for a romantic setting (special thanks to the barten-dress-artist there who, when asked, explained the significance of a painter's palette).

An excellent resource for my character "Sirena" came from the

1929 novel, *Passing,* by Nella Larsen. A recent film adaptation by the same name was written and directed by Rebecca Hall.

A special, posthumous thank-you to Pat Hemingway, whose voluminous collection of Monterey's visual history in his *California Views Photo Archive* gave me many visual ideas for scene locations.

# DISCUSSION QUESTIONS FOR
## *THE ARTIST COLONY*

1. How much do you know about women painters and the history of women's art? Has this novel inspired you to learn more?

2. Did you know who Robinson Jeffers and some of the other famous people mentioned in the novel were? If not, did you look them up while reading? Why or why not?

3. Art and creative writing share similarities as well as key differences. Discuss.

4. Is this a feminist novel? Is any novel espousing equal rights feminist? How does this novel address the issue of equal rights more broadly?

5. In *The Artist Colony*, women gather together to paint in Carmel-by-the-Sea. Do you think there were other artists' colonies elsewhere? How does gathering to work together matter to the creative process? To the reading process? Do you think artists' colonies remain important today?

6. Why is the setting critical to the story? Would you ever want to visit Carmel-by-the-Sea?

7. How does the theme of sisterhood affect the plot?

8. What is the role of critics and criticism in this story?

9. How are families portrayed in this novel? What kinds of families are depicted?

10. This novel is, in part, about how people see or don't see—landscapes, each other, and themselves. How do these various ways of seeing matter in this story?

11. Why is Albert important?

12. Why do you think the author added an introduction?

13. Included in "Notes on Sources" is a reference to Nella Larsen's 1929 novel *Passing*. One of its characters, Clare Kendry, was a resource for this novel. How does the recent film adaptation of the same title, written and directed by Rebecca Hall, portray Clare's motives as being different from Sirena's?

# ABOUT THE AUTHOR

© Michelle Magdalen

J oanna FitzPatrick was born and raised in Hollywood. She started her writing habit by applying her orange fountain pen and wild imagination to screenplays, which led her early on to produce the film *White Lilacs and Pink Champagne.* At Sarah Lawrence College, she wrote her MFA thesis, *Sha La La: Live for Today*, about her life as a rock 'n' roll star's wife. Her more recent work includes two novels, *Katherine Mansfield*, Bronze Winner of the 2021 Independent publisher book award (IPPY) in Historical Fiction, and *The Drummer's Widow*. *The Artist Colony* is her third book. Presently, FitzPatrick divides her time between a mountaintop cottage in Northern California and a small hameau in Southern France, where she begins all her book projects.

For more information, visit www.joannafitzpatrick.com.

# SELECTED TITLES FROM SHE WRITES PRESS

She Writes Press is an independent publishing company
founded to serve women writers everywhere.
Visit us at www.shewritespress.com.

*Talland House* by Maggie Humm. $16.95, 978-1-63152-729-6
1919 London: When artist Lily Briscoe meets her old tutor, Louis
Grier, by chance at an exhibition, he tells her of their mutual friend
Mrs. Ramsay's mysterious death—an encounter that spurs Lily to
investigate the death of this woman whom she loved and admired.

*The Silver Shoes* by Jill G. Hall. $16.95, 978-1-63152-353-3
Distracted by a cross-country romance, San Francisco artist Anne
McFarland worries that she has veered from her creative path. Almost
ninety years earlier, Clair Deveraux, a sheltered 1929 New York debu-
tante, becomes entangled in the burlesque world in an effort to save
her family and herself after the stock market crash. Ultimately, these
two very different women living in very different eras attain true ful-
fillment—with some help from the same pair of silver shoes

*Estelle* by Linda Stewart Henley. $16.95, 978-1-63152-791-3
From 1872 to '73, renowned artist Edgar Degas called New Orleans
home. Here, the narratives of two women—Estelle, his Creole cousin
and sister in law, and Anne Gautier, who in 1970 finds a journal
written by a relative who knew Degas—intersect . . . and a painting
Degas made of Estelle spells trouble.

*A Girl Like You: A Henrietta and Inspector Howard Novel* by
Michelle Cox. $16.95, 978-1-63152-016-7
When the floor matron at the dance hall where Henrietta works as
a taxi dancer turns up dead, aloof Inspector Clive Howard appears
on the scene—and convinces Henrietta to go undercover for him,
plunging her into Chicago's gritty underworld.